CAPTURED FATE

EVA CHASE

SHADOWBLOOD SOULS - BOOK 3

Captured Fate

Book 3 in the Shadowblood Souls series

First Digital Edition, 2023

Copyright © 2023 Eva Chase

Cover design: Sanja Balan (Sanja's Covers)

Ebook ISBN: 978-1-998752-16-4

Paperback ISBN: 978-1-998752-17-1

ONE

Riva

A painful tightness fills the middle of my throat. Before I've even opened my eyes, the urge to clear it grips me.

But I can't seem to swallow. I can't make a sound.

It's not a lump *in* my throat but something squeezed against my neck from the outside.

My eyes want to spring open. My muscles are braced to jerk into attack mode. But instead my body reacts as if I'm moving through mud.

My eyelids lift sluggishly. My arms and legs squirm against a firmly padded surface.

And jar to a stop when they hit restraints clamped around my wrists and ankles.

I blink with the same blurry sluggishness, fighting to clear my hazy vision. A room comes into focus around me: shadows along the walls but bright light streaming over the center of the space where I'm trapped in this seat.

It's like a dentist's chair. Except I don't think those normally lock you in place.

Of course, I've never been to a proper dentist before, only seen them in TV shows and movies. It could be the reality is much more frightening.

But why the hell would I have been kidnapped by a *dentist*? Some psycho tooth doctor was so desperate to clean my teeth?

My head's been filled with mud too. My thoughts seep along dampened circuits.

There was something, right before—

We were in the facility—we'd gotten a bunch of shadowblood kids out—

Running down the stairs after Jacob, urgency thrumming through my nerves. Dashing down a hall and into a room—

Unbreakable walls thudding into place around me. And Jacob—

Not Jacob.

He called me *Moonbeam.*

My heart lurches, and my limbs yank against the restraints even though I can already tell they're built to withstand my supernatural strength. But as the resurgence of shock and anguish crashes over me, I'm remembering what happened next. The gas that poured down from the ceiling in a thick lavender gush, blotting out the man I was staring at and clouding my mind into nothingness.

That's where the memories stop. I have no idea what happened between that moment and waking up here, now.

Panic trickles through the sludge in my head, sharpening my senses.

Where are my guys? Were they caught too?

What happened to the kids we got out—did Rollick and his people get them to safety?

Where the hell *am* I?

I open my mouth, wanting to call out, but the pressure against my throat chokes off any sound beyond a slurred mumble. A fresh chill winds around me.

I won't be able to scream like this. I can't defend myself with my strength, my claws, or my killing shriek.

Whoever's holding me knows exactly what I can do and figured out a way to chain all of my talents.

I clamp down on the jolt of terror with the instinctive discipline honed by years of training and combat in the ring. Freaking out isn't going to help me.

I have to focus.

When I draw my awareness inside myself to settle my nerves, I pick up on the faint prick of sensation in the two thumbprint-sized blotches that mark my collarbone. The marks that formed when I slept with Andreas and Dominic for the first time.

They're here, wherever here is. Somewhere nearby, anyway.

But I can't tell any more than that they're within maybe a hundred feet of me in different directions, and that they're alive. What state they're in beyond that, I haven't got a clue.

A soft rasp from behind me jerks me out of my thoughts. A shift in the air that tells me a door has opened.

My pulse stutters, and I hold myself still to track the sounds.

Careful footsteps tread across the floor toward me. As I turn my head toward them, an unfamiliar man comes into view.

He walks until he's nearly in front of the chair and stops there, facing me. His blue eyes study me assessingly.

I assess him right back.

He's decently but not epically tall, with a fair bit of muscle under his polo shirt and slacks. Strong but no match for me if it comes down to hand-to-hand combat.

A military-short cropping of carrot-red hair tops his face. His features have a hardness to them that makes me think of military discipline too.

Faint wrinkles mark the corners of his mouth and eyes, and when he shifts his weight from one foot to the other, the light from overhead catches on a few faded strands amid his red hair. I'd guess he's in his late forties.

He isn't wearing the typical metal helmet and vest that the guardians usually do. But I was captured in the depths of a facility. He must be with them, right?

I manage to push a few words from my throat, rough and faint but audible. "Who. The fuck. Are you?"

His thin lips form a reserved smile. "Someone who believes you can be more than what's been offered to you so far, Riva."

What the hell is that supposed to mean? I grimace.

"Someone. Who can't. Talk?"

He lets out a light chuckle that makes me want to punch him in the face. I wasn't making a joke.

Then he motions to my throat. "I'll take the clamp off

as soon as I'm sure you aren't going to turn that unexpected power of yours on me. It really wouldn't be in your best interests, and I'm sure you'll realize that for yourself. But I'd rather not take my chances before then, having seen how dire the consequences can be."

Yes, enduring one of my screams should not be on anyone's top ten lists of how to go. My power craves all the pain it can provoke while it's breaking its targets' bodies.

That doesn't mean this prick doesn't deserve every bit of the pain I could deal out.

"Where. Guys?" I force out. My throat is aching just from the little bit of conversation I've been able to carry out.

"Your fellow shadowbloods—the ones you grew up with—are being held in their own rooms. They'll be given the same opportunity. But you do seem to make a lot more trouble when you're all together."

His tone is dry, but I catch the more ominous implications. If we're kept apart, we can't plan a joint escape.

And escaping alone would leave the others in this man's hands, possibly to punish for our rebellion.

If I scream this guy to pieces, I have no idea whether I'd be able to even get out of this room afterward, let alone get to Dominic, Andreas, Jacob, and Zian. Or how many other people might be working in this place who'd make me—or them—pay for my actions.

But the thought brings back the image of the guy who led me into the trap at the last facility I entered—the guy I grew up with but believed was dead.

My throat constricts for more reasons than just the restraint before I croak out, "Griffin?"

"I don't think it's time to get into that subject just yet," the man says evenly. "Let's focus on getting you out of that chair. I don't want to hurt you or the others. I've been trying to get control over the Guardianship for years so that I could take our endeavors in a different direction. This is your second chance. But you have to show you're willing to give *me* a chance."

Every word coming out of his mouth sounds like bullshit to me. I narrow my eyes at him.

"Not. Trusting. Anything. Until. I see. Guys."

By the end of that sentence, my vocal cords are outright throbbing. I'm not sure I'll be able to say much else.

The man's mouth tightens. His gaze flicks away from me, toward the door, as if something has drawn his attention there.

His frown deepens, but he steps to the side as another set of footsteps approaches.

He wasn't the only one who came in. Someone's been listening from just inside the door.

My body tenses all over again, not that it ever really relaxed. And then the last face I ever expected to see appears in front of me.

My heart stops.

My brain wants to think it's Jacob I'm looking at. That's what would make sense given everything I believed.

But just as in that final moment in the facility, I can pick out the differences. The slightly longer fall of his blond hair. The posture that looks a tad looser than Jacob seems to be capable of these days.

The emptiness in the sky-blue eyes that used to shine with every bit of shared joy we could scrounge up in our old prison.

"I've checked on the other guys," says the man who must be Griffin, in a measured voice that holds no hint of emotion whatsoever. "Precautions have been taken when it comes to their powers, but they haven't been harmed. I wouldn't be here talking to you if I thought Clancy meant to do that."

He glances at the older man—Clancy?

My captor raises his chin. "There. You've heard it from one of your own."

Is the guy in front of me 'one of my own' anymore? He doesn't sound like the Griffin I knew.

I watched that Griffin take a bullet that tore right through his back and chest. I watched the blood burst out of him, the mix of crimson liquid and black smoke that earned us the name "shadowbloods."

I saw him crumple like a rag doll as if all the life had already left his body.

My face twitches with a wince, but I manage to cough up one more word, my gaze trained on the impossible figure before me.

"How?"

Clancy answers. "The Guardianship has always had excellent technology at our disposal. The shot only nicked Griffin's heart rather than puncturing it. It took some time, but between our doctors' expertise and the innate shadowblood ability to self-heal, he made a full recovery."

He nods to Griffin. "Why don't you show her the scar?"

Griffin's face remains completely placid, almost dazed, as he reaches for the collar of his button-up shirt. Has he been drugged like the other guys said the guardians did to them after our first escape attempt?

He eases open the top two buttons on his shirt and pulls the fabric down and to the left.

He's healed, but a reminder of the injury remains. A whorl of darker, ridged scar tissue marks the pale skin of his upper chest.

Right where the bullet hit him in my memory of that night.

"She's confused," Griffin says to Clancy in the same empty voice. Whatever they've done to him, apparently he can still read my emotions. "And scared. I think we should let her talk properly so she can ask whatever questions she's got. I don't get any sense that she's preparing to attack."

Clancy pauses and then nods again, this time toward me, though he's still speaking to Griffin. "You can loosen the clamp."

I guess he trusts Griffin to give an accurate assessment. How mixed up is Griffin with the "Guardianship," if that's what this bunch is calling their organization?

If he even really is Griffin. Who knows what else the guardians could be capable of that we don't know?

He steps toward me and fiddles with something by the side of my neck. His presence, so close to me but not quite touching my skin, sends a jitter through my nerves.

The shadows in my blood wake up and tug at me. An

itch to reach out to him races through my arm to my hand, not that I can move it even if I wanted to.

Some part of me, below the level of conscious thought, believes it's really him.

But I'm not totally sure I can trust even that impulse. So when the pressure at my throat eases and I can swallow again, I aim my full attention at the man claiming to be Griffin, who's stepping back again with his infuriatingly vacant expression.

My voice comes out hoarse but unimpeded. "Tell me something only Griffin could know."

Griffin pauses, his gaze shifting but becoming distant in a more focused way as if he's giving the matter serious thought. When he brings his attention back to me, his eyes look a little more alert than before.

"A few months before the escape attempt, one of the guardians distracted Jacob during a training exercise, and he started mouthing off at the guy, swearing and stuff. You snapped at him afterward and told him off, but you weren't really angry, even though you were acting like it. You were scared. Probably that it'd mess up the plans we'd been making somehow."

My arm muscles clench with the urge to hug myself. I remember that moment in the training room—the frustration seeping from my mouth while my gut was knotted up with an edge of panic.

"When we left to go back to our rooms," Griffin goes on, "I found a chance to give your hand a quick squeeze when the guardians wouldn't see. I wanted to reassure you."

I remember that too. A pang of loss echoes through

my chest even though the man I thought I'd lost is standing right here in front of me.

Only Griffin would know those things. It really is him.

But it couldn't be stranger to hear him talk about reassuring me in a voice that offers no tenderness at all, only flat facts.

Then again, maybe I'm feeling enough for both of us right now.

The pang swells into a wave of grief and guilt, sending a burn of tears into the back of my eyes. "I'm sorry. I didn't know—I thought I saw you *die*. If we'd had any idea you were alive—"

"It's okay," Griffin says, perfectly matter of fact. "There was no way you could have known."

Like he doesn't care. Like he wasn't ripped away from us for those four years just like I was from the other guys.

I don't understand.

What have they done to the boy I knew? The boy I *loved*?

I blink hard, pushing back the tears I can't move my hands to swipe away, and another question surges up from inside.

"Why were you at the facility when we— Why did you help them capture us?"

Griffin dips his head as if he's trying to indicate that he recognizes my turmoil without actually showing any regret himself.

"I've seen some of the things you did after you got out. And to get out. All of you. It became obvious that… it wasn't for the best for you to be out there in the world as you are. You were hurting too many people."

I flinch at his last words as if he's punched me in the stomach. In that moment, it's like the clamp is strangling me again. I can't find my words.

We were hurting too many people?

But even as he says that, images flash behind my eyes.

The mangled bodies in the cage-fighting arena. Most of those people died without ever having actually harmed me.

The buildings toppling into a Havana street with a yank of Jacob's power.

Billy the faun's delicate body turned into a crumpled, disjointed heap.

People *have* gotten hurt who shouldn't have.

"We were only trying to protect ourselves," I protest. "If they'd just let us go free…"

Somehow, Griffin still sounds calm. "Maybe. But even when the guardians weren't after you, there were others who wouldn't leave you alone. And then you'd lash out. It would have happened over and over. What Clancy wants to do is better."

My gaze jerks back to the older man. The military-styled dude offers me another tight smile.

My fingers curl toward my palms. "What exactly do you want?"

He's obviously going to tell me eventually. Might as well get it over with as quickly as possible so I can figure out where we go from here.

What avenues I might have for reaching the other guys. For breaking out of our new prison.

And if Griffin thinks this man is worth listening to, is it possible he's right?

But I don't know how much to trust this altered version of my old love.

Clancy takes a step toward me, putting himself just inches away from my restrained feet. "I should introduce myself properly, Riva. My name is James Clancy, and I've been part of the Guardianship since its inception, alongside my parents. It's only been in the past several months that I've had a chance to take the reins and present a better vision for our shadowbloods."

I resist the urge to make a face. "What vision?"

His posture pulls even straighter. "Chasing after monsters that rarely leave a lasting impact on society is pointless when there are so many bigger issues that human beings face. There are much greater challenges your skills could be put toward resolving. You and your friends have the opportunity to make the entire world a better place."

Two

Riva

To make the entire world a better place.

James Clancy says the words with total confidence, as if he's presenting me with an award or something. As if I should be fucking *honored* that he's chosen me to be trapped in a dentist's chair and half-strangled.

I glower at him. "What are you even talking about? I thought that was already the idea: we protect the world by fighting the 'monsters.'"

Not that the shadowkind—as I've learned those monsters prefer to be called—act beastlier than the guardians do, at least not the ones I met. But I don't see the point in rubbing that fact in just yet.

Clancy shakes his head. A gleam of enthusiasm has come into his eyes.

"The three founding families believed hunting monsters should be your purpose. But I've seen a lot over the years. I know you could accomplish so much more than that. You should have the chance to become more than monsters yourselves."

Griffin nods along, and I can't stop a flutter of hope from passing through my chest despite my wariness.

I don't want to like what my new captor is saying. But to be more than what the guardians made us and expected from us—that's a dream I've been chasing from the moment I fled the cage-fighting arena.

On the other hand, this asshole does still have me locked in a chair.

Clancy starts to pace, but it isn't an anxious motion. I don't pick up the slightest hint of nervous pheromones in the air.

He strolls back and forth in front of me like he's gathering momentum, pulling out a phone as he does. "You must have some idea of the larger problems we face from the media you were allowed to consume. There are totally human horrors that run rampant around the globe. Children dragged into slavery. Terrorists killing thousands. Cartels spreading violence and addiction. Extremists carrying out genocide."

He halts and holds out his phone so I can see the screen. His thumb swipes through images that wrench at my gut almost as much as my blood-soaked memories do.

Wide-eyed little kids holding guns. Bombed out buildings. Fields mottled with broken bodies.

So much more devastation than I've ever caused... so far.

I lift my gaze from the screen to Clancy. "And you think we could do something about this?"

His little smile comes back. "I know you could. If you have the skills to battle literal monsters, why couldn't you take down the worst of humanity? You shadowbloods have the ability to turn the tide against the evil forces in this world, to save the innocents they're harming, the lives being destroyed every day... Bring something good to society on a massive scale. Wouldn't you *like* that?"

The truth is, part of me would. If I had the opportunity to prevent even one of those images from becoming real, I'd jump at it.

But I don't trust the man in front of me.

"And I'm going to do all of that while shackled to a chair?" I say pointedly.

The corner of Clancy's mouth twitches. I think he suppressed a larger smile.

Does he find me *amusing*? My teeth set on edge.

The next thing I know, he's walking over to me and pressing buttons on the side of the chair.

The cuffs click open from my neck, wrists, and ankles. A breath of relief rushes into me.

I sit up straighter, rubbing my wrists, fully registering my clothing for the first time. I've lost my mock turtleneck with its Kevlar protection, but given the amount of blood splattered on it during our raid of the facility, it'd probably be rank by now anyway.

I've been left in the wide-strapped black tank top I had on underneath, my pendant necklace tucked beneath the neckline, and a new pair of black sweats. I run my finger along the waistband just enough to confirm that I've got on the same panties as before.

They invaded my privacy, but I can admit it could have been a lot worse.

I glance up at Clancy again. My captor doesn't look frightened of me, and I'm still not picking up any whiffs of anxiety.

He has Griffin monitoring my emotions. Griffin knows I'm not angry enough to go on the attack just yet.

I have the other guys to think about. What happens to them if I let loose my claws and slice open this man's throat?

What if this is the best opportunity we're ever going to get, and reacting with violence would mean consigning us all to a lifetime of total imprisonment and torture instead?

Clancy tilts his head toward the door. "Come with me."

Cautiously, I peel myself out of the chair and follow him.

Griffin trails along behind. As we step out past the steel door into a hallway that I realize looks as if it's roughly carved into stone, I glance back at him.

He offers me a smile of his own, but it's the same stiff kind he gave me right before the gas knocked me out in the facility. Not the way he used to smile, the expression lighting his whole face up.

Did *Clancy* do this to him, or was it the other guardians? Because if the man giving me this grandiose talk was responsible for killing the light in the boy I loved, he's going to end up with his throat severed eventually, one way or another.

As soon as I can figure out how to do it without screwing things up for the rest of my guys.

Panels on the ceiling send an artificial glow over the hallway. More steel doors are imbedded in the rocky walls, labeled with numbers.

I peer at them as we pass. The faint tingle in my marks tells me Dominic and Andreas, at least, are farther behind me.

My claws itch at my fingertips. "Where are my friends? When do I get to see them?"

Clancy casts his voice over his shoulder. "Like I said before, the bunch of you make a lot of trouble when you're all together. I don't think we'll be arranging a full group reunion until you're more settled in. But you'll have the chance to see them one or two at a time once I know where you stand. Assuming you're on board."

"On board with saving the world?" I mutter.

"Something like that."

We turn a corner into a wider hallway with a set of double doors just ahead. Clancy presses his thumb against a panel at waist height while offering his face to another scanner higher up.

The steel slabs whir apart. Daylight and a warm breeze spill through the opening.

My heart lifts of its own accord.

I hadn't realized how dim and cool the rocky interior was until now, as I stepped out onto a stone platform under the bright sun. I stall in my tracks just beyond the entrance, my jaw going slack at the scene before me.

The walls of the building I've just exited are rock because it's carved right into the face of a mountain. A mountain that's part of a range looming in craggy peaks all around a small but lush valley spread out some fifty feet below our vantage point.

Immediately in front of us, water burbles in a crystalline spring. A few acres of cleared land gleam with vibrantly green grass.

Some of that area has been left as a totally open field. Other parts have been set up for training activities: an elaborate jungle gym-slash-obstacle course, shooting or throwing targets, a trampled track.

A couple of running trails veer off into the tropical forest that fills the rest of the valley. I can't make out much through the dense canopy of leaves.

Bird song trills through the air. A flash of red-and-yellow feathers darts through the branches.

A faint perfume drifts on the breeze to my nose, sweet florals with a mossy undertone.

"The Guardianship owns this island," Clancy says, gazing out over the valley with a satisfied expression. "A long time ago, this spot was a crater smashed into the mountains by a meteor. Now it's become a place where life can thrive."

He shoots a pointed look my way. "Even the most desolate things can transform into something spectacular."

I'd wrinkle my nose at the blatant insinuation about my own usefulness, but my attention has been drawn to the figures who are moving amid the training equipment.

My pulse stutters at the thought that I might see my guys among them, but I don't recognize any of the current trainees. They're all young, I determine after studying them for a minute. Mid to late teens.

As that thought passes through my head, one of the

guys slips on the climbing ropes. The girl ahead of him jerks around at his yelp and flings out her arm—and an invisible force shoves him back into balance.

My mouth goes dry. "They're shadowbloods. You're training them here now?"

Clancy nods. "I've gathered as many of our subjects as I can at this facility. Those who were away from their facilities—in the interests of tracking your group down—are on their way now. That will be all of them... except the six you led to the monsters."

The six we helped escape from imprisonment, he means.

My mouth tightens, my appreciation of the gorgeous setting fading. I turn toward him, the words to tell him off rising up my throat, and find him already watching me.

"Do you want to know what the creatures who pretended to be your allies did to those children?" he asks in a low voice.

An uneasy prickle ripples over my skin. "What do you mean?"

Clancy takes out his phone. "Some of them can be very persuasive... but we consider them monsters for a reason."

When he points the screen toward me again, my stomach flips over.

It's a photograph of four bodies sprawled on the forest floor under muted daylight. I can't see much of the two farther figures other than that there's blood splashed across them.

The closer two are clearly dead. Eyes staring vacantly, flesh drained to white. Scarlet flecks dapple their cheeks.

I know the girl. She's one of the two I led out of the facility.

Clancy gives me several seconds to take the image in and then slides to another, showing the other two forms. There's the boy I escorted out, equally limp, his arm torn right from its socket.

In my shock, my voice breaks. "But— How did that happen? Who—"

"The beasts you brought them to must have felt it best to eliminate the threat the shadowbloods represented as quickly as possible." Clancy tucks the phone away, his tone now grim. "I'd imagine they only left *you* alive as long as they did in the hopes you'd help them eliminate more of your kind."

My stomach roils. No. That doesn't make sense.

I can't imagine Pearl, the bubbly, curious succubus, planning a slaughter. And Rollick, the demon who was overseeing our mission—he proved over and over that he was on our side.

Could that really have all been an act?

It doesn't need to have been, does it? Other shadowkind working under Rollick tried to kill us in spite of his protection before.

Maybe they were less scared of our younger counterparts—maybe they jumped in and murdered the kids before he realized they were rebelling against his orders.

We gave those kids freedom—for what? A few minutes? And then…

Guilt congeals in my gut. I grapple with the nausea churning inside me.

"That doesn't mean *you* were right," I say roughly. "The things you put us through, everything you forced us to do…"

All the anguish I've witnessed on my guys' faces and heard in their voices as they talked about the four years we were apart, even worse than the time before. The four years when *I* was stuck fighting for my life every week and in shackles every other hour of the day, because the guardians sold me off.

At least the shadowkind didn't torture the kids.

"I haven't had much control over your training," Clancy says. "It took time before I really had a voice, and more time for everyone involved to listen. I don't agree with everything you've endured. But it's toughened you to withstand the worst the villains out there can throw at you."

I scowl at the training equipment below. "And what are we doing here? More toughening up?"

Clancy's voice softens. "I don't think training needs to be torturous. You've already had enough of that. The five of you are more than prepared to go out into the field already. We'd only go through exercises designed to confirm you have specific skills needed for a given mission —and that you're committed to seeing it through. As well as some exercises for increasing your control over your powers."

My gaze jerks to him with a jolt of surprise. The whole reason we turned to the shadowkind to begin with was for help harnessing our supernatural abilities.

"You *know* how to help us control them? Better than we learned before?"

"Your past keepers were mainly concerned with provoking as much ability out of you as possible, not reining it in. My colleagues who've supported my cause and I have developed some strategies that appear to help with focus and moderation."

So I could make sure I only let out my scream when it was deserved? Modulate it to decide how much to hurt, whether to kill?

The guys have been struggling with the wilder side of their abilities too. We've all been longing for this.

Clancy studies me. "It wouldn't take very long before you could start making a difference—a real one, for the people who need it most."

I don't like the lump that's risen in my throat. But the photos he showed me mean I have even more to make up for than I knew before.

If I can believe anything he says.

I cross my arms. "You said there were three founding families. I guess Ursula Engel was part of one of those, and she got pushed out. Did you manage to convince... your parents? And whoever the other founders are to go along with all this?"

Clancy's mouth slants at an uncomfortable angle. "My parents passed away in the last few years, and their other co-founder stepped away during their illnesses with his own concerns. It's become clear he won't be returning. The direction of the Guardianship rests solely in my hands now."

I can't claim his idea sounds like a totally horrible direction, at least not if he's telling the truth. That doesn't mean I'm going to leap to sign up.

"And if we don't commit to your missions?"

He offers a slight shrug. "Then you'll be confined to your room and contribute with the tests we'll run on you, physically and mentally. I'd imagine getting out into the world and taking matters into your own hands will be more satisfying, but the choice is up to you."

Do things his way or go back to being a total prisoner. Such fantastic options.

I hold in my snark, my hand rising instinctively to my necklace. My fingers tug out the cat-and-yarn shape and curl around it.

The feel of it against my skin makes me glance toward the other man standing on the ledge with me—the one who gave this necklace to me years ago.

Griffin hasn't said a word since we came out. He stands there under the warm sunlight, his stance easy but his expression just as blank as it's been since I first saw him.

What would it take to get a real reaction from him?

I raise the pendant so the light flashes off it. "I've held on to your necklace all this time. It helped me get through a lot."

There's no real joy in his smile. "I'm glad it served you that well."

I can't help reaching toward him with my other hand. Maybe it's an echo of the moment he referenced when he offered me that quick squeeze of reassurance.

My fingers brush his, and a spark quivers across my skin and into my veins. My pulse hiccups.

Whatever the guardians have done to him, I'm still just as attuned to him as I am the other guys.

Griffin swivels toward me, moving his hand out of reach with the same motion. He considers me like I'm an interesting piece of art hanging in a gallery rather than one of his closest friends.

Still, I can't hold back the question. "Do you think this is a good idea?"

Griffin inclines his head. "I think we should help. We can, and there aren't many people who could—not as much, not on the same level. I want to know I've done something good with my life. We haven't really had the chance before."

No, we haven't. But it's hard to feel totally convinced when Griffin delivers his answer in that vacant voice.

Clancy motions me back toward the hallway. "Let me show you your actual room here, and you can take some time making your decision. But I hope it won't be a difficult one."

THREE

Jacob

I hate this fucking room.

There's nothing in it. Just me and a floor, ceiling, and walls that all look and feel like rock.

A steel door I can't budge with my powers, no matter how hard I pull.

A light fixture sealed behind layers of some translucent material that's so well-secured I can't wrench it out either.

Of course, if I could break it, then it'd be just me and the dark. But at this point I'm too pissed off to care how practical the strategy would be.

I prowl through the small space, my sneakers smacking the flat but rough ground, my hands clenched into fists. My power zings this way and that, snatching at every surface around me for something to catch on to and snap.

The guardians screwed us over somehow. Some stupid trick that I didn't recognize until it was too late.

When we'd gotten the kids out of the facility we

invaded, I had the strongest sense that I needed to keep digging, keep searching—that there was something else important there. I remember opening a door with a rush of exhilaration that I'd finally found whatever that was.

Then the door slammed shut behind me, tossing me forward as a hissing sound filled the air. A chemical smell filled my nose.

And before I could do shit about any of it, my mind went black.

Am I still in the same building? The stone surfaces make me think of the cave the other one was built into, but all the rooms and halls there looked like a regular building, not something carved right out of the rock.

When I get my hands—or my powers—on the fuckers who're caging us now...

I march up to the door and pound my fists against it, even though I know it won't budge. Let them know how fucking furious I am.

They're going to have to face me eventually. I can't see them going to the trouble of knocking me out and shutting me in here just to leave me to starve to death.

What have they done to Riva? To the other guys?

I should have been with her—protecting her. If they've gotten her too...

God fucking *damn it.*

I slam my clenched hand into the door once more, hard enough that a lance of pain shoots up my arm. The renewed surge of anger and frustration sends me storming in another circuit of the room.

The guardians have always come down hardest on her.

She was the one they took away when we first tried to escape.

They left her on her own to fight for her life at some crime boss's whims. How much worse will they do this time?

"Fuck!" I shout, flinging an invisible force at the wall, which of course doesn't budge.

I'm just coming up on the door again when a panel I didn't notice slides open on the ceiling and a screen whirs down from it.

All I register is a middle-aged man's face on the screen, hard angles topped by short orange hair, and his mouth moving to form words. "Hi there, Jacob. This seems like the safest way to—"

My power whips out of me at the first viable target it's gotten since I woke up on the uncomfortable floor.

The screen shatters. Bits of glass rain down on the floor. Sparks sputter from the electronic frame that held it.

It occurs to me a moment too late that I should have been a little more careful. I should have cracked the glass so I'd have a larger piece to work with as a weapon.

Fuck it. I've got a dozen spines that'll spring from my arms, as sharp as any glass and poisoned on top of that.

I stomp through the glass-littered part of the room for good measure, taking a tiny pleasure in the crunch of the shards under my feet. The panel starts to hum shut again, but I snatch at it too.

With a heave, I bring the camouflaged covering and the metal frame crashing down too.

That's what I think of their attempt at conversation.

They want to say something to me, they can come look me in the eyes.

"Where's Riva?" I yell in the vague direction of where the screen once hung. "Where are my friends? Let me out of here, you assho—!"

A current of electricity jolts through my body from the floor and cuts off my last word with a rattling of my jaw. My body spasms.

My legs give, and I fall to my hands and knees. The brief zap has dissipated, but every nerve in my body continues to vibrate with the discharged energy.

I've bitten my tongue. The tang of blood trickles over it.

I grimace and shove myself, wobbling, back onto my feet. I'm going to tear those pricks apart and dance on their fucking—

The roar of anger reverberating through me simmers down like a pot taken off the stove. A strange rush of cool, soothing calm muddies it.

I should be raging. Why the hell am I—

This tantrum is silly. Everything is okay. The others must be okay too.

No, *that's* ridiculous. The guardian bastards grabbed us and—

Another cool wave rolls over me, numbing the searing flames. I suck in a shaky breath.

What is going on in my head?

I'm bewildered and chilled out enough that when the lock in the door clicks, my power doesn't immediately jerk to the ready. I just stand there, staring, somehow sure that I need to wait and get the answer I need when it swings open.

There's a soft hiss of escaping compressed air. The door slides partway into the side of the stone frame rather than swinging inward.

For an instant, I think it's opened to reveal a mirror. That's a reflection of me, gazing back at me with the same pale blue eyes.

But reflections don't walk on their own like this one steps into the room, the door thudding shut behind him. A reflection wouldn't be wearing a green shirt when mine is black.

A reflection wouldn't aim an awkward-looking smile at me while my jaw hangs slack.

"Jake," the other man says in a mild voice that seems to sweep over me on a third swell of calm. "You need to stop fighting. Let's try talking. You can talk to me if you don't want to listen to anyone else yet."

I think I've swallowed my tongue. I can't seem to find it, and a choking sensation constricts my throat.

I cough and sputter and find my voice again as my heart thumps on with an erratic beat.

"Griffin?"

It's hardly more than a hoarse whisper. I'm almost afraid to have made his name audible, as if I'll shatter the illusion by addressing it.

But the man in front of me doesn't fracture. He looks steadily at me, not denying my naming of him.

"I'm sorry it's been so long. Things have been… complicated."

"They—*what*? You—we thought—I saw you—"

A different surge of emotion sweeps away all my

words. My gut knots up, and the rest of me lurches forward.

I wrap my arms around my brother and tug him close. Absorbing the warmth of life from his skin, the even rhythm of his pulse thumping in his chest.

He's really here. Right here with me, speaking, breathing.

But not quite the way I remember. The way I know down to my bones that my twin is supposed to be.

Griffin would have laughed, because I'm usually not a hugger, and hugged me back tightly. Griffin would have overflowed with his excitement at the reunion.

The guy I've embraced has lifted his arms to return the hug, but more in a comforting way than with any clear enthusiasm. He stays quiet as I pull away.

I stare at him, trying to connect the figure before me with my expectations and memories. Nothing quite makes sense. My mind feels as if it's been buried under a landslide.

"Where have you *been*?" I blurt out, which maybe isn't the best question to lead with when I should be singing Hallelujah that he's alive at all, but it's the one that careens out first.

Griffin smiles in his new, tight way. "Another facility. It took them a long time to heal me and to make sure that I was prepared for everything I might have to face. And then the guardians said it would be better if I didn't come back and disrupt the habits you all had gotten into. I asked… You know what they were like."

He didn't die. We thought we saw his life leave him in

the video they showed us, but his injury wasn't quite so bad that they couldn't patch him up.

He was alive all this time, and they kept rubbing it in our faces that supposedly Riva arranged his murder. That it was her fault he was dead when even the dead part wasn't true.

The realization and my brother's last words spark a renewed flare of frustration. "What they *are* like. Those assholes—"

But Griffin… shakes his head. "New management. Things are changing. We're *here*, and together. It's a fresh start. I'd really like to embark on it with you—with all of you, but especially you, Jake."

I'm gaping at him again, wishing I had Zian's X-ray vision so I could peer inside his skull in case I might find a little gremlin sitting at a set of controls where his brain should be. "A fresh start? What the fuck are you talking about?"

"Someone new has taken over the guardians," Griffin says. "He's got different plans—he's going to let us run missions that actually matter. Take control over our lives. Have a say in our training. You have to give him a chance to explain."

"Whoever he is, he shut me in this prison! He took away the others—Riva—"

Griffin's voice gentles. "They're all here. I just talked to Riva a half hour ago. She's fine. Everyone's fine. You'll be able to see them, talk with them and the younger shadowbloods who are here, go outside—everything. When you've calmed down and we don't have to worry about you hurting anyone by accident. Or on purpose."

Something about that last sentence makes my pulse hitch.

He knows. He knows the people I've already hurt—in both ways.

Griffin never wanted to hurt anyone. He'd feel their pain as well as his own.

He can't understand.

I raise my chin. "I was protecting us. I'd do it again."

"You won't have to," Griffin says. "We're safe here. We don't have to go out and tackle the real villains until we're ready."

I scowl at him. "I'll believe it when I see it."

Griffin sighs. It's a mild sound, but it conveys enough disappointment that I want to cringe away inside my own body, away from the sense that I've let him down.

I let him take lead in the escape—I let him be the one to race out first, where the bullets started flying—

How much of the strangeness I see in him now is my fault too?

I suck in a breath through my teeth. "We can't trust them. We can't trust any of them. Even Engel, the one who *made* us, turned out to hate us."

"Clancy isn't like that." Griffin steps back toward the door. "Show that you're ready to talk and listen, and then we'll get somewhere."

He slips out before I can get another word in, leaving me behind in the cold, empty room.

FOUR

Riva

The swaying, reed-like strands of plastic sparkle with pink glitter. I eye the narrow opening, tracking their movements in the breeze.

There's a dip in the ground under them. If I roll into it —a little to the side to avoid that root—at just the right moment...

I brace my limbs and then launch myself. As I hit the ground, I tighten my muscles to squish my compact body as small as it'll go.

The pink-and-green strands flash by over my face. Then I'm shoving forward and leaping onto a jutting tree branch to avoid a pool of more glitter—this stuff neon yellow—on the far side.

I crouch there for a moment, breathing hard but with a sense of satisfaction I wasn't totally prepared for. The branch starts to wobble, warning me that it's part of the course's training too.

With a rasp of my feet against the bark, I spring off and slip along a narrow path between the trees. I spot the trip wires seconds before I reach them and hop nimbly over each, just dodging a spinning disc that's careening back and forth along one of them.

It's done. I dart out into the field beyond the jungle with a sigh of relief.

The sun beams down over me, comfortingly warm. My nerves jangle from the high alertness I kept all through the stealth course that's part of this island facility's grounds.

Flopping down on the soft grass, I breathe the warmth and the new stillness in deeply.

I *can* do this. I can lie back and rest, knowing I made it through the course successfully.

Knowing I got to choose to run that course to begin with. Clancy escorted me from my room in the mountain facility this morning after a brief talk, but once we reached the grounds, he told me I could explore and try out anything that interested me.

He *wanted* me to get comfortable here. To see what he's offering and what the life he's talking about could be like.

I'm still having trouble wrapping my head around the idea of a guardian offering me a choice.

I told him I'd give his training style and his missions a try, because it was either that or stay locked up and be prodded like a lab rat. The decision was pretty simple.

But is it possible this option could actually be... good?

I'll feel surer about that when he lets me see my guys

again. How much can I really trust him when he doesn't totally trust us?

Of course, he's right not to trust us. If I knew how to reach the guys and had a clear way of getting us and the other shadowbloods out of here, I'd take it in an instant.

But the mountains that surround this crater-turned-valley look ominously steep. I don't know how far we'd have to go beyond their ridges to find the island's shores—or what avenues for further escape we'd find there.

How is Clancy bringing in people and supplies? Helicopter? Boat?

I have no idea which direction we'd even want to go in.

So for now I'll play along, make whatever observations I can, and stay ready.

And if he really can help me get a proper handle on my sadistic talent while I'm here, I might actually leave better than I arrived.

Footsteps rustle across the grass toward me. I sit up in a snap and find two of the younger shadowbloods wandering over.

They hesitate at my sudden motion before continuing toward me. The younger-looking one, who I can't imagine is even in her teens yet, strides forward boldly even as her eyes widen to take me in. A cloth bag swings from one of her hands.

The older one, who I'd guess is in her late teens, comes at more of a stroll, her eyebrows slightly arched beneath the fringe of her dark pixie cut. The wry expression contrasts with her statuesque bearing, tall and solidly built but elegant as well. But what stands out the most is her neon pink T-shirt.

"Did you make it through the whole thing with no glitter at all?" the younger one asks breathlessly, swiping her fawn-brown hair back from her pale face.

I guess they were watching my explorations.

"I think so." I get up and hold out my arms for them to examine me.

They both circle me. The younger girl leans in to tap something on my black tee that I grabbed from the assortment of workout clothes I found in my room and giggles. "Nope, that was just a bit of lint. You really made it! I always get a little dusted."

I look her up and down. "I'd imagine I've been training a while longer than you have. Also, it helps being tiny."

Even the preteen has a couple of inches and maybe ten pounds on my five-foot-one frame. Her companion is at least half a foot taller than me.

"And fast," the older girl says with a smile, and dips her head, the sun shining off her high brown cheeks. "I'm Nadia, and this is Tegan. You're one of the First Gen shadowbloods, right?"

The capitalization of the words comes across in her tone, like it's an official rank. A shiver that's a weird mix of uneasy and proud tickles under my skin.

I shrug. "Yeah. I guess I am. My name's Riva. Have you been here on the island for a while?"

Nadia shakes her head. "I think it's been a week? I'm not great at keeping track."

"Yeah, same." Tegan peers at me again with those big

eyes that I'm starting to think are just permanently wide. "Is it true that you and the other Firsts were going around with the *monsters*?"

I blink at her. "You know about the shadowkind?"

The guardians never told me and my guys anything about the "monsters" we were supposed to be training to fight. We only found out what our expected purpose was when we confronted Ursula Engel.

Nadia's eyebrows arch higher. "Shadowkind?"

"That's what they call themselves," I say. "The beings the guardians call monsters. They helped us. Well, some of them did."

My mind darts back to the photos Clancy showed me of the dead kids. The bodies that could have been the two girls in front of me if they'd been held at the facility we broke into.

Tegan claps her hands together. "Of course we know about them! The guardians told us that's why they're working us so hard. So we can go out and stop them. Nadia's even done missions to *kill* them."

The older girl grimaces with a tug at her vibrant tee. "That wasn't anything wonderful. I don't even know what the ones I took out had been doing. I shot them with some special bullets from far away... But it was better than what the guardians would have done if I'd argued about it."

I can imagine—they probably threatened her friends, her fellow shadowbloods, like they did with me and the guys.

Why did the guardians send our younger equivalents

out so much sooner than us? What made them change their approach?

The two girls obviously don't realize there's anything strange about it. I swallow that question.

Curiosity itches at me about their talents, but if I ask about theirs, they'll want to know mine... and the thought of trying to explain my brutal scream to sweet Tegan makes my stomach clench up. Instead, I focus on something more immediately important.

"How's it been since you got here? No one's treated you badly?"

"It's great!" Tegan crows. "We get to come outside all the time, and the guardians working with Clancy are way nicer than the ones before. And the food is SO much better."

Nadia nudges her. "You forgot to get out the snack."

"Oh, right!" The younger girl grabs the cloth bag she set down and opens it up. "One of the kitchen staff made brownies for a treat. I was going to see if you wanted one. Or two. However many you'd like."

She smiles at me so shyly but eagerly that I have to smile back. Then my stomach gurgles.

"Sure. Seems like I've worked up an appetite."

She lays the bag down on the grass between us, spreading the opening wide so we have easy access to the several slabs of chewy chocolate stacked inside. I pick one up with instinctive wariness, but it smells and feels like perfect fudgy goodness.

When I take a small bite, it tastes like that too, chocolate heaven melting in my mouth. Normally I'm more of a sour-flavors gal, but I can go for sweets when they're this delicious.

But as I chew, a pang shoots through my chest.

Dominic would love these. Has he gotten to have one?

I can sense that he's somewhere within the mountain facility right now, but nothing about how he's feeling or what he's doing. I guess he can't be in too much distress, because I seem to pick up a trace of particularly strong emotions, but that's not a huge comfort.

It'd be awfully nice if these marks operated like walkie talkies.

As Tegan hums happily over her own brownie, two other teens who look around Nadia's age amble toward us. The guy, whose tan skin and spiky blond hair make him look like he's walked out of a surfer movie, tsks his tongue in mock-offense.

"You didn't think to tell *me* you had the goods?"

Nadia scrambles up in a much more awkward motion than I've seen before, her cheeks reddening as she sweeps up the bag. "Of course you can have one. And you too, Celine."

She nods to the girl who's trailed behind him. From her features, I'd guess she's got a lot of Chinese or Vietnamese in her genetics.

The guardians seem to have liked to experiment with a variety of human ethnic heritages. I suspect Nadia is mostly Native American in background—as much as you can call it a background when we were constructed in a lab rather than out in the real world.

Celine smiles widely with a swish of her long ponytail,

the red flecks in her black hair catching the sunlight. "Thanks so much!"

Something about her tone jars me. Like the chipper inflection should remind me of Pearl's bubbly personality, but it doesn't hold as much warmth as I'd expect.

But then, who could blame her if she's a little on edge in this place? It might be nice compared to other facilities, but we are still technically captives.

Nadia is mainly focused on the guy anyway, her gaze lingering on his face as he raises the brownie to his full lips.

I might not be the most socially experienced person ever, but soap operas have more than prepared me to recognize a crush. And that, ladies and gentlemen, is what I'm looking at right now.

Did they train together like I did with my guys? Nadia isn't acting like they have quite the same level of closeness already.

"Nice," he says after swallowing the first bite, and lifts his hand to me in greeting. "And nice to meet you, Firstie. I'm Booker."

"Riva," I reply. *Firstie?* Is that what they're all going to be calling us now?

Celine aims her smile more directly at me. "I'm glad you're all back with us, safe and sound."

Tegan, who's gotten up too, bobs on her feet. "Celine was out with the guardians trying to help you get away from the monsters."

Oh. My lips part, but my words have dried up.

Should I say thank you when I didn't really want to be "helped"?

Celine laughs as if it's no big deal, but her eyelids flicker down for just a second. I think I catch a flash of discomfort, maybe even sadness, before she's smiling fully again.

What did the guardians put her through during their hunt? It's no wonder she'd be struggling, even if she's doing her best to put on a cheerful front.

Before I can figure out how to talk to her, a twinge at my collarbone brings my gaze jerking to the facility entrance. My heart leaps.

Two figures are just walking out onto the ridge in front of the entrance, over the broad stone staircase that winds around to the valley floor. It only takes one glimpse for me to recognize them.

It's probably horrendously rude of me, but I can't stop my feet from bounding forward. I sprint across the field and up the steps as the two men who stepped out hurry down to meet me.

"Drey!" I throw my arms around the leaner guy the second he's within reach, knowing he'll welcome the hug.

Andreas sucks in a hitch of breath and squeezes me hard. He smells like he always has, warm and a little spicy, like cinnamon.

When I force myself to ease back to scan his face, he looks the same too: dark coiled hair, gorgeous brown face, sparkling dark gray eyes. I don't see any injuries on him.

Then he's cupping my jaw and pulling my mouth to his, and there's no part of me that can resist the kiss.

I loop my arm around his neck and kiss him back hard with a giddy quiver through my veins as if the shadows in me are rejoicing at our reunion.

This is something different too. I never would have dared to show this much physical affection in any of the other facilities.

But I don't give a fuck what Clancy thinks. These are my guys, my loves, and I'm not going to pretend they're anything less.

Well, they're my guys to varying extents. As Andreas releases me, keeping one arm slung around my back, I turn toward Zian with a smile that's both joyful and a little cautious.

Zee hasn't generally reacted all that well to even brief touches, let alone a full hug. But he did offer me a very careful embrace right before we set off on our last personal mission.

He's staring at me with so much emotion blazing in his dark brown eyes that it lights up my skin. His brawn flexes all across his broad shoulders.

He reaches out and brushes his fingers tentatively over my shoulder. "They didn't hurt you, Shrimp?"

The question comes out gruff, the silly nickname offset by the concern wound through his voice.

"No. I'm okay. Just… not really sure what to make of all this." My gaze darts between the two of them. "Are you both totally all right? Have you seen Dominic or Jacob?"

Andreas flicks his gaze toward the facility with a trace of the same wariness I feel about our new situation. "We're… as good as we can be. I got to talk to Dominic at breakfast this morning—he wasn't happy that we're being kept apart, but otherwise fine."

Zian knits his brow. "Neither of us has seen Jacob. You haven't either?"

"No. You two are the first." My stomach sinks. "Clancy hasn't been letting us out until we commit to running his missions. Maybe Jacob isn't giving in."

It's way too easy to imagine the rigidly stubborn guy refusing to even pretend to play along if he's angry that we were captured at all. And there's also—

I pause for a second with a constricting of my throat. "You know—Griffin…"

I don't have to say anything more than that. Andreas's face somehow manages to brighten and fall at the same time, and the furrow in Zian's forehead deepens.

"All this time," the bigger guy says in a disbelieving tone, and swipes his hand back over his short black hair.

Drey nods. "That's got to have thrown Jake for a loop. Especially when Griffin is definitely… different, too."

"Yeah." My gut knots at the memory of Griffin's oddly vacant demeanor.

I haven't seen him since the talk with him and Clancy yesterday. I have no idea how he's been spending his days.

How closely do the two of them work together?

"At least this place seems better than many of the alternatives," Andreas says with a hesitantly hopeful note in his voice. He glances across the valley. "I saw a place like this once in some backpacker's memories. He went around scaling mountains, soaking in lagoons, and gorging himself on tropical fruit until he gave himself a stomachache. Even then, he called it paradise. It never occurred to me I'd get to visit somewhere like that in person."

He's fallen into his storyteller's lilt. Andreas has always been our memory-keeper—both of our own past and all kinds of lives that were beyond our reach except through his talent.

His attention comes back to me with a knowing expression. "And it's also a little less restricted. Can't complain about that."

"Nope," I agree. Not when that lack of restriction means more opportunity for escape if we don't like the other opportunities Clancy offers us.

As if drawn by my thoughts, our grand leader himself steps out onto the ridge above us. He sets his hands on his hips and smiles down over his domain and all of us within it.

"All right, folks," he calls out. "You've had some free training time. How about something a little more structured? Capture the Flag—the whole valley's your arena. Three Firsts against the rest of you. That should be fair enough."

An excited murmuring rises up from where the younger shadowbloods—including another two who've joined the bunch I talked to—are gathered below. I glance at my guys and swallow hard.

Clancy is working so hard to make our time here feel like recreation rather than torture. He's given us a home some people would consider paradise.

But he's still one of *them*.

Just how dangerous would it be to trust him?

FIVE

Riva

However skeptical I might be about the intentions of the new man in charge, I have to admit that mealtimes in the mountain facility are a big step up from our past imprisonment.

No more trays of bland food chosen only for nutritional completion shoved through a slot in a door to be eaten in solitude. We get our choice from a spread of dishes set out in shifts, with a random assortment of about ten fellow shadowbloods in the cafeteria for company.

The buffet isn't anywhere near as extensive or gourmet as the meals Rollick provided us with on his yacht, but everything I've sampled so far at least tastes good. And there's something to be said simply for getting to pick.

For this morning's breakfast, I'm debating between omelets stuffed with cheese and fried veggies or bowls of steaming oatmeal laced with berries and brown sugar. I kind of want one of each, but I don't think my stomach will thank me after I've stretched it to twice its regular size.

I end up grabbing a plate with an omelet, add a small scoop of hashbrowns and a bottle of orange juice for good measure, and turn toward the tables.

The rock-carved room holds five rectangular tables that comfortably seat six each, but I've never seen them full. Because we eat in shifts, I have no idea exactly how many shadowbloods are staying here.

Right now, the two of the tables on the left hold three and four of the younger shadowbloods respectively. I spot Nadia and Booker at one, her laughing hard at something he's said and then covering her mouth as if embarrassed.

Today her shirt is neon green. She obviously has a thing for bright clothing.

Everything in my wardrobe is darker shades... Did she ask Clancy for those tees specially?

Did he give her new clothes simply because she asked?

As I'm working through my new debate of whether to be friendly and go sit with them or huddle on my own at one of the empty tables, a familiar blond head passes through the doorway at the right side of the room.

My pulse skips a beat, and my plate wobbles in my hand. For an instant, I'm not sure which of the twins I'm looking at.

Then his gaze collides with mine, and any doubt flies out of my mind. Only Jacob could look at me like a dam's just burst open behind his eyes.

Before I can even part my lips to speak, he's hurtling forward, straight toward me.

He doesn't even veer around the vacant tables between

me and him. With a flick of his arm, he sends them flipping over to clear his path.

Both tables clang against the stone wall. Jacob strides by without a split-second of hesitation, his gaze still fixed on me.

Then he stops right in front of me and raises his hand with a gentleness totally at odds with the aggression of his approach.

As he touches my cheek, my fingers tighten around my plate and the neck of the juice bottle as if I'm clutching them for dear life.

My heart pounds against my ribs. I'm too choked up to speak.

To say that Jake and I had a stormy time with our original reunion is like referring to a hurricane as a light breeze. But in the last few days before we ended up here, I came to understand how he acted a lot better than I had before.

To recognize that no one could hate how he first treated me more than he did himself. To see just how far he'd go to ensure nobody ever hurt me again.

And how far he'd go to make me feel *good*, when I'd let him.

The maelstrom of emotion in his sky-blue gaze matches the turmoil his presence has stirred up inside me. He strokes his fingers over my cheek with nothing but tenderness, staring at me as if he can read my experiences of the past few days through my skull.

"Are you okay?" he asks in a low, taut voice, either because he can't tell or he wants me to confirm it.

I manage to get enough of a grip on my internal state

to locate a trace of my sense of humor. "I'm fine. I don't know if the tables are."

Jacob doesn't spare the pieces of furniture he upended even the briefest of glances. "Fuck the tables."

I'm not sure Clancy's staff are totally on board with that attitude.

A man and a woman have stepped into the room to eye the results of Jacob's arrival. Like Clancy himself, the guardians working under him don't wear the protections we're used to—but then, we know those are useless against our powers anyway. But they're the only people around who are older than me and my guys, so they're easy to identify.

I tense, expecting them to march over and yank Jacob away from me—Lord only knows how big a catastrophe *that* would turn into—but the woman simply shakes her head in apparent consternation. She and the man heave the tables onto their feet, study the new but small dents along the edges, and nudge the chairs back into place.

Huh. I guess they're choosing their battles.

I have no idea what the younger shadowbloods are making of Jacob's dramatic entrance. I only manage to watch the guardians for a matter of seconds before my attention swings back to him as if drawn by a magnet.

I move as little as I can manage to set my plate and my juice down and then rest my hands against the front of Jake's shirt. "Are *you* okay? You must have— Did Griffin—?"

He nods with a tightening of his mouth, cutting off the question I'd only started. "If you can even call him Griffin anymore," he mutters.

A tremor passes through his body, and he brushes his fingers farther across my face to stroke them over my hair. He hasn't moved one inch closer since I set aside the meal I was holding.

He's waiting for my welcome—or lack thereof. I can feel his tense anticipation like a vibration in the air.

I ease forward and tip my head against his chest.

A breath rushes out of Jacob with a shudder, and his arms encircle me. He hugs me to him tightly but still with a sense of restraint, as if he's afraid he'll hurt me even now.

But if our new prison has proven anything to me so far, it's that Jake has never really been my enemy.

He fucked up, and he shouldn't have treated me the way he did. But the guardians fucked him up first.

They did it on purpose.

And having seen the new Griffin, drained of any noticeable emotion, devoid of warmth, I know just how thoroughly they can break a person.

I may never fully understand exactly how much they wrecked the man I'm holding.

Jacob's voice comes out in a rasp muffled by my hair. "I'm sorry."

I frown and raise my head. "What for?"

I hate how familiar I am with the anguish etched on his chiseled features. "I was supposed to be looking out for you in the other facility—I swore I'd keep you safe—and they still managed to— I got distracted. I wasn't thinking."

"Hey." I touch his cheek the way he cupped mine. "You know that Griffin was *there*, right? He messed with our emotions to get us where the guardians—at least the ones on Clancy's side, I guess—wanted us to be."

Jacob blinks at me, and a muscle ticks in his jaw. Maybe he *hadn't* realized that part.

"Shit. I should have recognized—I should have known—"

"No." I tap the side of his face firmly to emphasize my protest. "We all got caught. It's all of our faults or none of ours. I haven't for one second blamed you. So you're not allowed to blame yourself for this."

Jacob's mouth twists, but he can't seem to find a way to argue with me.

I pull away from him a little reluctantly and pick up my breakfast to bring it to the nearest undented table. Jake snatches the first plate in reach and follows me.

As he sits down across from me, I hover my fork over my omelet. "So, you decided to give Clancy's missions a try? We've been a little worried about you since we hadn't seen you yet."

Dominic joined in my outdoor training session yesterday morning, and I saw Zian and Andreas again at separate meals. Jacob's absence has been weighing on all of us.

Jake shrugs a little stiffly and jabs his fork into the fried egg. "It wasn't really much of a choice, was it? It was the only way they'd let me see you, or the guys. They still made me wait a whole day for that after I said I was in."

Clancy must have been watching him, evaluating whether he could trust Jacob's intentions enough. "They just left you in your room all that time?"

He shakes his head. "I think they take us outside in shifts just like the meals. Clancy and a couple of his underlings brought me out to a training area that's a ways into the forest, along with some of the kids. We didn't see anyone else going to or from."

I haven't been taken to any separate areas of the valley yet, but his explanation doesn't surprise me. Zian said that he and Dominic were escorted to a rock-climbing area yesterday afternoon while I was in the field again.

Jacob takes a bite and considers me over the table as we chew. "We have to get off this island for one of these missions. See how it all works. Then we can make more of a decision."

Exactly what I've been thinking. I offer him a crooked smile in return. "Yeah."

We eat for a few minutes in silence, wary of who might be listening unseen. Then Jacob motions his fork at me.

"You said 'we.' How many of the others have you seen?"

"All of them, now. But only here and there. And never more than three of us together at once." I swallow a lump of cheese-saturated egg, the flavor turning sour as I think about my answer. "Clancy made it clear that he doesn't think it's in his best interests to let all five of us have a chance to collaborate."

Jacob lets out a disdainful huff. "Because we'd run fucking circles around his operation here."

He could be right. But we're not getting to find out, are we?

Even though the omelet is perfectly enjoyable, my stomach has twisted into a knot by the time I've finished eating. I get up to put my dishes away, knowing that in a matter of minutes some of the staff will come by to usher us to our various next destinations.

But I've barely set my plate down in the bin when Clancy himself pokes his red-topped head into the cafeteria.

He walks over to my and Jacob's table at a briskly professional pace. "The two of you appear to be settling in."

Jacob eyes him, looking like he's grappling with his self-control. "I'd like to see the rest of my friends."

"We'll get to that. I'm sure Riva's already told you that they're perfectly fine, as she is." Clancy motions to us. "I was hoping to talk to just the two of you in my office for a moment."

Jake and I exchange a look. Our new captor makes the request sound voluntary, but somehow I don't think he'll be pleased if we refuse.

We'll get more chances to figure out this place and how to leave it the more we dance to his tune.

But I'm not going to let him call all the shots either—at least, as much as he'll let me have a voice.

As we follow him into the hall, I clear my throat. "There were a few things I wanted to ask you about too. Just to understand how we ended up here better."

I don't know whether to be relieved or suspicious that Clancy answers without hesitation. "That's completely fair."

Of course, after we've stepped into an office room that's got the same stone walls as the rest of the mountain facility, it's Jacob who speaks up first. He doesn't even wait until Clancy has moved behind the desk at one end of the room.

"In the other facility, the one we broke into—you set us up to get caught, with my brother's help. How did you know we'd be coming there? Why did you let us get the kids out first?"

I've been wondering a lot along the same lines. I study Clancy's face as he sinks into the simple office chair behind the desk, leaving us standing.

"About your brother's part in things, I think that's something you should discuss with Griffin, as much as he's willing to. As for the rest, I didn't intervene right away because I wasn't sure how the situation would play out. Not everyone working at that facility was completely on board with my approach. I hoped their strategy would work and that I could arrange your transfer to the island regardless."

The knots in my gut pull tighter. "But it didn't work, so we slaughtered a bunch of people who were causing problems for you." How convenient.

And technically, *I* slaughtered most of them.

Clancy doesn't show any reaction to that statement. "I'm not happy about the loss of life. It is what it is. We did have to resort to a certain amount of trickery in the end, but I'd known that if brute force wasn't going to do it, we'd have to be as smart as possible instead."

They'd waited until we'd started to split up and then divided us even further.

"What about the younger shadowbloods—all of them?" I ask. "The ones I've talked to here all already know about the sha—the monsters we're supposed to be fighting. Some of them have already been sent on missions directly against them. That never happened with us."

Clancy folds his hands in his lap as he leans back in his chair. "We've made some modifications to our process from generation to generation. We were able to train in the younger shadowbloods faster because we'd learned from our experiences with you. And after your escape attempt, a significant portion of the Guardianship felt it would be too dangerous for the six of you to leave the facilities under any circumstances."

Modifications in their process. He probably doesn't realize what we learned from Ursula Engel's computer files —that she never gave the rest of the guardians her full formula for creating us.

The kids have weaker powers than we do. *That's* at least as much a part of why the guardians worried less about sending them into the field.

But it also means they'd have been less equipped to actually fight the shadowkind they were up against.

"What are we doing here if you're not actually going to give us anything to do other than train more?" Jacob demands, scowling.

A hint of a smile touches Clancy's lips. "I said a significant portion. I didn't say *I* felt that way. I actually brought you in here so we could discuss your first potential assignment."

SIX

Riva

The first moment when I emerge from sleep in my new bed always feels a little empty. It's comfortable enough, with layers of covers I can bundle under against the cave-like chill, but I'm all on my own.

Sometime over the past few weeks, without even realizing it, I got used to waking up next to my guys. Mostly Dominic, but one time him and Andreas both, and once, after a particularly tumultuous evening, Jacob.

We have more freedoms here, but I'm no longer allowed the simple pleasure of a cuddle to greet the day.

I pull myself out from under the covers, wash at the sink in the corner, and dress with quick movements. I'm just slipping on my sneakers when a knock sounds on my door.

I don't cross paths with any of my guys at breakfast, but when I'm ushered out to the facility entrance, Clancy is waiting with Jacob, Dominic, four of the younger shadowbloods, and several other guardians.

Seeing Jake, my heart skips a beat. This must be preparation for the mission we agreed to yesterday.

Clancy confirms my assumption with a nod toward the kids, who look to all be from the oldest of their generations, around seventeen. "This group will perform some secondary work as part of your assignment off the island. It should be relatively straightforward, but we want to make sure we've covered all the bases before sending you into the field."

Celine is there, flashing me one of her bright smiles as she teases her fingers through her ponytail, but I don't know the others by name yet. As we set off down to the clearing and then along a jungle path, she chatters energetically with a couple of her companions.

Here and there, I think I catch glimpses of that sadness I thought I noticed earlier. I feel like I should apologize to her for the last mission the guardians forced her to take on, even though it wasn't my idea that they should hunt us down across the continent.

Behind them, the three of us "Firsts" walk in silence. I'm too keyed up to make any kind of small talk.

Dominic takes my hand and interlocks my fingers with his. Jacob sticks close to my other side, scanning the wilderness.

Despite the sticky humidity, it isn't really an unpleasant hike. Birds twitter in the trees, and the hazy sunlight dances between the rustling leaves.

It doesn't take long before we stop in a small clearing. Three of the guardians direct the younger shadowbloods off between the trees at the far end for whatever they need to work on. Three others and Clancy stay with us Firsts.

Clancy strolls back and forth in front of us, his hands clasped behind his back. "I know the three of you have already been through extensive training, including some missions outside your facility. And obviously you've added to your real-world skills in the weeks while you were on the run."

Real-world skills that included killing a whole lot of his colleagues. My skin creeps uneasily despite his calm tone, and Dominic squeezes my fingers reassuringly.

His closer tentacle slips around my wrist as if to duplicate the casually affectionate touch with the gentle graze of its suckers. Both times I've seen him since arriving on the island, he's had his strange new appendages uncovered like he'd started to feel comfortable doing on Rollick's yacht.

I catch a couple of the younger shadowbloods glancing his way and nudging each other. My jaw sets on edge, and my grip on his hand tightens in return.

They might be like us, but I'm not going to let *anyone* make him ashamed of the features that are now part of him. Especially not when he's finally found a kind of peace with his situation.

"This operation will require a few very specific skills that will need additional testing and training." Clancy halts and turns to face the three of us. "Riva and Jacob, you'll be taking lead, which will require immense stealth and speed. Dominic, if your healing ability is needed, time will be of the essence there as well. We'd like to see where you're currently at."

He points to a blotch of orange through the trees in the opposite end from where the teens are doing their training. "Start by that marker and run as fast as you can, regardless of the obstacles, to the one you'll see ahead of you." His arm swings to indicate the direction we'll be running.

Then he fixes his gaze on us again. "Please give it your all. I don't want to waste time on additional exercises that aren't really necessary."

I don't want to hang around here training any longer than I need to either. Less than a week, and he's already opened up the possibility of getting off the island.

I have no idea how we can make use of that opportunity, but I want to find out as soon as I can.

This once, we have to leave Andreas and Zian behind. But maybe we'll learn something that could bring us back together, one way or another.

We head toward the marker, Jacob positioning himself between me and the guardians like a shield.

As we turned, we put our backs to the younger shadowbloods with a sway of Dominic's tentacles. A shocked gasp carries after us, followed by nervous giggles and a muffled "What the *hell*?"

Dom's fingers tense momentarily in mine.

"Ignore them," I say under my breath. "They'll get used to it."

They'd better.

Dominic's grip has already relaxed again. "I know. And I do look strange. It's worth the trade-off."

He told me the first night we got together that he'd never want to try to remove the tentacles because then he might not be able to heal me properly if I needed his help in the future.

I raise his hand in mine to press a kiss to his knuckles, and then to the back of his tentacle still tucked around my wrist. Dominic beams at me, and I don't give a shit that the guardian who's following us clears his throat as if to remind us to stay focused.

Jacob shoots a death glare over his shoulder at my critic, so that helps too.

The guardian veers away from us toward the other orange marker that I can now make out through the trees. "Get ready and wait for my signal."

We spread ourselves out in a reasonably straight line in front of the tree that has the first marker, my hand parting from Dominic's reluctantly. I drop into a sprinter's starting stance.

The guardian gives the standard "Ready, set, go!" and I launch myself forward alongside the other guys.

Between the three of us, it's no real contest. I could probably outrun even Zian's similarly super-powered strength here in the forest, where my small size makes it easier for me to slip between the tree trunks and through the underbrush.

My feet thump over the uneven ground in a swift rhythm, finding their balance instinctively. I fly past bushes and low branches and skid to a stop just past the second marker, barely winded.

Jacob charges after me, hurtling forward as fast as his muscular legs can propel him. Dominic follows several paces behind him with his tentacles coiled close to his back.

But even though Dom's always been the least coordinated of us, all our past training has still served him well. He reaches the two of us just seconds behind Jacob.

The guardian gives his timer a third click and studies the results. "Better than you were looking for," he shouts back to Clancy.

"Then we can move on," Clancy says. "Come on back, you three."

When we tramp over to him, he motions Jacob toward another of the guardians. "Lin has some models for you to work your powers on. We want you honing that telekinetic accuracy so you can dispatch enemy combatants with no chance for them to sound a warning."

Clancy turns to me. "I'd like to see if your claws can let you climb up a brick wall without the need for a harness. We've got a setup for that over here."

Then he beckons over the last of the guardians who've stayed with us, who's been lugging a large sack. The man peels it off to reveal a short, dense shrub in a thin plastic pot that's trailing fabric straps.

"You," Clancy says to Dominic, "need a guaranteed energy source if you're going to be healing on the fly. So we're going to see about making an effective harness for you, with the largest plants you can carry that won't interfere with your movements."

Dominic studies the shrub with a slight rise of his eyebrows. "I'm going to be porting bushes around like a baby in a carrier?"

I can't stop a short laugh from slipping out at the image that forms in my mind. "Whatever works, right?"

It's actually a pretty smart idea, even if it'll look funny.

Clancy and the guardian who handled our race lead me over to a section of layered bricks they've set up in another clear patch of forest. I flex my claws out far enough that tufts of fur spring across the shell of my ears too and launch myself at the mottled surface.

After a few tries, I figure out the trick for sinking the tips far enough into the mortar between the rough blocks at the right angle to hold my weight. I can't hold myself in one spot for more than a few seconds, but by quickly jerking my hands upward one by one and scrambling with my feet catching on whatever small notches they can find, I make it to the top of the ten-foot structure in the space of a few breaths.

I push myself off and land on my feet on the ground.

Clancy nods with a satisfied air. "Give that at least ten run-throughs until you're totally comfortable, and then we're going to work on refining your other supernatural talent."

My pulse hiccups at the thought of bringing out my fatal shriek. I glance toward Jacob, his pale hair partly visible through the trees, and think of the task he was sent to do.

By "dispatch," Clancy meant "kill."

"Are you going to tell us who we're going up against and why?" I have to ask.

"We'll get to that."

He turns on his heel and leaves me to it.

I tackle the wall twenty more times just to make sure I'm fully prepared. I might have kept going if the last joints of my fingers didn't feel ready to fall off by that point.

I stop to catch my breath, flexing my hands to stretch out some of the soreness. Clancy returns with a smaller sack I didn't notice the guardians carrying.

He pulls it open to reveal a wire cage containing eight white mice.

I recoil instinctively. "I don't want to kill them."

Clancy gives me an evaluating look. "I don't want you to either. I think your power could be much more useful than that, in ways you might be more comfortable putting it to use. From the video footage I've seen—you can only break one body at a time, but you can hold dozens of them frozen while you work your way through them. Is that right?"

"Yes." I swallow against the sudden dryness in my mouth.

"Then if we can modulate that scream of yours, you should be able to maintain it at lower levels of influence. Simply paralyze your targets without inflicting any damage. Possibly even seek them out without touching them at all, like a sort of sonar."

His even words steady my nerves, but doubts coil in my gut. "I don't know. It... It really *wants* the pain."

Clancy doesn't object to my characterizing my talent as something separate from myself. "It's in you. You can control it. You simply need to learn how."

I drag in a breath. "What did you have in mind?"

Clancy motions for me to sit and sets the cage in front of me. "We'll pull back from your innate impulses by degrees. Can you damage one of the mice without outright killing it?"

I give him a sharp look, and he smiles apologetically.

"We have to start somewhere. If you can manage it in one go, we can scale back even more."

Every molecule of my body balks at torturing an innocent animal, but I remember Rollick's admonishments far too well. If I don't learn how to control my power, then it's going to control me when I least want it to.

Like when I nearly tore apart one of the shadowkind who'd been most welcoming to us.

The memory of Billy's twisted, smoking body congeals inside me, stiffening my resolve. "All right. I'll do my best."

SEVEN

Riva

I kill the first mouse.

I don't mean to. I summon the furious vibration in my lungs, remembering the other guardians chasing us down, the cage-fights in the arena, the attacks of the monster hunters, and part my lips, letting only the thinnest shriek slip out.

But maybe the vicious thing inside me is too hungry after all the days it's lain dormant. Or maybe other parts of me crave the rush of power a little more than I want to admit.

The scream jolts out of me faster than I intended. The mouse twitches and spasms, the flavor of its agony hitting me in a swift smack like a gulp of cold water on a hot day.

The next thing I know, it's lying in a disjointed lump on the cedar chips covering the base of the cage.

I flinch at the sight, but Clancy sets a careful hand on my shoulder.

"It's going to take time. After everything I've heard and observed, I think your problem might be how much you're resisting the urge."

I stare at him, barely holding back a glower. "Isn't the point to resist?"

"Then you're fighting against yourself. You'll only make yourself weaker." Clancy tips his head thoughtfully. "What if you focused on how you *will* get what the power wants? Stretching out the pain so you can absorb more of it—and then you'll have more time to pull back as well. Even holding a creature in place with the sense of something horrible to come is a pretty painful act, if you think about it."

I wet my lips and look at the dead mouse again. I don't know if what he's saying makes sense, but it's true that my past attempts at control haven't gotten me very far.

I've managed to get more specific in *who* I target, but how... not really at all.

Gritting my teeth, I brace myself to try.

The second mouse I don't kill outright, yanking myself out of the scream's trance at the last second. But its mangled twitching showed there'd be no point in keeping it alive if Clancy couldn't scoop it out and pass it to another guardian, telling him to take it to Dominic.

I still feel sick, but knowing I managed to rein myself in a little builds my confidence. With the third mouse, I encourage the demanding need inside me to inflict the pain slowly, drawing out every drop.

One bone snaps. A sliver of flesh rips.

I slam my mouth shut, and the mouse shudders. It's going to need healing too, but it can still walk.

A startled laugh of relief tumbles from my mouth, soothing the vocal cords still quivering from my last shriek.

The next time, I don't break anything at all. I narrow all my attention onto the panic I can sense in the rodents' beady eyes, the twitches of their bodies as my scream grips them, drinking in the thinner stream formed by the torment of that fear—and pull back before the scream can slice any deeper.

I practice again and again, until I've probably given the poor things PTSD. But I haven't done anything worse to them.

Finally, I sag back on my heels and realize that my shirt is damp with sweat.

Clancy's small smile looks almost friendly to me now. "That was good. Very good. You'll have a chance to practice more later. Better not to push yourself too hard all at once."

I find myself accepting his offered hand to help me to my feet. A whisper of elation tickles through me as we return to the main clearing.

He told the truth about at least this much—he's giving me the chance to be something other than a monster.

When I rejoin the others, Dominic still has his harness on. The straps of the shrub-carrier have been constructed well to work around his various appendages, angling under his tentacles and then across the outer part of his shoulders. Another strap around his waist holds the contraption steady, with the pot right in the middle of his back.

"It's not too bad," he tells me with a crooked smile.

"I'm going to leave it on for the trek back to the facility just to get more used to it."

Jacob rolls his shoulders, his expression impassive. I can't tell if he's been affected by the mock-killing he's been practicing.

"What now?" he asks Clancy.

Our captor-slash-trainer has brought out a tablet. "We'll go over more of the details of the mission back at the facility this evening. But I want you to start absorbing the key faces now so you're most likely to recognize them later."

He brings up a photograph of a man who looks to be in his sixties, grizzled with slicked back gray hair and lips that are both full and sharply carved in his craggy face. "This is the leader of a child abduction ring that's been operating for decades. His people kidnap vulnerable kids and teens and sell them off into work-slavery or worse."

A shiver of revulsion passes through me. "And there aren't any police or whatever who can stop them?"

Clancy grimaces. "He pays off local law enforcement and operates very carefully so there's as little evidence as possible. I think it's time someone took matters into their own hands."

He flips through several more photographs, pausing on each to give us time to study their faces. "These are his known associates that we've identified. Most of them should be with him in his home on the night we send you in."

"What about the kids?" Dominic asks, frowning.

"They never have more than one or two on their property at a time, and never for very long. And from what we can tell, they don't keep them at the private home. But to take every precaution, we'll pick a time when we're sure they're between transactions."

Clancy lowers the tablet and considers us. "There may be household staff on the premises. We'd prefer you didn't harm them if you can avoid it. I'd imagine you can differentiate between them and your real targets by their behavior and clothing."

One more factor to pay attention to. I won't be able to simply scream at the house and carve up every human being inside it.

This assignment isn't going to be easy. It isn't anything like our past missions, where we had no idea what real purpose the guardians had for sending us out.

But the quiver passing through my veins is as much anticipation as it is nerves. I *would* like the chance to put my deadly skills to use in a way that helps people rather than simply slaughtering those in my way.

And I'm starting to think that might be possible in ways I never imagined before.

How can I say that killing a bunch of child-slavers is a bad thing? These assholes have to know their work is evil, but they're doing it anyway.

If I was willing to shatter Ursula Engel and her men simply for trying to murder us, slaughtering this bunch should be barely a blip on my conscience. Hell, it's balancing the scales, making sure people who deserve it have real *lives* that these pricks would steal from them.

Good fucking riddance.

If we get a better idea of how we could get free again while we're at it, then it's an extra win.

I eye Clancy's tablet as he slips it into his shoulder bag, wondering about the cell reception out here. Would we be able to get our hands on a phone out in the wider world that we could bring back and use?

But who would I contact? I had Rollick's number programmed into my old phone, but I didn't memorize it.

And I'm not sure even our supposedly greatest ally can be trusted to have our backs—or to protect us from his fellow shadowkind—after all.

Well, there's no way to know what we'll have to work with until we get out there.

Clancy claps his hands together. "Riva and Jacob, why don't you two run back to the facility. We've highlighted the trail with more markers at intervals. Consider it a challenge to see how quickly you can get there ahead of the rest of us."

The corners of his eyes crinkle as if with amusement. As if he likes watching us rise to the occasion.

I have no idea what to make of this man.

Jacob jerks his head toward me. "Come on, Wildcat. They can eat our dust."

He springs forward, not waiting for me—but then, he knows I can catch up with him in a matter of seconds. Which I do.

We dash between the trees, noting each orange marker when they flash into view up ahead. I could pull past Jacob and leave him "eating my dust" too, but I only propel myself a few steps ahead of him where I'll have more room to maneuver.

It's more fun when I can hear him right behind me. Like it's a real competition.

And weirdly, for several minutes there, the extended sprint actually does feel almost fun.

The wind whips over my face and braid, the fresh forest air flooding my lungs. Our feet thunder over the ground in a complex joint rhythm that's close to a song.

We're not free. I know we're not.

But for a few moments there, I feel closer to it than I have the whole time we were out of the guardians' clutches but hunted at every turn.

Jacob called me a superhero after I tore down Engel's soldiers with my scream. I managed to believe I was acting like one while we broke those six kids out of the facility days ago, even if that went all wrong.

Could what Clancy's offering us really be our best chance at becoming some kind of heroes for real?

I spot streaks of brighter sunlight in the distance where I think the forest gives way to the main field around the mountainside. I push myself a little faster, our goal in reach—

And stumble at the sight of the guy I thought was behind me emerging from between the trees in front of me instead.

It's not Jacob, though. Jacob slows next to me as my run peters out into a hesitant jog.

The guy who's ambling through the woods, now heading our way after seeing us, is his twin.

I haven't seen Griffin, let alone spoken to him, since my first day in the facility. From Jacob's tensing and the whiff of startled pheromones he gives off, I suspect he hasn't had much chance to reacquaint himself with his brother either.

Griffin offers us a mild smile. "Back from training?" he says in that vaguely friendly way that feels as vacant as his gaze.

I don't know how to talk to him anymore. Is that awful, when I've spent years wishing I had him back?

"Yeah." I come to a stop a few feet away, not sure whether I should keep going, what else he might want to talk about.

Then Jacob barrels between us, his muscles and his voice taut. "You *helped* Clancy get his hands on us, Griffin? What the fuck were you thinking?"

Oh, shit. I forgot that Jacob hadn't realized that part until I told him yesterday morning.

Griffin blinks at his twin, but even his surprise at the outburst is mild. "It seemed like the best thing to do. The right thing to do."

"To see us stuck back in cages? What's the matter with you?"

Griffin's gaze veers around us. "This isn't much of a cage."

I think his calm demeanor is pissing Jacob off even more than he already was. "It doesn't matter how pretty it is—we're still trapped here. Partly because of *you*. You're one of us. Or at least you were."

Griffin studies Jake as if he's a little confused by the entire line of questioning. "I didn't want to see you get into even more trouble or do more things you might regret. I'm sorry that I had to trick you to do it."

"You're sorry?" Jacob rasps. "You betrayed all of us. Me. Riva. You loved her—I know you did—and you helped them drag her back— How could you turn on even *her*?"

A flicker of something passes through Griffin's expression, there and then gone before I can tell if it's anything resembling an emotion. His attention slides to me where I'm standing behind his brother's shoulder, and a pang shoots through my chest.

I loved him too. I don't know if there's anything left of the guy I loved behind those dazed eyes.

"I think I should give you more space," Griffin says, backing up a step. "Seeing me is getting you worked up. I hope we can talk more later."

"You—"

Jacob's hand twitches, and I grab his arm before he can lift it. I don't want him using his powers on his brother—I can't imagine he won't regret *that*.

"Let him go," I say quietly as Griffin strides off toward the clearing. "I don't think he *can* give us any answer we'd be happy with."

Jake's fingers flex and clench at his sides. "There's nothing okay about that."

"I know. It isn't okay at all. But yelling at him isn't going to fix it. Throwing around your power definitely won't."

Jacob lets his breath out in a hiss. His head droops. "Yeah."

Watching him, an ache expands through my chest, eating away all the momentary joy I found. I can remember the two of them together so easily, back when we were all in the facility together.

Any time Griffin faltered in a physical trial, Jacob

would be there, ensuring his twin made it through. Every time Jacob's determined incisiveness boiled over into frustration, Griffin would be there, talking him down.

They fit together perfectly, like two halves of a whole, made to complement each other—to balance each other out. I've never seen them argue.

Until now.

We stay there for a few minutes, just standing together as Jake's breaths even out. I figure it's better not to push him to go on to the facility until he's got his anger totally under control.

Just as he finally lifts his head, footsteps crackle behind us. We look over to see Clancy approaching us.

Apparently our captor is a fast walker.

He takes us in with a slight cock of his head that asks a question silently.

"We bumped into Griffin," I say in explanation. "It wasn't a good conversation."

"Ah." Clancy's mouth tightens.

I cross my arms over my chest, just shy of hugging myself. "What did the guardians *do* to him?"

Clancy takes a deep breath, his gaze sliding past us toward the mountainside and then back again. "It's over now. I'd focus on that."

Jacob's voice comes out in a growl. "But—"

The older man cuts him off with a shake of his head and fishes for something in his bag. "I realized there's one thing I wanted to go over with you upfront. While you're out on the assignment, we'll be tracking and monitoring your life signals the entire time. To make sure you haven't gotten diverted, and so we can alert Dominic right away if his powers are needed."

My spine stiffens. "What do you mean?"

He pulls out a couple of metal bands about as thick as my thumb. "You'll each be wearing one of these around an ankle. So you'll never really be alone."

EIGHT

Riva

The lit windows stand out on the face of the mansion like signal flares in the dark night. But we have to avoid those beacons until we're inside.

Jacob topples the last of the three men who were stationed outside the isolated home with a snap of a vertebrae straight through the spinal cord. His power catches the body so it slumps quietly on the ground rather than hitting the lawn with a thump.

That's what he's spent the past two days practicing, while I've been climbing more walls, slipping silently through shadows... and doing my best *not* to kill mice.

Oh, and one of Clancy's guardians did walk me through the fastest ways to kill a person with my claws using a dummy. But when she saw that my cage-fighting days had driven those skills home even deeper than my previous facility training, she decided I was good to go.

I always left my opponents alive if I could, but if it came down to me or them, I needed to know how to end the fight quick.

We stalk swiftly through the darkness to the back of the sprawling two-story mansion. Clancy showed us a rough blueprint of the place—there's a room at the back that the people he's sent to observe never saw the light go on in.

Whatever our targets do in there, they don't do it at night. It's our best chance at entering without alerting anyone.

The second-floor window is closed, and I bet it has a latch on the inside too. But Jacob simply stares at it, and after a moment the sliding pane eases upward with a faint rasp.

I don't even wait for it to be fully raised. I leap at the side of the building, digging my claws in the way I've rehearsed, and fling myself up toward the window.

My ears pick up the tiny scratching of my claws, but I don't think even Jacob will be able to hear the noise below, let alone anyone inside. The second I reach the window, I whip my arm over the ledge to brace myself and lift my other hand to carve open the screen.

I roll inside through the opening I've made, peer through the darkness to confirm that the small room holds nothing but scattered cardboard boxes, and whirl toward the window while unstrapping the coil of rope from my waist.

Jacob's always been able to move small things very precisely and larger things with great force, but he doesn't have enough control with something as heavy as a person to lift them fifteen feet in the air with no chance of them thumping against the wall. So he won't be flying himself or anyone else through windows anytime soon.

Although when Clancy talked us through this part of the plan, I got the impression that Jake was making mental notes to develop that skill too.

I drop the rope, and Jacob catches hold. Bracing his feet against the bricks, he heaves himself up with careful steps until he can scramble in after me.

We glance around the room, our eyes adjusting to the more enclosed darkness. He reaches into a box and lifts up what at first looks like a rag.

No, it's a shirt—a kid's shirt, that could fit a six year old.

My stomach clenches.

Another box I glance into holds an assortment of basic toys—dolls and plastic cars and building blocks. My throat constricts to match my gut.

Clancy said the slavers don't appear to bring the kids to this house, but they clearly stash some supplies to do with their business.

Jacob glances at me with a determined expression, and I nod, squaring my shoulders. I may have led the way into the house, but for most of the mission, he's going first.

He'll "dispatch" every person we see who's part of the slaving ring, and I'll stay ready to leap in if Jake's subtler approach to offing them goes wrong.

Zian's X-ray vision would have been helpful here too, though I guess he might not have even fit through the window. And Clancy is still determined not to let too many of our group work together.

As we steal over to the door, footsteps creak on the floor outside.

Jacob tenses. He cocks his head, judging the sound, and nudges the door open a sliver to get a look outside.

The next thing I know, there's another faint *crack*, and he's yanking a limp corpse into the storage room with his powers.

I catch the body to help break its fall, and we lay it together on the floor. Even slack with death, the face catches on a memory.

It's one of the men from the pictures Clancy showed us. Not the boss, though.

Jacob must recognize him too, because his mouth twists into a grim smile. He catches my gaze again as if to check that I'm still good and returns to the doorway.

The hall outside is empty now. We slip along the thick rug, finding the spots where we can set our weight without provoking creaks of our own, to a room farther down that voices are filtering from.

With my ears pricked, I decipher three different voices. I don't think Jake will be able to drop all of them before the last can sound an alarm.

He's going to need me too.

I touch his arm to catch his attention and hold up three fingers followed by a gesture toward myself. Jacob grimaces, but he nods in reluctant acknowledgment.

He isn't going to gamble both our lives by overestimating his abilities.

To my surprise, instead of leaping straight in, he reaches to me and clasps my hand. Tentatively at first, as if he's afraid I'll yank away—like I probably would have a couple of weeks ago.

But I squeeze his fingers in return with a strange wobble through my pulse.

We're going to do this together. We're *good* together when all the other shit is out of the way.

We position ourselves in front of the door. My muscles coil.

Then Jacob flings it open in one brisk motion.

I don't pause for even an instant to make sure he's handling his part of the problem. I spring straight at the man who's standing the farthest on my side of the room, my claws slashing out to strike his throat.

As I catch his fall while blood gurgles out of him, two more bodies slump at my right. One sways in Jacob's hold, but he manages to push it toward an armchair that muffles the impact.

I scan the faces in the lamplight and swallow a twinge of disappointment. All three were in Clancy's file, but none of these are the man in charge either.

He's the most important one. If we don't get him, he could just start his business all over again once he's hired more people.

Thumps carry up the stairs from outside the room, a voice rising alongside them. The words are in a language I don't know, but they have the cadence of a question.

Jacob and I fall into position silently.

The door still stands partly open. The moment the newcomer is close enough, Jacob grabs him with his power, snaps his neck, and drags him inside with the others.

We shut the door behind us and pause to listen in the hall. No other sounds of human presence reach our ears from the rooms around us, but more remarks travel up from the first floor, along with a tinkling of music.

We have to hurry. Who knows how soon the rest of the inhabitants might start to think it's strange that their companions upstairs have been so quiet?

The banister on the broad staircase only offers partial shelter. I spot a couple more men and a woman—one of the two women included in Clancy's photos—sitting on a leather sofa in a huge living room, laughing at something on the TV.

This time, I don't even need to look at Jacob. He reaches back and rests his hand on my foot, nudging me ahead of him.

He can do his work from here. I need to get closer if I'm going to be speedy enough.

I dart the rest of the way down the stairs and flatten myself against the wall by the living room entrance. When I'm ready, I make a quick gesture to Jacob without shifting my attention from the room's inhabitants.

I trust that he'll act the moment I signal him. And as I hurtle into the room, the first of the men is already crumpling.

The second man starts to yelp, but I cut off the sound with a swift slash, tearing open the woman's throat as well before she can do more than flinch. Blood spurts out over their sagging bodies and splatters my black clothes.

We still haven't found the boss. Is he not even home right now?

Clancy wouldn't have sent us in unless he was sure we'd find our main target, would he?

Jacob descends the stairs. We creep through an empty dining room and out into a wide hall that leads to a kitchen and a few other closed rooms.

The clink of dishes carries from the kitchen. We venture closer, our eyes peeled.

Two figures are moving around between the gleaming stainless-steel appliances and counters. Both the woman and the man are dressed in plain clothes, aprons tied over them, no jewelry or weapons.

And if that wasn't enough to suggest that they don't fit with the house's main residents, they're in the middle of unloading a dishwasher. They must be part of the household staff that Clancy mentioned.

I'm about to move on in the hopes that we can ignore them completely when a man walks into the kitchen from the back door, his confident stride and posher clothes marking him as a target rather than a servant. Shit.

We don't have time to retreat to an easy hiding place. And maybe it'd be stupid to try to continue our assault with the kitchen staff here anyway, when they could potentially wander into the other rooms and stumble on a body at any moment.

At least this way, we control when and how they find out.

Jacob focuses on the man, who's already ambled halfway across the kitchen. As the faint, fatal crack sounds, I hustle into the room.

The kitchen staff spin around, the woman letting out a

gasp of surprise at the sight of one of her employers toppling. I press my hands to both of their mouths.

"We don't want to hurt you," I whisper in as low a tone as I can manage. "We just want to stop them from taking more kids. Get out of here, and don't come back."

They both nod, wide-eyed. The man rushes out through the back door first.

The woman treads after him and steps out into the night. But she's only made it a few steps into the lawn before she whirls around and screams out a warning in that language I don't know.

Fucking hell. My claws spring from my fingers again, but I have more vital things to do than get revenge on her for her betrayal.

Heavy footsteps pound toward us—some from the hall and others up from a basement staircase I hadn't even noticed. Someone else is yelling now.

There's an oof and a bang from the hall. Jacob dashes into the kitchen after me.

Two men charge in from the other direction at the same moment, guns in their hands. I swing around, but I'm not close enough to strike either of them in time.

One smacks into the wall with a heave of Jacob's invisible power. He throws himself at me, tackling me to the ground just as the second gun fires.

We roll across the floor behind a storage cart. Nerves jangling, I squirm out from under Jacob just in time to see the gunman barging toward our momentary shelter.

He aims his pistol at Jake, who hasn't quite righted himself yet, and this time I am close enough.

I launch myself at our attacker, my knee slamming

into his elbow to send his shot wide, my claws snatching at his throat. With a hiss of breath, I tear the entire front of his neck right off of his body.

At another thud, my head jerks up. A woman who ran into the room, clutching a rifle, is just slumping to the ground, her head seeping blood against the wall from where Jacob cracked it open.

My gaze drops to the man who's just collapsed in front of me.

Slicked-back gray hair. A craggy face with harsh full lips above the gouged-out throat.

My heart leaps.

"It's him," I murmur to Jacob. "We got him. The main boss."

Jacob is staring at me as if he hasn't quite heard me. A shudder runs through his body.

His head jerks around, but no other footsteps reach our ears. That isn't enough of a guarantee that we're done, though.

I open my mouth and let a tiny shriek reverberate out of me, even softer than the ones I've practiced. Just enough to quiver through the walls, seeking out a target to latch on to.

In the middle of my adrenaline high, I don't know if I could have reined it in as well as I did in the controlled environment back on the island. Maybe I'd have ended up tearing into any body it touched.

But I don't have to find out. It flows through the whole house and catches nothing.

I gulp in a relieved breath. "That's it. We got them all."

"Then let's get the fuck out of here," Jacob rasps.

I couldn't agree more.

We race out the back door, scanning the night for assailants drawn by the sounds of the fight. The yard is empty.

The staff fled for safety after all—after the woman screwed us over.

I grit my teeth and run for the surrounding wall. Jacob is right behind me.

He offers me a boost up and I lean over to grab his arm, helping each other in turn. Then we sprint for the van we parked half a mile away in the cover of a short stretch of forest.

The metal band around my ankle shifts with my movements. Clancy will know that we left and that we made it through the attack okay. Dominic will be safe where he's waiting in his own van to find out if he'll need to rush to anyone's rescue.

Safe for now, anyway. I can only hope that the team of younger shadowbloods doesn't need to deal with too many late arrivals.

We leap into the van without breaking stride, Jacob having disengaged the locks from a distance. He starts the engine while I strap myself into the passenger seat.

As we tear off down the road to put even more distance between us and the site of our assignment, a message pops up on the touchscreen mounted on the dashboard between us.

Targets eliminated?

I tap in a hasty answer. *Several including the big one.*

Good work. Get to the rendezvous spot and wait there. Expect the others in approximately 2 hours.

At the command, I can't help looking down at my ankle. Jacob studied his tracking band on the way out here and indicated to me that he couldn't feel any simple way of removing it.

The knowledge passes through my mind that we could make a run for it. We don't have much, but we've gotten by with hardly anything before, and we'd have a two-hour head start.

But even if we can bash the anklets off before Clancy's people find us, even if we could navigate this country without a clue where the plane brought us... we'd be leaving the others behind.

I don't even need to voice the question to know Jacob would reject that idea just as vehemently as my heart is recoiling from it. I'm not even sure we aren't better off in our new circumstances, at least in some ways.

I paid attention during the trip leaving the island, though. I know where the runway the private jet took off from lies relative to the mountain facility, and that there's a harbor in sight within a few miles of it on the island's coast.

We've learned useful things for ourselves on this mission as well as taking out villains who deserved it. If we decide it's time to leave, hope isn't lost, not by a long shot.

Jacob pulls into the open field a short distance from the currently vacant airfield. The second he's turned the engine off, he twists toward me.

His gaze skims over my body. "Are you okay? None of them got to you?"

I adjust my position, cringing inwardly at the feel of the still-damp patches of blood on my shirt. "None of this is mine, as far as I know. We should get out of the bloody clothes, though."

Clancy didn't leave us much in the large space at the back of the van, but we do each have a change of clothes —and a bag where we're supposed to stuff the evidence of our mission for burning. I push into the back and tug at my long-sleeved tee.

Jacob follows me. I expect him to change his own clothes, but when I toss my bloody shirt into the bag and move to reach for the new one, he touches my arm to stop me.

The next sweep of his gaze over my nearly naked torso lights a flicker of heat under my skin despite the cool air. I open my mouth to say something about personal space and privacy, but the turmoil in his eyes when they rise to meet mine stops the sardonic remark in my throat.

"You're really all right?" he says, like he can't quite believe it.

He wasn't checking me out just now. He was confirming I don't have any wounds.

A little of my self-consciousness fades. I hold out my arms so he can see the sides of my torso clearly, everything that isn't covered by my sports bra or the slim chain of my necklace.

"Yeah. Not a scratch. Up until the end, they had no idea what hit them."

Another shudder like the one I saw in the kitchen ripples through Jake's frame. "The asshole with the fucking gun—he almost shot you. I almost didn't get there fast enough."

Oh. That's why he's so keyed up.

I touch his jaw in an attempt at reassurance. "You did. You were my armor, like you promised. And then I got to be yours. That's how it should be, right?"

Jacob lets out a strangled sound and lowers his head so his forehead brushes mine. "Yeah. Yeah. I just never want to see anyone get that close—"

His voice tightens. "I want to tear his head right off his fucking shoulders and dance on it."

"I think he's dead enough already," I say with a hint of dryness. "Are *you* okay?"

He doesn't seem like he's detached from reality the way he has a few times in the past when we'd gotten through a shitload of trouble. Tonight's incident doesn't really compare.

But he's obviously not jumping for joy either.

Jacob sets his hands on my waist, skin to skin, with a bloom of warmth. He swallows audibly. "Nothing you need to knock me out of, Wildcat. But I wish I could keep you out of anything this dangerous completely. What good is fucking armor when there's so many of them?"

His voice drops, getting hoarse. "I love you so much, Riva. If I could make sure no one ever fired another bullet at you to begin with, there's nothing I wouldn't do."

A lump rises in my throat. "I know," I say through it, and I do. I believe him with every fiber of my being.

So nothing could feel more natural than finishing my answer by tugging his lips to meet mine.

NINE

Riva

I've kissed Jacob before. More than once.

There was the time I used a kiss to snap him out of a frenzy he was caught up in, thinking he still needed to protect me from attackers.

And the time we started making out and I bawled all over him.

Not the greatest track record. But then, maybe that's to be expected when our entire reunion has been so messy.

I can feel the tension in him as he kisses me back. Part of it is hunger I know must be flaring in his veins just like it is within mine, our shadows straining toward each other.

And part is him battling that hunger.

His fingers flex where he's raised his hand to cup my cheek. A quiver runs through his body, every muscle taut.

I haven't wanted everything he could give me before. I've asked him to be gentle.

Just like every other moment since the one when he called me away from the train hurtling toward me, he's doing whatever he can to make me happy. Whatever he can to make sure he doesn't damage that happiness again.

But the only ache left inside me is the best sort of pain.

I break the kiss to draw back just a few inches, holding his face between my hands as I do. The words feel like they well up from the very center of me. "I love you too."

Jacob lets out a choked sound and dips his head for another kiss. It's all tenderness and giddy release, but I can still taste the restraint in it.

I need more.

I push him downward, and he moves easily at my prodding. As he sinks down to sit against the inner wall of the van, I straddle his lap like I have before.

Maintaining control. Taking the reins.

But that doesn't mean I'm going to be calling *all* the shots.

I tug at his shirt to pull the blood-dappled fabric off him and slide my hands down his sculpted torso.

Jacob's voice has gone rough. "Riva?"

My tongue darts out to wet my lips. I can taste how much he wants me in the desire that laces the air.

The shadows in my blood thrum with eager anticipation.

I look at him, straight into his blue eyes that smolder like pale flames. "I'm not afraid of you anymore. Let it all out. Show me what you'd do with me if you knew I wanted all of it. Because I do."

The flames flare into a full-out bonfire. Jacob trails his fingers under my chin to pull my mouth back to his.

His hesitation doesn't vanish in an instant. The heat of this kiss could melt me, fierce and demanding, but his hands stay careful as they travel over my body.

I kiss him back hard and splay my fingers over his bare chest, tracing every ridge of muscle, thumbing his nipples, caressing all the way down to the solid planes of his stomach. Taking in every part of him without any hesitation of my own.

With each stroke of my hands, Jacob's touch becomes firmer too. He curls his fingers around the back of my neck as he tilts his head, his tongue delving past my lips, scorching hot.

Then he traces my spine all the way down my back before returning to yank at my bra. I raise my arms so he can peel the stretchy sports bra off me, watching how he lifts it around my necklace so the fabric doesn't catch on the pendant.

The gesture brings his forearm near my face where I can't help tracing the scar just below the elbow with my gaze.

There's nothing I wouldn't do.

An echo of the anguish that hit me when he brought the knife to his arm all those weeks ago rises up through my chest. I grip his wrist and bring my lips to the pink line of the scar.

Jacob holds perfectly still as I chart the evidence of his attempted sacrifice with soft kisses. I hear him swallow.

I lift my head to meet his eyes again. "No matter what

you feel like you have to do, don't hurt yourself again. Not even for me. I want you here, every part of you."

Jake brushes a stray strand of hair back behind my ear, his gaze fathomless. "You've got me. Every part. I'm yours, whatever you want to do to me, whatever you want me to do."

I dip my head close to his. My voice comes out in a whisper. "I just want you to love me."

He raises his chin to fulfill that request. As his mouth crashes into mine, he cups my bared breasts.

My curves are just large enough to fill his hands. He swivels his palms against my nipples, cautiously and then with more force at my encouraging whimper.

Every increasingly urgent rotation sends a rush of pleasure through my chest. I can't stop myself from nipping at his lip and drinking in his groan.

The essence inside me is rioting now, clamoring for the connection it's already gotten to solidify with two of my other men. My claws tingle behind my fingertips; my hips rock against Jake's.

He grasps my ass, pressing me tighter against him as I grind. Even through multiple layers of clothing, the friction of my pussy against his stiffening erection makes us both growl.

We've gotten this close before, and I didn't let it go any further. But I'm burning up, and the man beneath me is both fueling the flames and absorbing them with his touch.

I want him. I want Jacob in all his fucked-up, damaged, obsessively devoted glory.

It's because of his damage that he understands the deepest wounds I try to hide.

I don't want to lose him again, not any of the ways it could happen. And when the shadows between us meld and merge, I'll always know where he is.

I'll always be able to find him... and I'll know he can always find me.

My hands drop to his athletic pants, yanking at the waistband. Jake's breath hitches, and he shifts his weight to help me drag them off him.

When I stroke my fingers over his rigid cock through his boxers, he groans—and the first aid kit in the corner of the van goes pinging off one of the walls.

Jacob winces in embarrassment and catches my gaze. "Sorry. I can keep better control."

I'm not sure if that's true, but it won't be his fault. My first times with both Andreas and Dominic, our powers came flaring to the surface of their own accord.

I give him a smile that I suspect looks a little wicked. "Just don't give either of us a concussion, and you can go as wild as you want."

Jacob's gaze turns blazing, and he yanks me back into his embrace.

Our kisses become hungrier, hastier, as he strips my sweatpants off me. The pulsing need between my thighs has me grinding against him again with a gasp at the surge of heady sensation.

Jake echoes the sound, his lips branding my neck, my shoulder. He lifts one breast to clamp his mouth around the peak and flicks his tongue over my nipple until I'm bucking in his arms.

He trails his fingers up and down my bare legs, torturously close to my panties, but he pauses to linger over the metal band around my ankle. He looks up at me with a ragged breath.

"Are you sure—"

Resolve burns in my chest alongside my raging desire. "If they can figure out what we're doing, let them. There's nothing wrong about this."

Those words bring a smile to Jacob's face that's so bright I swear my heart almost leaps right out of my chest.

He pulls me into another kiss, tender as the first ones but with scorching passion simmering underneath. My pussy throbs, and the shadows inside me stretch toward the man I've rediscovered my love for.

My pulse kicks up a notch with renewed urgency. I wrench at Jacob's boxers, and he helps me wriggle out of my panties.

But as I lower myself over his jutting cock, he catches me by my hips before I've quite reached him and exhales in a rush.

"I want you so badly. Once we get started—"

I brush my lips against his. "It'll be fine. It's how it's supposed to be. We're meant for this."

He kisses me hard, and I sink the rest of the way onto him. Jacob jerks upward to meet me, plunging deep enough to send a jolt of bliss all the way to my throat.

I cry out and kiss him fiercely so he knows the sound is all happiness. Our hips roll together, propelling him deeper, in and out, with the giddy swell of heat that rises to fill my whole body.

Another loose object smacks into a wall somewhere behind me. Jacob hisses, his fingers digging into my thigh.

When he adjusts the angle at which we fit together, his cock drives home so perfectly I can't suppress a moan. His grasp urges me on while his other hand traces across my scalp where my hair has loosened from my braid.

I know exactly where he's touching me. His fingers sear against my skin. But moments later, an impression of contact reaches other parts of my body, as if more hands have reached for me.

A careful pressure caresses my breasts. A similar sensation runs down my back and across my belly.

My breath stutters in surprise, and Jacob teases his teeth against the crook of my jaw.

"I want to make this as good for you as it possibly can be," he says in a rasp. "I know where it should feel good, but I can't tell— You've got to show me when I get it right."

He's caressing me with his power as well as his body. I'm too lost in the growing whirlwind of pleasure to fully comprehend what he means by "showing" him until the pressure condenses around one nipple as if in a pinch.

My nerves spark, and I sway faster with the rhythm of his thrusts. A needy sound slips from my lips.

"You like that?" Jacob murmurs in a wash of heat across my neck.

I whimper in answer, and he repeats the gesture, tweaking both of my nipples with his telekinetic talent simultaneously. The rush of bliss makes me buck faster.

My voice comes out in a mumble. "So good. More."

Jake chuckles, raw and jerky. "You feel so fucking good

too, Wildcat. Never going to let you down again. Never going to stop making you feel fantastic."

The invisible touch massages my ass and strokes my hair, toys with my nipples and wraps around my torso. I spur on his attentions with gasps and moans as he discovers every spot that sets me on fire.

Then the pressure dips right down to the place where we're joined to strum my clit.

Pleasure crackles through me in a rampant blaze. A louder moan of approval careens from my lungs.

Jacob growls and plunges up into me harder, faster.

I want to bury myself in him and swallow him up, all at the same time.

He thrusts up inside me just as his power seems to set off every point of pleasure in the rest of my body, and I hurtle into my release. My nerves sizzle with the smoky essence reaching to twine with his.

The wave of bliss hazes my vision. My claws spring from my fingertips.

Jacob grates out a curse with a twitch of his arms to angle the poison spines that've just shot from his skin away from me.

He slams home once more with a groan that reverberates through the van. The sound tosses me even higher.

I cling to him, riding the wave, shivering with the intensity of the moment. Feeling his heart thump in time with mine, our breaths mingling at the same panting pace.

We are one. Forever.

The tingling races all through my body, but I know it'll condense on my upper chest. This time, when I start to sag over him and glance down between us, I'm not at all startled to see the mark like a thumbprint-sized bruise that's formed at the top of his sternum.

A matching spot has bloomed on my left clavicle, next to the one that formed when I first hooked up with Andreas.

Jacob's chest is still heaving, but he touches the mark with absolute gentleness, his expression full of awe.

"I marked you. Like Drey and Dom did."

"Of course you did. We're blood. Our shadows *want* to meld together." I beam at him. "And now we'll always know how to make our way back to each other, no matter what comes between us."

He lets out a shaky chuckle. "I wasn't totally sure, after everything…"

"You're mine," I inform him, in case he wasn't already aware of that. As if he hasn't been telling *me* that over and over for the last few weeks. A pang of emotion cuts off my voice for a second before I can add, "And I'm yours."

Still inside me, Jake hugs me to him, tipping his head against my shoulder. "For as long as you want to be, Riva."

A quiver passes through his frame, but it feels different from the tremors that shook him before. More energized, less tense.

He tilts my head to claim another kiss. Then his attention falls to my chest again, but not to the marks on my pale skin.

Jacob curls his fingers cautiously around the cat-and-yarn charm dangling from my neck. The one his twin gave me all those years ago.

He lifts his gaze to meet mine. "We're going to fix this too. There has to be a way, and I'll find it."

He got one of the shadowkind to fix the charm itself already, but I know that's not what he's talking about. He means Griffin himself.

The memories of the times he's talked about his feelings for me and his recognition of his brother's send a tightness around my heart. Jacob thought he couldn't have me at all because he didn't want to get between me and Griffin.

I touch the side of his face, grazing my thumb over his cheek. "I know if there is one, you will. But I don't need him *more* than I need you, Jake. I don't love him more. I wanted *you*."

The corner of Jacob's mouth twitches into a hint of a smile. He hugs me again, and I nestle into his embrace for the short time we have before we need to return our minds to the end of our mission.

Before we need to head back into our new cage, gilded as it is.

TEN

Dominic

I stretch out my legs in the back of the van, then tuck them into a cross-legged pose, and pretend I don't notice our local contact shooting uneasy glances my way. He's sitting sideways in the driver's seat so he can alternate between looking out through the windows and over toward me.

I know I'm not much to look *at* right now. Clancy outfitted me with a track jacket even lighter weight than the trench coats I used to use to hide my tentacles.

It only falls to my hips, so I have to keep my unusual appendages coiled a couple of times over. But he must have had the jacket custom made, because the inner lining holds loops of soft fabric to help support them.

I hadn't realized that spreading out the weight across my body would make them feel like less of a burden.

In any case, all the stranger can see is that my back is oddly shaped. I've been holding the tentacles still—

holding my whole self pretty much still as we wait to see if I'll be called in to save any of my fellow shadowbloods.

He rubs his hand across his chapped lips and shoots me another glance. "Do you want something to drink? I have water bottles up here."

His accented voice should give me a clue about where Clancy has sent us, but all I can tell for sure is his native tongue isn't Spanish or anything in that family of languages. Maybe German? Or some variation of Eastern European?

Hell, it could be Swedish or Turkish and I'm not sure I'd know the difference. I don't even know if he's a long-time local to this place or a more recent transplant from abroad.

"That's okay." I pat the knapsack resting on the thinly carpeted floor next to me. "I've got a canteen."

He grunts in acceptance and goes back to gazing through the windows, though there isn't much to see out there in the night. With the van's overhead light on at its dimmest setting, the world beyond the windshield looks totally black to me.

I understand why Clancy arranged for his man as my sort-of guide. The de facto leader of the guardians needed to be in touch with people on the ground to find out exactly what we'd be dealing with.

If there's a problem, this guy will know the roads and the rules of them better than any of the guardians would. He'll get me straight to my friends if they need help.

He'll recognize the signs of trouble faster.

But I can't help wishing, for the first time in my life,

that I had a guardian for company instead. Someone who already knew about my strangeness and wasn't fazed by it.

What have they told this guy? What is he going to think if I do have to rush in and whip out my tentacles to pour healing power into one of the other shadowbloods?

God forbid.

I shift my weight, my pulse picking up a faster beat. Will Riva and Jacob already be inside the house?

How long will it take them to carry out their first part of the mission—the most dangerous part?

Has the man sitting with me and whatever colleagues he's had helping Clancy given us all the information we needed to keep them safe?

I brush my fingertips over the thin leaves of the shrub that's poised on the floor next to me, its harness ready to fling onto my back in a matter of seconds. The tingle of energy I can sense within them settles my nerves just a little.

I gave the plant a bit of water from my canteen right after we hunkered down here, about a mile from the house —not close enough to draw attention but not too far to cross the distance quickly if I have to rush in. Its crisp herbal scent tickles my nose.

Please, don't let me have to kill it. For all our sakes.

I'd rather not have to destroy any more life. Even a plant's.

The screen on the van's dashboard stays empty. No news so far.

I close my eyes, inhaling the smell of the shrub. My mind strays back to my new room at the island facility.

After our first training session for his assignment, I

asked Clancy if I could have some potted plants in my bedroom. I told him it'd help me feel more at home, since that seems to be what he wants.

I didn't really think he'd go along with it anyway, but by the evening, he'd come to escort me to a different room that must be near the face of the mountainside. My old one had no windows, but this one came with a skylight where one wall slanted into the ceiling.

Three potted shrubs of different types and an assortment of flowers waited for me, right where the sunlight would hit them best. A whole garden.

Just remembering it sends a little thrill through me. This isn't the life I expected to be living, and I'm not done sorting out how I feel about Clancy and his plans... but is it possible this new facility *could* be a real kind of home, eventually?

It already feels more mine than any other place I've stayed, both at past facilities and when we were on the run.

My guide is peering at me again. He lifts his chin toward the shrub.

"Your special power—you can make injuries better? But you need the plant?"

I brush my fingers over the leaves again. "If it's a big injury, I need to draw the energy to heal it from something else. Plants are... easiest."

They make me feel the least guilty about the life I've stolen. But I don't want this guy thinking about what else I might suck the energy out of.

He hums to himself and adjusts his weight in the seat.

I guess he's probably getting a little restless too, stuck in this van with a particularly strange stranger.

He's curious, though. Maybe I should be trying to make more of the opportunity.

Do more than sit here like a lump hoping I won't need to do anything else.

When we were first driving out to this spot from the airfield, I tried nudging him for clues about where we are, but he shut those down quickly. Clancy must have instructed him not to tell us anything identifying.

"It's safer for all of us," was how he put it to us shadowbloods.

But even having more of an idea about how Clancy is reaching out to people beyond his Guardianship could be useful to know.

"The man who set up this mission with you," I venture. "He told you about our powers?"

My guide shrugs. "Some. Not a lot. Enough to be sure that you should accomplish what you're here to do."

"It doesn't bother you? Or did you already know that people like me and my friends exist?"

"Many unexpected things exist in the world. Better to work with those you can when it benefits you, not dismiss them or run away."

He chuckles lightly, but his gaze flicks toward my back for just a second with the same wariness I've noticed before.

He's happy to *use* our services, but that doesn't mean he trusts us.

His mouth tightens with a momentary frown, and he twists a little farther in the seat to face me. "Your friends—

they won't touch anything they find in the house, will they? They only destroy the people."

"That's what we were told to do." I can't say whether Clancy might have given Riva and Jacob other instructions at the last minute. "Is there something important inside?"

He waves his hand dismissively. "Don't worry about it. That's for us. That was the deal."

An uneasy prickle runs down my spine at his words. Who is "us"? What "deal"?

I thought he was helping our mission because he wanted to see the child-slavery ring taken down too—for the good of his community. What would that have to do with anything the perpetrators are keeping in the house?

I try to tell myself that he could simply be thinking of records about the kids and where they've been sold or something understandable like that, but I can't quite shake the sense that he didn't mean it that way. Why would he avoid talking about it if that's all he meant?

"Our boss does take his deals seriously," I say carefully, watching the man's expression.

He lets out a guffaw. "He should, with what he's getting out of it."

The prickle jabs deeper under my skin.

I try to keep my voice even, but I'm not sure I totally succeed. "What exactly is he getting out of the deal this time?"

This time, the man's gaze darts toward my face rather than my back, with a flicker of panic as if he's realized he's said something he shouldn't have. Then he turns to face the windshield.

"That's between us and him. Not your concern, right?"

I'm sure as hell concerned now. "Are you saying that you *paid* him to take on these guys?"

That isn't necessarily so bad, right? They could be a group of outraged citizens who raised the funds to hire someone to deal with a problem they couldn't tackle themselves.

But the way he's acting is setting off my internal alarms. And Clancy never mentioned anything about getting compensation—or about being called by the locals.

He made it sound like he'd found the slavers and decided they needed to be taken out all on his own.

"Did he come to you first or did you come to him?" I ask.

The man shakes his head. "We're done talking about this."

"I just want to understand what's going on. I'm part of this too."

"You work for your boss. I work for mine. We all get what we want. That's all you need to know."

No, it's not, not when everything he adds to the puzzle makes the pieces look more ominous. He has a boss—helping with this mission is *work* for him?

I wish Andreas was here to peer right inside this guy's head and find out what's going on. But he's not.

It's just me.

"Please," I say. "I came all the way out here. It's my mission too—why shouldn't I know all of it?"

My guide keeps his mouth clamped shut. He appears to have decided he's not going to talk at all.

The old me might have given up. This me has faced off with literal monsters and murderous gunmen.

This me has watched the woman he loves torn apart and then melded her back to life.

If there's something going on here beyond what we know, I have to find out what that is. All of our lives could depend on it.

I'm not going to be the weak one. I can't let this slide.

I push to my feet, ducking my head under the low ceiling of the van. "How were you and your 'boss' involved in setting up this mission? I need you to tell me."

"You can ask your own boss if you want to know more."

I step toward the guy and take in his flinch with a wince of my own. But underneath my revulsion at his reaction, I know I can use it.

He's scared of me. And fear can be an incredible motivator.

"I don't need you," I say. "I can drive this van myself. I could tell my boss that you freaked out about my abilities and tried to hurt me. It was self-defense."

The man's head jerks toward me. "What are you talking about?"

I hate using my physical differences this way, like a threat, but it's the only thing I'm sure will work. I shrug off my jacket and let my tentacles rise on either side of my shoulders.

I aim a firm gaze straight into the man's twitching eyes. "I can use anything living to draw energy from. I can drain a whole human being in a couple of minutes. I know, because I've needed to before."

The man cringes in his seat against the door of the van. He snatches at the handle, but I whip out one tentacle and snag it around his nearer wrist.

"You're not going anywhere. Just tell me the terms of the deal, and we can go back to just sitting here like we never talked at all."

"Get that thing *off* me!" The man jerks at his arm, but my suckers and the sinewy muscles within the tentacle clamp tight.

"I can start siphoning off your life right now," I warn him, but he keeps struggling.

I need to prove it. I need to make him feel what he could be losing.

My mouth goes dry. I managed to take just part of a fish's life once, back when Rollick and his people were helping us get control of our abilities on his yacht. That last set of exercises I attempted with him, I was just starting to get the hang of refusing the deeper hunger.

But that was only once, in a perfectly controlled situation.

On the other hand, a fish has a lot less life than a human being.

I can do this. I *have* to do this, or what did I even start threatening this man for?

I clench my teeth and give a tug through my tentacle. My will catches hold of the streams of life energy that thrum through the man's body alongside his pulse.

The first spurt of it rushes through me with a giddying warmth, like drinking the richest hot chocolate in the world. I want more—I want to drown myself in it—

My mind flails, and for a second I almost do lose myself.

Then I yank up a memory of Riva. Riva smiling at me. Riva stroking the tentacles and telling me I'm not a monster.

With her, I'm not. Right now, I don't need to be either.

I cut off the flow of energy that was flooding me. The man's shoulders slump, a shudder passing through his body.

But he's alive. He's breathing properly, if rapidly. His skin hasn't lost his color.

I didn't take too much.

Only enough for him to know what it feels like. For him to get a sense of how far I could go.

My stomach lists queasily, but at the same time his now-watery eyes dart to mine.

"I'm sorry. I wasn't supposed to say. It's very simple. We give him the money, he clears out the house and leaves it for us."

I knit my brow, not letting up my hold on the man's wrist. "What do you want the house for? What's in there that's so special?"

My guide gestures vaguely with his free hand. "Not so much the house. Records, equipment, connections. They had a good business going. We move in and take over. Everyone wins."

I stare at him. "You're going to take over their business?"

The man starts squirming against my hold again. "Not

me. My boss wants to expand. That's all it is. Just business."

Acid burns the base of my throat. For a second, I think I might actually vomit.

It's not business to the kids who've been getting snatched and sold.

We aren't really protecting them. If I'm understanding this guy right, there'll be a brief respite, and then a new syndicate is going to take over where the group we're slaughtering left off.

And they paid Clancy for the opportunity. They paid him to send us in and do their dirty work.

How much does he even know about what they're planning?

What else that he's told us has been a total fucking lie?

ELEVEN

Riva

I expected to feel relieved the moment we all clambered back onto the private plane that's going to take us back to the island. One look at Dominic's face turns any joy inside me to dust.

He isn't like Jacob—he doesn't carry his discontent like a storm cloud wrapped around him. I don't think anyone who doesn't know him well would even notice.

But I see the way the corners of his mouth stay tight when he aims his smile of welcome at me. I notice the slight hunching of his shoulders, like he's reverting back to his old uncertain self.

Back in the old facility, he always withdrew into himself like that right before he had to say something hard. The memory rises up, as if Andreas is telling it to me, of the complex strategy game the guardians had us play maybe a year before we tried to escape, with the promise that we'd get a full day to train and relax outside if we beat it.

Dom looked like he does right now in the moment before he told us in a rough voice that he'd just realized we'd made a fatal mistake several steps back... one there was no longer any way of recovering from. Any chance of claiming the reward we'd all longed for was gone.

Those were the kind of stakes we usually dealt with back then. These days, it could be so much worse.

My gaze jerks to the other figures on the plane. Did one of the younger shadowbloods get hurt? That could have been awful to see—what if he couldn't even save them?

That can't be true, though, because all four of them are tucked into their seats in a cluster, chattering quietly but with an easygoing air.

"Everything went okay on your end?" I call over to them, leaning my arm on the back of a seat.

Celine laughs and brushes her hand over her shoulder with a swish of her black and red-flecked ponytail. "No one even came. We just sat there the whole time."

One of the boys shoots a grin at me. "You two must have done a good job. Made it easy for the rest of us."

Celine laughs a little louder, and I find myself thinking of her missions before, hunting us down.

I don't know whether she was ever close to the actual fighting. Maybe I'm assuming she must be bothered about it underneath when those were easy for her too.

"It's always good to have backup," I say, because I don't want them to think we didn't appreciate them being there.

If anyone else working with the slavers had shown

up while we were inside, they could have thrown the whole operation off. And having the teens monitoring the road for any late arrivals after the fact allowed Jacob and me our break, with all the unexpected enjoyment it brought.

"You shouldn't have to take all the responsibility on your shoulders," Clancy told us before, when we were going over the plan. "One of your greatest strengths is how well you rely on each other."

The private jet's seats are arranged in clusters of four along one side of the plane, two pairs facing each other with a tiny table in between. Narrow sofas and a refreshments cabinet stand along the opposite wall.

The teens have claimed one cluster for themselves. Jacob drops into a seat next to the window, across from Dominic.

I have the urge to follow him. To hold on to the new closeness we've formed between us.

But Dominic's expression tugs at me more.

I sink down beside him and slip my hand around his. "Everything went okay for you too, then?"

His smile doesn't reach his hazel eyes. "Pretty boring, but I'd rather that than needing to rush in to heal any of you."

He hooks his arm right around mine and leans in close, and I instinctively tilt toward him. His lips brush my cheek and then veer toward my ear as if he's making an intimate gesture.

"Pretend I'm saying nice things to you," he murmurs, so soft I'm not sure even Zian's sharp hearing could have picked up the words if he were in the seat across from me.

"I don't know how closely they're monitoring us on the plane."

I squeeze his hand in agreement and push my lips into a small smile, willing down the nervous twist of my gut.

Dominic keeps talking, low and steady but quickly as if he's afraid he might get cut off. "Clancy didn't come up with this mission out of the goodness of his heart. Some other gang paid him to eliminate those guys. And they're planning on taking over the business. They were just looking to off the competition."

With every sentence, my muscles tense more. It takes all my willpower not to clench my jaw in a horrified grimace.

So I don't have to hold the increasingly stiff smile any longer, I turn as if to nuzzle his head in response. My voice comes out in a thin whisper. "Are you sure?"

He nods without hesitation.

I close my eyes. The images from our mission waver behind the lids—bodies crumpling, blood splashing.

They still deserved it. We stopped them from doing horrible things.

But what if someone even worse steps in to fill the void?

How could Clancy be making decisions about what wrongs to set right based on getting *paid*?

When I look up again, Jacob is watching the two of us, but without a trace of jealousy. From the furrow on his brow, he's picked up on the fact that our PDA is a cover for a more serious conversation.

I could tell him the same way that Dominic just told

me—but I'm not sure Jake could hide his reaction well enough. I'm having enough trouble myself.

If the snack packets start bouncing off the ceiling, the guardians who've come along to escort us home will know something's up.

We can't keep quiet about this for long. I'm not going on another mission without understanding what the new leader of the guardians is really up to.

But I'd rather not hash it out with his underlings while we're thousands of feet in the air.

It'll be better if we can confront him without him knowing that we're on to him. Observe his unguarded response before he recovers from the surprise.

We can fill Jacob in at the same time.

I give Dom's cheek an actual kiss and whisper, "We'll see what Clancy has to say about it when we get back."

He nods again and slings his arm right around me to give me a brief but emphatic hug. The love we share seems to pulse through the mark on my collarbone.

After several minutes, I switch seats to cuddle up with Jacob, but all I tell him is, "There's something Clancy hasn't been telling us. We'll bring it up with him when we see him."

Jake manages to restrain a full frown, but his muscles tense even at that vague news. He glances at Dominic, who offers a small, crooked grin, and sighs.

Then he loops his arm around my shoulders as if he's determined to be some kind of armor for me even here. Even without knowing what he might be protecting me against.

I run through the possible scenarios dozens of times in

my head during the flight until I fall into a doze. At the jolt of the wheels hitting the mountain-top runway, I wake up with a jerk.

As we straighten up in our seats, everyone looking a bit groggy, the door swings open.

Another guardian appears in the glow of the jet's interior lights. "Clancy wants a briefing from each of you, in your own teams. Jacob and Riva first."

My pulse stutters. I assumed we'd all go together—that I'd have the backup of five other shadowbloods when we confronted him.

That Dominic would be able to say exactly what he found out.

There isn't time to hash out an alternate plan. The guardian is motioning to us impatiently.

I peel myself out of my seat and hurry over with Jacob right behind me.

It'll be okay. The two of us can handle the conversation ahead.

It's better for us to address it than to leave Dominic to take Clancy to task on his own.

Outside the plane, a warm breeze washes over us, carrying the hum of nighttime insect life. Dawn is just starting to tint the horizon.

We head down the path carved into the mountainside from the plateau that serves as a landing strip, our shoes rasping against the rough stone. Our escort leads us straight to Clancy's office.

In spite of the early hour, the head of the Guardianship looks perfectly alert standing behind his desk to greet us. Did he sleep while we flew, or has he been up all night?

As he motions us into the room, my gaze catches on the other figure waiting with him, and my heart hitches in my chest.

Griffin is sitting in a chair in the far corner, watching us with his unnervingly blank expression.

What's he doing here? The only explanation I can think of is that Clancy wants him to read our emotions, to make sure we're telling the truth.

I guess it's a good thing I decided I was going to call out our captor now, because I'm sure Griffin would have picked up on the fact that I was hiding something major if I held off.

We come to a stop in front of the desk, but Jacob's attention has fixed on his brother. His jaw works.

Griffin simply tips his head in greeting as if this is a totally normal situation. Jake wrenches his gaze back to Clancy without acknowledging the gesture.

Even with all the other concerns gnawing at me, grief ripples through my gut. Have the guardians managed to destroy their brotherly connection forever?

I make myself focus on the man behind the desk.

Clancy is studying us with an intensity that feels more penetrating than I remember from our past conversations. As if he already knows there's something we'll have to say beyond the basics of the mission.

My skin creeps in uneasy anticipation.

"It seems the assignment went well," Clancy says with typical briskness. "But I'd like to hear the full account

from your own mouths. It appeared that you had a bit of a
hiccup toward the end of your time in the house."

My mouth twists. He must have been able to tell
something went wrong from our physiological signals
broadcast from our ankle bands.

"We didn't have any trouble with most of the
mission," I start. "We took down the first several people
we found in the house before they even realized what was
happening."

I give him my account of our progress into and
through the house, trading the story back and forth with
Jacob, from our first kills to the kitchen staff's warning to
our ultimate victory.

With every word, the nausea gripping my stomach
expands. At the time, it *did* feel like a victory.

Dominic's revelation has drained all the justice out of
that triumph, turning it hollow.

Why did I ever trust this man even a little? The
guardians have never done anything except manipulate us
and betray us.

I should never have believed he was any different, no
matter what he said or did.

But I still need to hear what he'll say for himself. I
need to know just how aware he was of the shit he dragged
us into.

Clancy takes our account in with occasional nods and
sounds of encouragement. When we've finished, he
contemplates us with a satisfied expression. "It sounds as
though you fulfilled your tasks as well as I could have
hoped. There can always be unexpected obstacles along the
way—it's impossible to avoid them entirely."

"There was something else unexpected that came up," I say, girding myself for the conversation ahead.

Clancy arches his eyebrows slightly, almost as if he's amused. I don't think he can have any idea what I'm about to say. "Is that so?"

I cross my arms in front of me. "Yes. Why didn't you tell us that someone was paying you to send us in there? It wasn't a humanitarian mission."

Our captor's gaze flickers with a momentary tensing of his jaw. Oh, he had no clue at all that I was going to bring that subject up.

A faint whiff of stress pheromones reaches my nose, but he recovers quickly. "An organization on this scale requires funding. Our operations can be both humanitarian and paid for."

Griffin is looking at Clancy instead of us now, with a furrow on his brow. He didn't know about this part either, apparently.

I raise my chin. "Sure, that's possible. But not when the people paying you off only want you to get rid of the criminals so they can take over the same slaving business for themselves."

"What?" Jacob snaps. He narrows his eyes at Clancy. "You hired us out to *help* some child-abducting assholes?"

Clancy's whole expression has tightened now. "I didn't inquire about the plans of the group that hired us. They wanted to take out a target I was happy to see gone. If you heard something that led you to believe our sponsors had malicious intentions, you were probably mistaken."

I snort. "Probably? You don't even know. It didn't

occur to you to ask why these people were willing to spend who knows how much money for a mass assassination?"

Dominic wouldn't have told me with so much certainty if he hadn't found out enough to be totally convinced. And the fact that Clancy admits he didn't really know one way or the other only makes me surer that Dom was right.

"It doesn't matter," Clancy says firmly. "You did a good thing today—you removed people who were doing horrible things from the world. We can't control who might step in to fill a vacuum that's been created, but if someone else picks up where they left off, they can be dealt with too."

Jacob scowls. "As long as someone coughs up enough money to make it worth your while?"

Clancy gazes steadily back at him. "There's a lot of injustice in the world. I see no reason we shouldn't address it while also avoiding bankruptcy."

He makes the whole thing sound so reasonable, but every inch of my skin is crawling at his matter-of-fact tone.

Destroying awful things could be awful in turn if it's done for the wrong purpose.

Can't he see that? He must.

He just doesn't give a fuck as long as his bank account gets larger.

I catch Jacob's eye. We don't need to speak for me to recognize that we're on exactly the same page.

Being paid mercenaries is a totally different thing from acting as superheroes. We don't want this.

But as long as we're here under Clancy's control, we're

either carrying out his missions or he's going to lock us up as lab rats.

Which means we're going to have to get out of here, no question about it. All of us—the younger shadowbloods too.

And I have no idea how the hell we're going to pull that off.

Clancy steps around the desk toward us. I brace myself for another attempt at justifying himself, but instead he cocks his head, his gaze skimming over our bodies.

"That's not the only interesting thing that happened after you completed your part of the assignment, is it?"

My heart skips a beat. After Dominic's report, I totally forgot to wonder how much the guardians might have realized about my and Jacob's intimate activities.

"I don't think anything happened that would be interesting to *you*," I shoot back.

Jacob steps closer to me in solidarity. "You're just trying to change the subject from your shitty attitude."

Clancy tsks his tongue. "Or maybe you're trying to divert *me*. I did hear some very intriguing things while I was monitoring the missions."

He reaches out, a gesture I wasn't prepared for, and tugs down the collar of Jacob's clean tee. Just far enough to reveal the dark spot that's formed at the top of his sternum.

Jake is shoving him away a second later, but Clancy mostly dodges the blow with a backward step, anticipating it. He rocks on his feet, brushes himself off, and glances at me.

"I'm guessing you have a third of those now. A mark.

We made note of them when you arrived, but I didn't realize they were connected to your powers."

My pulse thumps faster. "What are you talking about?" I blurt out, praying that there's some chance he doesn't really understand.

Griffin stands up. "You're upsetting them," he says, his voice as calm as ever but the furrow on his forehead deepening.

Clancy ignores him. "I suppose I didn't mention that your tracking bands also transmit audio. I heard everything you said after your little interlude. Sex creates a connection between you? An extra awareness of each other? That's fascinating. We didn't anticipate anything like—"

"Shut the fuck up!" Jacob snarls, and throws himself at the other man with a clench of his fist that I think is directing a smack of telekinetic force ahead of him.

But Clancy is ready for that assault too. His arm whips out, and Jacob's body spasms with the crackle of a taser.

A cry bursts from my throat as Jake stumbles to his knees. "Stop!"

My claws spring out, but Clancy holds up his hand. "Let me remind you that you aren't gambling only with your own well-being but his and your other friends' as well."

I stop, the vibration of a scream burning in my lungs, my fingers curling.

I want to slash his throat out like I did to the thugs in the mansion we just invaded. I want to shriek pain through his joints until they break.

But I don't know what will happen to us—all of us—if

I give in to that impulse. I don't know how much worse things could get.

Taking in my stillness, Clancy rolls his shoulders, the taser still held between us. The door clicks as several more guardians enter the room to surround us.

"I think this conversation is over," he says. "You've simply opened a new avenue of inquiry—a process I'll need to study more closely to fully understand."

TWELVE

Riva

Nadia bobs on the balls of her feet in the grass, her latest neon T-shirt flashing under the sunlight in the yard. "I can't wait until I can get out there on a mission. They only let the non-Firsts who've already done a *lot* of fieldwork join in for that one."

I look up at her from where I've been stretching out my legs on the grass. The morning's exercise hasn't done anything to loosen the knot in my gut that's lingered since my talk with Clancy yesterday.

"You wouldn't want to go until you're definitely ready anyway," I say, not knowing what else to tell her.

You shouldn't want to go at all. Clancy's just using us. And I don't know how much worse it could get.

What would be the consequences of laying out the things I've discovered? Before I left Clancy's office, he warned Jacob and me to keep what we'd learned to ourselves… or we wouldn't get the chance to work with the other shadowbloods at all.

He's got his guardians watching us, I'm sure. How much could I even tell Nadia or the rest of them before I got dragged away?

I need to keep training, keep watching, and figure out a way to actually get us out of here. None of the rest matters as long as Clancy's calling the shots.

Nadia lets out a huff and swipes the short strands of her thick black hair back from her face. "I guess not. But even if it is nicer here than it was in the old facility, I want to see more of what's out there."

My chest constricts, knowing that longing for freedom so well. "Yeah. You'll get there."

On my terms rather than Clancy's, if I can manage it.

The carnage from the photos he showed me of the last kids we tried to rescue flashes through my mind, and the knots in my gut pull tighter. My terms have to be safer this time.

Booker saunters over from where he just finished a round of strength training. "When they send you on one of those missions, you'll have to trade in the neon for stealth-wear. Are you sure you can handle that?"

Nadia rolls her eyes at his teasing, but a hint of a blush appears on her brown cheeks at the same time. "Maybe, maybe not. My whole job is lighting things up."

Her words tickle my curiosity. "That's your shadowblood power?"

She nods and picks up the jump rope she brought out for an aerobics workout. "I'm a human glowworm. Lucky me."

She flips the rope over her head and starts up a brisk rhythm, moving her feet back and forth rather than simply keeping them in place. A shimmer appears beneath her skin.

Within a matter of seconds, the glow has risen to the surface, shining off her as if she's a signal beacon.

Booker laughs and claps his hands in approval. "We'll never get lost in the dark with you around, anyway."

As I get up, planning on taking another run through the stealth course—since stealth is definitely going to be key in working around Clancy's security systems—Booker glances at me. "The mission went okay, didn't it? You're all right?"

I hesitate, startled. The questions are perfectly straightforward, but his concern sounds genuine.

What's the best way to answer? I roll the words around in my mouth. "Things got more complicated than we expected. I'm still figuring out how I feel about that. Why? Did you hear something from Celine's group?"

Did the younger shadowbloods who came along pick up on something being off even though we never said as much in front of them?

But Booker shakes his head with a flash of sunlight off his pale hair. "Nah. Just your vibe." He waves vaguely around my body. "I see auras, basically. Like a haze that gives an idea of where a person's at, physically and mentally. Yours looks kind of uneasy."

Oh, shit. I had no idea he could pick up on my internal state while I've been doing my best to put a good face forward.

"I'm still not totally used to the whole setup here," I

say in the best explanation I can give. "This island isn't where I was planning on ending up."

He lets out another chuckle. "Yeah, I guess that's the same for all of us."

Nadia pauses in her rope-jumping. Booker bumps his knuckles against her shoulder in a playful but affectionate gesture. "I'm going to go tackle the ropes. See you around, Glowworm."

She watches him go, the rope swaying in her hands. I recognize the longing in her expression, all the way down to my bones.

"Were you in the same facility before?"

Nadia jerks her gaze back to me with an embarrassed purse of her lips. "Some of the time, anyway. When we were kids. There was a point when they started only letting girls train with other girls—and the guys with the guys. Until now."

A chill washes over me. That might be kind of my fault too.

When my guys and I tried to escape the first time, one of the guardians who caught me said something about it being a mistake to include a "female" in the mix. Maybe they figured the emotional connections forming between us had given us extra motivation to want to get out.

Apparently once they came to that conclusion, they applied their new principles to the younger shadowbloods.

"I'm sorry," I can't help saying.

Nadia shrugs. "Maybe it was better like that. It's not like anything could have happened in the kind of place we were before. I mean…" She trails off awkwardly, tensing as if she expects me to mock her for her romantic aspirations.

I don't really know how to do this whole role-model thing. I'm only four years older than her, barely more experienced.

But I want to be something like that for her and all the other shadowbloods. If the guys and I are blood, then we're connected to the rest of them too, if not quite as closely.

There's no one else in the whole world who could really understand what we've been through.

I offer her the best smile I can. "I know. I've been there. We'll get a real life eventually, where everything's… a little easier."

God, I hope I can fulfill that promise. Especially after the way she smiles back at me after my encouragement.

Another swell of cold wraps around my stomach. What if I end up leading them to their deaths instead?

Before I can shake off the thought and head over to the course like I intended, a couple of guardians jog down the mountainside steps. Their slacks shift with their brisk movements, and for the first time I notice a glimpse of a monitoring band around the man's ankle, just like the ones Clancy had us all wear on the mission.

The ones he made a point of taking off us when we returned. But the guardians wear them?

Understanding hits me like a slap to the face.

Clancy's monitoring the guardians—so that he knows immediately if any of us tries to hurt them. If I went on a rampage out here and slaughtered these two, no doubt an alarm would go off somewhere and the whole place would be locked down before I could get any farther.

Knowing the guardians are okay is more useful to him

than tracking our exact movements when we're confined to the valley anyway.

They let us shadowbloods go without those anklets to give us the illusion of freedom. The guardians don't need the illusion, because they *know* they're actually free.

All more of his manipulative lies.

As the two guardians stride toward me, I force my hands to unclench. It's clear from their gazes that I'm their intended target.

I move forward instinctively to meet them before they get closer to Nadia, even though I'm not really sure what I'd be shielding her from.

She and the other younger ones haven't had to see half of what the rest of us have. Haven't had to *do* what we've been forced to in order to survive.

And I'd rather keep it that way if I possibly can.

"We've got a different task for you, inside," one of the guardians says with a jerk of her thumb toward the facility.

I frown. "Right now? I thought I had the whole morning out here."

The other guardian rests his hands on his hips—by his electrified baton. "Change of plans. Clancy's orders."

A prickle of apprehension runs down my back, but I nod and go with them. Let's find out what the man in charge wants from me today.

The guardians lead me to a different part of the facility than the areas I've become familiar with. In a small room with a vaguely medical vibe, they have me take off my running shoes.

Then they wrap a band around each of my arms, just below the sleeve of my T-shirt. The outer material feels like fleece, but something more solid presses against my skin from within.

As they click into place, tiny bumps jut out against my skin with a faint prick that fades away almost instantly.

I study the gray fabric warily. "What are these for?"

"Monitoring equipment," the woman says. "They give a closer look at your internal state, but you'll forget they're even there."

I find that hard to believe. And something about her phrasing sets off a sharper alarm bell in my head.

The man opens a door at the other side of the room and ushers me into a slightly larger space. The door thumps shut the second I've stepped over the threshold.

Zian turns at the sound where he's standing at the far end of the room, his expression uncertain. Other than him, the room holds only a shag rug, a polka dot loveseat, and a double bed with two pillows and a duvet, all lit by a soft glow from the panel set in the ceiling.

My entire body is jittering with discomfort now. Something about this whole scenario feels way too wrong.

I glance at Zian, noting the matching bands against the peachy-brown skin of his bulging biceps. "Do you have any idea what this is about?"

He shakes his head, his mouth tight. "They didn't tell me anything. I don't get it."

I'm starting to wonder if anyone else from our original group will be sent in to join us when Clancy's voice warbles from a speaker set somewhere in the walls.

"It looks like we're all set up now. Why don't you two get comfortable? You can take things at your own pace, although of course the faster you move things along, the sooner you can go back to your typical day."

I peer at the stone wall in the general direction the voice seems to be coming from. "Move what along? What are we supposed to be doing?"

There's a slight hesitation. I can imagine Clancy clearing his throat as if preparing for a not-entirely-comfortable announcement.

"You've already formed this marked bond of yours with Jacob, Dominic, and Andreas. If we're going to study the mechanics of the process, that leaves Zian."

My gut plummets. Zian goes rigid, every muscle tensing as a shudder ripples through his body.

I glare at the wall, but my voice wavers. "You're ordering us to have *sex*? While you watch? Are you out of your fucking mind?"

The last two words crackle with a mix of anger and desperation. He wouldn't really go *that* far...

No, I can't say that for sure. I have no idea how twisted our new captor's mind might actually be.

Some small part of me is still hoping he'll chuckle and say I've got it all wrong. No dice.

"We won't be watching. There are no cameras in the room. The changes in your bodies and your shadowblood energies will be monitored through the bands you're wearing—that's the data we're interested in."

A process I'll need to study more closely. He practically told me he was going to do this when he dismissed me and Jake yesterday.

The fact that he isn't going to be sitting there directing us in his own personal porno doesn't really make the situation any better. Even if I believe him that we're not being secretly recorded.

Zian retreats from me until his back hits the far wall. He slides along the wall to the corner and wedges himself there, his massive frame outright quaking now.

Watching his obvious agitation, my heart wrenches even more than it had already.

"We won't do anything you don't want to do," I tell him in as soothing a voice as I can manage. "We don't have to listen to them."

I can't tell if Zee even hears me. His gaze has gone vague with horror, panicked pheromones flooding the air from his corner.

Clancy pipes up again as if I give a shit what else he has to say on the subject. "Allowing us to study the process will mean we can help *you* understand what the connection means too. What benefits there might be to it that you haven't discovered on your own, or any potential pitfalls."

My hands ball at my sides. "Don't tell us you're trying to force us into hooking up for our own good. Forget it. This whole thing is sick."

"I'm not going to force anything. The two of you care about each other—you're attracted to each other. Griffin has sensed as much in just the last few days. I'd imagine this would have happened before too long regardless. We're simply—"

"Fuck you!" I snap, and whirl around as if I can figure out where he and whoever's with him might be relative to this room. "Are you in on this right now, Griffin? You really think what this asshole's doing is okay?"

I don't get any answer. Zian rocks in little jolts between the two walls, a faint growl seeping from his throat.

"Take as long as you need," Clancy says, so fucking calm I want to tear his face off his skull. "You'll remain confined to this room until you decide to take that step. But be aware that your three friends will also remain in solitary confinement for the same length of time. It's up to you how long the process takes."

There's a crackle, and I have the sense he's shut off the mic.

I fling myself at the door, but even my superhuman strength can't yank it open. As much as I strain at it, I can't break the lock.

"No, no, no," Zian is muttering in his corner. He rakes his hands through his short hair, and I wince at the sight of the little red scratches he's drawn in their wake—from the claws that've poked from his fingertips.

My stomach is churning so wildly it's a wonder I haven't already spewed my breakfast on this nice rug. "We can wait him out, Zee. He can't make us do this."

I take a couple of steps toward him, groping for some way to reassure him more, and his head jerks up with a snarl. Fur has sprung up along the sides of his neck; the beginning of his wolf-man snout contorts his face.

"Get away from me!" he yells in a guttural voice that barely sounds like the Zian I know.

I freeze and then back up. If he needs space, I'll give it to him, even if it kills me to see his distress.

The last thing I want to do is add to it.

With a click, Clancy's voice drifts into the room again.

"There's no need to get so worked up about the situation. You'll both enjoy yourselves. If you—"

I don't find out what fantastic tips he has for us now, because Zian's roar cuts off our captor's voice. He barrels out of his corner with a ferocity that makes me flinch.

His full wolf-man face has taken over, fangs protruding from a wrinkled muzzle. His body looks at least half a foot taller and broader than his usual size.

He hurls himself at the bed and gouges his claws right through the duvet into the mattress. Chunks of fabric and foam career through the air.

I scramble backward and leap onto the loveseat, my pulse racing. I've never seen Zian quite this wild before— and I'm the only person in the room.

I don't want to think he'd hurt me, but if he's so upset that he isn't even aware of what he's doing...

His arms swing, smashing the bed's plain wooden frame. Splinters fly across the floor.

When he spins around toward me with a feral howl, my heart nearly stops. His eyes blaze with fury and anguish.

He lunges forward—and the door bursts open. Several guardians hurtle into the room, two zapping him with batons, another stabbing him with a syringe as his body spasms.

"Don't hurt him!" I shout through my constricted throat. Tears burn behind my eyes.

It isn't his fault. They pushed him until he snapped.

As Zian slumps on the floor, Clancy himself appears in the doorway. He meets my gaze with just a little regret in his expression.

"I'm sorry this attempt went so badly," he says. "Let's get you out of here. We can try again with a new approach another day."

"Are you *insane*?" I sputter.

Before I can say anything else, the prick of a needle radiates from my shoulder. I hadn't heard the guardian turning toward me.

I teeter over, the rest of my caustic words dying in my mouth.

THIRTEEN

Riva

I scale the mountainside with swift, efficient movements, ignoring the growing burn in my arms. Whenever the terrain ahead of me is predictable enough that I can risk it, I take swift glances around at my surroundings.

I specifically picked this training exercise today so that I could get a better sense of the island's landscape. Maybe even catch a glimpse of something that'd indicate a potential escape route.

We can't fly away using Clancy's private jet, since none of us knows how to pilot a plane. But if I could spot an obvious route through the mountains to a harbor or any sign of human civilization beyond the facility...

The latter option feels more and more impossible. It would make sense for Clancy to buy an entire island for his purposes rather than take the chance that we'd be discovered.

But surely they have *some* method of transportation other than the air route. He doesn't seem like the type to put all his eggs in one basket.

Hell, I'd be willing to attempt a swim to the mainland if it turns out there's some in sight.

Anything to not get dragged into more of his sick schemes.

When I reach the top of the climbing path and perch on the shallow ledge there, the view doesn't offer much. There's no easy way to scale the last fifty or so feet to the very top of the cliff, which is smooth and sheer probably by design, so I can't look over the other side of this peak.

All I see sprawled out in front of me is the dense jungle that once looked so appealing. Now it seems to glower ominously at me.

I worry at my lip in the few minutes I can reasonably rest before I should start the climb down to avoid raising suspicion. Maybe we do need to focus on getting a plane —hijacking it, forcing one of the guardian pilots to take us off the island.

Although if the jets they have access to are all the same size as the one that took us on our mission, I'm not sure we could safely fit all of the shadowbloods on it. There are at least a few dozen of us here, and I don't know if I've met all of the facility's inhabitants yet.

Not only are the training periods staggered and unpredictable, there could be just as many prisoners who aren't allowed out at all because they haven't agreed to Clancy's terms. Or he's decided they're even more volatile than the rest of us.

And I have no idea which of the guardians is trained as

a pilot, or how we'd threaten them into complying if I can figure that out.

A wave of hopelessness washes over me. I close my eyes against it and then propel myself onward.

I start the scramble back down, relying mostly on my clawed fingers and my feet in their flexible athletic shoes, keeping the safety rope loose. When I figure out a plan, I want to be ready for whatever it'll require.

Voices carry through the trees during the last short stretch before my feet hit the ground. Celine, Booker, and a few of the other older teen shadowbloods emerge along the path through the jungle to the climbing site.

The five of them keep chattering away as they stretch their arms and legs in a quick warm-up. The smiles flashing between them and relaxed tone to their conversation make my stomach knot.

I'm not sure how easily it'll even be to convince the other shadowbloods that we *should* escape. They haven't seen the darker side of this place—and Celine knows firsthand just how ruthlessly the guardians will hunt us down to reclaim their supposed "property."

Funny that Clancy spoke about the child slavers with so much disdain when he and his colleagues have treated us like slaves since we were old enough to walk.

The guardians here make a show of giving us our space, but I can pick out a couple of figures hanging back among the trees along the fringes of the climbing site. I can't talk safely here.

But I might be able to get a general sense of how content our younger counterparts actually are.

After I've stripped off the climbing harness, I amble

over to where the teens are stretching. "It's a good day for a climb," I say, just to start the conversation. "Not too sweltering for once."

One of the girls laughs. "I'm just glad to be getting out in the sunlight every day. It can swelter us all it wants."

Okay, no sign of mutiny there. I drift a little closer to Celine. "Too bad the guardians didn't give you more of a break to enjoy your new life here before sending you off on missions again, huh?"

I try to keep my tone light, as if I'm making a joke out of it rather than criticizing our keepers. Celine lets out a quick giggle with an energetic shake of her head.

"I like getting out there. Knowing I'm being useful. Maybe the next mission, I'll get to do more than sit in a van!"

She sounds upbeat enough, but a trace of apprehension tickles my nose with its heightened sense of smell. There's something about the subject she isn't totally happy about.

I prop myself against the side of the cliff while the first couple of climbers gear up. "You ever think about what you'd want to be doing if we weren't part of this whole Guardianship thing? Like what job you'd do or where you'd want to live?"

Booker snaps his fingers. "Hell, yes. I don't know about jobs, but New York City is where it's at. At least out of the places I've been. Could be there's someplace I'd like more outside of the US."

As he cocks his head with a contemplative air that clashes with his surfer-dude appearance, Celine shrugs. "I don't know. With the missions, we could end up seeing all kinds of places anyway."

"As much of them as you see from the inside of the van," I say.

She giggles again. "Well, yeah. I'm sure we'll have more action on other missions. And once we've proven ourselves more. Maybe Clancy will even let us take vacations or whatever!"

So she would like a chance to have more freedom, whether she's fully recognized how stuck we still are or not. That's a start.

And Booker seems to have dreamed about other things, despite his easy-going attitude.

"I like to think about that stuff sometimes," he says, his grin going a bit crooked, "but mostly it makes more sense to focus on what we've got right now. Especially when this is a heck of a lot better than we ever had it before."

I force a smile in return. "That's true." Though I'm not so sure I'd agree about the "a lot."

Celine wanders away to watch her friends on their climb, but Booker lingers near me, his stance turning unusually hesitant. Has he guessed why I was asking these questions?

He glances at the ground and then back at me, and asks in a lowered voice, "You and Nadia have gotten kind of friendly, yeah?"

Huh. Where's he going with that?

I dip my head. "Sure, I'd like to think so. Not that we've had the chance to get to know each other all that well yet."

"I just wondered—and maybe this is a weird thing to ask, so you totally don't have to say—has she mentioned anything I did that bothered her?"

I blink at him, feeling totally out of my depth. He thinks Nadia is *upset* with him?

At my startled silence, Booker barrels onward. "It's just, her aura gets kind of… strange when I'm around, like agitated or something, even though she always acts nice. If I did offend her or something, I'd want to apologize. I mean, I really like her."

He stops abruptly, a flush coloring his cheeks.

I've never had anything like a normal family, but in that moment, swept up in a rush of amused affection, I have the urge to ruffle his hair like I'm the worldly big sister in a sitcom. Except it'd be a bit of a reach when he's nearly a foot taller than me.

I can't stop a real smile from tugging at my lips. I'm not going to betray Nadia's secrets, but it seems fair to say, "I think she'd really like to hear that. She's definitely not upset with you."

Booker studies me as if trying to read more into my words and lets out a chuckle with a rush of breath. "That's —that's good to hear. Sorry if it was a strange thing to bring up—"

"No," I say quickly, meaning it. "I don't mind at all. I know most of us have only just met, but we're all kind of family, right? We should help each other when we can. At least, I want to."

"Yeah." He flashes me a more confident grin. "Thanks." Then he lopes over to join the others at the base of the climbing route.

I watch them for a moment with an uneasy twist of fondness and apprehension in my gut.

Maybe he and Nadia will find something special together like I have with my guys.

Maybe Clancy will force the issue if he realizes they're into each other, to see if they'll form the same kind of connection we have.

My teeth set on edge. I can't let that happen.

I don't know the best way to get us out of here or how to protect us once we're gone, but I know we can't stay here any longer than we can help.

I have a while yet before I'm due back at the facility for my lunch period, so I set off for my other planned training activity: firearms. I might prefer close combat where I can use my supernatural strength and claws, but when it comes to dealing with people as well-equipped as the guardians, weapons could definitely come in handy.

And I want to take into consideration all the weapons we could have access to.

The shooting range is set up in a cavernous room at the top of a carved flight of steps leading from the valley floor. A broad waterfall covers the entrance, the warbling of the water drowning out any sound that resonates out of the mountain.

When I duck past the waterfall, a guardian is standing several feet down the hall on the other side, keeping an eye on things. No doubt I was watched along the path I took to get here as well.

I could kill any of them if I wanted to—but that wouldn't do us any good. Clancy knows I'm not going to go rogue without my guys. And the second I attack any of his people, their ankle bands will let him know.

We're still shackled; he's just given us a longer chain.

As I step into the shooting range, my spirits lift a bit. Andreas is standing down by the end, next to a younger guy I don't know and little Tegan.

There is something deeply wrong about watching a twelve-year-old raise a pistol and blast away a target with cool focus.

Andreas brightens at the sight of me, and my pulse stutters with the sudden thought of all the things he doesn't know. I haven't seen him since getting back from my mission.

There's no sign in his expression that any of my other guys have filled him in on the pieces he's missing.

I grab a pair of earmuffs and examine the array of weapons on offer, presided over by another guardian. They're basic handguns and rifles, including a couple with sniper scopes.

I haven't done much work with long-distance shooting. I pick up one of those and move to a lane that's deeper, with a more intricate target at the far end.

Something about the process of positioning the gun and focusing on the stick figures I'm supposed to pick out in the target drawing is unnervingly reassuring in its familiarity. I sink into the same focused state Tegan must have found.

Squeeze the trigger. One, two, three, four times.

I miss one of the targets by half an inch, but the bullets tear straight through the others. The finished sheet whirs away, and another takes its place.

I've blasted my way through five of them when I notice Andreas heading over to the equipment area. As he takes off his earmuffs, I lower my rifle.

I have to talk to him. That's more important than just about anything.

We can't come up with any plan at all until we're on the same page.

Andreas waits for me and catches my hand as we head down the hall, away from the thunder of the range. He probably figures we'll hang out in the valley for a bit, but I stop him right by the waterfall.

Its noise can cover our voices too.

I bob up, looping my arms around his neck when he bends to meet me. For all my determination, in that first moment I can't help simply hugging his leanly muscular frame to me.

"Hey," Andreas murmurs by my ear, embracing me just as eagerly. "I missed you too."

I let out a rough laugh and squeeze him tighter, shutting my eyes against a sudden burn of tears. Cool flecks dapple our skin from the waterfall next to us, but I tune out the sensation.

I tuck my head against his shoulder so I can speak right by his ear like he did with me. "Things are even more messed up than we realized. Dominic found out that Clancy's picking missions based on what he gets paid to do. And he doesn't really care who's paying him or why they want the job done."

Drey kisses my cheek, but his mouth has drawn into a grimace. "He managed to tell me about some of that when I saw him yesterday. Not what the guy pitched to us, is it?"

"No." I let out a shaky breath. "But it's gotten even worse than that. He found out about our marks. Because Jake and I—after the mission, we…"

I trail off, abruptly uncertain of my words, but Andreas gives a low chuckle. "You don't have to feel bad about that. You told me right from the start how you felt about all of us. I'm glad Jake's done enough for you to trust him again."

I swallow thickly, simultaneously warmed by his response and sickened by the rest I have to tell him. "That's not the problem. Clancy didn't know any of us had formed that kind of connection before. He wants to study how it happens—*what* actually happens. So he stuck me and Zian in a room together and tried to make us put on a demonstration."

Drey's whole body goes rigid against mine. He pulls back just far enough for me to see the fury flashing in his dark gray eyes. "What the fuck? I'll kill the asshole myself."

He's managed to keep his voice low enough even in his anger that the guardian down the hall doesn't react, but my heart skips a beat anyway. I pull him back to me to hide his expression.

"Nothing happened. Well, Zian really freaked out. Have you seen him since yesterday morning? They tranqed him."

Andreas pauses, his muscles flexing with the tension coursing through his body. "He was there at breakfast this morning. Quieter than usual, but then, we don't usually feel comfortable talking all that much anyway."

A little of my own worry releases. "Okay. Good. I just

—I think Clancy's going to try again. Not the same way, but… He really wants to figure out why our powers are bonding like that."

Drey lets out a sound that's close to one of Zian's wolf-man growls and hugs me like he thinks if he can hold me tight enough, Clancy won't be able to reach me. Right now, I think if our captor stepped into view, Drey might actually murder the guy, consequences be damned.

"We can't stay here," I say. "But I haven't been able to figure out any way we could make a run for it without getting caught before we're even out of the valley."

Andreas's breath hisses through his teeth. "I've been searching the guardians' memories here and there when I get the chance, looking for anything that might be useful in case we wanted to break out. Nothing useful has come up so far, but I'll start pushing harder. There's got to be a chance."

He nuzzles my hair and squeezes me in another hug. "We made it so far before, Tink. We can do it again. I'm *not* letting him turn you into some kind of sex experiment. If you need to fight back in the moment, fight. Don't worry about the rest of us."

Pressed against his solid chest, I choke up with a swell of emotion. Because it just might come to that.

And deciding between my personal autonomy and my guys' well-being is the last choice I'd want to make.

FOURTEEN

Zian

When the pair of guardians who seem to have been assigned to me come to collect me after dinner, I assume they're going to lead me back to my room. That's where I've been locked up for most of yesterday and today other than meals, since my freak-out with Riva.

Instead, they direct me toward the entrance to the facility. I walk along hesitantly, my nerves on edge.

What is Clancy going to do with me now?

Fractured memories of my panicked rage yesterday morning flit through the back of my mind, but I do my best not to look at them too closely. I focus on what's ahead instead.

We step out onto the wide ridge into the warm evening air. The sun hasn't quite set, the sky cast with a golden haze.

A few shadowbloods are training in the field below,

but I don't recognize any of them. I haven't gotten many of the younger ones' names so far.

I'm always a little afraid that if I approach them, they'll see me as a threatening presence rather than a friendly one.

"This way," one of the guardians says. They both walk with me down the steps and along one of the jungle paths.

The sound of burbling water reaches my supernaturally keen ears well before I see the source. When we come to the edge of a glade between the trees, I stall in my tracks.

It should be a pretty scene. A waterfall, much thinner than the one that hides the shooting range, tumbles several feet down the cliffside into a clear pond ringed by polished rocks, obviously set up for swimming. Ferns and bushes with vibrant flowers frame most of the pool.

And Riva is sitting on the grassy patch near the bank, her knees drawn up to her chest, alone.

"Clancy thought the two of you should have a chance to talk after what happened yesterday," the guardian next to me says. "You'll be given your privacy. As long as you stay in this clearing, you won't be disturbed. When you're ready, you can walk back to the facility—or we'll come to escort you if you get off track."

Without waiting for my response, she and the other guardian vanish into the thickening shadows of the path. I stay where I halted, looking at Riva.

Clancy wants us to *talk*? He's giving us our privacy?

They say that, but Riva's got the bands around her upper arms like they put on us yesterday. Maybe the guardians never took them off.

They've left mine on, a faint weight against my biceps.

The fabric is a little scuffed on mine because I tried to tear them away after I woke up in my room. The metal bits underneath wouldn't give.

They're obviously still monitoring us. And I'd bet they want us to do a lot more than talk. This is just a different tactic.

Riva gazes back at me from where she's sitting. Her mouth forms a tight smile.

She tips her head toward a couple of baskets sitting on the ground next to her. "They left us swimsuits in case we wanted to get in the water and some snacks if we get hungry. I think this is Clancy's insane idea of a date."

Her tone is dry. I'd snort in amusement if I didn't feel so sick.

"Something like that," I mutter.

Riva studies me for a few moments longer, her pretty face turning so serious it sends a different sort of ache through my gut.

Her voice softens. "Are you okay after yesterday? They came at you so hard when you got upset—I've been worried about you the whole time."

The ache digs deeper at her phrasing, as if what the guardians did to subdue me was more violent than my destruction of the room. There was a point when my entire world dissolved into a frantic fury to smash every piece of Clancy's plan.

I duck my head. "I was fine after the tranquilizer wore off. Other than feeling pretty awful about the whole thing. I'm sorry if I scared you."

Riva makes a dismissive sound. "It wasn't your fault. It was a psychotic plan—of course you were upset."

She was upset too, but she didn't fly into an uncontrollable rage. I bite my lip and then force out the words.

"I can't do it. Even like this, without being so trapped. Even if he keeps pushing it on us over and over. I just—I *can't.*"

When I dare to look at Riva again, her eyes have widened. "Don't even think about that," she says firmly. "Even if you could make yourself go through with it, *I* wouldn't want to. Not like this. If anything… If anything's ever going to happen between us, it'll be because we both want to for ourselves, not to satisfy some sick tyrant."

Her gaze flicks toward the jungle around us, her chin lifting at a defiant angle, as if challenging Clancy in case he's watching.

A bit of the tension that's twisted up inside me loosens. I finally convince my feet to move again.

As I walk over, Riva pushes one of the baskets forward so that it can sit between us. A little shield, confirming that we aren't even going to touch.

The sight relaxes me even more. I sink down on the grass next to her and peer at the crystalline water of the pool in the fading sunlight.

"It is a nice spot."

"Yeah. Under different circumstances, I'd appreciate the gesture." Riva laughs roughly and then digs into the basket. "I guess we might as well make the most of it."

Under the cloth covering, we find raspberry and custard tarts, a container of popcorn, miniature sandwiches, and a couple of bottles of what turns out to be lemonade.

Riva sips hers and wrinkles her nose at it. "Not sour enough."

I find I'm capable of smiling at her. "You'll have to ask them to import some lemons so you can make your own, Shrimp."

"That's not likely to happen. I don't think Clancy is very happy with me right now in general."

I pause, my stomach clenching all over again. "I saw Dom at lunch. We talked a little."

I don't know how much I should say out loud in case Clancy's monitoring us. But Riva can obviously guess that Dominic told me about their mission—and what they found out about Clancy's approach to global activism—from my brief remark.

She sighs and takes a bite of one of the tarts. "It was too good to be true right from the start, wasn't it? We'll figure something out."

She's already working on a plan—I know her well enough to tell. She got us out of a facility before.

But that one wasn't on an isolated island. And it was only the four of us she needed to break out.

"At least we have the chance to train and improve our skills while we're here," I say. "I've been working on the exercises Rollick suggested for controlling my shifts. Obviously they didn't help yesterday, but in less tense situations, I think I'm making progress. He wasn't wrong about some things even if… things have turned out badly here too."

I wince inwardly as images come back to me of the pictures Clancy showed me when he was first pitching his new plan for us shadowbloods. Things went very badly before—there's no denying that fact.

Riva considers my expression. "You heard about what the shadowkind did to the kids we got free."

"I saw the photos he has."

She gives a soft hum but doesn't say anything else, her gaze going momentarily distant. I wish I could read her mind.

This whole situation would be so much easier if we all could communicate through thoughts alone. Although I'm not sure I'd want Riva seeing everything that's in my head.

She slips off her running shoes and socks before scooting onto one of the smooth stones around the pool. With a tug of her pantlegs to her knees, she dips her feet into the water.

"Not bad." She swishes her feet back and forth. "Not as warm as I'd usually like, but I guess it'd be a little much to expect a hot tub."

The rippling water tempts me. We spent all that time on the yacht sailing around the ocean, and I never really got the chance to swim.

I hesitate and then ease over to the pool's edge too. The water laps around my feet and calves, as warm as the tropical air around us.

I shoot Riva a sideways glance. "I don't know what you're complaining about. This is perfect."

She laughs more openly this time, the bright, buoyant sound that sends a giddy shiver right down the middle of me. "No one's stopping you from diving in."

I suppose that's true. I look down at myself and then at the other basket with the swimming clothes. But I don't really want to get changed with Riva right here, even though I know she'd avert her eyes for my privacy.

I don't want to deal with the feelings that'd rise up in me, getting undressed with her so close by.

But it's not as if I'm particularly attached to the tee and sweats I'm wearing. Without letting myself second-guess the impulse, I push off right into the water in my regular clothes.

Riva laughs again, the perfect soundtrack to the delight of the warm water closing around my large frame. I kick off from one end of the pool to the other, but it's only about fifteen feet across, so not much of a workout.

Oh, well. It isn't the swimming I like most anyway.

I stretch out on my back, flexing my muscles in the right places to keep me afloat. My body bobs in the peaceful water.

For a moment, I feel as if I weigh nothing at all.

I close my eyes, absorbing the sensation of floating free. My body drifts toward the spray of the waterfall, and I scull briefly to nudge myself away.

There's a soft splash and a shift in the water's gentle currents. I glance up to see Riva has joined me, leaving on her tee and sweats like I did.

Her silvery braid trails behind her head in the water. She grins at me and paddles around the pool.

I can't help following her movements, unwilling to return to the meditative state of my float.

Her slim arms dart through the water with both strength and grace. The water darkens her eyelashes, bringing out her bright brown eyes.

It's only about a minute before she paddles back over

to the bank where she was sitting before. She scrambles out and gives herself a quick rubdown with one of the towels from the basket before hunkering down at the edge of the water again. "That's enough of that."

Her damp top clings to her curves. My gaze traces them before I jerk it away, with heat flaring through my veins.

In my pants, my dick rises.

There's a part of me that wants to swim right over to her, yank her back into the water, and press my body against every bit of hers. Kiss her until our lips are on fire.

But I know that if I tried, I'd be recoiling in another jarring smack of panic before I did much more than graze my fingers over her leg. I'm not sure I could touch her at all right now, no matter how carefully, without setting off the instinctive jolt of horror that Clancy provoked so badly with his experiment.

Riva cocks her head, catching me staring. I turn, glad that the flush staining my cheeks won't show in the twilight.

How the hell is she ever going to understand why I keep pushing her away?

Andreas's voice travels up from my memories. *You've got to tell her, you know.*

Every particle of my being balks at the idea, still. But maybe he was right, because she's already gotten the wrong idea.

She pulls her legs up in front of her to hug her knees. "It's okay, you know. I'd *never* want you to do anything more than you'd want to. I love you, Zee, as you are, without you needing to do anything else. What we already have is enough for me. That's not going to change."

My throat closes up at the raw affection in her words. For a second, I'm afraid to speak, but I know I have to say at least one thing.

The statement seems to yank at my heart as I push my voice from my mouth. "I love you too."

The smile that springs to her lips could kill me.

She does need to know the rest. She *deserves* to know.

I don't want to be treading water while I'm doing it. I clamber out of the pool a safe distance from Riva and wrap the other towel around my bulky shoulders.

When I sit down with the picnic basket between us like before, my thoughts jumble together. I don't know where to start.

No, maybe that's not really true. My dick is still half-hard—it's taking conscious effort not to let my eyes trail over her body again.

I fix my attention on the water instead. "The worst thing is that I do want more. A lot more. Even now. I just don't think I'll ever be able to act on wanting it."

Riva gives me a moment and then ventures into my silence. "I heard from the other guys about what the guardians did after I left—how they brought in that woman... and something went really badly."

Should I be glad there's one part I don't need to explain? All I feel is the weight of the story pressing down on me.

"She took Andreas first," I say. "He said he told you about that. I could see afterward how sick he felt about the whole thing, and then she came to me. She was leaning into me and touching me to encourage me to come to the other room, and I—"

I stop, gathering myself, my gaze still glued to the water.

Riva's voice comes out painfully gentle. "It's okay. You don't have to talk about it if—"

I shake my head. "No. I do. You need to know…"

I inhale sharply and force myself to go on. "I've never wanted anyone other than you, Riva. And my head was a mess right then because she wasn't you, and that wasn't right, but the guardians had told us all that shit about you turning on us, so I didn't know how to feel about you anymore. And I was just so angry about everything."

"Anyone would have been."

"Maybe, but anyone else wouldn't have—" I close my eyes with a wince. "She started tugging on my arm for me to join her, and something in me just snapped. The wolfman came roaring to the surface all raging. I just wanted her to *stop*, I wanted her to be gone, to leave me and my friends alone…"

My voice trails off into the stillness around the pool. I inhale raggedly, my stomach churning as I put the memory that's haunted me for nearly four years into words.

"I was hardly aware of what I was doing. But then the guardians zapped me back to reality, and she was there on the floor… in pieces… all the blood…"

I press my hand against my face. "It wasn't her fault. They'd hired her, they'd told her what to do. She might not even have had any more of a choice than we did."

My whole body is tensed against Riva's reaction. But when her voice reaches me, it's quiet and steady.

"That's right. It was the guardians' fault. They should never have put you in that position."

"I shouldn't have lashed out that harshly. I shouldn't have lost control." My breath rushes out of me. "And now, when I'm in any situation that feels like that scenario even a little, all the feelings come back. The disgust and the anger and the horror about what I did. And I'm terrified. If I can't control the feelings, then how do I know I can keep control of myself?"

It could be Riva lying in a puddle of blood, chest gouged open and limbs strewn by my vicious hands. Not because she did anything wrong. Because I'm just too fucking messed up to protect her from myself.

And here she is, still trying to help me after everything I've told her. "That makes sense. Of course you'd want to be careful."

I manage to raise my head to finally meet her eyes. "It isn't fair to you. It's the *worst* with you, because even a totally innocent touch can set me off, because… because I do want you, so it always affects me more. But nothing's gotten better as we've spent more time together. I might be like this forever."

Riva's eyes glint with a shimmer that might be tears. For me?

"If you are, then that's how you are," she says. "But you haven't had that much time to see how we could work through it, right? We'll just have to take it as it goes and see what happens. When we're in a place where we can actually do that without any… pressure hanging over us."

A burn forms behind my own eyes. I want so badly to hug her right now.

Instead, I reach, ever so tentatively, to rest my hand on the basket between us.

Riva watches and carefully sets her hand just a few inches from mine. An offering, take it or leave it.

I swallow hard and evaluate the emotions whirling inside me. Then I let myself slide my hand that last short distance to curl my fingers around hers.

Riva responds with a gentle squeeze that sends a pang through my heart. Her smile is tight, but I know the pain in it is empathy for me, not her own distress.

"This is enough," she says, like she told me before. "It will always be enough."

I thought I already loved her as much as a person could, but somehow in that moment, the feeling grips me twice as hard.

How can I care about her so fucking much and still not be sure I won't destroy her?

Darkness settles over the glade. The warmth starts to fade from the air, chilling my damp clothes and probably Riva's too.

We grab another tart each and then pack up the baskets. Before we can set off for the facility, lights glow along the path.

Clancy arrives with another two guardians in tow. One moves to collect the boxes, while the other goes to Riva.

She offers Riva a poncho to warm her up—and removes the bands from her arms without a word.

As the guardian motions for Riva to walk along the

path, Clancy reaches for my own arms. I hold myself tensed as he detaches the bands.

"I'm sorry," he says in a low voice for only my ears. "I was aware of the incident at your old facility, but I failed to realize how deep the trauma ran. I shouldn't have put any pressure on you at all. Nothing like this will happen again."

I blink at him, but all he adds is a brisk nod. Then, without any sign of expecting forgiveness, he ushers me ahead of him down the path.

I follow the light that glimmers off Riva's hair, tension still humming through my body. Should I even believe his apology?

It's hard to imagine we've won any kind of victory here. All we can do is wait and see what Clancy and his guardians will try next... until we're free of them.

FIFTEEN

Andreas

It's another bright day, which means I can wear the
sunglasses I requested without looking at all strange.
I adjust the frames on my nose and lean back on my
hands where I'm taking a brief break from training in the
yard.

The dark lenses let me train my eyes on each of the
guardians monitoring our progress or moving to and from
the facility without them noticing the reddish gleam that
gives away my talent. For the past few days, I've been
riffling through as many memories as I can reach, at every
possible opportunity.

One of them has to have seen or experienced
something that could help us get off this island.

It's hard to narrow down my search. The only way I've
found I can focus my ability to pry inside people's heads is
by targeting a specific person.

I started by digging up memories involving me or my

friends, but those didn't get me very far. Glimpses of moments like the attaching of bands around Riva's arms and walking her into a bedroom to meet Zian only left me twisted up with fury and a sense of helplessness.

Clancy didn't get to see through his plan. Riva's okay. But just thinking about what he tried to force them into makes me want to batter him with my fists and feet until he looks worse than the victims of Riva's screams.

Who knows what messed-up plan he's going to come up with next? We have to escape.

I have to find a way how.

If I'd been paying more attention, we might not have gotten stuck here at all. If I'd taken a moment to scan Griffin's mind when the guy I thought was Jacob beckoned me and Dominic down that hall in the facility...

All it would have taken was a brief peek, and I'd have known it wasn't Jacob. That it was a trick.

I could have stopped us before we ended up trapped in that room, before he had a chance to go back to trick the others as well. I could have warned everyone.

And maybe we'd have gotten away.

I'm the only one with a talent that would have let me realize the problem before it was too late, and I fucking failed all of us.

Guilt gnaws at my gut as I adjust my position on the grass. I'm not going to miss a crucial detail like that again.

For my current quest, I've switched to homing in on memories involving the man in charge. Clancy gives the orders to the other guardians—he introduced most of his staff to this place.

He knows its inner workings better than anyone, so the things he told his underlings could hold the key.

The man I'm currently studying surreptitiously from behind my shades isn't offering anything all that useful, to my disappointment. I sink into a memory of Clancy telling him to escort a group of younger shadowbloods to the climbing course, leap from that to a moment seeing Clancy at the other side of the cafeteria, and from there to a conversation Clancy was a part of involving some sports team in the regular world.

I grimace and push myself off the coarse grass, knowing I can't rest for long without the guardians hassling me about keeping up my training. As if I'll be a willing volunteer for any of their missions now that I know their motivations are more about financial gain than making the world a better place.

We have to play along for now, or we'll end up shut away in our rooms, no chance to discover a way out at all.

I make my way through the trees to the rope course, knowing it'll allow me a vantage point where I can check out the guardians monitoring the area without them seeing what I'm up to all that well. It can't hurt to keep both my muscles and my agility in tiptop shape too.

After I've clambered up one of the ladders and set out across the hanging boards between my starting platform and the next, one of the younger shadowbloods emerges below me. Even from above in the mottled jungle light, I recognize him immediately from his skin tone, so dark it's almost literally black.

I've made a point of chatting with all the shadowbloods I've crossed paths with during training and meals. I *want* to find out what their lives have been like—and who knows when one of them might have something useful to contribute.

So I know that the kid down below is named Ajax, and that he's part of what appears to be the middle "generation" of younger shadowbloods: the ones who are currently fourteen or fifteen years old. The few times I've seen him around, he's been pretty quiet.

Now, he glances up at me, runs his hand over the stubble of hair on his scalp, and moves to the ladder on a tree ahead of me. He times it so that he reaches the platform just moments before I swing off the last board to join him.

"Hey," he says in a low voice the guardians on the jungle floor won't hear, with a careful but intent look at me.

He's positioned himself like this on purpose—because he wanted to talk to me?

I walk slowly around the platform as if considering my options for my next trek. "Hey. Everything good?"

"About as good as it can be, huh." Ajax rests his hand against the tree trunk. "You know, with my power—I've got a little bit of telepathy. Can't pick up much, but I catch bits and pieces of thoughts. Stuff people are thinking the most loudly."

A chill washes over my skin. I keep my voice quiet and even. "Oh, really? You must 'hear' a lot of interesting things."

"Nah, mostly it's boring—or I can't even make sense of it. But yours have gotten me curious." He pauses with a swift glance toward the guardians below. The only one in view isn't even facing us at the moment.

Ajax drops his voice even lower. "You really think we could leave?"

I grip one of the ropes, my mouth going dry. Can I trust this kid?

For all I know, he could turn tail and inform Clancy of anything I tell him.

I measure out my words. "Anything's possible. Why— are you thinking you'd want to?"

The boy gives a barely perceptible shrug. "I know a lot of 'em like it here. But there's someone who matters a lot to me that I hardly ever get to see. Back in the old facility, we were together every day."

My mouth tightens in a grimace. I can understand his frustration too well. "That sucks."

"Yeah. And it's not much fun being stuck around the guardians with the way they think about us anyway."

Ajax lifts his head, and I let myself meet his dark brown gaze. "I just wanted to say... If you find a way, I want in."

He doesn't sound like a schemer trying to manipulate me into a confession. He sounds like a nervous but hopeful kid.

I study him for a moment, slipping through his skull into his memories.

I see him sitting on his own in a corner, wincing at the insult that tumbles out of a guardian's mind into his head. I see him waving goodbye to a group of other kids, his other hand clenched, as he's escorted out of a facility's training room.

Emotions don't come through with my talent, not directly, but I can sense how unhappy he was in those memories from the feel of his body.

I pull back out and re-focus on him here in the present. "I'm just... considering my options. But if you pick up on any thoughts that might help with that goal, even a little, you should let me or one of the other Firsts know ASAP." I hesitate. "Well, any of the firsts other than Griffin."

Ajax makes a face. "He's always with Clancy anyway. What's his deal?"

I wish I had a better answer. "I don't know. He wasn't like that before."

I don't want to linger any longer in conversation in case the guardians take notice. Ajax turns toward a net-like configuration of ropes, and I set off along another path of hanging boards.

An ache has formed in the pit of my stomach. It isn't just Riva and my friends counting on me.

I've just given that kid a reason to hope. I need to have something more for him the next time we talk.

I've scaled most of the course when one of the guardians calls up that it's time for lunch. Ajax has already left, and I don't see him again on my way to the mountain facility.

They switch up our shifts and never let us know when we'll see each other again specifically to make it harder for us to plan anything. They pretend it's freedom, but really it's just another kind of cage.

As I'm climbing the steps to the mountainside entrance, Clancy himself appears. He gives me a brisk nod and gazes out over the training grounds for a moment before returning inside.

I have to take off the sunglasses once I step into the facility to avoid raising suspicions, but I can't resist fixing my gaze on him while I follow him down the hall. Imagine all the useful information that's tucked inside *his* memories.

But I only glimpse a fancy dinner someplace that's got to be nowhere near the island, with crystal chandeliers and people in tuxedos and evening gowns, and then a fragment of a childhood elementary-school test. Before I can dig any farther, a guardian steps out of the cafeteria ahead of me.

I jerk my gaze away, hoping she didn't notice me using my talent. When she doesn't say anything, only motions me inside, I exhale softly in relief.

Even if the quest feels pointless, I have to keep trying. Giving up *definitely* won't get us anywhere.

As subtly as I can manage, I flit through the memories of the guardian standing near the buffet table while I grab a hamburger, fries, and salad for my lunch. Clancy yelled at him one time for showing up late to his post, but I don't see how that could factor into our plans.

Keep trying, keep trying, keep trying.

My lack of progress makes it hard to appreciate seeing Zian walk into the room. How much of a friend am I if I can't get us closer to freedom?

Freedom he needs even more than I do.

He shoots me a small smile and makes a gesture to indicate he'll sit with me. My gaze slides past him to the guardian who escorted him in.

I've seen that guy talking to Clancy pretty often. Maybe he's a closer associate than the others.

But he stands there by the doorway watching all of us. If my eyes flare red for more than a few seconds, he's bound to notice.

Fuck. I don't want to let the chance go.

"Zee," I murmur when the bigger guy sits down across from me. "Could you go keep the guardian who came in with you busy for a bit? Ask him about your schedule for the rest of the day or something like that—just keep his attention away from me?"

Zian's forehead furrows. "I can give it a shot. I don't know how long I can keep him talking for."

"Whatever you can manage is fine."

He sets off without question or complaint. Trusting that I'd only ask him to do this if it was important.

Zian approaches the guardian from the side, and the man turns to better face him. His frown doesn't indicate much patience for the interruption.

I train my gaze on him and leap in.

Clancy, Clancy, Clancy. Grabbing breakfast together, a briefing on training progress, daily orders.

I'm aware of Zian shuffling his feet at the edge of my awareness, but I force myself to keep digging. He's doing his best, and I have to too.

Then I stumble into a memory of what looks like a facility control room, though with the stone walls specific to the island. Clancy is gesturing to a set of controls.

An emergency system? asks the guardian whose head I'm in.

Clancy nods. *Earthquakes in this region are infrequent*

and rarely severe, but we need to be prepared. If a tremor strikes that sets off the sensors, the rooms will automatically unlock. We'll need to get all of the shadowbloods out into the valley as quickly as possible. As few assets lost as possible.

My host stares at the pane Clancy pointed at with its zigzag symbol, so I stare at it with him. Sensors that'll make our rooms unlock?

Of course, we'd need an earthquake to make that happen.

But Jacob once toppled two three-story buildings with his power. Maybe…

Zian passes between me and the guardian on his return, cutting off my connection—and ensuring the man doesn't see the fading flash of red in my gaze. He drops back into his seat and gives me a curious look.

"Get anywhere?"

"You know, I just might have." A hint of a smile touches my lips. "I could use a little more help—from your X-ray vision this time. Look through the walls around here and check if you see this symbol anywhere."

I squirt ketchup next to my fries and scrape the tines of my salad fork through the scarlet liquid. Sketching out the emblem from the guardian's memory, that just might be the key we so desperately need.

SIXTEEN

Riva

I'm getting a little tired of the guardians' surprises. Especially the ones where I can't even tell whether the unexpected event is good or bad, like being ushered into a random room in the facility to find Griffin standing there waiting for me.

I stop in the doorway, my pulse stuttering.

Is this guy my friend or my enemy now?

Does *he* even know?

"Hey, Moonbeam," Griffin says, with the vacant smile that makes me want to claw the sound of the childhood nickname out of my ears.

I'm afraid hearing him say it like that will write over my memories of all the times he spoke it with real affection. Of when he was still himself.

I don't answer, tearing my gaze from him to take in the rest of the room.

It's a hotchpotch of furnishings: a sofa against one

wall, a utilitarian table along another, and a couple of round, ringed targets hanging at the far end. Like whoever set it up couldn't decide whether it was for lounging in or training.

The table holds a row of gleaming knives. My fingers twitch at my side.

Griffin is watching me. "You always liked practicing with throwing knives. And I thought you might feel more comfortable if you had weapons available while we talk."

My attention jerks back to him. "Are you planning on saying something that'll make me want to stab you?"

He lifts his shoulders in a gentle shrug. "I hope not. But I know the last week here has been a lot more stressful for you than any of us would have wanted. You have every reason not to feel totally safe."

I walk over to the table and skim my fingers along the edge while I eye the blades on offer. "What did you want to talk to me about?"

"Clancy knows he fucked up. I've told him how badly he did. He'd like to find a workable solution, but he thought you might prefer to talk things through with me first. Since you know me better."

I don't know the guy talking in that unnervingly even voice at all.

But I *would* rather talk to Griffin than that asshole Clancy. If only because there are questions that've been gnawing at me that no one except Griffin can answer.

I select one of the knives—a particularly slim one that looks sharp enough to slice through flesh like butter. "Are you just his puppet, then? You speak for him and not yourself?"

Griffin shakes his head. "I make my own decisions. But I still think what he's trying to do here could be for the best for all of us. It's a work in progress."

A work in progress that traumatized Zian more than he already had been, that forced me and Jacob to murder one gang on behalf of another that might be even worse...

My jaw tightens. I curl my fingers around the hilt of the knife and turn toward Griffin.

"Then you're on his side. And I've got a lot of reasons to be pissed off with him. Aren't you afraid I'll stab you no matter what you say?"

I could kill him for real. He knows I could. One slash deep enough through his throat, and he'd be too far gone before the guardians could rush Dominic in here.

With my supernatural speed, I could land the blow before Griffin even has time to try to deflect me.

But he simply gazes calmly back at me, without the slightest sign of being disturbed by my suggestion.

"You're not that angry," he says. "You don't want to hurt me."

I grit my teeth. I might not be feeling particularly murderous, but the fact that he can read my emotions irritates the hell out of me.

Especially when he doesn't appear to be remotely affected by them.

What the hell would it take to jolt a little emotion of out *him*?

I adjust the knife in my hand, willing myself into a state of calm focus that won't betray my intentions. Then I lunge at Griffin.

I slam him back into the stone wall he was standing

by, hard enough to bruise but not to break any bones, and whip the knife up to brace it at the base of his throat.

Griffin's expression twitches with the impact, but it settles back into its usual placid state a second later. I can't say the reaction was anything more than physical.

He gazes down at me with those uncomfortably blank sky-blue eyes.

If anything, he looks *curious*. Not rattled, not annoyed.

"Maybe I don't need to be angry to think we'd be better off if you really were dead," I snap, but I know even as the words come out that they aren't going to land right. Because just saying them sends a twist of guilt and horror through my gut that no doubt he can pick up on.

He is right that I don't want to hurt him, no matter what he's become.

Griffin cocks his head, not seeming to care that the blade nicks his skin with the movement before I tug it back a fraction. "You're upset with me, but not like that. What are you doing this for?"

I grimace at him. "You're acting like nothing matters. I'm trying to figure out if anything *does* matter to you."

He lifts his hand to set it over mine—the one that's pressed flat against his chest just beneath his shoulder. The second his fingers brush over my skin, a tingle races through my veins.

All the shadows in my blood wake up and quiver with anticipation. And something flickers in Griffin's eyes, the closest thing to an emotional response I've seen in him so far.

Huh. Does touching me affect him like it does me?

I guess that would make sense. The other guys all feel the same magnetic pull between us, the urge to connect physically and let our shadows meld together.

Whatever the guardians did to Griffin, maybe they couldn't stamp out that one aspect of his nature.

His gaze stays a little more intense, a little more *present*, as he tucks his hand around mine.

"You matter to me, Riva. The guys matter to me. All the shadowbloods here do."

The physical contact and our closeness are distracting me more than I like. I shove away from him, yanking my hand from his and lowering the knife.

"You have a funny way of showing it. We finally got out like we'd always wanted to—we'd have come for you too if we'd known you were alive—and you helped the guardians drag us back into their prison."

I regret stepping back when I see the vagueness creep back over Griffin's expression. Like he really was more here with me for a moment and now it's gone.

"I told you why I helped them," he says. "You were doing a lot of damage out in the world. Destroying things, killing people."

"People who were attacking us!"

Griffin is silent for a moment, studying me. When he speaks again, his voice has gone quieter.

"I didn't help right away, you know. Some of the guardians came to me and told me what had happened, showed me pictures from the place where they said you'd been doing cage fights, said you were the one who murdered all those people. I didn't believe them."

My throat closes up. It takes a moment before I can

speak. "That wasn't— I didn't *mean* to kill the whole audience. I didn't even know it was going to happen."

"But that's a problem, isn't it?" Griffin's tone has turned coaxing, as if I'm a wild animal he's working at taming. "Most of those people were just there to watch. They weren't the ones controlling you. Did they all deserve to die?"

My whole body tenses with the surge of anguish. "I had no idea I even had that power then. I'm learning how to control it."

"It wasn't just that," Griffin says. "It isn't just you." He pauses. "I didn't believe it until they showed me video footage from Ursula Engel's cabin. She had surveillance cameras, you know? So I could see the way you twisted and broke the bodies, just like at the arena."

"That's when you started tracking us for them," I say with a lurch of my gut as the understanding hits me.

After Engel's house—that was when the guardians started finding us so much faster. We couldn't stay anywhere for more than a day without them showing up.

Griffin inclines his head. "For a little while. But then, in Miami... Their strategy wasn't working. They couldn't take you in, and one of the shadowbloods died while they were trying, and I thought maybe I'd been wrong. That it was safer letting you go."

I swallow thickly. "But then you changed your mind again?"

"They showed me what Jacob did in Havana. All those people *he* broke—and then cut off their hands..." Griffin knits his brow as if the thought confuses him. "He was getting worse, being out in the world. More violent. And then Clancy came to me and told me how he was going to change things, so the Guardianship wouldn't work like it had before. So you wouldn't be trapped the same way. So you could use your powers to make things better."

"And you believed him."

"He didn't lie. Here we are."

I flip the knife in my hand and fling it at one of the targets. It smacks straight into the central ring, but I get no satisfaction out of the sight.

"Here we are," I say. "Working as hired goons for whatever criminals feel like paying him to take on their dirtiest work. How is murdering people for money better than murdering them to protect ourselves, Griffin?"

Griffin walks over to the table by the knives, but he only looks at them. He never liked weapons practice much even in our old lives.

"I didn't know about Clancy getting paid. But he does need money to keep things running—to keep supporting us. If he chooses the jobs that do the most good for the world at the same time, it doesn't have to be a problem."

I snatch up a smaller knife and whip it after the first. It strikes the target a couple of inches from the center.

"And how can you be sure he is choosing those jobs and not whichever get him the most money?"

"He's said he'll be more careful from now on about vetting who hires us."

I snort. "Funny. Somehow I don't automatically believe everything he says."

Griffin replies with the air of patience that annoys the shit out of me. "I've known him since before he managed to bring us here. He worked hard to give us this opportunity. And he *is* better than the guardians who were in charge before."

"Better doesn't mean good."

"But if there isn't any option that's good in every way, you have to go with the closest one."

I take another knife but simply toss it from one hand to the other, eyeing Griffin. "And what about how he treated me and Zian? How is that anything close to good?"

Griffin's voice firms. "That wasn't okay. At all. I didn't realize he was going to try something like that. But he knows it was an awful mistake. He hasn't pushed you two together again, has he?"

It's true that I've only seen Zian twice in the past four days, and those were during regular training sessions, no one forcing us to even work together.

"It was still sick that he tried to force us at all," I have to say.

Griffin's gaze drifts away from me, somehow going even more distant than before. "I think... the guardians aren't used to seeing us as people instead of test subjects. Even the ones who are trying to do the right thing. That might take time."

I swallow a growl of frustration. I'm obviously not going to get Griffin to reject Clancy's approach right now.

If we get a chance to make a break for it, using the emergency system Andreas told me about in a secretive murmur during dinner two evenings ago, would we even be able to take Griffin with us? Would he be willing to go or try to stop us?

But if we leave him behind... he'll point the guardians right to us like he did before, won't he?

I change subjects to get at the most vital information he could still give me. I'm not sure if he'd answer if I ask directly, but that doesn't mean I can't prod my way there.

"We're talking about the people who made you bleed all over the country tracing our movements too. I'm surprised they didn't drain you dry over all those days you must have been following us."

Griffin offers a faint smile as if he thinks he's reassuring me. "It wasn't like that. My powers have evolved and grown too."

I raise an eyebrow at him. "Our emotions led you to us?"

"In a way. We've determined that if I focus on someone I know reasonably well, I can pinpoint their location on a visual display like a map. I just… feel where they're feeling things, you could see it as."

He can pinpoint us on a fucking map? A chill races over my skin.

We'd never get far enough away from the guardians while Griffin's willing to serve as a tracking device. Even crossing the ocean only worked because he was momentarily refusing.

But I have no idea how to get through to him.

No, maybe that's not totally true. I know the one thing that's provoked anything close to a real reaction in him the entire time we've been in the room together.

Setting down the knife, I turn to fully face him. I reach out and take one of his hands in my smaller ones.

The simple skin-to-skin contact sets my nerves alight. They spark brighter when I stroke my fingertips over his knuckles, the shadows inside me flaring with the impulse to step closer.

And a hint of the same longing wavers in Griffin's suddenly uncertain gaze.

"You know me that well," I say softly, holding on to him. "You've always known me the best out of anyone. Can't you see that I'm not some kind of monster who needs to be locked in a cage? We were figuring it out—we were getting a grip on our powers. None of us would have hurt *anyone* if we'd been left alone to live our lives."

His mouth tightens. "I don't know that for sure. And if you lose control again—if Jacob goes on a rampage— I can't just let that happen."

I squeeze his hand, and his fingers wrap around mine in return. A pang resonates through my chest. "It wouldn't be your fault. Nothing we did was your fault."

Griffin laughs, a strangely rough sound after the eerie calm I've gotten so used to. His voice drops until it's barely a whisper. "You have no idea how much is my fault."

What is he talking about?

Anguish shines in his eyes, there and then gone so quickly I can't tell whether I only imagined it. I let myself step closer, lifting one hand, meaning to touch his face—

But Griffin pulls back, dragging his hand from my grasp.

Whatever tenuous connection I forged vanishes. He blinks, his expression evening out.

Before I can try again, the door behind him opens. A guardian pokes her head into the room.

"Griffin, Riva—since your talk is going well, Clancy wants me to move you on to dinner."

Your talk is going well. The words roll over me, and something clicks in my head.

Horrified certainty spikes through my veins. I jerk my gaze back to Griffin. "For fuck's sake. You know what this is, don't you?"

Griffin knits his brow. "What *what* is?"

I can't read his mind even as much as he can read mine, but I think he genuinely didn't realize.

I step farther away from him and cross my arms over my chest defensively. "You said Clancy learned from his mistakes? He's only gotten sneakier about them. This is a fucking *date*. He wanted us to get friendly again—why now, after he couldn't force me to hook up with Zian? Why would he care other than because you're the only other guy from our original six I haven't already been with?"

Griffin stares at me. Before he can respond, whether he'd deny it or argue in Clancy's defense, I decide I can't stand to hear any more from him.

I march over to the guardian at the door. "I'd like dinner, but I'm not having it with Griffin. Let me go to the cafeteria. *Now.* And tell Clancy he can fuck off to the goddamn moon, if he isn't already listening to hear me say it himself."

SEVENTEEN

Griffin

The twining melodies of violin and piano swell through my room. They wind around me as I lean back in my armchair.

The music stirs emotion in some people. I've seen videos of audiences weeping while listening to this song.

But nothing rises up inside my chest. My heart beats on at the same steady pace.

I used to put on music like this to test myself. To confirm just how deep the guardians' training ran.

This is one of the rare moments when I can't help thinking I might prefer it if I noticed it getting to me just a little. If I knew the things that affect other people could still affect me, if only slightly.

A normal person would be irritated, even angry, that Clancy was taking so long to come talk to me. I told the guardian who tried to bring me and Riva to dinner that I wanted to see him immediately, in the firmest tone I'm capable of.

But it's been... hours? Definitely at least one of those.

My sense of time has gotten foggy with the fading of my emotions, as if feeling things about what was happening helped define those events concretely in my head.

By any measure, it's been a lot more time than *immediately*. My thoughts won't settle until I can address him directly.

And yet with each passing minute, my heart thumps on in the same steady rhythm. My gut stays relaxed.

The tension in my mind doesn't seep beyond my skull.

Maybe he's gone to talk to Riva first, which might be fair, and that's what's keeping him.

At the thought of Riva, one of my hands brushes over the other unbidden. The graze of my fingertips over my knuckles doesn't summon even a ghost of the sensation I'm unconsciously seeking, but it does provoke a flicker of memory.

Her hands, tucking around my own. Her fingers stroking my skin.

The tiny but heated quivers that shot through my nerves and had my pulse momentarily hitching.

The memory in turn provokes a faint twinge of aversion. No, that shouldn't happen. No, that's nothing I want.

The source of that reaction is buried so deep now that it doesn't contain any emotion of its own, only a dull impression of recoiling within my head.

What am I recoiling from, though? It was Riva— It was *good*.

The urge to walk straight to wherever she is and feel it again nibbles at the edges of my mind.

No.

Even feeling things because of her can be a problem. Those kinds of feelings could be the *worst* problem.

Couldn't they?

I rub my forehead as if the gesture will sort out my uncertainties.

All I know for sure is that Clancy created a problem much bigger than any turmoil inside me. How could he have thought it made sense to send me to Riva as if I could take Zian's place in his disturbing plan?

Unless Riva was wrong, and that wasn't what he intended after all.

If it wasn't, if he has nothing to justify, why hasn't he already come to tell me that?

Jacob would be furious. I've felt my brother's anger, sharper and harsher than it ever was when I knew him before.

I've felt it aimed at me. How am I going to make *him* understand that I was trying to keep him safe in my own way?

I thought, once we could see each other again...

At a plaintive meow, I lift my head. Lua is stalking over to me, her tail standing straight and her ears perked in anticipation.

My cat might not be able to talk, but I can instantly tell what she wants, although I can't read animal emotions at all. Even without the inner insight, she's so much simpler than any of the human beings I encounter.

As she rubs her cheek against my leg, I reach down and give her a gentle scratch down the length of her spine. With an encouraging meow, Lua jumps right onto my lap.

She stretches out in her favorite spot, squeezed into the narrow space between my thigh and the arm of the chair, and offers up her white-furred belly for more pets. A smile crosses my lips as I oblige.

It isn't the same as feeling something, but I get a general satisfaction out of knowing I can cater to her needs. Make *her* happy.

That the emptiness of my body doesn't stop me from showing I care in the ways I can.

When I told Clancy I was bringing Lua with me from the facility I'd been kept at before, he started to ask if that was really necessary. The look I gave him stopped him halfway through the question.

I'm not totally sure why the guardians who worked on me after the escape attempt brought her to me as a kitten, but she's mine now. She counts on me.

And maybe I need her a little bit as well.

At the knock on my door, Lua twitches in surprise and then goes right back to purring avidly. I scoop her up and get to my feet, reaching to switch off the music.

"Come in."

I know it's Clancy already, well before he opens the door. Every person in this place has a different feel to them, and I'm more familiar with his overall air than most.

He steps inside and stays by the door, his arms folded

loosely in front of him. The fact that I have no emotions roiling in my own chest makes me twice as aware of his own, as detached as I am from the visceral sensations of them.

He's apprehensive but mostly calm and determined. Prepared for this to be an uncomfortable talk but assuming everything will be smoothed over without much difficulty.

I hope he's right.

"I take it your visit with Riva didn't go all that well?" he says. "Is that what you wanted to talk to me about?"

I study him, watching the outward signs of his mood even as I monitor him from the inside out. "It was going fine until she got the idea that you were hoping us re-establishing our friendship would lead to something more. Was that the larger plan? That she might warm up to me enough that she'd want to have sex with me, since she isn't going to with Zian?"

My straightforward question sends a flicker of discomfort through the older man. As if his intentions would be any better or worse depending on how I phrase it.

He adjusts his weight. "I can see I pushed too hard with the two of them. I wasn't going to force anything. But if we'd reached that outcome, getting more data on the connections she's been able to form within your group would have been a welcome side benefit."

"And would you have encouraged me to talk with her at all if it wasn't for that possible 'side benefit'?"

Clancy simply avoids answering that question. "Griffin, you know the work we're trying to do here—how difficult it'll be. I'm looking out for all of you, searching for every possible advantage."

A pang of self-righteous defiance resonates through his emotions. He's on the defensive—because I'm getting at the truth, and he doesn't want to admit there could have been anything wrong about his plans.

My fingers continue their rhythmic stroking of Lua's fur where she's sprawled in my arms, but my thoughts jitter as the new information shuffles into my understanding of the situation.

He was using me like he tried to use Zian. He didn't even *tell* me he was trying to use me.

I wouldn't have thought he'd go that far. Just hours ago, I was telling Riva he'd realized his mistake.

Clancy sighs. "If you talk to her again, you could help her warm up to you with your powers, couldn't you? I know you couldn't intervene very well with Zian, but her hesitation is much less... aggressive."

I frown at him. "I tried to calm Zian down when he went into that rage because I was afraid he'd hurt someone, not to make it easier for them to hook up. To push Riva to feel happier around me..."

That would be just like forcing myself on her, wouldn't it? Worse than doing it physically, because she wouldn't be able to see the attack and ward it off.

A flinch ripples through me, my thoughts narrowing down to a surge of denial. "I don't understand why you'd ask me that. It'd be a horrible thing to do to her."

So horrible a twinge of nausea ripples through my gut, as if just for an instant I'm actually feeling that horror.

Clancy shakes his head. "Sorry, it was a reflexive

thought. Obviously as soon as you left, your influence would fade, and that could have adverse effects that would counteract any progress we made."

Adverse effects? How about the fact that she's one of my oldest friends, and there is no universe where coercing her into any kind of intimacy, even only renewed friendship, would be seen as anything but morally appalling?

The flicker of emotion has vanished, but my abhorrence at the idea hasn't wavered. I need to be completely clear about this.

I draw my posture straighter. "Even if it wouldn't fade, I would never do that to her. She's my *friend*. I'm here to stop people from being exploited, not to do it myself."

"Of course, of course," Clancy says, holding up his hands. "I won't mention it again."

He's uneasy, but I can tell from the way he's eyeing me that it's only about my response. He doesn't feel any concern or guilt at all about the tactic he just suggested.

What if Riva was right about that too? What if I've failed to recognize just how detached this man is from *us*?

Does he still see us as so subhuman that he can't be trusted to have even our basest best interests at heart?

The other accusations Riva threw to me flood through my head. I find myself saying, "You know, she'd be happier naturally—they'd all be happier—if the Guardianship gave them even more freedom. Chances to go out into the wider world for their own reasons, to do what they want, not just for missions."

Clancy exhales in a huff. "You of all people should realize how dangerous that could be. We can't risk it until we're absolutely sure they wouldn't give in to their more violent impulses."

I fix my gaze on him even more intently than before. "Well, what about me? What if I wanted to have some time for myself? I've never hurt anyone. My powers can't do any permanent damage."

"You're a key part of getting our operations into gear, Griffin," Clancy says without missing a beat. "I hope you wouldn't try to bow out on us when we need you to make sure we achieve everything we're aiming for."

He's dodging the question again. He could have said I could take a brief trip, or that he'd be willing to arrange something in the future, but instead he's saying no while doing his best to make it sound as if he's only being reasonable.

James Clancy is a very controlled man. I've never sensed his emotional state going wild the way Zian or Jacob can.

But the impressions I pick up from him still tell a story. And right now, I taste not just the fear I can assume is about what might happen to the world if shadowbloods were allowed to roam freely through it, but also an anxious twinge of anticipated loss.

He doesn't want to let go of us. And not because he cares about *us* all that deeply, it's clear.

Because we're the key to his grand master plan, and he can't carry it out properly without us. We're tools he's counting on putting to use.

He hasn't shown any concern about what I might be going through that I'd want to ask that question. Any sign that *my* happiness matters at all to him beyond carrying out his goals.

Has he ever? Or was I so caught up in the idea of fixing everything that's gone wrong, making a better future for us all in alignment with his vision, that I never paid enough attention before?

"I want to do what's best for all of us," I say, an answer that's both true and that I know he'll accept.

Clancy gives me a tight smile. "I'm glad to hear that. Don't worry about this whole situation anymore. Or about Riva. She just needs time to fully grasp the bigger picture."

He leaves without checking if there's anything else I hoped to ask him. The door clicks shut behind him.

Clicks shut and locks, because I'm never allowed to go looking for *him*.

For a few minutes, I stand in the same place, running my fingers over Lua's back and under her chin, gazing at the door without really seeing it.

This facility and the missions carried out from it were built off Clancy's vision… but they wouldn't have happened without me. Without me, I doubt any of the guardians stood a chance of catching up with my former friends, let alone capturing them.

At the time I was sure I'd made the right decision. That it really was best for them and me as well as him.

I have no gut feeling to guide me, no innate sense of whether these are the results I should have expected, but fuck, do I wish I did.

What if I've actually screwed up our lives all over again?

EIGHTEEN

Riva

The low, thin voice reaches my ears as I secure the last pieces of my climbing gear.

"Riva? That's your name, right?"

I glance around at the same time as Dominic does where he was gearing up a few feet away from me—more carefully to work around his tentacles.

A slim boy in his early teens has approached us, so quietly I didn't notice him coming. The bright afternoon sun gleams off the rounded planes of his dark face and the stubble of even darker hair over his scalp.

His intent gaze is fixed on me. I recognize him from seeing him here and there around the facility, but we've never spoken before.

I tip my head in acknowledgment. "Yeah, I'm Riva. Are you going to climb too? There's room for three on the course."

He steps closer with a flick of his eyes toward one of the guardians stationed at the edge of the jungle around the climbing site. His voice lowers so it's barely a murmur.

"Andreas told me I should let the Firsts know if I picked up anything that might give us a way out. I caught something from a guardian at breakfast—the supply helicopter is coming right after the last dinner shift tonight."

Understanding clicks in my head: this is the kid Drey mentioned to me, the one who can read thoughts, just a little. Ajax—that was the name he said.

I push a smile onto my face, keeping it as relaxed as possible for the sake of the watching guardians. "Thank you for the heads up. We might check out the course after we're done here."

Ajax's mouth twitches upward with a faint smile of his own, accepting the cover story I've offered. "I figured you'd want to hear about it," he says, and turns to go.

I meet Dominic's gaze and find it even more pensive than usual. He pauses and then nods to the cliffside in front of us. "We'd better get climbing."

We can't really talk while we're scaling the rocky surface. I push myself faster than usual both in anticipation of the conversation to come and to let the burn of the exertion focus my thoughts.

Of course, that means I reach the ledge partway up the cliff well before Dominic does. I brace my feet on it and lean my weight against the cliffside as I give him time to catch up, rolling my shoulders.

The guardians won't think there's anything strange about us taking a brief break here. That's the whole reason they included the ledge, even if on my own I'd clamber right past it.

Dominic scrambles up to join me with a huff of ragged breath and a weary smile. "I think you've gotten even faster since the old days."

I give him a crooked grin in return. "I've had a lot more motivating me."

He balances himself carefully on the ledge and lets one of his tentacles slip over to wrap around my wrist, the monstrous equivalent of holding my hand. "What do you think about the news?"

I bite my lip, gazing down at the jungle where I can only barely make out the forms of the watching guardians now. There's no way they can hear us up here.

The wind gusts over me as I consider my answer, whipping my braid across my neck. "I don't know. I guess a cargo helicopter must have a decent amount of room in it—but enough for all of us?"

Dominic strokes the tip of his tentacle over my palm in a soothing gesture. "You know we might not be able to get *everyone* out all at once. I don't even know how many shadowbloods are living here."

Neither do I, but every part of me balks at his suggestion. I push my thoughts toward other considerations. "We'd still have to figure out a way to *get* to the chopper and take it over without being caught along the way."

"Yeah." Dominic's mouth twists. "I guess we don't know for sure if Jake even can set off the emergency system. And we'll only get one chance to try that trick."

"He's got to make it feel like a whole earthquake. A *big* earthquake."

That seems like a lot, even for Jacob. I've seen him pull down two three-story buildings in one go, but nothing on the scale of shaking up an entire mountain.

Dominic chuckles roughly. "You know he'll try, even if he practically kills himself doing it. The number of times he ran himself to the point of injury in the last few years at the old facility, pushing himself past his limits like he thought he was proving something…"

A melancholy cast comes over his face. I wonder how many times Dom needed to patch Jacob up after he overexerted himself.

A tickle of inspiration ripples through me. We should probably start climbing again, but I have to put the idea out there.

"Dom… You told me that you can take energy out of things even when you're not using it to heal, right? That it makes you feel stronger, exhilarated, like my scream does for me?"

Dominic's shoulders tense, and I reach to grasp his actual hand in the hopes of conveying that I didn't mean any judgment in the question.

"Yeah," he says quietly. "Why?"

"I was just thinking… if you can pass energy on to someone else to heal them, maybe you could pass it on to boost them when they're already fine too."

Dominic blinks at me, and understanding dawns on his face with a strange mix of hope and horror. "If I can get to Jacob at the right moment, maybe I can pump up his powers."

"It could be worth trying. If you're okay with it."

He gives both my fingers and my wrist one last affectionate squeeze and turns toward the cliffside again. "If it would get us out of here, I'd try just about anything."

I take the second half of the climb slower, making sure I don't get too far ahead of Dominic. I still reach the upper ledge a couple of minutes ahead of him.

Stretching out my arms, I peer over the craggy landscape in the direction of the facility. The landing strip where our private plane took us to and from our mission lies above it. That's probably where the cargo chopper lands too.

Supplies must be delivered pretty regularly. It's not like this is the only chance we'll get.

I'm just not sure how much better prepared we could be. Or how much worse our circumstances might become the longer we delay.

When Dominic reaches me, he takes one look at my face and slings his arm around me. I hug him back, tucking my head against the crook of his neck and breathing in his familiar tangy scent, sharper now with the sweat he's worked up during the climb.

"We'll figure it out," he murmurs to me. "One way or another. One time or another."

I wish I could feel as sure as he sounds.

He cups my cheek and brings my mouth to his. My skin lights up from head to toe as our breaths mingle.

I haven't gotten to kiss any of my guys more than briefly since I hooked up with Jacob in the van. The soft but determined press of Dominic's lips against mine leaves all my nerves tingling—and aching for more.

He draws back only far enough to rest his forehead against mine. His voice comes out with an unusually husky note.

"I've missed getting to be this close with you."

My throat chokes up. "Me too."

"One more thing to look forward to when we get out of this, Sugar."

The new nickname heats me up even more. I can't resist claiming one more lingering kiss before we head down the mountainside again.

We chuck off our gear for the trio of preteen shadowbloods who've come for a climb and set off toward the facility. My thoughts spin in my head.

Dominic doesn't push for further answers. He knows that a problem like this needs to be contemplated carefully.

We come out into the clearing beneath the facility in time to see a procession scaling the winding path higher above the entrance.

I stop in my tracks, squinting at the figures who are just cresting the peak of this part of the mountain range. My heart thumps harder, but I don't make out the forms of any of my guys—or any other shadowbloods I recognize.

I do catch the ruddy gleam of the short-cropped hair on the man at the back of the line. I'd know that color and the confident gait anywhere.

Clancy is directing a bunch of the shadowbloods off somewhere.

"Another assignment?" Dominic murmurs next to me.

"Must be." My stomach knots with the question of what mess he's bringing them into this time.

Dom hesitates before he speaks again. "It means some of the kids won't be here... but he won't be either. And last time he brought at least a few other guardians with him. You were gone until the next day, weren't you?"

The knot clenches tighter. "Yeah."

I know what he's saying. The mission gives us an additional opening.

The facility's leader will be away, out of easy reach to give orders, when the supplies arrive. There'll be fewer guardians in general to tackle a rebellion.

How many opportunities are we going to get like *that*?

One of the guardians still here strides over to us with a curt air. "Riva, you're having lunch now. Dominic, you have another hour of training time."

Splitting us up as they always like to do. They wouldn't want us to have too long at once to feel comfortable in each other's company.

Except when they're trying to force me to fuck one of the guys, that is.

I grab Dominic's hand for a quick squeeze before the guardian gets insistent. He surprises me by tugging me right to him in an embrace.

The jolt of pleasure at his kiss mingles with my apprehension. We've avoided most overt PDAs in front of our captors.

But the gesture isn't really about stealing a momentary make-out session. Dom's lips brush my cheek next, and the faintest whisper travels to my ears.

"It's your call. Say the word, and we'll be with you."

He steps back at the guardian's clearing of her throat. I shoot him a nervous smile and hustle up the stone steps to the facility.

The knot in my stomach feels like a boulder now. Why is it up to me?

But I already know the answer to that. I'm the one who instigated our last escape and our attempt at breaking the younger shadowbloods out of a different facility.

I'm the one who has the most need to escape from here, the one Clancy has imposed on the most.

My men don't want to drag me into a plan I don't agree with. They trust me to judge when the balance of opportunity to risk skews right.

Too bad I'm not sure how much I trust myself. That last escape we carried out is what got us captured.

It led to those gory photographs Clancy showed me.

We definitely won't be able to bring everyone with us, not when a bunch of the shadowbloods are on this mission. Hell, for all I know Clancy did bring one of my guys with him and I just didn't spot him. I can tell Andreas and Jacob are still in the area, but I don't have that kind of awareness of Zian.

I slip into the cafeteria in a daze and am hit with a wave of relief seeing Zee by the food table. He notices me at the same moment and gives me a smile so bright and yet shy that it wrenches at my heart.

I hurry over to fill my plate next to him, careful not to stand close enough to touch. He tilts a little toward me as he snatches an enchilada off a platter with a pair of tongs.

"I saw Jake last night. Told him where I've spotted the markings Drey showed me for the emergency system."

My pulse stutters with this new piece of information added to the puzzle of "What the hell am I going to do?" All the factors are starting to line up, pointing toward a conclusion I can't ignore.

It isn't really a sudden decision. We've been prepping for a moment like this for days.

"Good," I murmur in response, taking an enchilada of my own.

As I drop some salad onto my plate, Zian backs up abruptly to make room for a younger shadowblood who's darting to the dessert tray. In his haste, Zee's elbow brushes my forearm.

He jerks his arm close to his chest like he's been burned, the now-familiar panic crossing his face for an instant before his jaw tightens.

I swallow thickly as I give him a slight nod to indicate that I'm okay. That I'm not offended by his reaction.

And anger sparks in my chest.

The flames of my fury smolder while I add a cookie to my meal, while I walk behind Zian over to one of the tables, while I sit across from him and take in the longing I can now recognize in his gaze when he looks at me briefly before digging into his lunch. The burn spreads all through my abdomen.

He's gotten worse—he's still worse than he was before, even though Clancy finished his sick games almost a week ago. The guy in front of me, the guy I *love*, has taken even more damage in the short time we've been here than he'd already endured before.

How long can we let them keep manipulating us, using us? How much farther will they go?

Who will they hurt next? How many of the younger shadows have they already screwed up without my even knowing it?

The anger sears into a swell of resolve. We can't stay here any longer.

Every day, every hour, each of us dies a little more.

And it isn't just me. I might be lighting the signal fire, but we made this plan together.

We all have a choice. Me and my guys and the other shadowbloods who can join us or not. We won't force them.

I tap my fork lightly against my plate, and Zian looks up.

"Tonight," I mouth, not even a whisper.

The way his face lights up tells me this is right.

As I gulp down my lunch without tasting it, I focus on the marks dappled across my collarbone. On my sense of Jacob and his taut, brutal energy.

He's outside right now, but not far. In the clearing just outside the facility, I think.

I construct an excuse in my head. When I stand up from the table, I make a show of patting my hip pockets.

Then I jog over to the door, where one of the guardians is monitoring, as always. "I think I dropped one of my earbuds outside while I was training. Can I quickly check the clearing?"

The man eyes me, but I really do have a portable radio and a set of wireless buds that Clancy supplied me with back in my room. I've been on good behavior my whole time here.

They have no reason to think I'd be up to anything nefarious—and they'll be watching me the whole time anyway.

"I want you back inside in five minutes," he says brusquely.

"Thanks!"

I dart out the entrance and down to the clearing. Jacob is poised near the trees with a couple of weights from a rack the guardians have set out, but the second I appear, his attention snaps to me.

To avoid being obvious about my real intentions, I stalk over to the edge of the jungle by the path that leads to the climbing area. I don't need to do more than be here —Jake joins me a moment later.

"What's up?"

I keep my tone casual. "Dropped something. Help me look?"

I crouch down as if peering through the underbrush. Jacob squats next to me, his shoulder brushing mine.

"Tonight," I say under my breath. "Right after last dinner. Dom might help you."

Jacob reins in any reaction he might have to the news other than the glitter of his cool blue eyes. "You got it, Wildcat."

We veer in separate directions, and then I let out a huff as if in frustration. "I'll have to look by the climbing range next time I'm out."

As I lope back to the facility, my heart thuds in my

chest. We're really doing this—if we can get coordinated in time.

My hand rises to my cat-and-yarn necklace, flicking over the silver surface without quite swiveling the joints. And a different thought jabs through me like an icy spear.

If we're going to get out of here and stay free from Clancy's grasp, we're going to have to deal with Griffin.

NINETEEN

Riva

We don't have watches or clocks, but I know my dinner is one of the middle shifts. A few shadowbloods are heading out of the cafeteria when the guardian escorts me over, and more are just arriving when I'm ushered out.

Back in my bedroom, the door thuds shut behind me with the hiss of the lock engaging. My pulse skitters through my veins as I sink down on the side of the bed.

It's not even a bad room. It's three times as big as the cells we were confined in at the old facility, with a soft-toned overhead fixture that mimics daylight and a cupboard to store the possessions I've actually been allowed to hold on to.

A few changes of clothes, picked by me out of the selection Clancy offered us—all practical and flexible, but that's how I like them. The radio he gave me, programmed to only offer stations with no hosts talking about the outside world, just music.

A couple of novels from the small fiction library we're allowed to borrow from, that I tried to read to pass the time but lost interest in. An assortment of weights, bands, and other exercise equipment so I can work on my strength and flexibility between outside training sessions.

How is it possible that our new captors have treated us both better and worse than any before?

Maybe that's why it's most important that we get out of this place. The better parts lulled me into enough complacency that the worse parts took me by surprise.

No matter how people like Clancy dress up the situation, no matter what grand ideals they announce, in the end, we're still prisoners as long as the guardians have us.

I should never have let myself feel like somehow that could be an okay life. Like it wasn't reasonable for me to want to make my own choices beyond someone else's tight restrictions.

I turn on the radio and switch it to a station playing a soft but steady beat and lowkey melodies. Nothing that makes me want to dance. Just enough to focus my mind without distracting me.

It occurs to me that it might be smart to have some extra clothes along. Even the radio could be useful in some way.

But I don't have anything to carry them with. And even though I can't see any, I'm sure the guardians have cameras monitoring the room.

Just like the first time, we have to act normal, or we could betray our plans before we get to act on them.

And I won't think about how badly that first escape attempt ended.

The flickers of memory bring my mind back to Griffin. A new ache forms in my stomach.

I wish I could talk to the other guys properly—make a real strategy, confirm that we're all on the same page. We'll have to scramble to organize ourselves once the doors open.

At least four of us can find each other through our marks.

But we have to bring Griffin with us too. It's either that or kill him, and no matter how he's helped Clancy or what he's agreed to, every cell in my body recoils from the thought.

I can't imagine the others will feel any different.

As long as he's with the guardians, he can pinpoint our location almost instantly. The only way to make sure he isn't with them is to keep him with us.

I'm just not sure how we're going to accomplish that when I doubt he's going to come willingly.

As that uneasy thought passes through my head, the floor beneath my feet vibrates with a faint tremor. My breath catches in my throat.

That's got to be Jacob. He's starting to shake the whole fucking mountain.

When I concentrate on my marks, I can sense that he and Dominic are together, somewhere near the facility entrance. Twinges of strain resonate from both of them.

They must be pouring a ton of effort into the attempt

if a hint of it is seeping through our connection. Will their powers be enough to trigger the emergency system?

Or has all my worrying been pointless?

As I get up to turn off the music, the tremor expands. The quivering sensation spreads through my bones from the floor.

My heart pounds faster alongside it. What if the guardians realize what's happening?

For a few seconds, the vibration plateaus, not getting any stronger or weaker. Then the stone floor lurches so hard I have to smack my hand against the wall to catch my balance.

An unnerving creaking sound resonates through the air, followed by a distant peal of an alarm—and the whir of my bedroom door sliding open.

Adrenaline jolts me into action. I dash into the hall, my attention split between possible threats in the hall outside and my awareness of my three guys through our marks.

Dom and Jake are rushing deeper into the facility, toward me. Andreas is… farther down the hall in the opposite direction, around at least one bend, but hurrying toward me too.

A few confused faces appear around the doorways nearby—younger shadowbloods trying to figure out what's going on. Before I've taken more than a step toward them, two guardians hurtle into view.

They're carrying their electrified batons and a tranq gun, but I don't give them a chance to use either. With only a slight pang of guilt, I shriek at the one who's slightly closer—a short, sharp scream designed to tear right through the most vital parts of him as quickly as possible.

He crumples, and the other guardian slams into the wall headfirst. Not because of me. As she slumps to the ground amid pooling blood, Jacob charges up from behind her with Dominic at his heels.

"Come on!" I shout to the younger shadowbloods, darting down the hall and beckoning them. "Everyone out —out to the facility entrance. We're taking off!"

Nadia and Tegan venture from nearby rooms, their eyes wide but chins up. Other kids duck back into their rooms as if more afraid of escaping than staying.

Why wouldn't they be? They have no idea what we'll face out there.

Most of them don't even really know me.

Andreas dashes around a corner farther down with Zian beside him. Relief flickers through me, but it isn't enough just to have my guys.

"Let's go!" I call out. "You don't have to live with guardians controlling everything you do, forced to go on missions and train and the rest. We can find something better."

My guys peer into the open rooms, motioning to the kids who are hesitating. Booker and Ajax must have joined Andreas and Zian as they rushed this way, because I spot them in the increasingly crowded hall.

Another guardian sprints into view, only to be tossed aside by a shove of Jacob's power. Jake comes up beside me, his hair sweat-damp along his forehead and his jaw tight.

"We've got to get moving quickly while they're still confused."

"We need Griffin," I say.

The darkening of Jacob's eyes shows that he understands why without me saying anything more. He pauses for an instant and then strides onward. "I can find him."

As Jake's twin awareness leads him around the bend in the opposite direction from where Andreas came, the other guys fall into step with us. We point every shadowblood kid we pass toward the entrance, hoping they'll listen, and hustle onward.

"We have to be ready," Jacob says. "I don't think Griffin can push emotions on more than one or two of us at the same time. You see it happening to someone, jump in there and interrupt him."

Zian frowns. "I don't want to hurt him."

A shudder runs down my spine. "None of us do. But we'll all be hurt if he can track us down for the guardians again. Knocking him out would be better for everyone in the long run."

Two guardians appear in the hallway up ahead. Zian barrels forward to crash into one; I cut the other down with another truncated shriek.

Then Griffin emerges from a room just beyond their broken bodies.

He looks at the corpses and then at us, and like so often now, I can't read the slightest emotion in his gaze. But he can obviously tell what's going on.

"You're breaking out," he says in that new, vacant voice of his.

Jacob grabs his brother's arm. "And you're coming with us. Get moving."

I tense, waiting for Griffin to put up some kind of fight. But after a second's hesitation, resolve tightens his expression. "All right. I just need to get Lua. I can't leave her here."

Lua?

My momentary confusion is broken by a meow from just inside the doorway. Griffin shoots Jacob a look of appeal, and his twin nods.

Griffin's fast about it. He ducks into the room and emerges within a matter of seconds, a backpack slung over one shoulder and a cat's white-furred face poking from the unzipped top.

As we hurry toward the entrance, I check the other guys. I don't see any sign of him warping their emotions.

Would he have grabbed his pet if he was only planning to turn the tables on us at the right moment? Or is it just to convince us to trust him?

I turn and narrow my eyes at him. "No argument? You're happy to join us?"

Griffin blinks at me. "I don't know if happy is the right word, but it's become clear that none of us are better off staying here."

It has? Since when?

As much as I'd like to badger him with questions, this isn't the time for it.

A particularly young-looking kid with spiky white hair flits past us toward the entrance, his body seeming to stutter as he blinks out of view and reappears a few feet farther ahead in an instant. I catch sight of Celine braced in the doorway to her room, her expression taut with worry.

I wave to her as we pass. "Come with us. There's room for everyone who'll come."

At least, I hope there is.

She wavers a second longer and then sprints ahead of us. Her dark hair swings as she veers into a room near the entrance, but she's returned by the time we've caught up.

I guess, like Griffin, she had something here she didn't want to leave behind, although I can't see any sign of what that was.

A dozen or so younger shadowbloods are gathered on the dusk-draped ledge outside the entrance. *Is that all?* a voice in the back of my head murmurs, but I don't let myself dwell on my disappointment.

We have to get the kids who were willing to flee out of here ASAP. That's what matters most.

Especially because feet are thundering in the halls behind us. The guardians must be regrouping, preparing to recapture us.

There's no time to go back and try to convince the others to join our escape if we want to escape at all.

"Up the path!" I shout over the racing of my pulse, jabbing my hand toward the narrow, shadowy track that weaves back and forth up the mountain over our heads.

Jacob and Andreas push to the front of the crowd, dragging Griffin with them.

"Follow us," Jake calls out, and the kids start to stream after them into the thickening dusk.

Good. Whoever reaches the plateau first will need to deal with the helicopter's pilot, and my guys are more equipped to do that than the kids. I should have thought that part through more carefully.

But when did we have time to put our heads together and really plan?

I hustle along at the back of the group, ushering the kids ahead of me with Dominic and Zian on either side. When the spiky-haired boy I noticed earlier stumbles, Zee grabs his elbow to steady him.

We're not moving fast enough. As we swerve around the first bend, some of the kids already slowing as the unexpected climb saps their energy, a squad of guardians hurtles up the path toward us.

I spin around and let out a shriek, but one of our pursuers fires a weapon at the same time. A projectile whizzes through the evening and smacks me right in the throat.

My voice fizzles out with a squeak. I try to force another sound out and only rasp.

Shit.

As a chilly wave of panic washes over me, Zian throws himself at the guardians—only to hurl himself backward, barely dodging the bolt of electricity that shoots from one of their batons.

"Go, go, go!" Dominic hollers to the kids ahead of us, urging them onward, but my stomach has started to sink.

More shots blare through the night. Zian smacks a dart to the side with a swing of his hand.

Another plunges into the back of a kid just beyond him. The boy crumples, and I stumble as I avoid stepping on his slack form.

We can't afford to stop and try to carry him, or the guardians will be on us.

One of them must hit a control, because the next thing I know, a section of path in the middle of our frantic procession crumbles away. Three of the younger shadowbloods tumble down the mountainside to a thick net that's waiting to confine them below.

"Jump!" I manage to force out in a thin voice. Zee and I catch Dominic between us and spring at the same moment.

It's at least a five-foot gap, but we clear it. Unfortunately, the guardians were prepared for that possibility too.

One of them jabs the side of the mountain, and a new ledge of rock protrudes to fill the gap so they can continue their pursuit. Another arc of electricity whips through the air, close enough that my fingers jitter.

I cough and try to propel a shriek from my mouth, but my throat is throbbing from the impact. The strangled noise that pops out of me does nothing at all.

Just in front of us now, Tegan sways on her feet, her fawn-brown hair sticking to the sweat that's broken out on her neck. Her breaths are so ragged I can hear them over the pounding footsteps around us.

I'm considering swinging her small form onto my back —or gesturing for Zian to do it—when she spins around. Her eyes have stretched even wider, but her mouth is set in a line of total determination.

"I can stop them!" she says. "I can give you enough time."

She squeezes between us before I can say a word.

When I jerk around, she's already facing off against the guardians—with her mouth open as she exhales in a rush.

I never asked what her power was. Now I get to see it up close.

A current of dark smoke like the shadows that bleed from our veins gushes over her lips. The cloud sweeps over the guardians, setting off shouts of alarm that make me think it's doing more than obscuring their vision.

"Tegan!" I rasp, taking a step back toward her, but Zian tugs me in the opposite direction.

"We have to let her. We might not make it otherwise."

I know he's right. But the sense of abandoning her yanks at my heart with every step I take away from her toward the top of the cliff.

As we veer around another bend and race the last distance to the top of the mountainside, Dominic's breath breaks into panting. I'm not sure how much longer he can keep up this pace.

But we've arrived. We burst onto the air strip in the midst of the cluster of younger shadowbloods who've made it this far—who are staring at Jacob where his hand is pressed against the helicopter's windshield, lit by the glow of its running lights.

It's a huge chopper with a propeller on the tail as well as one over the long main cabin. The pilot gapes at us from inside, both in shock and because Jake's power has a grip on his throat.

"Open the fucking doors!" Jacob snarls.

Griffin steps up beside him, his presence weirdly calm amid all the turmoil. "Force isn't working. Let me try."

Jake narrows his eyes at his twin. "You—"

Andreas cuts him off with a grasp of his shoulder.

Griffin doesn't appear to be paying much attention to the other guys anyway. He peers through the window at the pilot, and my skin prickles with the sense of exuded power.

The pilot's expression shifts, loosening other than the worried slant of his mouth. "What do you need? How can I help?"

Griffin only offers the slightest of triumphant smiles. "Open the doors and let us on."

The hatch halfway down the body of the chopper opens up. I wave the remaining shadowbloods on board, my mouth gone dry.

Will Griffin really be able to manipulate this guy into doing everything we need? Should we even believe Griffin is looking out for us?

But then, how else are we going to get a flight out of here? Jacob and Zian can't beat the guy into submission and then expect him to coherently direct an aircraft.

If it seems like something's wrong during the flight... we'll just have to deal with it then.

We squeeze into the dim, metallic-smelling space alongside several plastic crates and cardboard boxes that must be the supplies the guardians were expecting. Griffin comes around to the cockpit, leaning against the back of the pilot's seat.

Jacob stations himself right beside his brother, poised for potential trouble.

"Take us into the air," Griffin says in a voice that's almost hypnotic in its smoothness. "We need to leave this spot."

He may as well have hypnotized the pilot from how quickly the man moves to follow his suggestion.

As the helicopter lurches into the air with a whir of the blades, Griffin glances back at me. His backpack wobbles as his cat squirms inside it, her head ducked down in the chaos.

"Where do we want him to go?"

God, that is the question, isn't it? I can't see anything but darkness beyond the windshield right now.

I freeze up, both because I'm not sure what the right answer is and because I don't know if I could say it loud enough for Griffin to hear me anyway.

Dominic catches my hand and answers for me. "The nearest major city on the mainland. As quickly as we can get there."

Griffin nods at the pilot. "You heard him."

The helicopter swings around with a bob of the floor beneath our feet. I snatch at the corner of a box for balance and glance around at our fellow escapees.

A few of the kids I know have made it—Nadia and Booker, Celine, Ajax. The spiky-haired kid is here. And then a few others I haven't specifically noticed before.

They're all huddled together in the cramped space. Booker is gripping Nadia's hand like Dominic has mine, but she looks too frightened to appreciate the gesture of affection. Ajax has wrapped his arm right around another boy who looks about the same age, with dark hair, brown skin, and features that make me suspect the human part of his genetic heritage is Middle Eastern.

"What do we do now?" Celine asks from where she's

sitting against a stack of crates, her normally perky voice
gone a bit shaky.

I swallow and find I can speak a little more loudly,
though it's not much better than a croak. "I guess we get
to the city and get our bearings, and then make more
decisions."

I can reach out to Rollick without telling him where
we are. Find out exactly what went down after our break-
in at the other facility.

Zian stiffens abruptly. "Tracking devices."

I stare at him for a split-second before my gut lurches.

Right. When we made our first escape, he'd figured
out that we all had trackers embedded in our teeth.

We got rid of them by yanking the molars out of our
jaws—or having Zian do it, for those who didn't have the
same brutal strength. The thought of asking all these kids
to do the same makes me queasy.

But if we don't take care of them quickly, the
guardians will be able to figure out exactly where we've
gone even without Griffin's help.

Celine has gone rigid too. "What?"

Andreas comes up beside me, resting his hand on my
back. "We all had tracking devices in our teeth. We dealt
with ours before, but you probably still have them. We'll
need to do something about that."

"Something like what?" Booker asks in a wary tone,
adjusting his grip on Nadia's hand.

Dominic answers in a gentle tone. "Zian pulled the
tooth out for each of us. It isn't fun, but I can heal you all
up as soon as it's done."

Celine shivers, and the boy Ajax is embracing cringes

in his arms. Ajax looks down at his friend—boyfriend?—and then his gaze jerks up to meet mine.

"Devon might be able to do it another way. The devices are made out of metal, right? He can create heat... Not a lot if it's a big space, but if he concentrated it on something really small, he should be able to melt circuits."

He glances down at the other guy with a fond but concerned expression that clearly indicates *boyfriend*. "Don't you think so? If you want to try."

Devon lets out a halting sigh and offers a crooked smile. "I guess it'd be better than having my teeth yanked out. How do we know which tooth it is?"

Zian's shoulders come down at hearing there's an alternative to him disfiguring all these teens and preteens we're trying to save. He moves over to the young couple. "I can find it. Let's start with the two of you to see how it goes."

For the next fifteen minutes or so, Zian's eyes flash as he uses his X-ray vision to locate each tracker and then confirm that it's sufficiently melted by Devon's power. The knots in my stomach gradually unravel.

Maybe we're actually going to be okay. Maybe the worst part is over.

It doesn't matter that the radio crackles with questions about where the pilot is going. Jacob silences the device with a bash of his power.

It doesn't matter that I'm not totally sure about what we're going to do once we've landed. We'll figure it out once we're there.

This time, the guardians don't have Griffin as an ace up their sleeve. They tracked us down once without his help, but only after we'd stayed in the same place for a whole week.

Then Zian steps away from Celine, who submitted herself to the heat treatment last, and she points a finger at Griffin. "What about him? He's got a tracker too, doesn't he? He never ran away before."

We all glance over at the twins. Jacob shoots his brother a grim look.

"She's right. Let's destroy whatever you're carrying too."

As Zian and Devon move to flank Griffin, who raises no protest, Booker raises his eyebrows. "Are we sure we should have this guy along at all? He was helping Clancy."

"If we left him behind, then he'd have been able to help track us down," I say in my roughened voice.

Griffin turns toward Booker. "I'd rather be here with all of you. Clancy misled me about his plans too. I apologize for anything I've been a part of that's harmed you."

"You don't *sound* sorry," one of the other kids mutters.

"I—I'm working on that."

Griffin opens his mouth wide for Zian and Devon to do their work. Watching them, Booker abruptly pushes to his feet.

I don't know if he isn't satisfied with Griffin's answer— I don't think *I* am.

Whatever his intentions, the movement must distract Griffin. Because just as Devon turns away, the pilot yanks on the controls.

"What the fuck are you doing?" Jacob demands, his gaze snapping around.

The kid who muttered about Griffin being sorry jumps up. "He pretended to be on our side, and now he's letting the guardians catch us again!"

The pilot whips a phone I didn't know he had to his ear. "Yes," he gasps out in the frantic tone of a man who knows his time is limited, "They've got me—"

I don't really know who's to blame for what happens next. Jacob whirls all the way toward the pilot and sends the phone flying from his hand. At the same moment, the spiky-haired boy launches himself toward the cockpit with a cry of, "I'll stop him!"

He blinks a few steps forward like I saw him do in the hallway and slams into the pilot's seat as he appears, his arm whacking the guy across the back of the head in a blow that doesn't look totally intentional.

As the boy yelps, the pilot careens forward. His head bashes into the controls.

The helicopter heaves. Those of us standing bang into the walls and boxes.

Griffin's even voice cuts through the chaos of gasps and exclamations. "You can still do this. Get the helicopter steady."

The pilot has straightened up a little, but he lets out a pained moan. Blood is trickling down his forehead and from his nose.

"I can't—I can't see—it's broken."

"Just try. Try your best. There, you're doing so well."

It doesn't feel like anything's going well. The next lurch tosses me right onto my knees.

"Hold on to something!" I call out hoarsely to the kids.

A plummeting sensation melds with the forward momentum. The darkened sky beyond the windows tilts.

We're falling—faster, faster, rushing onward at the same time. All at once, branches crackle against the windows.

Then there's a boom of impact, and we slam to a sudden halt.

TWENTY

Riva

My head smacks into the box I'm crouched against. For a few seconds, my thoughts spin as pain splinters through them.

Something creaks. Gasps and a few sobs fill the air around me, along with a panicked feline yowl.

I shake myself out of my daze with a hitch of my pulse and peer through the darkness. "Is—is everyone okay?"

I can't tell if my voice is still strained from the thing the guardians shot at my throat or if it's all the shock of our crash now. In the dim moonlight that seeps through the windows, I vaguely make out the younger shadowbloods amid the tumbled boxes and crates.

A bag of rice has fallen out and split open, pale grains spilling across the floor. Celine has her hand pressed to her beige forehead, a trickle of blood streaking down from beneath her palm.

"Dominic!" I cry out automatically, and feel his hand on my shoulder.

He squints at me in the dimness and touches the side of my head where I smacked it. The tender spot makes me wince, but there's no coolness of blood.

"I'm all right. The kids…"

"I'm on it," he murmurs, and moves deeper into the helicopter's cargo area with a slight sway to his steps that makes me wonder if *he's* completely all right.

"Riva!"

It's Jacob's voice, taut and ragged.

I spin toward the cockpit, the direction where I last saw him. "I'm here. I bumped my head, but not too badly."

Zian staggers to his feet near me. Andreas catches my arm, his fingers curling around my elbow.

Jacob, silhouetted by the faint light through the shattered windshield, takes an urgent step toward me and then glances back at Griffin. His jaw tightens.

He still doesn't trust his brother enough to feel comfortable leaving him to his own devices. I'm not sure I do either.

I push myself toward them instead. "The pilot—"

The words snag in my throat. With just a couple of paces, I've come close enough to see the full consequences of the crash.

The front of the helicopter rammed right into a thick tree trunk—right at the pilot's seat. The metal and glass there have crumpled inward.

You can't tell that the man's nose was bleeding before because now his entire body is bashed beyond recognition.

My stomach flips over.

Griffin is staring at the pilot from just behind him, blood smearing the back of his hand from a thin cut— maybe from the breaking glass. Hugging his backpack and the quivering cat inside it to his chest, he blinks and glances over at the rest of us.

"I didn't mean for— I was hoping we could still land properly."

"It's okay," Andreas says in the warm voice that comes so naturally to him. "The crash could have been a lot worse."

Jacob scowls. "At least this way we know he won't be reaching out to the guardians."

With a twitch of his fingers, he summons the phone he wrenched from the pilot's hand just minutes ago. As his power tugs it through the air to us, his scowl deepens.

Cracks form a spiderweb on the screen. He pushes the wake button just in case, but no light flickers on the fractured surface.

Zian looks around. "Where are we?"

All that's visible through the windows are the shadowy shapes of more trees. I can't make out any sign of civilization, not the slightest gleam of artificial light in the distance.

"No way of telling from the navigation screen," Jacob says. "But we were heading toward a city like Dominic told him to. I could see a big patch of lights in the distance."

Andreas nods. "North… northwest. It was just to the right of where the sun was setting."

A flicker of hope rises in my chest. "How far away?"

Jacob shakes his head. "I don't know. It wasn't *close*."

"We won't be able to tell which direction is northwest until the sun's back up," Zian says.

Griffin's voice comes out calm but more tentative than usual. "I know where it is."

All our gazes jerk to him.

Jacob's eyes narrow. "How?"

His twin gazes back at him steadily. "There are a lot of people there. A lot of emotions. I can only pick up on a general impression, and faintly, but there mustn't be much of anyone else around, because it's mostly coming from that way."

He points at an angle from the windshield, into the jungle outside.

Zian lets out a rough guffaw. "Griffin can be our compass."

From Jacob's expression, he isn't happy about the idea. But we can't be beggars and choosers.

"He did help with the escape," I remind Jake. "And we've got to get moving in some direction as soon as possible. We'd only just disabled the last tracking device when we started to crash. The guardians might be able to find us here if we stay with the chopper all night."

Jacob sighs in frustration, but he doesn't argue. He just shoots his brother another steely look.

I scramble back to the cargo area where Dominic is tending to the younger shadowbloods' injuries. Devon and the spiky-haired kid who hit the pilot were tossed back by the impact, squatting on opposite sides of the bay now.

Devon winces and then relaxes as Dom grips his ankle

with a healing hand. The spiky-haired kid, who can't be more than twelve, watches with darting eyes.

His gaze catches on me, and his shoulders curl in on himself. "I'm sorry. I didn't mean to run right into him. I didn't mean to hop at all. It just *happens* when I'm worried."

I'm not anyone to criticize people for having erratic control over their powers.

I crouch down across from him. "Hopping—is that what you call it when you flash forward like you're not even there for a second?"

He nods. "The guardians said it's teleporting. But they were always mad I couldn't go farther."

Of course they would have been. Skipping a few steps isn't going to make that much difference on a mission.

"We're here now," I tell him. "And we're going to keep going. What's your name?"

He swipes his hand across his eyes like he's rubbing away tears before they fully formed. "George."

When I turn around, Dominic has finished healing Devon, and Ajax has come over to help his boyfriend to his feet. Booker and Nadia are standing close together, his hand at her back, her face tight with worry.

Booker rakes his fingers through his pale hair, his expression too serious now to conjure the surfer dude impression he gave me when we first met. "What now? Can the guardians find us here?"

"I don't know," I admit. "So we're moving out. But…"

My gaze travels over the jumbled assortment of supplies, and I manage a small smile. "At least we shouldn't have to worry about going hungry. Let's quickly dig through all of this and grab whatever's easiest to carry and doesn't need cooking."

A girl whose name I haven't caught points toward the back of the helicopter. "There are some things that look kind of like backpacks that would help for carrying stuff. I think they might be emergency parachutes, but we could tear the parachute part out."

Celine, the scratch on her forehead sealed, lets out a tinkling laugh that doesn't hold much real humor. "If we can even see what we're doing in here."

Nadia perks up, the tension falling away from her face for the first time since we ran to the helicopter. "Finally, it's my time to shine! Literally."

As she grins, her brown skin lights up the way she showed me before.

In the daylight of the clearing, it was hard to tell just how potent her inner light is. Now, the warm glow washes over the entire interior of the storage bay as if the overhead lights have turned on.

"Wow," Booker says with admiration that's obviously genuine. "You're really something, Glowworm."

As we all get to work digging through the boxes and crates, Dominic turns pensive. "Can you adjust how strong the light is? To make sure you don't wear yourself out—and so it'll be harder for anyone to spot us from above?"

"Oh, sure." Nadia pauses, and her glow fades as if she's pushed down a dimmer switch to halfway. "Is that good?"

Andreas shoves open the hatch and takes in the jungle beyond. "I think that'll be safe enough. The tree cover is pretty thick, at least right around here."

In the end, the six of us "Firsts" end up carrying most of the supplies in the limited number of makeshift backpacks. I stuff mine full of crackers, cheese, apples, carrots, and a couple of jugs of juice.

We might be relying on that to stay hydrated, since it doesn't appear that the supplies included water, and we have no way of making sure any streams or ponds we pass are safe to drink from.

Each of the younger shadowbloods gathers a small assortment of their own, tying swaths of parachute fabric around their backs and shoulders however feels most comfortable as makeshift carry-sacks. When we're all loaded up, I glance over our motley group again, holding tightly to the spark of hope that lit when Jacob said he'd seen a city.

"Is everyone ready to go?"

There are nods and murmurs all around. They don't exactly sound enthusiastic, but then, I don't think any of us would take this trek if we had the choice.

We just know it's better than the alternative.

Nadia leads the way with her innate light, Booker sticking close to her side and Zian tramping along at her flank in case we encounter any threats. The rest of us Firsts spread out through the procession, monitoring the kids for signs of faltering.

I end up at the rear of the line, making sure no one falls behind. Andreas eases back next to me as we tramp over the uneven ground, weaving between the trees and scrambling over jutting roots.

"We won't be able to keep this up all night," he murmurs. "None of us has slept since yesterday."

The stress of the escape has worn at my nerves enough that exhaustion is already nibbling at the edges of my awareness. "I know. But we should get as much distance from the crash site as we can."

"Yeah, let's see how they do. I think we can get away with a fairly short rest and then keep going as soon as it's daylight. We can have a longer break the next night, if it takes that long. It'll be better not to let Nadia drain herself too badly—and we'll be harder to find when we won't stand out against the darkness anyway."

I dodge a waxy-leafed bush and rub my arms. A fly buzzes around me and starts to land on my elbow before I swat it away.

The jungle air is humid, nearly as warm at night as it was on the island, but my fears send a chill through the sweat on my skin.

I told these kids we'd get them to someplace better than the facility. I have to make sure that this time I keep my promise.

As we push on through the brush, the minutes blur into hours. Stars glint overhead in the small gaps in the canopy of leaves.

From time to time, Andreas lifts his voice with his storyteller's cadence. Because of course he has stories to go with even this trek.

"One time, I came across a woman who'd done a hike all the way from one end of the States to the other," he says. "All on her own. It took weeks, and most of that time some part of her was aching, and she'd get hungry for food she couldn't have carried on the trail. But when she got back, if anyone asked, she'd tell them the worst part was the loneliness. She said she'd do it over again if she had the right company."

He glances around at us with a weary but honest smile. "We don't have anywhere near that far to go, and we've got each other. I think we've got this."

His assurance helps steady me, so I hope it does the same for the younger shadowbloods as well.

But even my supernaturally strong legs are feeling the burn by the time the ground starts to slant upward in an increasingly steep slope. I notice George and Devon wobbling as they trudge onward.

Have we come far enough that it's safe to stop? How can I possibly know?

The sound of trickling water is what decides the issue. Zian turns his head toward it, no doubt hearing it much more clearly than I can.

"I think there's a waterfall," he says. "Running water is safer than still, right?"

Dominic nods. "Let's take a look at it and see if we want to risk it. Either way, this might be a good time to set up some kind of camp. We'll tackle the hill better after we've gotten some rest."

I don't miss the sighs of relief that carry through our younger charges. Yes, it was definitely time to stop.

We veer toward the sound of the water and halt our march when Nadia's light glints off a current about a foot wide burbling down a sheerer section of the hill. As she heads over with Dominic and Andreas to inspect the water, the rest of us hunker down among the trees.

"Have a snack if you're hungry, and then I guess curl up wherever you can make yourself decently comfortable,"

I tell the kids. At least it's warm and reasonably dry for the moment.

I don't want to think about what we'll do if it starts raining.

Our three water analysts return with uncertain expressions. "It looks pretty clean, but there are flecks of dirt in it," Andreas says. "I took a gulp, and if I'm still okay by tomorrow, we can all have a drink." He nudges Dominic. "Otherwise I'm relying on Dom to cure me."

I don't love him using himself as a test subject, but I guess we don't have a lot of choice. "Juice for tonight, then, anyone who's thirsty."

Celine stretches out a hand. "I could use some of that right now!"

As she drinks, Griffin hunkers down near me, watching her with an intentness I don't understand. I wait for him to make a comment to explain his attention, but he doesn't say anything, even after Celine passes the jug on to Ajax.

After a moment, he reaches into his old backpack and guides out the white cat and a tin of cat food he must have snatched up when he grabbed her. He peels back the lid, and Lua sniffs it tentatively before taking some cautious bites.

I've been drinking regularly along the trek, so my throat isn't too parched, but my skin feels uncomfortably grimy. I push to my feet with a quick glance around at my guys. "I'm going to wash up a little before I try and sleep."

It only takes a minute to walk the last short distance to the waterfall and its winding stream. The hillside there is rockier but still has clumps of soil clinging in pockets.

I can see why the guys hesitated to trust the water washing over those rocks for ingestion. But to splash it on my face shouldn't be a big deal.

I dampen not just my face but my neck as well, then swipe under my armpits for good measure. As I give my hands a final rinse, the brush rustles behind me.

When I glance over my shoulder, I find Griffin emerging onto the rocky bank next to me. Not who I would have expected.

My stomach shifts with a hitch of uneasiness. It feels wrong to be this wary around the one guy I once trusted more than anyone in the world... but completely necessary at the same time.

"Hey," I say in a low voice, adjusting my weight to stand. "The stream's all yours."

Griffin catches my wrist before I can rise more than a few inches, his grip firm but careful. "I didn't come for the water. I wanted to talk to you."

I settle back into my crouch, studying his face in the dimness. As usual, I can't read his intentions in it—but for once he does actually look concerned, if only vaguely. "What about?"

Griffin glances at the ground and then back at me, leaving his fingers curled gently around my wrist. "I'm sorry. For getting you caught, in the facility, before—I need to apologize to everyone for that—but especially for trying to tell you that you should still work with Clancy. For not realizing what he was doing when he had us meet up."

The words are right, but I don't hear any anguish in them.

I frown. "Are you saying that because you really mean it or because you know I'd want you to be sorry?"

"I mean it. I just—" He sucks in a breath, and his mouth tightens. His thumb glides over the underside of my wrist, sending a tingle shooting up my arm.

"I don't feel very much," he says, low and even. "I pick up on what others do, but inside *myself*... I haven't felt anything in years. The guardians decided I was too affected by the emotions I absorbed, it was a liability, and they decided to fix that problem. And for a while, I thought I was better off that way too."

My throat constricts. "Feeling nothing could never be better. What did they do?"

Griffin shakes his head. "It doesn't matter. The point is... I do feel something, when we're touching. I don't know why, but the contact seems to wake up something they didn't totally suppress."

He traces the fragile bones of my wrist again, setting off a more heated tingle. A flush courses over my skin.

"You pulled away from me, before," I point out, remembering our conversation in the training room.

Griffin's fingers go still. "I—I wasn't sure if it was a good thing. It's been a long time. I've gotten used to having my head clear."

He pauses. "But I don't know if it ever really was clear. I was missing something all along. I'm starting to think I can't actually make the right decisions if I don't have any emotional reactions to guide me along with pure information."

I swallow thickly. "I think everyone needs both."

"I have to find a good balance. I can't let—I still need

to be careful." He knits his brow. Then he strokes his hand right up my arm from wrist to elbow, provoking a full-out flare of heat.

When Griffin meets my eyes again, I catch a flicker of longing there. A clearer emotion than anything I've seen in him since we reunited.

"I'm not going to ask for anything from you," he says. "You're upset with me and confused, and that makes sense. But every time we touch, I feel a little closer to where I need to be. So... if *you* want to—to hold my hand, or sit close to me, or anything like that, I hope you will."

Sudden tears prick at the back of my eyes. I *am* upset and confused, but I can also hear the boy I loved so much in his halting admission.

Griffin has been just as much a victim of the guardians' schemes as the rest of us. Maybe more so, if they somehow managed to sear every feeling out of the guy who was once the most compassionate person I've ever encountered.

Part of me balks, but not enough to override the urge to lean toward him right now—to wrap my arms around his slender but toned shoulders and hug him hard.

Griffin lets out a shaky breath and hugs me back, his bare forearm resting against my neck, his hand skimming the band of skin where my tee has ridden up at my waist. Keeping that bodily contact in place.

"I'm sorry," he whispers again, and this time I feel it as well as hear it.

I rest my head against his, absorbing the rhythm of his breath and the warmth of his body. "The people who really should be sorry never will be. So we just have to make sure they can't hurt any of us ever again."

"Yeah." His breath tickles against my ear. His arms squeeze me a little tighter. "Ever since the other day with the throwing knives… I've been dreaming about the night we broke out. The moment when you kissed me."

I wince inwardly. "When they shot you. That must be an awful memory."

"No. It's not. I wish everything after had gone differently, but the pain I went through is nothing compared to the joy before. Right then—that's the best I've ever felt in my life. And for years, I never even thought about it. They took it away from me."

My threatening tears rush back with a vengeance. I'm too choked up to speak.

My hand rises of its own accord to Griffin's jaw. Nothing could feel more right than tilting my head so I can brush my lips against his.

The kiss stays butterfly-soft. Griffin barely seems to breathe, but a tremor runs through his body as he kisses me back so tenderly I want to melt right into his arms.

But I don't know if I trust him quite that completely just yet.

And before I can decide either way, he eases back and turns his head. I follow his gaze.

Jacob is standing between the trees just a few steps from the waterfall. Watching us with eyes so stormy I can make out the turmoil in them despite the darkness.

Griffin releases me from his embrace as we get up. He offers his brother a lopsided smile.

"I'm not trying to get between you—any of you—and

Riva. If she had to choose right now, she wouldn't pick me anyway."

He's probably right about that, but the comments Jake's made in the past—about knowing he had to stand back so his brother could be happy with me, about believing that I'd rather he'd died instead of Griffin—form a lump in my gut.

"Jake," I start, not sure exactly what I'm going to say. We found a peace with each other in the past few weeks, but it suddenly feels so tenuous.

Jacob breaks in before I can get any farther. "It's fine. I only came to make sure you're okay. I'm going to take one of the first watches. Everyone who's going to sleep should stick together."

I nod. "We'll head right back."

Griffin strides ahead of me through the trees on our way back to the campsite, not touching me at all, but Jacob's gaze trails after us with a prickling sensation down my spine.

TWENTY-ONE

Jacob

I thought the island we were stuck on was fucking hot, but somehow the jungle we've crashed into is even worse.

The interlacing branches overhead, heavy with leaves, block out most of the direct sunlight, but humidity saturates the air underneath. Trudging along feels more like wading than walking.

Bugs buzz past, some of them stopping to nip at us. I guess the island breezes kept the worst of them away back by the facility.

Our group skirts a patch of huge ferns, the edges of the fronds tickling over my arm. I swipe at the sweat collecting on the back of my neck and scan our surroundings.

I used to like the occasional opportunities the guardians gave us to explore the forest beyond the facility where we grew up. Gazing up at the leaves and breathing in the wild scents loosened something inside me, like a trace of freedom.

I'm not sure I'm ever going to feel the same way about the jungle. Between our training on the island and this trek, I can't help associating the dense vegetation and heavy warmth with restrictions and perils rather than peace.

We've been walking since sun-up, other than a short snack break partway through the morning and a slightly longer break for lunch a couple of hours ago. The younger kids appear to be drooping with the sticky heat, but the older teens are carrying themselves pretty well, I have to admit.

Well, they've been through the same brutal training as the rest of us. At seventeen, they're practically adults, not kids at all.

We were around that age the first time we made a run for it.

The thought brings my gaze veering back to my friends.

Andreas is loping along as quickly as the dense underbrush allows, no sign of sickness from the jungle water he drank last night. We filled up two emptied juice jugs at the waterfall before we moved on from our campsite.

He's got a cord he picked up somewhere wrapped around one hand. On the easier stretches of terrain, he's fallen into a rhythm of twisting it into knots and loosening them again, like he used to do sometimes back at the old facility. Maybe it helps him focus.

Zian pushes ahead at the front of the group, snapping

branches and crumpling shrubs to allow easier passage for all of us behind. And probably terrifying any wildlife that might notice us into giving us a wide berth.

Well, other than the damned bugs.

Dominic has stuck to the middle of the group, his head swiveling periodically as he conducts a similar scan to mine. Any time one of the younger shadowbloods so much as stubs their toe, he's there, siphoning life out of a twig or a wildflower to set them right again.

His short ponytail clings damply to his neck. I hope he's keeping *his* health in mind just as much as everyone else's.

Riva prefers to stick to the rear of the group where she can monitor the whole bunch more easily, so I've hung back too. It means I'm close by if the brush happens to trip her up, although she's scrambling through it perfectly fine so far even with her tiny frame.

And it means I can keep an eye on my brother wherever he happens to drift through the group.

Griffin does drift quite a bit. One hour he'll be at the left of the pack, the next at the right. Sometimes he presses forward until he's just behind Zian and other times he slows until he falls into stride with Riva.

When that's happened, she's reached out and taken his hand. Nothing spoken, not much more than a brief glance exchanged, but something in his expression softens just a tad when her fingers curl around his.

It makes him look almost like he really is my brother again.

Can I trust that impression? Is he actually coming

around, snapping out of the demented stupor the guardians inflicted on him?

Or is he simply making the best moves he can to win us over so that he can then betray us when he has an ideal opportunity?

I can't read the answers in his face or his behavior. And the knowledge that he can sense my uneasiness without even trying gnaws at me.

We always thought that Griffin was the weakest out of us, at least when it came to combat skills. But knowing how your enemies are feeling, being able to twist those emotions to your will if you want to…

I'd rather deal with another guy like me, with telekinetic talents and poison spikes, than face off with my brother.

At least I haven't seen any sign that he's manipulating us. Riva might have kissed him last night, whatever he said to her that encouraged the gesture of affection, and she's offering moments of companionship now, but her gaze stays wary when she looks at him.

She isn't convinced he's really come back to us either. And if he was going to mess with anyone's emotions to his benefit, presumably it'd be mine or hers.

The kids in front of us clamber over a fallen tree that rises to my thighs, and I extend my hand automatically to heft Riva with me over it. She accepts the help with a soft smile that rearranges my insides and gives my hand a squeeze before she lets go on the other side.

Even when we're not touching, it feels like we are through the mark now burned into my flesh at the top of my collarbone. I can sense exactly where she is in an instant.

I'll never really lose her again.

But somehow I can't convince myself that even that closeness is enough. Can't shake the vague impression that there must be something more I should offer that I haven't worked out yet.

It turns out that not every wild creature around has been warded off by Zian's might. We're just ducking around the low branches of a vine-draped tree when one of those "vines" lifts its head with a threatening hiss.

The huge snake's head swings toward Riva. With a jolt of panic, I hurl out a surge of power that smacks it backward but doesn't dislodge it from its perch.

Before I can launch a more aggressive defense, Riva sets her hand on my shoulder and parts her lips. The sound that seeps from them echoes the snake's hiss with a hint of one of her deadly shrieks.

A flinch ripples through the snake's body. It recoils and slithers away higher into the tree.

Riva shoots me another smile. "I appreciate the protection, but I wanted to see if that would work. I'd rather not kill the animals if we don't have to."

She looks so pleased with herself—with the control she's gaining over her powers, with the kindness she was able to offer that beast I'd have smashed to pieces—that my heart just about bursts.

I rein in the urge to grab her and pour all my adoration into a kiss of my own. We've both got to stay alert.

But the longing lingers as we tramp onward.

The jumpy kid with the spiky white hair does one of his teleporting hops and nearly trips onto his face. Riva dashes forward in an instant and catches him before he hits the ground.

She walks on next to him, getting into a murmured conversation. I'm torn between wanting to catch up so I'm close at hand if *she* needs help again—not that she ever needs that much—and knowing she'd rather at least one of us was at the back of the pack to keep track of all the kids.

Then Griffin drifts backward again, falling into step beside me. The weird pang that hits me every time my twin is nearby radiates through my chest.

It feels wrong to still be grieving him when he's right *here*. But he's not exactly. Not one piece of my body has come to grips with that fact.

"You don't miss the comforts of the facility?" I hear myself saying before I've considered the question. It's not a bad one, though. If I could assume he'd answer honestly.

Griffin shakes his head without hesitation. "It wasn't really that comfortable when you got down to it, was it? I just… I was looking at things too narrowly."

I guess that's one way of saying he royally screwed us over.

As if he's read that thought as well as my emotions, he glances over at me. "I am sorry, you know. I made mistakes—I misjudged the situation. I hope… I hope that none of us will have to hurt people the way you had to before, but I can see why you didn't feel you had much choice."

I gaze back at him, letting my gaze harden. "Anyone

we hurt, it was to make sure they couldn't kill us. Or turn us back into slaves."

"I know. I know you did the best you could."

He pauses, a crease forming in his forehead as if he isn't sure of what he's going to say next. He exhales softly.

His voice comes out quieter. "I'm sorry I wasn't there, too. It always seemed... wrong, being apart from the rest of you. Especially *you*. I tried to tell the guardians, to convince them. We supported each other in a way they didn't seem to understand. And I didn't know what you were thinking with me being gone, how that would affect you, but it bothered me, so it couldn't be good."

Another pause. His head bows. "I'm not sure it would really have made things much better if they had let me come back the way I am now, though."

"It would have been better," I burst out. "I wouldn't have been thinking you were *murdered* because of a plan I helped come up with. They couldn't have messed with us making us believe that was mostly Riva's fault."

I aim a scowl at my twin. "You realize that's the main reason they kept us apart, right? It was an easy way to lie to us, to fuck us up even more than they already had."

"I didn't know what they'd told you," Griffin says. "If I had, I'd like to think I'd have fought harder to get back to you. Maybe I wouldn't have trusted Clancy at all, even though he acted like he wanted nothing to do with the group who'd been handling me since the escape."

I can't conceive of what our lives would have been like if Griffin had turned up, in his currently vacant state or not, before Riva crashed back into our lives. If we'd known from the start that the guardians had lied to us about his fate—and therefore probably hers too.

It kills me even trying to picture it in comparison to what actually went down.

"All we can do is go forward from here." Griffin glances over at me tentatively. "You're going to be angry at me for a long time, just like the others, and I don't resent that. But I'm doing *my* best to figure out how to head in a better direction. And if you feel like you could lean on me for anything, in any way… I want to be there like I wasn't all those years. As well as I can."

I can't tell how earnest he is when his tone holds only the faintest trace of emotion, but the words make my throat tighten anyway.

Lean on him? I always saw myself as the one he leaned on. When the training pushed us hard, when the guardians wouldn't let up.

But I know that's not really accurate. Something about his knowing but compassionate gaze, the ease to his words, could settle the rest of us down no matter what upset us, even when we were little. He kept us centered.

Where has that guy gone?

Before I have to decide how to respond, my brother's gaze slides forward, to where Riva is just giving the teleporting kid a reassuring pat on the back.

"She loves you so much, you know," he says. "Every time she looks at you, it's there, shining like an entire full moon, not just a moonbeam. She wants you to be happy. Whatever you're worried about when it comes to her, I don't think you have to be anymore."

He picks up his pace, leaving me grappling with a tangle of my own emotions.

It isn't as if Riva hasn't told me how she feels. I'm not sure I've totally believed it, though.

After everything I put her through…

I might not completely believe in Griffin, but hearing him say it so confidently smooths out a few rough edges inside me that I hadn't even noticed scraping at my heart.

So maybe he hasn't totally lost his centering gift after all.

When Riva returns to her position at the back, she gives me a curious look. "Are you and Griffin okay?"

I rub my mouth as I debate my answer. "I don't know. But it's possible we could get there."

Our afternoon break stretches a little longer than the morning one. Some of the younger shadowbloods massage their calves and stretch their arms in attempts to relieve the strain.

New hope comes in the form of a strip of thinner underbrush we stumble on maybe an hour after our stop.

Zian steps out into the clearer stretch cautiously, his shoulders flexing as he glances up and down it. The rest of us follow.

I toe the grass-choked ground and make out faint ridges in the packed soil. Bits of gravel rasp against the sole of my sneaker.

"It was a road," Dominic says, coming to the same conclusion I have a little faster. "Just a small one, like a private lane or something, and obviously not used in a while."

Andreas peers along it into the distance. "That's got to

mean there are people around *somewhere* not too far away."

He turns to Griffin, whose eyes go even more vague as he must tap into his empathic sense. My twin's mouth slants crookedly.

"Other than our group, I'm not picking up on anyone really close. I'm still aware of the big population northwest of here. But that doesn't mean there isn't anyone closer. At longer distances, I can only pick up on a whole lot of emotion condensed in the same place, unless it's someone I already know."

Riva cocks her head, her eyes glinting with sudden inspiration. "Can you tell where Clancy is?"

Griffin takes another moment to focus inwardly. "Nowhere near us. Someplace south. I'd need a map to pinpoint him."

"Nowhere near sounds good enough to me." I motion toward the section of overgrown road that heads in approximately the same direction we were already headed. "We might as well walk along this route while it's taking us where we need to go, right? We'll move faster with fewer obstacles."

"I'll watch and listen for any sign that we're getting close to the locals," Zian says, his face settling into a mask of concentration.

I'm not surprised that none of the younger shadowbloods argue. Some of them even get more of a spring in their step as we set off along the easier terrain.

I start to doubt my suggestion when the road takes on an upward slope. But unless we wanted to spend an extra day or two walking all the way around the looming hill ahead of us, I guess we'd be stuck scaling it either way.

The sun has sunk below the level of the canopy when Zee lets out a low shout to alert us and stops in his tracks.

"There's a building up there," he says, squinting through the trees. "I can see part of a roof."

We all gather around him. A couple of the kids shift nervously on their feet.

"Any sign of people?" Riva asks.

Zian shakes his head. "I can't make out a whole lot from here, though."

Griffin gazes off in the direction Zee indicated. "I think I'd be able to sense if anyone was over there. I'm not picking up any emotional impressions strong enough to be coming from a building that close."

Andreas steps to the front of our pack. "I'll take a quick look around incognito."

He tips his head jauntily and vanishes from view in a blink.

The lanky, blond-haired guy near me—Booker, I think his name is—sucks in a breath of surprise. A startled murmur passes through the younger shadowbloods.

I forgot that most of them aren't familiar with our powers. I don't think I'll be showing off my spines anytime soon.

Zian moves a little farther ahead to keep scanning the area while we wait. Riva pulls a jug of water out of her pack and passes it around, checking on the kids with Dominic flanking her, ready to treat any injury.

Seeing her dote on them sends another quiver through

my chest, not as heated as the impact of her smiles but with a soft glow of warmth I'm not used to.

She's been so worried about her powers, about being someone destructive. A monster. Does she even realize how easily she's taken on this nurturing role?

She's a badass, brilliant superhero of a woman, but I bet she'd be a fantastic mother someday too, if that's something she wants.

Whether I'd be much of a dad...

That idea leaves me unsteady enough that I yank my mind back to the present.

Andreas reappears in the lengthening shadows with a grin. "It looks like it was some kind of eco hotel. Solar panels on the roof, a cistern that's set up for catching rainwater. It's been abandoned for a while, and the jungle's crept in on it, but there's still some power going and the plumbing works. And it's got actual beds."

My instinct is to balk at the idea of staying anywhere it looks like people would want to stay, but the relief that crosses several of the kids' faces keeps my mouth shut.

Dominic is already thinking cautiously for all of us anyway. "How noticeable do you think it'd be from above?" he asks.

Andreas motions to us. "You can all come take a look, but there's tree cover over a lot of the roof now. The building was only a couple of stories tall anyway. I don't think we'd want to have the lights on once it really gets dark, but otherwise I doubt it'd stand out."

We tramp on up the road for a few more minutes before the hotel comes clearly into view.

The trees have grown right up against the tan walls, in

some places jutting through windows or broken sections of thatched roof. They block what was once probably a pretty view over the hillside. But they also camouflage the place to a degree that satisfies the worst of my worries.

We slip inside onto the dirt-strewn hardwood floor of what was once the lobby. The boards sigh under our feet.

A vine has crept over the reception desk and around a couple of sagging armchairs. A little monkey chitters at us and darts out through a broken window.

The air flow through the space has kept it from getting musty, though. The faint perfume of jungle flowers laces the breeze that washes through the hallways.

Andreas leads us to the kitchen, which is deep enough inside the building that it's remained mostly unaffected by the jungle's imposition. At his twist of a fixture, clear water burbles from a tap.

"The stoves have power," he says, pointing to a couple of rows of burners. "And there's a little food left in the pantry that might be edible—rice, dried beans, and lentils that I don't think would really go bad."

The tall girl who lit our way through the night lets out a low chuckle. "I could go for a real dinner."

Riva takes in the space with a contemplative air and gives a short nod. "I think we should spend the night here. Get some real rest before we keep going with the journey. But we'll need people keeping watch at all times just in case."

Zian moves closer to her, his expression turning abruptly fierce. "The guardians aren't getting their hands on us again."

Riva beams at him, so much affection shining in her

eyes that my chest clenches up—even more so at the hesitant but bright smile Zee offers in return. At the momentary lifting of his hand as if he's thinking of offering her a brief touch, only to jerk his arm back to his side at the last second.

I don't need Griffin's talent to know how much he wants her... or how hard it is for him to grapple with that longing. My stomach twists in pained sympathy, and I find myself remembering Griffin's comments to me in the jungle.

He tried to make it easier for me to embrace everything Riva's been willing to offer me. To help the two of us understand each other.

If she wants to see me happy, I want the same for her at least as much. For all of my friends, including Zian, who has so much trouble reaching for that happiness himself.

But just telling him how much Riva cares about him wouldn't be enough. I'm pretty sure he already knows. That isn't the problem.

I keep part of my attention on Zian as I move to help the others sort through the kitchen equipment, the gears in my head spinning.

Maybe I don't have to only be the guy who races into a fight and bashes any possible threat. It's not like those impulses have been helping my friends or the woman I love a whole lot recently anyway.

Maybe I could be as generous as it seemed Griffin meant to be—fill the hole where Zian has faltered.

I just need to figure out how. For both him and her.

TWENTY-TWO

Riva

Our mishmash of rice, lentils, and the few spices we scrounged up isn't fit for a five-star restaurant, but after twenty-four hours of crackers, hard cheese, and bruised fruit, I have to hold myself back from licking the plate when I'm done.

We've hunkered down in the vast kitchen, one of the cleanest rooms in the abandoned hotel. The terrace on the other side of the hall looks like it served as the main dining area, but it's been consumed by jungle: tree branches jutting through the broken railings and vines strangling the chair-and-table sets.

The daylight has almost completely faded. As I glance around at my fellow shadowbloods, I catch a couple yawning.

I raise my voice to carry to the entire group. "We should get some rest while it's dark. It wouldn't be safe to turn on any lights at night anyway. And as soon as the sun comes up, we'll want to get moving again."

Mumbles of agreement reach me. Dominic stands up with the more confident air that's starting to come naturally to him.

"There are lots of bedrooms farther down the halls," he says to the group. "Pick one that's reasonably neat, and stay at least in pairs so you have someone to turn to if there's a problem. I think we should avoid the second floor since the roof obviously isn't in great repair."

"And give yourselves a good wash if you want," I add. "Running the water shouldn't give us away, and we don't know when we'll have another chance."

After another day of trekking, the dirt and dried sweat on my own skin itches at me.

A few of the younger kids drift out of the room, Ajax and Devon hand in hand. Celine gets to her feet with a swish of her ponytail and manages a smile that only looks a little tired.

"You Firsts should get a break. You've been running yourselves ragged looking after the rest of us—you organized the whole plan to get us out. We can take the first watch."

She motions to herself, Booker, and Nadia—the oldest of the kids who escaped with us. Nadia nods without hesitation, but my stomach dips uneasily.

"I think at least one of us—" I start.

Griffin interrupts so smoothly it barely feels rude, looking up from where he's stroking Lua's fur. "I can watch over the younger shadowbloods for the first shift. I don't think I'm ready to sleep yet anyway."

I hesitate again, appreciating the offer but not sure it's quite what I needed. If Griffin has actually been lying about his intentions, this would be a perfect opportunity to work against us.

My instincts tell me he's been honest. But what if they're wrong?

I thought we could trust Rollick to keep the other kids safe, and look how that turned out.

Andreas steps close to me and lowers his head by my ear. "I've had Ajax monitoring Griffin's thoughts as well as he can. He told me he's only picked up things that confirm his story. Ideas about how to help, worries about how his past actions might have hurt us."

I exhale slowly, releasing a little of the tension that's gripped me since we first got the opportunity to flee the island. I don't think Griffin is skilled enough to conceal every suspicious thought, if he'd even realize that Ajax would be searching his mind.

I can believe that my instincts were right this time with that outside confirmation.

"Okay." I offer Griffin a slightly guilty smile because of my initial uncertainty and aim a brighter one at Celine. "Thank you. A couple of us will take over in a few hours. You should spread out so you can keep an eye out all around the hotel."

Booker gives me a playful salute. "We're on it, Captain. Don't worry—we've been training our whole lives for this."

The wryness of his tone makes Andreas's lips twitch. "Hopefully we'll find something better to do with our lives once we're out of the jungle."

Celine cocks her head, her tone still light. "Are you thinking we'll go to the monsters to see if they'll help us like you did before?"

I hesitate, my regrets about my past decisions still stark in my mind. "I—I don't know yet. We can't turn to *anyone* without being really careful about it."

She nods and casts her gaze away. I hope my uncertainty won't add to whatever worries she must already be grappling with.

Most of the kids have already shuffled out of the kitchen. The five of us Firsts meander down the hall after them.

I'm not totally sure what we're searching for. We pass the first several rooms that've already been claimed by the younger shadowbloods and then start peeking through doorways at random.

I skip past a bedroom with a large water stain in the ceiling and another where some jungle creature appears to have crashed through the window and made a nest out of the bed. Then Zian lets out an awed sound from farther down the hall.

The rest of us hustle over to join him.

He's stepped inside a massive suite that must have been reserved for honeymooners and high-profile guests. In the dim moonlight that seeps past the vast windows, the four-poster bed in the center of the far wall is bigger than any I've ever seen, the duvet barely wrinkled.

One window is cracked, a vine winding its way partway to the floor, but only a thin smattering of dirt and dust has coated the floor. The mirror mounted on the ornate vanity still gleams.

But Zian's attention has been captured by the tub.

A huge jacuzzi bathtub stands across from the bed, half embedded in the wooden floor. Its white walls are dappled with dirt, but Zee gazes at it like it's the most glorious thing he's ever seen.

I can't stop a fond grin from crossing my lips. He's always been drawn to the water on the rare chances we had to appreciate it.

The image of him floating in the jungle pond near the island facility drifts up from my memory. He looked so peaceful, so content, just for those few minutes.

I walk over and prod the controls on the side of the tub. "I bet we could rinse it out and then fill it up. You can have first dibs, Zee."

At a twist of a knob, water gushes from several of the jets. It carries the dirt in swirls down the drain. With a few swipes of my hand over the smooth surface, I bring back a faint gleam of white.

When I look up, Zian is watching me, not the water. Watching me with an expression that brings back other memories from that night by the pond.

Desire glimmers in his eyes, and uncertainty twists his mouth. The signs of his inner turmoil bring a lump to my throat.

"We'll give you your privacy, of course," I say, and lean down to push in the stopper so the tub will fill. "There are lots of other rooms where we—"

Jacob clears his throat, stopping me in mid-sentence. "I have a better idea."

We all glance over at him, and he gives the rest of us an unusually soft smile. "The tub's big enough for us all to share, don't you think? What have we got to hide at this point?"

He holds my gaze for a moment with a warily hopeful air and then shifts his attention to Zian with a flicker of concern. Jake must know as well as I do that Zee has the most reason to balk at the idea.

Zian shifts his weight, peering at the water and then the group of us. His eyes linger on me, the mix of longing and uneasiness only starker now.

I pause. "We wouldn't have to get totally undressed. I'll stay at the opposite end of the tub."

Andreas taps his knuckles against Zee's arm. "We'll all be in there, just hanging out. No pressure, no expectations."

Zian wavers for a few seconds longer and then squares his shoulders. "Yeah. Why shouldn't we?"

A gentle smile curves Dominic's lips too. "Why don't you get in first so you can enjoy a good float before the rest of us join in? We should scrounge up some towels anyway."

We leave Zian by the jacuzzi to prowl through the rest of the room. Dominic checks the actual bathroom and emerges with a stack of fluffy beige towels that he shakes a little dust off of.

Andreas and I give the bed the same treatment, stripping off the duvet and fluffing it out. The sheets underneath look almost pristine.

I'm tempted to sprawl on them right now, except *I'd* get them all dirty.

Jacob returns from his own search through the bathroom with a crow of victory. "Biodegradable bath oils.

Now we're living in real luxury."

He carries the glossy green bottles over to the tub, where Zian has stripped down to his boxers and gotten in. His brawny body just barely fits without bumping against the sides, drifting on the rising water.

It's nearly reached the overflow drain now. Zee reaches to tweak one of the controls, and a hint of steam puffs into the air from the jets.

He dunks his head to slick his short hair back and grins at Jake, looking much more relaxed now that he's actually in the water. "Well, pour that stuff in then. We should have the full experience."

As Jacob drizzles the oil in the tub, a thin froth of bubbles forms on the surface of the water. Andreas shucks off his facility-issue tee and athletic pants and slides into the jacuzzi kitty-corner from Zian.

I guess we're all getting in now. All four of these guys have seen me at least partly undressed, and the room is dark enough that I'll be mostly cloaked in shadows anyway, but all at once my skin tightens with self-consciousness.

They don't pressure me either, though. Dominic tugs off his shirt with a little extra effort to work around his tentacles, not even glancing my way. Jake sheds his pants like it's no big deal at all.

With the attention off me, I relax enough to peel off my own tee and pants, leaving my necklace on like usual. The air is so warm that I'm not at all chilled even in my sports bra and panties.

They're like a bikini. Like I'm just going for a dip in a pool.

No big deal at all.

As I promised Zian, I slip into the water at the far end from where he's settled. We form a ring around the edges of the tub, my calf brushing Andreas's next to me, one of Dominic's tentacles coiling around my elbow beneath the bubbles.

Zee's set the temperature nice and warm. I let out a sigh and sink a little deeper until the bubbles tickle my chin.

"Maybe a soak will make tomorrow's hike a little easier," Jacob says, stretching one arm and then the other in front of him.

Zian leans back against the smooth wall. "Are there any other roads around this place that aren't so overgrown? If they left any vehicles behind…"

Drey shakes his head. "I did a circuit of the whole hotel when I was first checking it out. There is another road, a little wider than the one we came along but just as choked. And I didn't see any cars around anyway."

Dominic hums to himself. "We could head that way tomorrow and see where it takes us."

"It's a totally different direction from where we were heading before," Andreas says. "I don't think it'll take us to the city."

I tip my head back, letting the water seep through my braid and up my scalp while I consider the possibilities. "Griffin hasn't sensed any large populations any closer than the city we knew about. And a little town might not have the resources we'd need to make a real escape."

However exactly that's going to work once we see what we have to work with.

Drey gives my braid a teasing tug. "You've led us well so far, Tink. I trust your judgment."

The brush of his fingertips against my neck sets off a heat much more potent than the water's steam. As my face flushes, he traces his fingers across my cheek.

All at once, pheromones of desire lace the air from all around me. A shiver of need travels through my body, the shadows in my blood quaking with it.

I've been forced apart from my guys, from the most concrete manifestation of our connection, for too long. And I can tell they feel it too.

But one of them isn't ready to act on that longing.

Zian must sense the shift in the air, because he straightens up with a slosh of the water. Even in the dimness, I can tell his peachy-brown skin has taken on a ruddier cast that I don't think is just because of the bath.

"I can give *you* guys some privacy," he says in a rough voice, turning to heft himself out.

Jacob stops him with a hand on his arm. His blue eyes blaze with sudden intensity.

"What if you could be a part of it too? Without risking any of the things you're scared of?"

Zian's gaze jerks to him, his eyes widening. "What are you talking about?"

Jake pauses as if he's still figuring that out himself. He glances at me with a look so scorching my nerves tingle.

Then he turns back to Zee. "Use us. We can be your hands, your mouth. Tell us what you'd want to do to her, and we'll do it for you. Like you're acting through us. That would work without setting anything off in you, wouldn't it?"

A fresh wave of heat courses through me at the idea.

Zian draws in a breath, his pupils dilating with unfulfilled hunger. "That would— I mean—"

His gaze sears into mine. "Would you even be okay with that?"

Every nerve in my body is trembling with anticipation. I've collided with Dominic and Andreas at the same time before, but only the once. And never more than the two of them.

The possibilities flooding my head light me up from the inside out.

"Yes. If you'd like it too."

Zian's next inhalation comes shakily. The other guys remain silent, Andreas's hand gone still by my cheek, all of us giving Zee the space he needs to come to his decision.

He wets his lips, the smolder in his dark eyes deepening. Then he nods to Drey.

"Kiss her. Kiss her until she's squirming for more."

A sly grin curves Andreas's mouth, and he tips my chin up so my lips can meet his.

It doesn't take much for him to summon a needy whimper out of me. His mouth claims mine with weeks of bottled passion neither of us has had the chance to really let out.

I clutch at his coiled hair and kiss him back hard. My lips part instantly at the flick of his tongue, welcoming him in.

Through the eager thundering of my pulse, Zian's voice reaches my ears, gone ragged. "Dominic, you know how to make her squirm too, don't you? Touch her— everywhere she likes it."

Dominic chuckles softly and presses a kiss to the peak of my shoulder. Both his tentacles glide around me, one across my back and the other over my belly, the suckers stroking my skin in a multitude of puckered kisses.

His hand glides over my chest at the same time. When he swipes one thumb over the tip of my breast, my breath stutters into Drey's mouth.

As I arch into Dom's touch, Andreas makes an urgent sound low in his throat and deepens our kiss. Our tongues tangle together, bliss racing through me from the melding of our mouths all the way down my body over the terrain Dominic is caressing.

Dom massages my breast with swivels of his thumb over the peak until my nipple is straining stiff against the fabric of my bra. A growl escapes me with the growing ache between my thighs.

I pull my mouth from Andreas's and catch Zian's gaze for just an instant. Hoping he can feel through the heated glance how happy I'd be if he really were joining in too.

Then I can't help seeking out Dominic's lips, pulling him tighter against me.

Jacob hasn't moved toward me yet, but his words travel over the water in a low purr that sets the shadows in my veins shivering twice as giddily. "Look at how much she's enjoying it, Zee. You've got three mouths to work with. Six hands. A couple of tentacles as a bonus."

He stops, and his voice dips even farther. "Why don't we get her out of the water so you can see just how well she's responding?"

"Yeah," Zian says roughly. "Bring—bring her to the bed."

I don't put up an ounce of protest when Dominic and Andreas lift me between them. They set me on the edge of the tub, clamber out themselves, and then Jake is there behind me, scooping me up in his arms.

"My turn," he says, blue fire dancing in his eyes.

I cup his jaw, remembering the uneasiness I saw in him when he caught me kissing Griffin and all the ways he's still been trying to make up to me what I've already forgiven.

"I need you just as much," I say quietly.

His arms tighten around me. He strides toward the bed, his head bowing to catch my mouth with his at the same time.

I could burn up in the feral demand of Jacob's kiss. The electric shock of his hunger races all the way to the tips of my fingers and toes.

He lowers me onto the sheets we cleared and drags his lips away, staying by my shoulder. The dampness of my body seeps into the silky fabric.

Dominic and Andreas follow us, Dominic sitting at my other side and Andreas sinking down next to my knee. In the faint moonlight drifting through the windows, their eyes shine with intensity.

The water warbles as Zian heaves himself out too. He walks right past the stack of towels to stand by the foot of the bed, heedless of the rivulets trickling over his sculpted brawn.

I want to lick the droplets right off his burnished flesh. I rein in the urge but lift my gaze to his face.

"What would you do with me now?"

His hands flex at his sides as if he's imagining his

fingers trailing over me for real. He watches Dominic trace the band of my bra.

"Take it off of her, Dom," he says hoarsely. "I want to really see her. You and Jake—touch her, kiss her there."

I push upward a little so Dominic and Jacob can pull the sports bra up over my head together. I've barely leaned back into the sheets before Jake has lowered his head to suck my nipple into his mouth.

As I gasp, Dom takes a more gradual approach. He rolls the other peak between his thumb and forefinger and then slides one tentacle across it.

Each sucker that grazes my pebbled nipple gives it a firm squeeze. In a matter of seconds, I'm moaning at the flashes of delight.

Having Zian's gaze on me feels like another caress in itself. Will it help him, seeing that he can call the shots and direct my pleasure without any disaster crashing down on us?

I hope he's enjoying the moment at least half as much as I am.

My thighs have started rubbing together of their own accord in an instinctive attempt to relieve the ache between them. Andreas strokes his fingers up and down my leg.

"I think she needs more, Zee."

A sound like a strangled groan escapes Zian. "Take the rest of her clothes off. And then—get her off, whatever will feel best for her—hands, mouth…"

As he trails off with another strained noise, Drey yanks my panties down. He teases his fingers over my clit and my drenched folds beneath.

My head pushes back into the pillow as a soft cry of longing breaks from my lips. The familiar burn of desire courses all through my body, my nerves and my shadows forming a chorus clamoring for *More, more, more.*

Andreas massages my pussy until I'm rocking with his strokes, one hand twined in Jacob's hair and the other clutching Dominic's arm. When Drey delves two fingers right into my slit, a blissful shudder runs up my spine.

He plunges them in and out of my slickness a few times before holding the digits, gleaming with my arousal, back toward Zian in his taut pose. His own voice has gone ragged. "You can taste her."

Zian freezes, but only for an instant. He hurtles the last couple of steps to the foot of the bed and bends in to accept Drey's offering.

The sight of his tongue swiping over Andreas's fingers, lapping me off the other guy, has my breath hitching to the point of panting. Zian gazes down at me with so much conflicted emotion in his expression my nerves crackle with it.

"Keep tasting her," he says. "Right at the source. Until she comes."

Andreas doesn't miss a beat following that directive. He leans down and melds his mouth to my sex.

Oh, fuck. The rush of sensation floods me alongside the pleasure Jacob and Dominic are already summoning from my body.

Dom chooses the same moment to latch his mouth around my breast. I'm being devoured from three angles, lips and tongues and careful scrapes of teeth playing a symphony of bliss all across my body.

Andreas laps his tongue right inside me, and my hips buck up to meet him. As he works over every sensitive place I need it most, my gasp blends into a whimper and then into a louder moan.

Jacob raises his head and caresses my cheek. "Better not to get too noisy, Wildcat. Wouldn't want the kids to realize what we're getting up to. Clamp down when you need to."

He slides his fingers past my lips, between my teeth, muffling my next cry.

I don't mean to take him up on his suggestion. But he pinches my nipple with increasing friction, and Dominic's tentacles strum even more pleasure from my skin while he worships my other breast.

And then Drey is sucking so hard on my clit it's like he's dragged a tidal wave of ecstasy smashing through a dam I didn't know I'd built inside me.

My throat vibrates with a muffled moan, and my jaw clenches on Jacob's hand. The tang of blood that laces my tongue somehow heightens the rush of my release.

I jerk against Andreas's mouth and then sag with the gentler swell of the afterglow. Jacob withdraws his hand without hiding the streak of scarlet from the imprints of my teeth.

My gut lurches with guilt. "Dom, you need to heal—"

"It's fine," Jacob interrupts, in a tone so thick with satisfaction I can't doubt his claim. He grins down at me, as ferally devoted as the night when he poured the severed hands of my enemies at the foot of my bed. "I hope it leaves a scar—another way you've marked me."

Zian exhales with a groan. One of his hands is braced

against the bedpost now, the other balled against the bulge in the front of his boxers.

"She needs someone inside her," he rasps. "Properly. Until she comes all over again."

I have no idea how the guys decide, and maybe they don't know either. Like one being, they shift around me, with Dominic settling between my splayed legs.

He looks up at me as if in question, as if he doesn't realize my heart swells with affection at the matching desire in his gaze. I reach up to tangle my fingers in the auburn strands that've come loose from his damp ponytail and beam at him.

"Please."

As he tugs off his boxers, Jacob captures my mouth with a kiss. Andreas applies his talented lips to my breast.

I'm completely encompassed in their joint embrace, their arms around me, Dominic's tentacles stroking along the sides of my torso.

Jake releases my lips just as Dom slides into me. My moan catches in my throat at the feeling of total fullness.

My knees lift to encompass his hips automatically, welcoming him deeper. He bows over me, the two other guys drawing back to make room but still keeping up their combined caresses.

"Love you," Dominic murmurs, with a hitch of breath as he drives farther into me that sets off a gasp of my own. "So much."

Joy radiates through my chest even though I've heard the words from him more than once before. "I love you too." I cast my gaze around to the other guys around us. "All of you. Always."

Andreas nips my earlobe, his words a warm wash of breath. "You're everything I'll ever want."

"Going to keep doing everything I can to deserve it, Wildcat," Jacob mutters, his fingers squeezing briefly around mine before he cups my breast again.

Zian's voice carries to me from the end of the bed, little more than a rasp. "Riva…"

He's gripping himself through his boxers now, his hunger etched across his handsome face. As Dominic surges into me again, propelling me toward another heady release, I manage to hold Zee's gaze.

"Come with me?"

He sputters a curse, every muscle tensing. Then he delves into his boxers to pump his erection skin to skin.

The slap of his palm against his cock merges with the rhythm of Dominic's thrusts inside me, the warble of all our broken breaths, the whirlwind of pleasure racing through me. He might not be touching me himself, but right then, it feels as if he's just as close to the others, just as much a part of this.

The thought sets off a brighter spark inside me. Its glow expands alongside the rising wave of bliss, on and on until the shadows are dancing in my veins and my body is trembling.

I press up to meet Dominic, urging him into me harder, faster. Tip my head to invite Drey's kiss. Tease my fingers down Jacob's chest.

And then shatter apart in time with Zian's final groan.

As I quake between the other three guys, our director slumps toward the mattress, spilling himself. His shoulders heave.

Then he drops his head a little farther and presses the most careful of kisses to the ball of my foot where I've just lowered it.

Right here with me. Where they're all meant to be.

But the peal of joy comes with a twist in my gut.

I have to figure out how to make sure they stay with me this time—that none of the villains beyond these walls ever come between us again.

TWENTY-THREE

Zian

I t sure would have been nice if the hotel had come with some kind of vehicle. I guess that would have been too much to ask.

Instead, we're tramping along through the dense jungle vegetation again, slapping away bugs and stubbing our toes on stones hidden in the underbrush.

I push forward in the lead, because with my size and strength it's easier for me to smash through the worst of the obstacles than it would be for any of the others. But that also means I don't have the greatest sense of what's going on behind me.

Even my supernaturally keen ears are focused more on any hint of danger from farther away than the murmured conversations and weary sighs of our group of shadowbloods.

So I have no idea that George's teleportation talent is on the fritz until he jolts into view a step ahead of me and promptly trips over a tree root his foot slammed right into. He sprawls forward with a whoomph of breath and then a growled swear word that twelve-year-olds probably shouldn't know.

I reach out to help him up. "You okay?"

He swipes his hand through his odd white hair and grimaces at me. "Yeah, fine. I didn't mean to do that. It just starts happening when I want to be moving faster than I am, whether that's actually a good idea or not."

His whole face is shiny with sweat, his hair's usual spikes drooping with dampness. His shirt clings to his skinny frame in patches.

I give him a quick onceover and decide I can pitch in a little more without it affecting my endurance all that much. "Here, why don't you take a breather on me?"

I heft him up onto my shoulders in a piggyback ride, balancing him over the bulge of my pack. He's so scrawny I barely feel the extra weight.

"You don't have to do this," he says as I tramp onward. "I can manage."

I shrug—carefully so I don't dislodge him. "I can too. Just keep your head low so I don't accidentally brain you on any of the lower branches."

George ends up resting his forearms gently on the top of my head, letting out a soft sigh that suggests he appreciates the rest more than he's letting on. He might be the youngest kid here—it's not surprising he's tiring out the fastest.

His voice reaches me in a low mutter I don't think he wants anyone else to hear. "Just for a few minutes. I'll keep up, really."

Something about his tone tugs at my gut. I wish I could see his face now to judge his expression, not that I'm the best at reading emotions even then.

"It's no big deal for me," I assure him. "I could keep going like this for hours."

His head droops closer to mine. "You shouldn't have to. It's my fault we're here at all."

As I snap a few vines that crisscross our path, I frown. "Why would you say that?"

"We wouldn't have crashed if I hadn't hit the pilot so hard—because I made that stupid hop when I wasn't even trying to. I'm always screwing up like that, but that time—that time I screwed things up for everyone."

Oh. The thread of emotion I caught in his voice before must have tugged at me because it's so uncomfortably familiar from my own life.

But with the recognition comes an unexpected sense of certainty. The words leave my lips without any hesitation.

"I think all of us have had issues getting control over our powers. The guardians never really taught us how to use them properly."

Clancy's done a little work with us, but only to serve his missions. I don't know if he's even bothered with this kid.

George lets out a soft huff. "Yeah, well, no one else made the helicopter crash."

I consider his statement. "No, but a bunch of us could have. And some of us would be more likely to screw up in different ways that could be just as bad. As long as... as long as we're *trying* to help rather than hurt people, I think we'll end up doing more good than bad in the end. The balance will be more right than wrong."

The kid is silent for several seconds. "Are you sure? I do try."

"As sure as I can be about anything," I say, and realize as I'm saying it how true that is.

Is this the first time I've thought of my own mistakes and not immediately started beating myself up over them?

I'm not happy about my fuck-ups. I wish I could take back the pain I've dealt out that wasn't deserved.

But I didn't ask for this power or the feral defensiveness that's intertwined with it. I can put more good into the world than pain myself, can't I?

I'm doing a little of that now by giving this kid a hand. And maybe not just by taking some weight off him in the literal sense.

A smile crosses my face, and my own steps feel even lighter. For a little while.

The direction we've been heading in, based on Jacob's observations from the cockpit before the crash and Griffin's emotional compass, is taking us toward a range of tall hills. Maybe even small mountains, from the looks of the green-draped peaks I'm getting glimpses of through the leaves.

The breaths of my companions become rougher as we veer upward again. How high are we going to have to climb this time?

We can't count on stumbling on another abandoned hotel for shelter.

I skirt a clump of jutting boulders with the others

trailing behind me and knock a path through a grove of sprouting saplings. George sways on my shoulders.

My calves are starting to prickle with exertion now. I'm going to have to put him down soon after all.

I glance up at the sun, just past its peak in the sky and searing even through the thin haze of clouds, and then back at the others. "Are we sure we definitely want to keep going this way? I haven't gotten us off-course?"

Dominic peers up at the sun too. "I think this is still northwest."

Griffin nods with that unnervingly vague expression of his. "It feels like we're going the right way to me, if we want to reach the biggest city around."

I guess we just keep trudging for as long as it takes, then.

I turn back to face the jungle, debating whether I can handle carrying George a while longer or should preserve my strength by setting him back on his feet now, and realize one of the other kids has sidled up next to me. The mousy-haired girl looks to be about fourteen, but she's been so quiet throughout the trek that I haven't caught her name.

"I, um," she mumbles, her head dipping shyly. "I think I might be able to tell where we could walk more easily."

I'm not going to say no to that offer. I smile down at her in an attempt to offset my imposing size, in case that's part of what's making her nervous. "How's that?"

Her hands twist together in front of her. "Well, I—my abilities have to do with the earth. Like, dirt and stuff. And I've been noticing I can kind of *feel* the ground around us. Where it's steeper or... not so steep. Where there are more roots in it or less."

"Less roots would mean less plants to push through," Booker pipes up. "Sounds good to me."

Jacob's voice reaches me with an impatient note. "We don't want to get too far off track. An easy path could still take longer if we wander off the wrong way."

Before my eyes, the girl deflates. The sight gnaws at me just like George's admission of guilt did.

She's trying to do something good for us too. Jake's just a natural skeptic.

"Do you think you could tell how far we'd need to go to get to the better routes?" I ask her. "Make sure it's not too long a diversion?"

She peeks up at me, biting her lip. "Yeah. I can't feel things very far away anyway. There's a spot that's pretty close that we could try."

"We might as well give it a shot," Andreas says in his easygoing way. "Especially with how much more walking we've got ahead of us."

A murmur of general agreement passes through the group. I give the girl's shoulder the gentlest pat I can manage.

"Why don't you take the lead for a bit? Sounds like you know where you're going better than I do."

The swift grin she flashes at me makes the gamble worthwhile all on its own. She darts a little ahead of me, picking her way across the terrain so deftly my confidence in this plan has grown before I'm even walking again.

I check behind me to make sure everyone's on board. My gaze collides with Riva's, and she shoots me a wider smile that makes my pulse wobble in the best possible way.

She's been championing these kids from the moment she found out they existed. But she doesn't have to be alone in it.

She doesn't have to be alone any way at all. A flicker of heat washes through my veins at the memories from last night—her taste on my lips, her face flushed with bliss.

I played a part in giving her that pleasure, and I didn't have to push myself too close to my limits to do it. Even if that's the best I can ever offer her, it's more than I thought I could.

The shy girl guides us onto a narrow but trampled path that I'd bet animals use to traverse the jungle more quickly. My strides lengthen as we set off along it, the strain easing back.

"This is great," I tell her, and she smiles a little longer than before.

"I feel like it's going to take us on a lower path between the higher hills," she says. "So we won't have to go right up any of them."

Nadia lets out a whoop of approval. "I'm all for that. No pain, no gain is definitely not my philosophy."

At our faster pace, we find ourselves surrounded by the looming peaks within a couple of hours. The ground keeps veering upward with plenty of hillside still to cover, but my spirits are high.

Of course, the others still need their breaks even with an easier hike. Andreas calls for a pit stop when we come up on a couple of fallen trees that can act as benches, and he and Riva pass around the drinks and snacks while Dominic checks everyone for possible injuries.

Griffin scoops his cat out of his pack and scratches her shoulders while she cuddles on his lap. As I watch him, wondering what's going on in that head of his now, he focuses on the perky girl from the older kids.

"I think we know everyone's talent now except yours, Celine," he says calmly. "What powers do you have? It'd be good to know in case they might come in handy."

She lets out a giggle with an awkward dip of her head. "I'm not sure how likely that is out here. The guardians say my abilities have something to do with magnetism... I can manipulate certain metals a little, and sometimes I pick up on things like radio waves, cell phone signals... Haven't heard any of that on this trip."

She motions to the wilderness around us with a wry grin.

Nadia gives her a teasing nudge. "We'll have to put you to work once we make it to the city."

"It could definitely be useful there." Jacob stretches his arms over his head and then considers the mousy girl with the earth affinity. "Any chance you can tell us how much farther we've got to go before we're heading down again instead of up?"

Her shoulders come up a bit at his demanding tone. "I —I can't really feel that far ahead. It's farther ahead than I can tell, anyway, but I think that only means it's not, like, ten minutes away."

Andreas cocks his head, studying the peaks on either side of us. "From the looks of things, I doubt it's more than a few hours farther. We're not going to make it all the way down the other side before it gets totally dark, but it'd be good if we can push on until we reach the highest point. We might be able to see the city from there. It'll give us something to inspire good dreams before we set off again."

Riva stretches her arms out in front of her with a gleam in her eyes. "That would be amazing—to know our goal is in sight."

Once we've reached civilization, we can find out where we are. Start making more plans. See if we can gather more allies.

My heart thumps faster in anticipation, even though those events are at least a day in the future. Then my attention snags on Riva's next movement.

She sat down a couple of feet away from Griffin, and she's just slipped her hand around his.

As he looks at her with a quiet smile, my hackles rise automatically.

He's been helping us with the escape. He hasn't given me any reason to distrust him since we fled the facility.

But he hasn't really explained himself either. Justified all the ways he worked against us with Clancy and whatever other guardians.

He helped Clancy form his plan to shove me and Riva together. Shared some of my most private feelings—and hers.

A growl forms at the base of my throat.

I don't care if Riva's decided she can trust him. He should *prove* it—to all of us. Or at least to my three friends who are tied to her as completely as anyone can be with the marks I might never be able to take on my own skin.

Maybe it's not his fault. The guardians could have put him through all kinds of hell that we don't know about.

We still need to hear it.

I confessed all my past shit to her. It was a good thing I did.

He should want to for all of our sakes, including his.

I stand up abruptly, my wolf-man features itching at my face. I'm not going to threaten him into it, even if part of me would like to.

When the others glance up at me, I jerk my head toward the area to the left of our path. "I can hear a stream somewhere off that way. Why don't those of us carrying the jugs go see if it's worth refilling them."

That's just us Firsts. We've shouldered the heaviest packs. And we've each got at least one empty jug by this point.

We wouldn't really all need to go, but Dominic gives me a thoughtful nod as he gets to his feet as if he understands I must have some other motivation. Jacob's eyes flash with sharpened alertness, and Andreas's easy grin fades.

Riva looks around at the kids with a slight frown. "You're all okay on your own for a few minutes?"

"Hey, we're not toddlers," Nadia says, her tone light enough to show she isn't offended. She swipes the fringe of her dark pixie cut away from her damp forehead. "And I don't think any of us would argue with having a plentiful supply of water."

Griffin has stayed seated on the log. He ruffles his cat's

fur. "I'll be here with them."

I fix him with a firm stare. "You should fill up too if it looks like a good source. Come on."

Griffin gazes back at me, and I know he can pick up on how I'm feeling. The threads of aggression, the determination behind my demand.

Riva makes a small noise as if she's about to speak, but then Griffin gets up. He lets the cat leap out of his arms and go to the empty can he filled with water for it.

"That's no problem. I want to do my fair share."

I have to lead the way, of course, since I'm the one who can supposedly hear the running water. But when I check to confirm that the others are all with me, Riva has twined her fingers with Griffin's again.

My fingers flex, my claws prickling with the urge to spring free. I keep walking in as straight a line as I can manage until the chatter of the younger shadowbloods has completely faded into the rustling of the leaves and buzzing of the jungle insects.

If my wolfish ears can't hear them, they definitely won't hear us.

I turn to face the others, folding my arms over my chest. "There isn't any stream—at least, not that I've heard. I just thought we should talk. The six of us, alone."

Riva knits her brow. "About what?"

I can protect her and my friends with more than my brutal strength. I can protect her from the secrets we need to be sure won't come back to haunt us.

I lift my chin toward Griffin. "I think it's time you told us exactly what happened to you in the past four years —and why we should believe anything you tell us now."

TWENTY-FOUR

Riva

Zian's words come out with the edge of a snarl. I instinctively step even closer to Griffin, my fingers tightening around his.

I don't know how much of a chance he's gotten to talk to the others—to apologize, to explain... Does Zian have any idea at all of the reasons Griffin decided to side with the guardians over us?

But then, *I* still can't totally wrap my head around his reasoning either, can I? I've been willing to do what I can to see the hints of the boy I knew rise to the surface through the robotic being he's become, but I wouldn't put my life in his hands.

Not now. Not yet.

A beam of sunlight streaks between the leaves overhead to glare off Griffin's blond hair. He's still standing calmly beside me amid the jungle vegetation, but a whiff of nervous pheromones reaches my nose.

What is he afraid of?

Should I be worried that he's unnerved or happy that he's capable of being scared at all?

He keeps his attention on Zian, though all five of us are watching him now. "I've tried to explain it. Clancy acted like he wanted to take the Guardianship in a new direction, one that sounded like it'd be good for us. You all thought that might be possible too, when you first got to the island."

He isn't wrong, but Jacob's lips pull into a grimace. "I wouldn't have dragged my friends back into captivity after they'd gotten free, no matter what I thought was 'possible.'"

"It made sense at the time. I—I didn't know what to think about everything he was showing me, about what you were doing, the people you'd hurt. *How* you'd hurt them. And my sense of who you all were was muddled. I hadn't seen you in so long."

"But you *knew* us," Zian insists. "Riva hadn't seen us in four years, and she did everything she could to help us even after we'd been assholes to her."

Griffin swallows audibly. "It's not the same. I don't know how to describe how it's been. Like everything was flat but also blurry at the same time…"

As he trails off, the shade of sadness in his expression wrenches at my heart. He obviously doesn't want to talk about how he ended up in his current state, but I'm not sure there's any other way of unraveling the tension between us.

I stroke my thumb over his knuckles in an attempt at reassuring him. "What did the guardians do to you that erased all your emotions, Griffin? How did it even happen?"

His mouth twists, and he grips my hand harder. There's pain in the answer to my question, and I've never really wanted to hurt him.

But maybe because he can tell that, he doesn't refuse me.

His gaze trails off toward the wilderness as if it's easier for him to bring back those memories when he isn't looking at any of us. "They called it 'desensitization.' The basic idea seemed to be to make feeling things worse than not feeling them."

Dominic brushes aside a fern frond that grazes his arm with the heavy breeze, his hazel eyes shadowed. "How did they do that?" he asks quietly.

Griffin's stance stiffens a little more with each word. "They started small. Showing me video clips that would provoke a little generic emotion in most people: a kid having a happy birthday party, a tense car chase, stuff like that. And they had me hooked up to a machine with different sensors. When they could tell that I was having an emotional response—from my heartrate and my breathing and I don't know what else—they'd overwhelm it."

Jacob's posture has turned equally rigid, as if he's matching his twin's discomfort. "Overwhelm it with *what?*"

Griffin's mouth twitches. "Physical pain. Electric shocks or chemicals that set off different types of aches or burns."

Andreas's eyes widen. "Fuck."

Griffin blinks hard, a tremor running through his body. I set my free hand on his arm a little above our clasped hands, doing my best to steady him.

"It was a long process," he says in a thin voice. "They'd show a clip, catch a reaction, lance the emotions like a boil. Then they'd play the same clip again. Over and over until my body just... didn't register whatever had made me feel something before. Like a connection was snapped. And then they'd move on to the next clip."

Jacob's fingers flex at his sides. A branch cracks overhead, whipping against the trunk of a neighboring tree.

"Those fucking pricks," he spits out. More rage burns in his blue eyes than I've seen in weeks.

My own anger at the guardians sears through my gut, but what chokes me up is a thicker anguish. "That must have taken a long time."

"Yes." Griffin swallows again, his eyes gone even hazier than usual, as if he's retreating inside his head. "They had to—to work up through every possibility to the most intense, and destroy those automatic reactions too. I didn't have much concept of time. During it or after. It was more than a year, at least."

More than a year of constant agony for every emotion that stirred inside him. Tears prick at the back of my eyes.

"I still don't understand why they wanted to do that in the first place," I say roughly.

"So my own emotions wouldn't confuse what I was reading in other people. So I wouldn't be affected by the things I read."

Jacob scowls. "And your feelings are just gone? You can't bring them back?"

Griffin raises his shoulders in an awkward shrug. "I'm not sure I even know how to try. By the end, the whole concept of what it was like to feel things wasn't something I could grasp." He pauses. "And by then, I—I kind of thought maybe they were right. Maybe it was better like that."

"What?" Zian sputters. "How could them torturing you be good?"

I feel Griffin bracing himself in the shift of his stance. Another whiff of anxiety reaches my nose.

His jaw works, and then he glances around at each of us with obvious effort. "It's because I couldn't control my emotions that they caught us. The first time. I gave away that we were going to try to escape."

Andreas's forehead furrows. "What do you mean?"

A rasp creeps into Griffin's voice. "They showed me the surveillance video when they told me. The afternoon before we were going to break out—right before we went back to our cells. I must have been thinking about getting free, and just for a moment I smiled at all of you. So bright they couldn't miss it."

I shake my head. "One moment couldn't have given everything away."

Griffin hangs his head. "They said they already suspected we were planning something. I guess it would have been hard to completely hide the conversations we were having, no matter how careful we were being. But they didn't think we were ready to make a move until they saw that. I guess I normally looked sad when it was time for us to leave."

His free hand clenches, and then he raises his chin. "I'm sorry. I'm so fucking sorry. I can't even—I can't even *feel* how sorry I know I am, but I ruined everything, and none of this would ever have gone so wrong if my emotions hadn't been so noticeable, and—"

My chest hitches with a sob I can't totally suppress, and I yank Griffin into a full embrace. He bows his head next to mine, his jaw coming to rest against my cheek.

"They were probably lying," I insist, my voice shaking with vehemence. "They couldn't have been that sure just because you *smiled*. And even if it was that, it wasn't your fault. You couldn't help being happy."

"They made it so I wouldn't be any more. I couldn't be happy or sad or angry or anything."

"And that isn't better. That isn't *you*. If we couldn't have escaped without you being broken, then it wasn't the right time to escape. You weren't the problem."

Andreas clears his throat, sounding pretty choked up himself. "In case it isn't clear, we all agree on that point. I'd never have blamed you, Griffin."

Zian's foot scuffs against the uneven ground. "I'm sorry for coming down so hard on you. I didn't realize—"

"It's okay." Griffin pulls a few inches back from me, his hands coming to rest on my forearms. "I wasn't sure how much I should talk about it—if you're going to accept what I did, it should be because I've made up for it *now*, not because you feel bad about what happened to me before."

Jacob's eyes still blaze with fury, but I don't think that

rage is directed at his brother anymore. "Can we fix it?" He glances at Dom. "Can you heal whatever they fucked up inside him?"

Dominic extends a cautious tentacle to rest on Griffin's elbow and pauses. "I can't pick up on any physical damage. It's not like a typical injury."

I turn my hands to grip Griffin's arms like he's holding mine. "You said that you're starting to feel things again."

He nods, gazing down at me. "The more I'm close to you, the more things are reemerging. It's—it's a little unsettling after all this time, and I'm still figuring out how to sort through all the sensations, but I think it's better than staying numb."

It makes sense that it took the draw between our shadowy essences to get through to him. I've never experienced anything like the urgent clamor in my blood except when I'm physically close with these five men.

The guardians could never have provoked that one feeling in him to torment it out of him.

Imagining the torture they inflicted on him makes my stomach plummet. "The feelings that are coming back—are they triggering the pain the guardians put you through?"

It's got to all be tangled up in a big mess inside him.

Griffin manages to give me a smile that's only slightly strained. "That's part of what I'm sorting through. But I have to deal with it before it can get better. You've been helping a lot. Don't feel bad about it. I want everything you're willing to offer."

He sounds so sure that I only hesitate for a second before giving in to the urge that sweeps through me at his words. Bobbing up on my toes, I press my mouth to his.

As he kisses me back, one of his hands rises to the back of my neck. The stroke of his fingers over my skin stirs up all kinds of hungry emotions inside me, not that this is a good time for indulging in them.

When we ease apart, I don't see a trace of disapproval in any of the other guys' expressions.

Jacob wavers on his feet and then steps toward his brother. As Griffin turns to meet him, Jake yanks him into a hug of his own.

"I should have been there," he mutters. "I'd have done everything I could to stop them."

Griffin hugs him back hard. "I know you would have. I can feel how angry you are on my behalf. I haven't blamed you for being angry with me at first, Jake. I deserved it."

"They fucking deserved it."

"They're gone now. I don't even know if they're still working with the Guardianship. Clancy told me what they'd done was barbaric." Griffin frowns as he draws away from his brother. "But he might have just said that to encourage me to trust him."

"It doesn't matter," I say. "We have plenty of other reasons *not* to trust him now. And we're not going to have anything to do with him again except to get the other shadowbloods free."

Zian reaches out to squeeze Griffin's shoulder. "Thank you for telling us everything, even if I kind of bullied you into it. I guess we should be getting back... and explain why we don't have any more water."

Andreas waves his hand dismissively. "We'll just say it looked too muddy to risk it. Simple enough."

I might have liked to have topped up our supply of hydration, but my spirits have lifted as we tramp back to the path anyway. The simmering tension between all of my guys has melted away, the vibe between us feeling almost as companionable as back when we were teens.

We rejoin the younger shadowbloods just in time to see Celine slipping through the trees toward the group from the other side.

Griffin aims a pointed look at her that I don't totally understand. "Where did you go on your own?"

She laughs with a tug at her clothes. "Needed a trip to the 'ladies room.'"

Griffin still seems pensive, but then his gaze travels across the group, and his eyebrows draw together. "Where's Lua? My cat?"

Booker, Nadia, and Devon look over from where they were standing in a cluster farther down the path, matching guilt on all their faces.

"I'm sorry," Nadia says, her shoulders slumping. "She was hanging out with us getting pets all around, and then all of a sudden she freaked out. Fur puffed out, hissing at us. She raced off this way."

"It was only a couple of minutes ago," Booker adds. "Maybe she saw or smelled something weird that freaked her out a bit, and she'll come back when she realizes there's no problem."

Zian's head jerks around in response to something I didn't pick up on. "Unless there is a problem. Everyone, stay where you are."

We all freeze, our voices fading into the humid air. My heart thuds so loud I can barely make out the twitter of the birds overhead.

Then I catch a hint of movement between the trees. A striped, muscular body prowling through the jungle several feet from the path.

We've got a feline companion, but it's not Griffin's little housecat. No wonder Lua panicked.

I glance at the guys, not sure what to say. How do you deal with a tiger on the hunt?

I don't want to risk pissing it off and making it more inclined to attack.

"Let's get moving, slowly and calmly," Dominic says. "Stick close together, and—"

"What's there?" The girl who found our path interrupts him with a nervous shiver, her gaze scanning the jungle. Then she lets out a squeak and scrambles farther down the path.

As if her fear has lit a fuse in the youngest shadowbloods, Ajax, Devon, George, and a couple others dash after her, George blinking in and out of view every few steps. But clearly that's the wrong move.

Paws thump over the ground. The tiger barrels through the jungle toward the fleeing kids.

"No!" I cry out, throwing myself after them.

The giant cat lunges onto the cleared path right at their heels, and a shriek jolts up my throat before I can even think about it.

The tiger's body seizes up. My power radiates up from my lungs, latching on to every nerve and bone in its immense body.

I've shattered a shadowkind monster before. A mortal jungle creature is nothing.

The energy vibrates through my body as the scream peals louder. This beast was going to hurt the kids—the kids I swore I'd protect.

I can't let it get another chance.

The tiger's legs crumple with a groan of agony.

Its tail kinks. Its back twists. Its jaw snaps open and sideways.

The crack of its skull resonates through my veins with a rush of power. In that instant, I feel as if I've just woken up fresh for the day, not a single step taken yet.

The furry creature slumps in the middle of the path, limp and deformed.

The young shadowbloods huddle together, staring at the tiger and then at me. My stomach knotting, I glance behind me to find similar shock etched on the faces of the older teens.

They had some idea what I can do, but they've never seen my power on full display before.

They've never seen the sadistic edge it takes… or how much satisfaction I take from the torment, even if I wish I didn't.

None of them have abilities anything like this. They couldn't have been prepared.

Jacob sets his hand on my back and lifts his voice. "You got it just in time, Riva. That thing would have mowed all of them down if you hadn't hit it so fast."

His steely gaze dares anyone to complain about my methods.

"Let's grab our things and get moving," Andreas adds, brisk but warm. "We've had enough of a break."

And we don't want the kids spending any more time gaping at the tiger's mutilated body than they have to.

Ajax squares his shoulders and meets my eyes. "Thank you, Riva."

The girl who ran first nods shakily, though she's clutching George's arm. "Thank you."

But as we skirt the tiger's broken body, a gloom seems to have fallen over our group that not even the brilliance of the late-afternoon sun can beam away.

TWENTY-FIVE

Riva

Our pathfinder—whose name she's finally told us is Lindsay—lifts her head abruptly in the thickening darkness.

"I can feel it. The land slopes down again right up ahead. Like it keeps going that way, not a little dip."

She's gotten our hopes up over what was just a dip a couple of times already in the past hour. This time she sounds a lot more confident than before, though.

At the skeptical looks a couple of the younger shadowbloods shoot her through the dusk, she raises her chin. "It's clearer than last time. And we *should* be getting almost to the highest spot by now, right?"

Nadia smothers a yawn. "I sure hope so."

Zian and Lindsay tramp on at the head of the pack. Andreas eases back along the line to where Jacob and I are bringing up the rear like usual.

Drey glances over the motley procession before turning to us with a low voice. "I think if we haven't reached the top yet this time, we should make camp anyway. Everyone's getting pretty tired."

My mouth twists. "Yeah."

We took another short break about an hour ago after Lindsay had to divert us from one animal track that veered off along the side of the hills to a clearer passage continuing upward. At that point, I think Dominic killed half a dozen twigs healing blisters.

My shoulders are aching under the straps of my pack. The pain is faint compared to the sharper sensation digging into my chest that has nothing to do with the exertion of the hike.

We've finished off all the juice, and we're getting low on water. The sky clotted with more clouds for part of the afternoon, but they burned off before any rain fell.

At this point, I'd rather we got rained on so we could collect some of it even if we all end up drenched.

And of course there's also the memory of the kids' shocked stares after my scream wrenched through the tiger, hovering at the back of my mind.

Jacob frowns. "The kids will have an easier time resting if they know the goal's in sight."

I swallow down the worry it's probably better I don't voice—that our goal might not be in sight at all. That we could reach the crest of this section of hills and see nothing but more jungle.

And then what?

"If we push them to total exhaustion," Andreas murmurs, "it's only going to—"

Zian's excited shout cuts him off, an eager squeal from Lindsay mingling with it.

"You've got to see this," he calls back to us.

We all hustle forward, breathless remarks passing between the younger shadowbloods. My pulse kicks up a notch, partly spurred by the whiffs of anticipation lacing the air from the group.

Zian and Lindsay have stopped up ahead, eased off into the thicker vegetation to make room for the rest of us to come up alongside them. The gasps and exclamations of our younger companions as they reach that spot wash away most of the gloom that'd fallen over me.

The three of us arrive at their heels, and for a second I lose my breath.

The landscape below us is draped in the same black as the shadowed jungle around us—except for a broad patch of gleaming lights piercing the night. In the darkness, I can't tell how far away from the hills it is, but it's definitely *there*: a big, vibrant city.

We'll be able to get food and water, one way or another. We'll have access to vehicles and phones.

The worst part of the trek is nearly behind us.

The kids let out soft whoops, grabbing each other in a jumble of hugs in their relief. Andreas shoots me a grin.

"Guess I didn't need to worry after all. Let's figure out a good place to hunker down for the night and who'll take first watch."

"I'll go first," I offer automatically. "I'm too keyed up to sleep right away anyway."

Jacob nods. "Then I'm with you. We'll get one of the older teens too—that should be enough eyes."

Settling into camp is a chaotic business. We hand out a little more food from our stash and try to make sure each of the kids has a decently comfortable patch of ground to curl up on.

We brought some sheets from the hotel, but anything heavier like an actual blanket would have been too much cargo. They bundle part of those up as thin pillows and drape the rest over their bodies.

The jungle terrain hardly makes for a cozy bed. I know that from our first night.

But everyone makes the most of it without complaint, maybe with dreams of finding actual beds again by the end of tomorrow.

I pick out a perch on a stump overlooking the other side of the hill and the city below. Jacob is still prowling around the perimeter of our camp, checking for immediate threats, but I suspect he'll stick close to me once he's done.

At the rustle of brush, I turn my head, but it's Nadia venturing toward me, her statuesque frame giving off a faint glow to help light her way.

"Hey," I say, abruptly hesitant. Nadia is probably the closest to a new friend I've made among the younger shadowbloods, but I have no idea what she thinks of me now. "Did you want to take first watch?"

She rubs her mouth. "Yeah. I'll keep an eye on things at the other end of the camp once everyone's settled. I just wanted to look at the city a little more first."

I can't hold back a smile. "Sure. I get that. If you want to take this post, I can cover the other side and—"

Nadia cuts me off with a shake of her head. "Nah. I'll get too distracted if I have that view in front of me the whole time. But... thank you."

She sounds a little uncertain too. I shut my mouth and simply gaze off over the darkened landscape with her, trying to chart the path we'll take even though that's impossible when I can barely make out the trees.

After a minute or two, Nadia inhales audibly. "The other Firsts... Do you all have abilities like what you did to the tiger? I mean, that strong?"

Oh. Yeah, it does make sense for that question to be on her mind. She'll never have seen any of her facility-mates pull off something like that.

"We've all got different powers," I say carefully. "But they're all pretty strong. That's the only reason we were able to escape—before and now. Jacob had to basically set off an entire earthquake to get us out, you know."

"Wow." She gazes at the city lights for a few beats longer and then looks at me. "None of the rest of us can pull off anything like that. At least, I've never met any shadowblood my age or younger who could even get close to that kind of impact."

She hasn't asked a question outright, but it's implicit in her words. I roll my answer around in my head, debating how much to tell her.

But she deserves the truth as much as we did, doesn't she?

I swallow down my doubts. "When we escaped the first time, we tracked down one of the founders of the Guardianship—a woman who worked with Clancy's parents. She's the one who figured out the process for merging humans with… with what they think of as monsters. She told us that when we—the Firsts—were very young and she saw how we were developing, she decided she'd made a mistake. She wanted us dead."

Nadia's eyebrows shoot up. "But they kept making more of us."

"It seems like the other founders and whoever else had control by then didn't agree with her. They shut her out more and more."

I tilt my head, thinking of the laptop we stole from her home in the Canadian wilderness, the one that's either still in Rollick's hands with the rest of our old supplies or tossed in the trash if he didn't bother to hold on to our packs.

"We found some records from her work," I go on. "We couldn't understand much of it, but as far as we could tell, when the other guardians pushed her for her process, she left out some parts. She might have been hoping it wouldn't work at all. It looks like what actually happened was the later shadowbloods they created had a lot less of the 'monstrous' stuff working for them."

Nadia hums to herself. Then, to my surprise, she lets out a dry bark of a laugh. "Well, that sucks."

It's my turn to have my eyebrows shoot up. "You'd rather you had more power?"

"Sure." She runs her hands through her thick black hair, rumpling the short strands. "Right now I can just glow a bit. If I could set off a whole solar bomb or something… We'd have a lot easier time keeping out of the guardians' hands, wouldn't we?"

Somehow it hadn't occurred to me that she might feel that way.

"It isn't always a good feeling," I have to point out. "I don't really like seeing what I've done, even if it helps us."

"But you wouldn't get rid of the power if you had the choice, would you?"

I open my mouth and close it again.

There was a time when I'd hoped the real monsters, the shadowkind, might be able to tell us how to carve our monstrous parts out of us. That was before I knew about all the younger shadowbloods who needed our help to escape.

Before I realized just how far-reaching the Guardianship's influence extended.

"No," I admit. "Not right now. Not as long as we might still need it."

Ajax's measured voice travels from behind us, making me startle. "I wish I could read a lot more of people's minds. Even if I'd probably see stuff that's disturbing."

I turn to face him where he's standing a few steps back on the path, chiding myself for getting so caught up in the conversation that I didn't hear him coming. Although he'll have trained in all the same non-supernatural skills like stealth that the rest of us have, so maybe it's not totally my fault.

I guess I haven't horrified the younger shadowbloods after all, at least not all of them.

"You might get stronger," I say, shifting my gaze between him and Nadia. "The six of us all had our powers expand over time, especially once we were technically adults. I didn't know I could scream like that until a few months ago."

Nadia perks up visibly. She rubs her hands together with a smirk that looks a little devious. "Maybe we'll figure out ways to develop the talents more when we get to decide how we train for ourselves."

I suppose that's possible, although I'd imagine the guardians have prodded as much ability out of the younger shadowbloods as they possibly could already. It seems kinder to keep that thought to myself for now.

"You never know."

Ajax yawns and drifts away. After giving the city one last longing glance, Nadia does the same.

As their footsteps rasp off through the jungle, Jacob rejoins me. He rests his hand on the back of my head, the gesture still tentative after everything we've been through until I lean into his touch.

"They'll be okay," he says. "We'll all be okay. Because you're making sure of it."

I don't know how to answer. Do I even think that's true?

But looking out over the glow of the city we've pushed ourselves so hard to find, it's a little easier to believe it than before.

I wake up on my uneven bed of soil and fallen leaves to a sorrowful *meow* that carries through the underbrush.

As I push myself upright, Griffin is already shoving through the nearby bushes. "Lua?"

The cat meows again, and a moment later he's turning with his pet tucked in his arms. Her white fur is mottled with bits of debris, but she nestles against his chest with a purr I can hear from five feet away.

Griffin smiles down at her, his expression so tender with affection that my pulse skips a beat. He really is coming back to us bit by bit, just like Lua found her way back to him.

Our fellow shadowbloods are stirring throughout our hasty camp. Dominic approaches Griffin, his tentacles unfurling from their coils against his back.

"Do you want me to check her over? In case she got any scratches or sprains that aren't totally obvious?"

Griffin hesitates, whether because he doesn't want to loosen his hug yet or because he knows what the healing costs Dom, I'm not sure. Maybe some of both.

Then he takes a step toward Dominic. "Yes, that would be a good idea."

I get to my feet, gathering my meager belongings, and raise my voice to carry through the jungle around me. "Let's have a quick breakfast and then move out. We're almost there!"

Energetic murmurs rise up after my reminder. I weave through the trees back onto our narrow path and peer down the opposite hillside again.

The city doesn't stand out as much amid the jungle greenery by daylight. But it's still undeniably there, a grayish blotch that feels even more within reach now that I can distinguish actual buildings.

And maybe a highway cutting through the trees

running parallel to the hills? If we can reach that, the hike will be even easier.

I turn back toward the camp with a lighter heart—and freeze at a rhythmic whirring that reaches my ears in the same moment.

Farther down the path, Zian has already stiffened. His head swivels as he knits his brow.

"That sounds like—"

A big military-style helicopter veers into view around one of the higher peaks nearby. From the expanding cacophony of sound, it isn't alone.

"Shadowbloods," a voice blares from a loudspeaker. "Stay where you are and prepare to be collected."

"What the fuck?" Booker says, staring up at the swiftly advancing chopper.

Griffin whirls around, Lua still clutched in his arms. His gaze latches on to… Celine.

His voice comes out cool with certainty but a little shaky. "You. You signaled them somehow. You're *happy* that they're here."

My stomach lurches. Griffin's been keeping an eye on Celine, questioning her here and there from the start, hasn't he?

Was he picking up on something in her emotions that made him suspicious? I guess not enough that he felt confident mentioning it to the rest of us until now.

Celine stares back at him, her hands clenched at her sides, her usual sunny smile vanished with the flattening of her mouth.

"How is this better than what we had before?" she bursts out with a wild gesture toward the jungle around us. She jabs a finger toward me. "She—she wants to take us back to the fucking *monsters* like she did before. I've seen what those things can do."

More nausea bubbles up inside me. "I wouldn't—it was just a possibility. We'd have been careful about it."

Celine narrows her eyes at me. "You can't be *careful* with those things. I saw what they did to one of my friends when we tried to help the guardians bring you back in Miami. I saw the pictures of what they did to the shadowbloods you thought you were 'rescuing' afterward. They're psychotic beasts."

Oh, no. The image flashes through my mind of the girl slumped in a pool of blood at the parking garage where we were attacked with Rollick.

I didn't want that to happen. When we asked Rollick and his people to help us push back the guardians, I asked them not to hurt any of the kids.

But they did anyway. I can't even promise her that it was unavoidable or a mistake, because I honestly don't know.

I don't even know which of the shadowkind killed her.

Nadia gapes at the other girl. "Are you kidding me, Celine? We came all this way—"

Celine glares at her. "We've been attacked by a tiger, almost ran out of water—we're sleeping in the dirt—to get to what? Maybe I don't love the facility, but we're a hell of a lot safer there."

She jogs forward toward the crest of our section of hill, raising her arms as if to beckon the helicopters, a second of which has swung into view.

"Celine!" I cry out, not even sure what I want to do, and spring at her.

A *boom* resonates through the air from the closer chopper. An invisible force smacks into me in mid-leap and hurls me into a tree trunk.

TWENTY-SIX

Dominic

As the thunderous sound splits the air, I throw myself into the shelter of two broad tree trunks. That might be the only reason I escape being knocked right off my feet.

As it is, I sway and clutch at the nearest branch to keep my balance. Shrieks and grunts carry through the air from all around me.

The mark on my sternum prickles with echoed pain. Riva's fallen somewhere out there—fallen hard.

My heart lurches. I push myself around the trees, searching for her slim form in the chaos.

My gaze catches on Jacob first. He's sprawled on his ass in the middle of the path, his hands raised, his face tight with fury.

He's aiming his telekinetic power at the helicopter. But the same instant that becomes obvious to me, the chopper sweeps by overhead—and drops something from a hatch in its belly.

A strange, glinting net plummets over the path, large enough to slam into Jake and a few of the younger shadowbloods who'd tumbled around him. An electric hiss ripples through its metallic strands, and their bodies jerk with spasms.

Fuck. He won't be able to toss the helicopters away while he's being electrocuted.

Where's Riva? I can't tell if she's even okay.

But if she can aim a scream at the guardians—

I scramble forward through the jungle and glimpse her farther up the path near the crest of our section of hill. She must have fallen to her hands and knees, but she's shoving herself upright with a wobble.

Zian has reached her already. He grasps her elbow to steady her—and the helicopter whips by again with another glittering release.

Riva and Zian try to spring out of the way, but they don't quite clear the edge of the net. The electric current jolts through their bodies with a searing pain that jabs into me.

The helicopter circles around. Clancy's voice booms from the loudspeaker. "Stay where you are, and we will collect you. There's no need to make this a fight."

My jaw clenches. He's already turned it into a fight himself.

But how the hell are we going to hit back when the shadowbloods with the strongest talents are tangled up in electrified cords?

I shove through the underbrush toward Riva, careful

not to expose myself on the path where another net could catch me. She's struggling, trying to claw her way free.

But the moment she jerks one shoulder out from under the twined ropes, another electric shock sizzles through her limbs. Her cry hollows out my gut.

She slumps next to Zian, whose head is lolling with a dazed expression.

I have to help her—I have to help everyone. But what can I do that won't get me shocked and stunned too?

I swivel around, hastily taking stock of who's stayed free of the nets.

Up by the crest, Griffin has pulled back into the shelter of the trees on one side of the path. Celine stands across from him, only about ten feet from where I'm poised, her face lifted toward the two helicopters as they hover in search of a landing spot.

She's obviously not going to be any help. She's the reason the assholes found us.

Ajax and Devon crouch deeper in the jungle beyond Griffin, but neither of them have talents that could destroy or deflect a helicopter. Glancing farther down the path, I spot Andreas several feet behind me with his arms out as if to shield George, who's ended up next to him.

Drey is staring up at the choppers. Then his gaze drops to meet mine, his face taut with strain.

"I can't see any of them to mess with their heads. I can't project memories unless I'm looking at my target."

Maybe it doesn't matter. If the helicopters can't land anywhere nearby, we'll have a chance to make a run for it.

The thought has just passed through my mind when another earth-shaking *boom* reverberates from one of the choppers. With an unsettling creaking sound, several trees topple over farther along the crest of the hill, past Griffin's position.

With another thunderous impact, the same thing happens beyond Celine. She teeters on her feet but spins toward the sound with a smile that looks like relief.

The helicopters descend in unison toward the makeshift landing pads they've apparently created for themselves. My pulse drums frantically in my veins.

The second they're on the ground, who knows what else the guardians will throw at us.

We're running out of time. I have to do *something*.

I've got to use the talents *I* have, however I can.

I haven't formed more of a plan than that before I'm sprinting forward, charging toward Celine.

She brought them here. She's loyal to Clancy.

If I'm going to take back some kind of leverage for us, who better than her?

My tentacles fling forward over my shoulders in anticipation—but before I'm close enough to touch her, Celine flinches.

In the same instant, a rush of thrilling energy smacks into me.

My steps stumble. Did I just suck away some of her life without even touching her?

If my powers work from a distance now… I don't even know how to grapple with the mix of awe and revulsion that rises up at the possibility.

There isn't time to mull it over now. I flick a tentacle in the helicopter's direction but feel nothing at all.

It only worked across a distance of a couple of feet.

Still not all that useful in a fight… except as I intended to use it anyway.

But taking a hostage only works if the threat is obvious.

As Celine sways on her feet, I hurtle the last few steps toward Celine and slam my tentacles around her.

One grips her by the throat. The other pins her arms to her sides.

I yank her toward me, staying in view of the closer helicopter that's just touched down but partly sheltered by the trees. I'm not risking the chances that they have some way to fling one of those nets at me even from the ground.

Celine gasps and struggles in my hold. I tighten the tentacle around her neck enough to make it hard for her to speak, holding back the urge to drink in more of the energy my suckers can sense thrumming through her frame.

"Stay still, and we all get out of this," I say in a low voice that's more ragged than I'd like. Even going this far has made me queasy.

She might have betrayed us, but she's really still a kid. I can't totally blame her for being scared after everything she's experienced.

But I can't think of any other way to get us out of this standoff—or at least buy us enough time that one of the others can figure something out.

The roaring whir of the helicopter blades cuts out. I pitch my voice to carry as far as possible.

"Don't come any closer! I'll kill her if you try to take us."

Celine starts to squirm again, and I drop my voice so

only she can hear. "They don't want any of us dead. If you decide to go back to them after the rest of us have gotten away, I won't stop you."

The guardians have always avoided any kind of attack that could kill us in the past. We're valuable property, after all.

With so few of us shadowbloods, they wouldn't want to lose any of us completely. Especially not one who's both proven her loyalty to them and shown that her skills have a clear use in the field.

Celine doesn't appear to believe me, though, because she keeps twisting against my hold, forcing me to tense my extra appendages even tighter.

Clancy's voice resonates from his loudspeaker. "I don't think you want to do this, Dominic."

I can only make out the front half of the helicopter from my current position, its windows tinted too dark for me to decipher any figures inside. Even if Andreas joined me, he won't be able to help.

"I don't want you to take us back to the island," I holler back. "You try to grab any of my friends, and you can say goodbye to the rest of your shadowbloods."

He doesn't know what I'm capable of, not really. Sometimes *I'm* not even sure what I might do.

Celine lets out a choking sound. A shudder I do my best to suppress ripples through me.

The guardians have to back off—they have to—

Clancy breaks through my frantic thoughts. "If that's the price you want to pay, it's up to you. It's the six of you who matter the most."

The creak of a hinge and the thump of multiple sets of feet travel through the air. My heart stutters.

He doesn't care. Are the younger shadowbloods really expendable to him?

Celine whimpers in my grasp, a hopeless expression coming over her face. That's obviously how she's taken his words.

She thinks I'm actually going to murder her now.

My gambit wasn't enough. He's calling my bluff—and I'm not sure killing her would do us any good even if I wasn't bluffing.

A tiny whisper in the back of my head asks if maybe I should find out. I've never sapped all the life out of another human being purely for my own satisfaction before.

And this girl has already betrayed us once. Should I give her the chance to do it again?

I recoil from the impulse, yanking back my tentacles as a cold sweat breaks on my back.

No. *No.* I'm not a fucking murderer, no matter what else the guardians made me into.

At the same moment, Griffin steps forward, across the path, where he'll be in view of both helicopters. There's an unnerving intensity in his gaze.

He must have set down his cat sometime before. His arms are empty, one hand pressed close to his side as if he's concealing something against the fabric of his pants.

"Let's stop all the resisting now," he says, cool and even but loud enough for everyone including Clancy to hear him. "You should have known you were never getting away from the guardians. I led you to them before, and now I've led them to you."

I stare at him in bewilderment. But he said—he said it was Celine who signaled them somehow. She *admitted* it.

He was upset with her. She ran to greet them.

And now he's saying—

Celine whirls toward him. "You traitor! You ruined everything."

Fury vibrates through her hoarse voice, and understanding hits me in an icy smack.

Griffin's using his power on her—he's making her angry at him. He's tricking the guardians so they'll trust him and not her?

Or was he using his ability to manipulate her before, when she confessed, and he's been working on a way to get us back to the facility all along?

After everything Griffin's told us and how well I once knew him, my kneejerk reaction is to reject that thought. But I have no idea what his full plan is either way.

I never would have thought he'd have turned on us in the first place.

The only thing I'm sure of is that the guardians are the biggest threat we're facing. I take a step back into the trees, watching for their approach and bracing myself to fend them off if need be, as well as I can.

Celine marches part of the way toward Griffin and stalls there, wavering. "You're such a fucking asshole!"

"I've done what I needed to do to get by," Griffin replies, so calmly it's hard to imagine he could be generating all the rage she's showing at the same time. "Now it's time to go home."

"I don't want to go anywhere with *you*."

Clancy's voice carries through the jungle, unaltered by the loudspeaker this time. He's close.

"Let's keep our tempers cool and think this situation through rationally. We can all go back to the facility. No one will be punished."

Griffin nods as if agreeing with him. "It's for the best for everyone."

Celine lets out a sound that's close to a growl. She snatches a rock off the ground, large enough that she can't totally close her fingers around it.

"All you think about is yourself. You let us go through all this shit, and now you're laughing at us."

My pulse kicks up another notch. Should I try to use my power?

I twist my tentacles, testing the atmosphere around me, but no one's close enough for me to latch on to their energy now. Maybe Griffin will lure Clancy close enough that I can take him down?

But if that's what Griffin intended, it isn't how things go down.

"It was silly of you to think you could ever have things your way," Griffin tells Celine.

She barks out a wordless rasp of fury and launches herself at him with the stone raised.

As she comes, Griffin jerks up his lowered hand. A blade flashes in the sunlight.

He's got a small knife, maybe taken from the hotel kitchen. He's prepared to stab her with it—in what will look like self-defense.

It isn't really, though, it occurs to me with sickening

clarity. He's basically reeled her straight toward that blade like a fish hooked on a line.

Is this some kind of revenge for her betrayal? Or—

"Griffin!"

A body hurtles up the path, singe marks darkening pale skin and hair, arms heaving forward.

Jacob managed to break free from the net to race to his twin's protection.

The wallop of his power slams into Celine before Griffin's knife can. Her body whips backward, her neck wrenching to the side with a crack of her spine that rings through the air.

"Jake," Griffin says in a pained tone, his eyes wide with shock.

Jacob stumbles onto his knees. "I couldn't let her…"

Then a stream of electricity crashes into my back, and my brain short-circuits to blackness.

TWENTY-SEVEN

Riva

As the guardians usher us back into the island facility, I steal as many glances at Griffin as I can. My gut has been tangled in queasy knots since I woke up with my wrists cuffed and the clamp around my neck that squashes my throat, braced with my fellow shadowbloods in the back of a helicopter.

Griffin wasn't locked up like that then, and he strides along beside Clancy and the guardians now as if he's one of them. He holds his head high, his gaze steady.

My memories of the guardians' assault on us are blurry, bits and pieces scrambled by the electric jolts of the net that caught me. I saw Griffin claiming that he called Clancy to our spot—I saw Celine fly into a rage and lunge at him.

I believed her when she confessed before. I don't know how he could have provoked those specific details out of her about the girl she saw die and her fear of the "monsters" I might turn to for help.

Is it possible he somehow found the right emotional button to push on to make her admit to a betrayal she hadn't committed? Or was it only in the end he was manipulating her, so he could take credit for that betrayal?

Even if it's the latter, even if he was honest with us every moment before then… why did he do it?

He had a knife ready. I think he'd have killed her, with the excuse of self-defense, if Jacob hadn't thrown himself in there first.

None of it makes sense. All I know is that in the next few frantic seconds, I squirmed in the net, which zapped me hard enough that my vision whited out.

And then there was a prick on the back of my neck, and everything went dark until the helicopter.

The guardians obviously overwhelmed the shadowbloods who escaped the nets. All of us from our group of escapees are cuffed alongside me in our procession—except for Celine, of course.

I don't know what Clancy ordered the others to do with her body. He wouldn't have left it as evidence.

Even though chances are high that she's the one who ruined our chance at freedom, a twinge of guilt runs through my stomach, remembering her frantic expression and her neck snapping with the force of Jacob's power.

She didn't want to be there with us. If I hadn't pushed for all the kids we encountered to come with us, if I'd realized how hesitant she was sooner…

It's too late for that now. One more death that's at least partly on my conscience.

Ahead of me in the line, Jacob sways and shakes his head as if trying to clear it. I think they drugged him like the guys told me the guardians used to after our first escape attempt, to dampen their powers.

They've wrapped a heavy blindfold around Andreas's face so he can't aim projected memories at anyone. He's relying on Dominic to keep him on the right track, a tentacle tucked around his hand like a lead.

I can't see Zian, who's behind me now, but from his glazed eyes on the chopper, I'd bet they drugged him too. There aren't many ways to contain his combination of brawn and monstrous strength.

The cuffs are pretty solid on their own, though. The guardians have had lots of time to experiment with what can hold us shadowbloods back. I can't feel the effects of any drug, but I can tell from my furtive tests that I wouldn't be able to snap the chain.

Clancy stops partway down the front hall, just past the door to the cafeteria, and the rest of the procession halts with him. An older man stands there, looking over the line of us captives with a dour expression that fits perfectly with his sagging features and posture.

Despite the sense of deflation he gives off, his voice comes out crisp and firm. "This is all of them, then?"

Clancy holds his posture with easy certainty, as if he isn't the slightest bit ruffled by the events of the past couple of days. "We lost one of the second generation. Not an especially valuable talent."

The older man grunts, his frown deepening. "We'll talk about it later. You'd better get them shut away before they flee on you again."

"If they do, we'll simply round them up like we did this time," Clancy says without showing a hint of concern.

I grit my teeth at his dismissiveness. He *wouldn't* have rounded us up if Celine—or Griffin—hadn't signaled him.

But what are the chances we'll get another opportunity as good as the one we just lost? He'll have figured out that we triggered the emergency system—and he'll have adjusted it to prevent the same gambit.

Every helicopter delivery will be heavily guarded from now on, no doubt.

We had our chance, by far the best chance we were ever going to get, and it's been wrenched from our grasp.

The guardians march us on down the hallway, pausing here and there to direct one kid or another into their rooms. I think we've passed mine, although it's a little hard to tell when the rocky walls look so similar throughout the facility.

My nerves prickle with uneasiness when the last of the younger shadowbloods, a drooping Lindsay, disappears behind her thudding door.

It's just the six of us "Firsts" now. Does Clancy have something else in mind for us?

Most of the guardians have drifted off during our walk. Only four remain with Clancy, two up ahead with him and Griffin and two others bringing up the rear.

They all grip the gun-like weapons that can shoot streams of electricity like something out of that ghost-capturing movie we all watched years ago. Although the sizzling bolts zap our bodies rather than our spirits.

The end result is the same—trapped and under their control.

I never expected to relate to the ghosts.

Clancy escorts us into a slightly larger room with a row of five chairs spaced wide apart along the middle of the space. As the guardians lead each of us to a chair, they position themselves between us.

Our collaborating is always what Clancy's been most worried about. He's not taking any chances.

Will he let us even be in the same room together again after this?

My worries form a pulsing ache in my stomach. I swallow against the collar and wince at the choking sensation.

Clancy strides to the front of the room where a large screen about five feet across hangs on the wall. He picks up a control from a small metal side table and paces past the screen.

Griffin hangs back by the side table, watching. His face remains as blank as it was during our first reunion here.

I can't tell if he's still feeling anything at all.

Even if his ploy with Celine was meant to help us, could the chaos of the fight have screwed up the progress he's made? Sent him back into his closed-off state, every flicker of emotion automatically dismissed?

Clancy clicks a button, and the screen lights up, though it's only a flat, pale gray at the moment. He swivels to face the five of us.

"You have not abided by the terms of our agreement. I've offered you the opportunity to do something incredibly constructive with your powers while learning how to use them in the best possible ways, and you threw that generosity in my face."

The choke-collar suppresses my derisive laugh.

Generosity? He was using us to fill his bank account.

No awareness of his hypocrisy shows in Clancy's expression. He taps the controller lightly against his thigh, considering all of us like a professor contemplating the expulsion of a bunch of disruptive students.

"You must see now how impossible striking out on your own is," he goes on, with a condescending edge that raises my hackles even more. "You were never meant to have normal lives. You *aren't* normal. But if we work together, you can have something better than anyone else in the Guardianship would be willing to offer you."

Does he expect a response?

Jacob and Zian stare at him dully. Andreas can't see him at all.

Dominic sits in the chair next to me, a shiver running through his tentacles and his mouth set in a flat line. His gaze darts around the room, but I'm not sure what he's looking for.

And with my voice cut off, I can't answer even if I wanted to.

Clancy squares his shoulders with an imperious air. "I'm hoping that you've learned your lesson, and we can move forward as I planned. But I can't allow more diversions. I have a mission that some of you will be sent on, one you should want to see fulfilled as much as I do. You can accept that challenge with full cooperation, or I'll assign you to continued testing until we find an effective way of harnessing your powers and ensuring your compliance."

That doesn't sound ominous at all. I contain a shiver of my own.

Jacob manages to cock his head with a trace of alertness. But there's still a faint slur in his voice from the drugs. "What mission?"

Clancy brings up an image on the screen—a video, panning through a dusty village of ramshackle huts and a few cars that look at least three decades out of date. The only detail giving away the modern time period is the high-tech army tank standing off to the side in the first shot.

The scene is mostly brown and gray except for the blotches of deepening red that scatter the ground... and the bodies slumped there. The camera takes in a few dozen corpses, fresh enough that blood still seeps from some of their wounds.

Men. Women. Children. All of them dressed in simple tees or blouses, ratty jeans or canvas slacks.

Despite my resistance to anything Clancy wants to show us, my chest clenches up in horror.

Clancy motions toward the video. "The national government of the country where this slaughter took place has been dealing with a large group of hostile insurgents for several years. The group's current MO is to hold an entire rural village hostage, killing the civilians one by one until the government complies with their demands. When the military has attempted to intervene, the insurgents use the villagers as shields and have mostly escaped unscathed... while leaving no survivors behind."

He rests his cool gaze on us. "Government officials heard of my services and reached out to me. They expect based on past behavior patterns that the terrorists will strike again within a week. To ensure the villagers' safety and push back against the insurgents to discourage or even prevent future attacks, they need a team with skills beyond their own."

And that's where he wants us to come in.

The worst part is that the sight of the decimated village tugs at my heart. I *would* want to protect people like that if my powers could shield them.

But how can we trust anything Clancy says now? Who knows what other ulterior motives he could have?

Those officials are probably offering him a huge fee, for one thing.

Does it really matter, though? Would I rather go back to being prodded and tested, knowing I let a bunch of innocent people die that I could have saved, just to spite him?

That's exactly the dilemma Clancy wants us to face.

He crosses his arms over his chest, his blue eyes turning penetrating. "You'll need to agree to take on this mission without knowing which of you will actually be sent out. And understanding that if you agree and you sabotage the assignment, your friends *will* suffer for it. There are lengths I'd have preferred not to go to, but if that's what's necessary for you to respect the responsibility you're being given, so be it."

My skin turns clammy beneath my shirt.

Of course, he's made it clear that if we *don't* agree, we'll all be tormented regardless.

We've gotten out of every tight spot we've found ourselves in before now... but my scrambling mind can't identify a single shimmer of hope.

Clancy nods to the guardians around us. "I'm sending you back to your rooms to recover and think on it. Any harm that you inflict on my people will be inflicted on yours twice over, so be careful how you use your powers. You have twenty-four hours to make a decision. Choose wisely."

With a rasp of his heel, he turns his back on us.

TWENTY-EIGHT

Andreas

At the sight of Riva sitting at the far end of the cafeteria, my heart just about leaps out of my chest.

I haven't crossed paths with any of my fellow Firsts since Clancy gave us his little presentation two days ago, even though yesterday I agreed to go along with his mission.

The others must have too. I can't imagine any of them consigning themselves to total isolation and torture instead.

At least this way we might have some wiggle room to decide our fate.

But I was starting to think he wasn't going to let us mingle with each other at all anymore. Not on the island, anyway.

As I walk over, holding myself back from sprinting to her side in case that would provoke the guardians, Riva glances up from her plate and sees me. The brightening of her face washes away the stress of the past two days.

At the same time, my stomach dips. I glance around the room, noting the two guardians in their usual posts near the door.

Nothing about the cafeteria looks different. I can't believe that Clancy is offering us this opportunity to talk out of the goodness of his heart, though.

The fact that he's letting it happen means it could benefit him in some way. He's got to be monitoring us even more closely than he was before.

We'll have to watch every word so carefully. Not let a single hint of mutiny show.

A wobble of doubt runs through my pulse, and there's an instant when I almost avoid Riva's table altogether, as desperately as I want to bask in her presence. What if I'm misjudging the situation even with my sense of caution?

Wouldn't it look more suspicious if I *don't* even talk to her? Any problems we had in the past were nothing to do with things I said.

I shoot her a smile and a nod, passing by, and quickly spoon chili onto my plate from a tureen. The hearty, spicy scent does nothing to settle my nerves as I sit down across from her.

"It's good to see you."

Riva smiles back at me, but the corners of her mouth stay tight. "Same. You've been okay?"

She's taking the same careful approach I meant to. Good.

"Yeah." I dig my fork in among the beans and bits of

ground beef. "I haven't seen anyone except the younger shadowbloods until now."

"Me neither." She takes a bite from her mostly cleaned plate and scans the room warily. "I guess Clancy decided *everyone* here was better off if we still had some contact."

"Everyone" as in him too. Yep, she's definitely come to the same conclusions about his motivations as I have.

"Wouldn't want morale to dip too low," I say with forced wryness.

Riva's head droops. She tears a chunk off her roll but then just holds the piece rather than bringing it to her mouth.

Then she drags in a breath. "I guess we're stuck with this place. Might as well make the best of it."

The strain in her voice and the quiver of anguish that touches my chest through my mark fill in the blanks in her words. She's afraid of how true those statements might be.

A similar hopelessness swells inside me. I've been thinking it over since the moment I regained consciousness on the helicopter, heading back here—how could we pull off another escape?

No brilliant plans have occurred to me. Or even mediocre plans, for that matter.

Every spark of an idea that lights in my mind sputters out before I follow it more than a couple of steps from its instigation.

Clancy has too much power. He'll have safeguarded all the weaknesses of the facility that we've discovered.

And the very fact of being on an island with little means to leave it limits our options to barely any.

"We'll make the best of it," I agree, attempting to push a little energy into the words. A nudge of encouragement that if there is an opportunity to turn this situation around, we'll find it.

Riva aims another smile at me, smaller but softer, so I think I've succeeded. She pops the bit of roll into her mouth and chews thoughtfully. "Have you found out anything more from Clancy about his mission or whatever else he's working on?"

Her wording and her tone give me the sense that she doesn't mean finding out only by conventional means. She thinks I might have learned something interesting from his memories.

But I haven't dared to sneak a peek inside the facility leader's head since we've gotten back. I've only seen him briefly anyway, when he came to collect my answer yesterday.

I shake my head. "No. He hasn't come around to talk to me."

She hums to herself, her gaze going momentarily distant. "I wondered a little about the older man from the Guardianship who talked to him when we got back. It sounded like he might have some say in the missions or other things." She pauses. "I guess you didn't even see him to recognize him—they had your eyes covered at that point."

"I didn't." But she's caught my interest. I did hear a fragment of conversation between Clancy and a gravelly voice I didn't recognize.

Is there still someone else who has authority over Clancy himself? Could there be a weakness we could exploit not in the facility's construction but in the hierarchy of the guardians?

"I'm not sure I could describe him all that well," Riva goes on in a casual tone. "I've never been as good at bringing memories to life as you are."

She flicks her gaze toward me, a meaningful look, and understanding snaps into place. If I wanted to search the other guardians' memories for this man, I could get a solid impression of him by looking inside *her* mind first.

My spirits lift, but the rest of me balks with a twinge of uneasiness. I obviously don't do a good enough job suppressing my discomfort, because Riva's brow knits with concern. "What's the matter?"

"I…" I grapple with the words and decide that it doesn't matter if I express this regret. The past has already happened—Clancy can't expect me to feel *happy* about how our escape fell apart.

Swallowing thickly, I meet Riva's gaze. "It's been bothering me that I didn't figure out what was going on with Griffin in time. I *should* have been able to pick up on these things—I'm supposed to be good at reading people in all kinds of ways—but I totally missed something so important…"

The previous time we were caught, I missed recognizing that Griffin was there at all, pretending to be Jacob. This time, I missed what he'd picked up on: that Celine wasn't actually happy about gaining her freedom.

That she was looking for opportunities to signal the guardians and screw the rest of us over.

I'd been searching *his* memories when I got the chance, checking for any sign that his efforts to help us weren't genuine. My guilt about my previous lapse made me extra conscientious… but in the wrong way.

I know that his act in the end, when they caught us, really was an act. Claiming he'd called them in was the first lie he told through the whole trek.

But I was so focused on confirming his loyalty, it didn't even occur to me to worry about the younger shadowbloods. I got misdirected all over again, and now I can only blame myself.

If I'd checked the kids earlier, if I'd noticed the signs of Celine's discomfort, maybe we could have stopped her before she alerted Clancy. Maybe we'd have made it to the city, however things would have played out from there.

Riva doesn't challenge my implying that Griffin was the one who betrayed us—for all I know, she thinks it's actually possible. "It was a chaotic situation, and we were dealing with a lot. We all had the chance to notice that something was off, and none of us did. You can't take the responsibility."

That's not what I'm really stewing over, though. I'm afraid that if I try to get us out of this mess again, I'll miss yet another crucial detail.

But as Riva gazes back at me with the taint of sorrow in her bright brown eyes, a renewed sense of resolve grips my chest.

It's better to try than to give up, right? We definitely aren't getting anywhere if we all throw up our hands and roll over.

I want to turn the sadness in Riva's expression into hope.

I reach out to take her hand, leaning closer as if with a

lover's intent. But really it's to make it harder for any outside party to spot the ruddy gleam I know comes into my eyes as I slip into her memories.

She doesn't have all that many of Clancy, considering we've only been here for a matter of weeks and his appearances have been sporadic. I flit through the images that I know don't match our arrival yesterday, wincing inwardly at a glimpse of a bedroom where Zian crouches with obvious agitation in a corner.

There. We're walking down the main hall in a line, Clancy in the lead, me with the blindfold I've only worn one other time—when I first woke up in the facility.

I linger in the recollection, focusing as Riva did on the grim white-haired man Clancy pauses to talk to. Etching his doughy features in my own memory.

To look for him again, I don't have to know his name. I only need a clear sense of his presence.

When I'm sure I've absorbed every detail, I pull back out of Riva's skull, squeezing her fingers as I do. She returns the gesture, studying me.

"We still have each other," I say. "That's what's most important."

And we'll keep working with each other to get away from Clancy. Let her hear that underlying message, the one I don't dare say out loud.

Clancy makes no further appearances throughout the rest of that day and the next. When I'm ushered into my stone-walled bedroom in the evening, my stomach churns with impatient tension.

He expected to be sending us on his new mission within a week. We're almost halfway through.

How can I get a glimpse inside his mind without him realizing that I'm up to something? If he catches me at it, I have no idea how he'll punish me... or the others, knowing their torment will hurt me more.

I sprawl on my bed and stew on the problem, running through possibility after possibility for both bringing him to me and ensuring he's otherwise occupied enough that I can get a good fix on his memories. Maybe I'm not giving up, but I still have to make sure I consider every angle if I'm going to do this right.

It must be at least a couple of hours before an inspiration strikes that I don't immediately dismiss. I turn the idea over, poking and prodding at it.

It's by far the best I've thought of, but that doesn't mean it's *good*. Fuck, I wish I could talk to Dominic for his thoughtful insight, or even Jacob with his incisive logic.

Even if I could see them, I wouldn't be able to talk about this, though. So it comes down to me.

I take a few slow, deep breaths, summoning the image of Riva's face in my mind. Reminding myself of why it's so important that I get this done.

Then I wrap my arm around my abdomen and double over on the bed.

A fake groan spills from my mouth. I twist and shudder as if in the grip of a wave of nausea.

The play-acting isn't enough. I need a blast of reality to really sell the performance.

I've told my friends dozens of stories from the minds I've dipped into over the years, across our early missions. Always picking the amusing or intriguing.

But there've been darker memories I've uncovered, that I never wanted to think about myself, let alone inflict on anyone else. Moments of the violence and horror humans are just as capable of as monsters.

They linger on in the back of my head where I've buried them as deep as I can. I dredge up one of the worst now and hug my belly tighter.

Gore. Gurgled cries. Slashes of a knife. A spray of blood, and organs jumbling—

I lurch right over the side of the bed to vomit onto the floor. The acid sears my throat as I gag and sputter.

The guardians have been watching me, because of course they have. I've barely had time to let out another groan when the door to my room hisses open.

Two guardians lift me onto a rolling hospital-style cot, murmuring urgently to each other as they do. I keep my eyes closed and jerk one way and another as if in the throes of internal agony.

They hurry me to a room that holds brighter lights and a woman who speaks in puzzled tones as she takes my temperature and a blood sample. I figured they'd have a doctor on staff somewhere in this place.

But shadowbloods don't generally get sick. Our enhanced bodies come with hyperactive healing skills. I can't remember ever having more than a brief sniffle growing up.

Clancy will have to come—out of concern for his "resources" if nothing else—won't he?

I lie there through a couple more spells of gagging and mumbled answers to the doctor's questions. My heart gradually sinks.

I could have miscalculated. Maybe I haven't accomplished anything beyond giving myself a stomachache.

Then brisk footsteps rap outside. The leader of the facility strides into the room—and he's brought a bonus I hadn't even let myself hope for.

Through my lowered eyelashes, I see Dominic trailing behind Clancy, my friend's mouth tight with worry.

"See if you can sense any internal injuries," Clancy orders him.

Dominic comes up beside me and rests his tentacles gently on the bare skin of my wrist and neck. I crack my eyes open just enough to make out Clancy behind him— turned mostly away from me in hushed conference with the doctor.

He's let down his guard. He doesn't suspect anything from me. Perfect.

I give Dominic's hand a light tap, the tiniest of nudges to the left so he'll completely block the doctor's view of my face if she happens to glance our way. That's all it takes.

The connection we each share with Riva might be marked on our skin, but the five of us—no, the *six* of us— all know each other down to our bones. Deeper than I think Clancy can even conceive of.

Dom's eyebrows rise just a smidge. He shifts over without a word.

Keeping my eyelids low, I stare at the back of Clancy's head—and tumble into it.

I hold the image of the man Riva saw at the front of my thoughts and prod the whirl of Clancy's past impressions with it. One after another, memories float to the surface of him speaking to that older man: in a video chat, in person, on the phone.

In every conversation, tension runs through Clancy's body. He keeps his voice smooth, but I can feel the urge in his throat to become terser.

He calls the other man Richmond. And Richmond has a lot of ideas about how Clancy should be running things, often referring to "the board" of the Guardianship that it sounds like he speaks for.

I push harder, faster, for a snippet of anything relevant to our current situation. And then I slide into a vision of Clancy's cave-like office here, Richmond wearing the same clothes Riva saw three days ago.

"Even with all your precautions, thirteen of them made it right off the island," Richmond is saying in a patronizing tone. "Including the six that are by far the most valuable."

Clancy stands stiffly behind his desk. "I retrieved all of them before there was any trouble."

Richmond snorts. "Any trouble other than two deaths and a whole lot of manpower expended. Look, the board has given you the leeway to try your approach, but a misstep like this calls the whole endeavor into question. There's been talk of superseding your right to direct the Guardianship. You know you'd never have taken it at all if Balthazar hadn't vanished on us."

Balthazar? My focus momentarily wavers, but then I remember the conversation Riva related to the rest of us, asking Clancy about the three founding families of the Guardianship.

He told her that one of the three founders had pulled back from the guardians. I have to guess that's who Richmond means.

At the implied threat, Clancy's spine goes even more rigid. Richmond is purposefully not mentioning his own opinion, but I can taste in his tone that he's been a vocal participant in the "talking" he mentioned.

"I've just landed a major contract," Clancy says quickly. "Now that I have a better idea of how the shadowbloods operate, I'll be able to keep them in line— and show just how much I can accomplish with them. You have to give me the chance to prove it."

Richmond rubs his fleshy chin. "I'll discuss the matter with the others. You can be sure we'll be watching closely. If you—"

A tug of my arm brings me back to the present. Dominic is leaning over me, his gaze intent.

"Thank you," he says over his shoulder.

Clancy is approaching, carrying a glass of water. Through my cluttered awareness, I piece together what must have happened: Clancy was going to come over earlier, but Dominic diverted him for long enough to snap me out of my power's daze.

Dom pats my shoulder. "Can you sit up?"

I push myself upright with a sway to sell my performance and sip the water. Clancy inspects me with his penetrating gaze.

"The best we can determine, something you ate must have disagreed with you that's now out of your system," he says in a clipped tone. "There's no sign of illness or internal damage. You can sleep here for the night while we get your room cleaned."

I nod my thanks and lie back down as he escorts Dominic out of the room. My thoughts keep buzzing, louder than the hum of the overhead lights.

Clancy is in danger of losing his grand dream. He's got a lot riding on this upcoming mission.

I don't know what we can do with that yet, but it gives us a foothold. If he's desperate, then we have leverage.

But who the hell can I tell that to without giving any budding scheme we could form away? I can't plan a coup and pull it off all by myself.

I roll onto my side on the thin cot mattress, closing my eyes again. The answer comes to me like a ghost rising from the grave.

Griffin. Griffin is at the middle of this mess, tangled between Clancy's objectives and ours.

He's just proven his loyalty to the guardians—in Clancy's eyes, anyway.

I don't know what the others think, but I've looked inside our former friend's head. I've followed the reasoning in his words and the cadence of his voice.

He understands us just as well as we do each other. He's with us.

And now he's the only one I can turn to.

TWENTY-NINE

Riva

I hear Nadia before I see her—her dry laugh carrying from between the trees by the row of obstacle courses. I recognize it, but there's a dull edge to it that wasn't there before.

It's harder to spot her than I expect. I find her standing with one of the other older teen shadowbloods and Ajax near the climbing course, dressed in black sweats and a dark gray tee that blend with the shadows between the trees.

Before I've even spoken to her, my heart sinks.

The three of them glance over at me as I emerge into the clearing by the first of the rope ladders. I nod to them all, my gaze holding Nadia's.

"Hey. No neon today?"

She rubs her toned arms self-consciously. "I guess I just haven't been feeling all that bright lately."

Her mouth tilts into a half-smile, but I can't find even

a hint of good humor in it. If my heart was heavy before, now it feels like it's morphed into a lump of lead.

Ajax runs his hand over the sheen of stubble on his dark scalp, but he can't seem to think of anything to say at all. Only the third kid, the one who wasn't part of our escape, shows any energy.

He claps his hands together. "Come on! Are we going to climb or what?"

The form of a guardian stirs farther away along the edge of the clearing, with a clearing of her throat. "This is time for training, not talking."

I hold back a bitter snort. When have they ever given us much time to talk—to do anything other than train and bodily necessities like eat?

The guy who clapped his hands grasps the ladder, and Nadia and Ajax shuffle into line behind him automatically. The droop of Nadia's shoulders and sluggishness of Ajax's movements send a jabbing sensation through my gut.

I touch Nadia's arm. "Your brightness got us through a lot. Remember that." And Ajax's shoulder. "You heard things the rest of us couldn't."

I don't know how well my attempt at raising their spirits lands. Nadia only dips her head, and the smile Ajax shoots at me is fleeting. The energy in the clearing remains downcast.

What else can I say?

A weird sense of homesickness winds through me, missing the brief days we had our freedom. Not because I loved tramping through the jungle with not much more than crackers to eat, but because we did all help each other.

It's not just the six Firsts who can accomplish a lot together. All of us shadowbloods make an amazing team.

When we have the chance.

As I watch Nadia and then Ajax scale the ladder with obvious reluctance, my heart seems to plummet all the way to the ground.

As difficult as our trek on the mainland was, it was better than this. We deserve to be free.

We aren't the tools Clancy sees us as or the experimental property we are to most of the other guardians. We're *people*—we shouldn't be owned by anyone.

We sure as hell don't owe the Guardianship anything after the hell we've already been through at their hands.

Who would Nadia and Ajax and all the others be if they could simply... *be*? Have the space and peace to explore what a regular human life could look like, on their terms?

I want to give them that, so fucking badly. But I don't have a clue how.

I'm just reaching for the ladder myself—not that I really want to go through the course, but I've got to do something to look like a participant and not a rebel— when the underbrush rustles behind me. "Riva?"

My pulse hiccups before I even glance back. It's Griffin's voice, soft and even.

As I turn around, he comes to a stop at the end of the path.

It's hard to imagine that I confused him with his twin just weeks ago. All I can see now are the ways they differ— the shagginess of Griffin's slightly longer blond hair in contrast with Jacob's smoothness, the gentler lines of his face.

The distance in his eyes, as if the whole sky really is contained in their blue irises.

I clamp down on the urge to hug myself. "What's up?"

His mouth forms a small smile. "I was hoping we could spend a little time together. We haven't seen each other since... everything. There are some things I'd like to explain."

Searching his gaze, I grapple with my response. I'm pretty sure he did what he did to protect the rest of us, not because he was the real traitor among us. But not one hundred percent sure.

And either way, I'm *supposed* to believe he betrayed us. What reaction would the guardians expect to see to keep up that ruse?

I raise one shoulder in a partial shrug. "I'm not interested in hearing your explanations."

He holds out his hand. "Please. For old time's sake?"

Have I resisted enough to sell my wariness? I'm also supposed to be trying to cooperate with the new status quo, to avoid me or the other guys getting punished.

I settle for ignoring his hand, as much as I'd like to take it, but stepping toward him. "Fine. What did you have in mind?"

Griffin's expression twitches as he lowers his hand, a trace of discomfort crossing it that I wouldn't have expected to see even a week ago. The feelings that've woken up inside him haven't vanished, then.

He motions for me to follow him and doesn't speak again until we're partway along the narrow path. "You seemed to enjoy tossing the knives during our last meeting. Clancy agreed to give us private use of the shooting range."

I press my hand to my mouth to contain a sputter of laughter. "And you're not worried you'll end up with a bullet in you?"

Griffin's tone lightens—just slightly, but any break from his new typical monotone is a relief to hear. "You managed not to stab me last time, so I think my chances are good."

We cross the stone bridge over the thin but deep river that courses away from the waterfall and climb the damp stone steps to the hidden entrance. The cool spray flecks my skin, sharp against the tropical heat.

Just inside the entrance to the shooting range, with the water rushing down inches away, Griffin stops me with a careful grasp of my wrist. He leans in so I can hear him over the warble of the falls.

"We aren't being directly monitored here. Clancy went along with a lot of concessions... because he thinks I'm trying to get him the data he wants."

He pushes up one sleeve to reveal a band like the ones the guardians made Zian and me wear—in the hopes of monitoring the forming of our marked connection.

My stomach clenches. "I—"

"It's okay," Griffin murmurs. He takes my hand, interlacing our fingers, and lets out a sigh that speaks of days of bottled tension releasing. "I wouldn't want to 'help' him like that anyway. It just buys us a little privacy. He said it only records physiological data, not voices, but I thought we should be extra careful."

Hence talking by the waterfall. I nod.

Griffin's head dips closer, the side of his face grazing mine. "I'm sorry. This isn't—I didn't want us to end up back here. I don't know…"

He trails off, but the anguish in his words is unmistakable. Any lingering doubts I felt disintegrate.

I ease closer to him, slipping my arm around his back in a loose embrace. The crisply airy scent that clings to him fills my lungs and tingles through the shadows in my blood.

"Why didn't you tell us you were worried about Celine?"

Griffin exhales raggedly. "I couldn't tell if there was really something to be worried about or if I was misreading her. It wasn't anything obvious. Just here and there, especially when we were in the helicopter, I got flickers of emotion from her that felt upset, or defiant, in ways that didn't match everyone else. I didn't want to accuse her of anything when I had no idea what was actually going on with her."

"You were sure in the end, though."

"Yeah." He swallows audibly. "She was so relieved —*happy*—when she heard the choppers coming for us. And a little triumphant. It was obvious then that she'd done something… I think she'd brought a device that would send out a location, but one that couldn't be set up properly if she was trying to carry it on her. I was watching her pretty carefully before Zian pulled us away."

I have a vague memory of Celine darting out of sight in the middle of our rush out of the facility. She could have grabbed something then.

But I also remember what she said to me when she acknowledged her betrayal. "It might not have been you stopping her before. It's possible she wasn't totally sure if she should use it or not... until after I admitted that we might turn to the shadowkind for help."

"Either way..." I feel Griffin's wince in the movement of his features next to mine. "I didn't want her dead. It was just—in the moment, when they'd arrived and they'd already incapacitated most of you, and Dominic's strategy didn't work—all I could think was that the guardians were going to take us back either way. And the only way I'd be able to fix things was if Clancy believed I was still on his side."

"And he wouldn't have believed that if Celine was alive to tell him she'd signaled them," I fill in.

"But maybe I was wrong. Maybe there was some way we could have still escaped. It was hard to see clearly with my feelings and my ideas all jumbled together—I'm not used to sorting through them anymore. I thought I saw our best chance, so I took it, because I thought I had to, but I can't say that was right."

A tremor runs through his lanky frame. "I'm going to get better. I'll get used to balancing both again. Andreas managed to arrange to see me yesterday—he's found out a few things—I have some ideas for using this mission to turn things back in our favor."

Hope flutters up through my chest. "What?"

"I'll have to see what I can pull off. Clancy might believe I'm standing with him, but that doesn't mean he listens to me all that much." Griffin pauses. "I don't think we can end this while *he's* still alive, though."

I absorb that statement with only the faintest twinge of uneasiness.

The current head of the guardians is willing to torture us to bend us to his will. Why should we give a shit about his well-being?

"Whatever you figure out, let me know as much as you can," I tell him, my nerves thrumming with the possibility of a new plan within reach.

"I'll do my best. He seems to still trust me, but he's being even more cautious with the rest of you." Griffin brushes a tentative kiss to my forehead that lights up my nerves in a totally different way and then eases back. "We should probably do a little shooting so he doesn't wonder why we'd have skipped that part completely."

I cock my head. "A chance for me to let out my aggression before you start your supposed seduction."

Griffin chuckles, but his cheeks flush at the same time. "Something like that."

Farther into the cave, I pick a pistol off the rack somewhat at random, set a pair of earmuffs in place, and let out a few rounds at one of the targets. Griffin takes a more measured approach, selecting his gun with care and then firing each shot with a moment of contemplation in between.

Even so, my bullseyes end up tattered while his shots dapple the two inner rings more haphazardly.

His mouth twists as he studies the result. "Blasting things apart was never something I took to naturally."

"We all have our own talents," I say, with a fond smile to show I think that's a good thing.

He reloads his gun and then gazes down at it. "Do you want to keep going?"

I consider my new target and wrinkle my nose. "I think I've worked through all my urge to shoot things. You're definitely safe now."

Griffin laughs. "Then maybe we could talk a little more? If there's anything else you'd want to ask me to feel better about how things went down, you can go ahead."

I recognize his phrasing as being for the benefit of any guardians listening in. "Yeah. I'm ready to hear you out."

We set aside our guns and earmuffs before meandering back to the waterfall. Griffin turns to me, setting one hand on my waist with his thumb stroking up over the bare skin beneath my tee.

"I— Can I just hold you for a bit?" he murmurs. "I never feel as much like myself as when we're touching."

Affection swells inside me so abruptly I lose my breath. "Yeah, of course."

He lowers his head next to mine again until we're cheek to cheek, sliding his arm around me so his whole forearm rests against my lower back where my tee has ridden up. His other hand traces along my arm to align them side by side, his fingers loosely cupping my elbow.

His warmth wraps around me, and every inch of my skin tingles with his closeness.

A breath shudders out of him as if he's found some peace in me that he's been missing for ages. He hugs me a little tighter.

"I missed you so much. All that time before… I didn't even know how much I did because I couldn't *feel* it—but it was all there underneath, and now all that pent-up loss is hitting me."

Tears well behind my eyes. "I missed you too. Every single day."

"I want to be everything I should have been before. I want to give you what you really needed. I don't know—I don't know if I'll ever be totally back to normal, but I'm going to try."

I choke up at the rawness of his voice. "I know you are. You've already done a lot. We've all made mistakes."

We've all had to do things we'd rather not have done in the fight for our freedom. I can't blame Griffin for the life he meant to take without condemning the rest of us dozens of times over.

Griffin's fingertips trace a gentle circle on my back. "My moonbeam, lighting the way for me."

Suddenly the tears that welled up before are flooding my eyes. I blink hard and turn my head to seek out Griffin's mouth.

Our lips collide with a rush of heated breath. He kisses me tenderly at first and then harder, as if he's pouring himself into the embrace.

As if he's offering himself up to me in every way he can, showing me I've got all of him.

Desire flares low in my belly. I wrap my arms around him, and he nudges us backward with a stifled groan.

My shoulders press against the rock wall of the hall. The need blazing through me sears away the brief chill of the damp surface.

I force myself to pull back a few inches, to gaze up into Griffin's face. He stares down at me with a wildness in his expression that I've never seen before, here or in the past.

The storm of adoration and hunger in his brilliant eyes unravels me. I'm bringing him back to his old self with every touch, every embrace.

Every brush of skin against skin.

I want more. I want to see every bit of the boy I lost surfacing through the frightening emptiness of the guardians' torture.

My hand rises to his cheek. My voice comes out in a whisper. "How much would you like to feel right now?"

Griffin wets his lips, the intensity in his gaze only deepening. "Everything I can."

I reach for the hem of his shirt and tug. Griffin lifts his arms to help me peel it off him, peering at me avidly.

When I reach for my own tee, his chest hitches. "Riva…"

"We won't give him what he's looking for," I say, tipping my head toward one of the bands that circle his upper arms. "There's so much else we can do."

For a second, Griffin's expression shifts with a trace of what might be fear. I hesitate, knowing the awakening of his emotions has come with a heap of pain.

Then he sets his hands over mine, and we strip off my shirt together.

Griffin lets out a low sound from deep in his throat and bows his head to kiss my shoulder. I slip one arm around his leanly muscled back and tangle my fingers in his rumpled hair.

Everywhere our chests touch, bliss sparks. The dark

essence twined through my body roars louder than the waterfall.

This man is meant for me, and I am meant for him. Just as much as the others.

Maybe it makes sense that I lost him first and found him last.

I yank Griffin's mouth back to mine. He trails his fingers along my spine and around my waist.

They pause at the band of my sports bra. I nip his lower lip between my teeth, reveling in his stuttered breath, and yank that off too so I'm completely bare from the waist up.

Griffin traces the soft ridges of my abdomen up to the curves of my breasts. He curls his fingers around the slopes carefully.

I've never seen anything as miraculous as the interplay of tender devotion and scorching lust etched across his features.

"I don't—I don't know exactly what I'm doing," he admits haltingly. "I've never—I imagined, before, but that's all. But I can feel what makes you feel good."

It hadn't occurred to me that he'd have even less idea about sex than the other guys. Of course the guardians wouldn't have exposed him to provocative videos and encouraged that kind of release while they were attempting to erase every emotion from him.

They didn't have to worry about giving him an outlet for his urges because they were stealing his entire capacity for desire.

"Your approach seems to be working just fine," I reassure him. "We've all been figuring it out as we go."

Something inside us calls to each other—directs our desire toward completion. I can already tell that the hardest part won't be enjoying this interlude but avoiding giving in to the hunger to fully consummate our connection.

Griffin kisses me again, teasing our mouths against each other until he finds just the right angle to press harder. When I whimper against his lips, he starts caressing my breasts.

He tests every bit of that terrain with his palms, his fingers, his thumbs. Stroking softer and harder, back and forth and in quickening circles.

When he catches one nipple between two of his fingers with a swift squeeze, the moan that tumbles from my lips is echoed by his matching groan. He repeats the gesture, kissing me harder as if drinking down the pleasure he's conjuring in my body.

My hips rock toward him of their own accord. Griffin drops one hand to trace the curve of my hip.

His voice comes out in a ragged murmur. "You need more. But we can't—"

He cuts himself off as if coming to a decision on his own—and hefts me against him braced between his body and the passage wall. The rough stone digs into my back, probably leaving a dimpled impression, but I can't find it in me to care when I'm melded this tightly with the man I've loved for so long.

As my legs splay around him, our groins locking together through our clothes, a different sort of need grips me.

I kiss him again and hold my face close to his. "I love you."

The second the words come out, I feel abruptly sheepish. "But you already know that, don't you? You always knew."

Griffin nuzzles the side of my face, his breath washing over me in its own caress. "This is the first time I've gotten to hear you say it out loud. I—I love you too. I don't think I even know how much yet. The feeling just keeps growing."

I close my eyes against a renewed rush of tears, bittersweet. The joy of being back with him; the pain of knowing how trapped we still are.

The darkness inside spurs me on, desperate for the merging I'm going to refuse it. I grind against the erection straining at Griffin's pants, and he muffles a groan in my hair.

We can't have that ultimate fusion yet. I'm not sure either of us is quite ready for it anyway, regardless of what ideas our bodies might have.

But we can still claim a different kind of satisfaction.

My fingertips skate across Griffin's back. He works over one breast with an increasingly confident hand as he keeps me balanced with the other.

We buck against each other through frantic kisses. The friction against my pussy floods me with waves of giddy heat.

And Griffin can sense every swell of delight. He adjusts his angle by increments, finding just the spot to send me spiraling higher.

Oh, God, to actually *fuck* this man—

I bury that thought under the rising whirlwind of bliss. We rut and groan and devour each other, my heart drumming out a desperate rhythm.

My essence screams out for him—and my release crashes over me. I quake in Griffin's embrace, biting his lip hard enough to draw blood.

Griffin lets out a growl low in his throat, his hips still bucking. Then his shoulders stiffen.

A final groan reverberates from his lungs. He clutches me to him, mumbling a litany of devotion by my ear.

"Riva. Love you. Love you. Moonbeam."

We stay clasped together for a few minutes, simply breathing in tandem. I don't want to let him go.

But Griffin draws back with an embarrassed glance at the wet splotch that's formed on his pants. "Well, that's… a bit of a mess."

His uncertainty only intensifies the love humming through my chest. I smile up at him. "Good thing we have this handy river to wash off in, huh?"

His gaze catches mine. He leans in again to bring our foreheads together.

"It is good. It's all good. Everything you give me."

My throat tightens, but there's a glow of hope in my chest that wasn't there before.

THIRTY

Griffin

I didn't remember how much feeling my body was capable of containing. Or maybe it never held so much emotion before, when our existence was so strictly regimented, when I'd never shared anything more with Riva than smiles and the occasional hug.

Now my adoration radiates through every pore, like I'm shining with it right down to my soul.

It's incredible and also overwhelming. I don't want to let go of her, even just to walk down the path to the river.

The slide of my arms around her bare back sends fresh shivers of sensation through my body. Slivers of pain lance through the joy here and there, punishing me for the indulgence, but the eager thunder of my pulse drowns those out enough that I can ignore them.

I can't keep all this happiness in.

"I love you," I murmur, kissing her forehead, her cheek. "I love you. I love you."

Can I say it enough times to make up for the years when I wasn't there to say it at all? For all the time I've been aware of her and then around her in the last few months when I couldn't even feel it?

My mind slips back to images from our shared past— to a younger Riva tucking herself next to me on the sofa in the facility's lounge area, trusting me not to betray the eagerness only I could sense to the others. To the spirited arguments with Jacob that neither of them took too seriously back then. To the strength that flowed through her body when she pushed herself through a challenge.

But with each of those memories, sharper shocks of pain jolt through my nerves. My stomach starts to cramp.

I have to clamp my jaw against the other memories that try to rise up, that the guardians seared into my brain in tandem with every image they could find that provoked the slightest emotional reaction in me.

But every memory since we came to the island is safe. I can revel in the hunger that winds through my veins at the touch of her, not satisfied even after the intimacy we just shared.

I can think of the compassion in her gaze and the tenderness of her kiss after I first told her what her touch was doing for me. Of the flash in her eyes when she told off Clancy for profiting off us.

I don't think there's any part of her I don't love.

A matching emotion shines from her into me. She was right that I don't need her to say it for me to know her heart, but my pulse still skips when the words pass from her lips again.

"I love you too, Griffin. I know... I know now that all

six of us are back together—really *together*—we can figure this out eventually."

I capture her lips, losing myself in their softness and heat—but not totally. Her last comment echoes through my mind.

Eventually isn't good enough. I screwed this up—it's because of me that she and the others ended up under Clancy's thumb to begin with.

I will make this right. I was willing to end Celine's life to make sure I was in a position to save us, as sick as *that* memory makes me feel.

I would give up my own life if it comes to that. There's no sacrifice that wouldn't be worth it.

Better to die knowing I gave them everything I could than to live with the awareness that I was nothing more than their downfall.

The unsettling thoughts finally loosen my need to hold on to her. What we're doing here isn't going to save anyone.

I take a step back, ignoring the protests of my desire pleading for more. "I guess we'd better get on with washing up."

Riva smiles bright enough to almost compensate for the loss of her embrace and tugs her bra and tee back on. I collect my shirt from the ground and pull it over my head reluctantly.

But I haven't lost her yet. She curls her fingers around mine to walk with me down the mountainside.

The guardians keeping watch have stayed far enough back in the jungle that I'm not sure Riva will see them. I can sense their presence, their mix of boredom and apprehension—and the jolts of alertness when they spot us coming into view.

I head straight for the riverbank at the base of the waterfall and slip over the coarse grass along the water's edge to plunge in waist deep.

Riva dips her feet in with a wince, though nothing on the island is really cold. It's more lukewarm.

I wade around, adjusting my pants so the current will carry away the outcome of our interlude and trying not to think about exactly what I'm doing. But Riva's gaze follows me, and my face gradually flushes hotter until I think it might burn right off.

I sensed her with the other guys that night in the abandoned hotel. I didn't set out to pry, but with the invisible bonds we've already formed, it's hard not to pick up on how they're feeling when they're nearby.

I know how much pleasure they gave her and how much enthusiasm they brought to the task. *They* all know that side of her so much better than I do, even when I can read her from the inside out.

How can I catch up when I'm not even totally sure how to feel anymore?

But I also know that she doesn't care. There's nothing in her now as she watches me except the warm glow of affection and a little worry that I can tell is for my own well-being, not hers.

And when I walk over to where she's sitting on the bank, my clothes clinging to my frame and my hair slicked back, a flare of desire sears through her too.

She doesn't let it show other than the brief flick of her

tongue over her lips. The tiny movement acts like a magnet, drawing me in.

Without speaking, I step right up to her, set my hand on her cheek, and kiss her.

Riva trails her hands down my chest, the heat of them seeping through the damp fabric of my shirt. I wish it was off again—I wish I'd never put it back on.

Maybe Riva's thoughts are traveling along similar lines. When our mouths part, she leans close so only I can hear her whisper. "There are a lot of places I haven't gotten to touch you yet."

I swear my dick rises to half-mast in an instant, as if volunteering for duty.

I lower my head to nibble her jaw where I know I can set off a spark of bliss before answering. "I've missed out too."

"Hmm. But I bet the guardians are monitoring us out here."

"Yes." I drink in her heat and the flavor of her desire, and an impulse grips me that I can't shake. "But we could work around that."

She cocks her head, but before she can voice her question, I scoop her off the bank. As Riva lets out a gasp of startled laughter, I push through the current to the waterfall—and propel us right under it.

The torrent washes right over us and then we're mostly beyond it. I press Riva up against the wet rock beneath, heedless of the current streaming down my back.

I was already soaked anyway. And back here, no one can see what we're doing.

No one can hear the breathier gasp that escapes her

when I trace my fingers right down the center of her to the apex of her thighs.

When I stroke over the spot that before I only bucked against artlessly, Riva's fingers clench in my shirt. If I had any doubts about whether I'm moving too quickly, she dispels them with the yank of my mouth to hers.

I don't know how much more time the guardians will give us. So I'm going to make sure I leave her with the best possible memories of our reunion.

I delve my hand under the waistband of her track pants and her panties. At the feel of her slick folds, I groan against her mouth.

She already came for me once, but I can make this one better. I can make it as close as possible to the total joining we're both craving but resisting.

I tease my fingertips over her sex until I've charted every spot that provokes the greatest rushes of pleasure and exactly what kind of pressure works best on each. The exact bodily sensations don't pass into me, but I can trace their intensity echoing through the flashes of satisfaction, exhilaration, and impatience whirling through Riva.

As my confidence grows, I delve two of my fingers right inside her wet heat. The physical evidence of her enjoyment sets off a thrill in me that's almost as intense as her quake of need.

"Griffin," she mumbles, burying her face in the crook of my shoulder. Begging for what I'm only too happy to give her.

I match her pose, kissing and nipping the sensitive spots on her neck while I pump my fingers in and out of her. The rhythmic swivels of the heel of my hand send even more desire flooding through both of us.

Riva whimpers, swaying into my hold. I can't even feel the waterfall behind me anymore.

Everything is her and us and the intoxicating symphony of our coming together.

My hand grazes a spot inside her that makes her cry out. I stroke it again and again, fanning the flames until she's shaking.

And then it happens, even more delicious than the first time. Ecstasy crackles through her, electrifying both of us.

She quivers and sags against me, wrung out. My erection throbs, but I want the moment to stay only about her.

I want her to know through every particle of her being how much I'm here for her, in every possible way.

"I love you," she says again, barely audible through the roar of the waterfall. Then she looks up and catches my gaze, as if she's read something inside me that I didn't realize would be obvious. "If we make it out of here again, you're coming with us. It's only worth it if it's all of us."

A lump rises in my throat. "Okay."

The urgency that brought me down to the river sweeps through me again. I carry Riva back to the bank and clamber out next to her.

The guardians adjust their positions among the trees, but don't move to stop us as we head down the path.

No one steps out to intercept us until we reach the clearing outside the facility. A woman raises her hand toward Riva.

"You're still in a training period. You'll go in for dinner in an hour."

Riva catches my gaze, and I nod, a gesture that feels totally inadequate. I carry her quiet answering smile with me all the way up to the facility and down the stone halls.

I need to find out what I can about Clancy's plans so far and see if I can direct him down a path that would benefit us. I can tell him that I found out something useful from Riva—that'll get his attention and kick off the conversation.

My clothes are still damp in the warm air, but it'll sell my story better if I go straight to him rather than stopping to change. Convince him it's important.

When I reach his office, a sense of keyed-up tension flows right through the door to me alongside with the hasty ruffling of papers. Something's already happened.

"Clancy?" I say with a knock.

"Come in."

His voice is curt. I step into the office to find him jabbing at the keys on his laptop while he stands over his desk, his face rigid.

I need to exercise plenty of self-control even seeing him in his regular moods these days. Keeping a tight rein on the flares of resentment and anger his presence provokes.

He lied to me, hid things from me. Tricked me into dragging the people I care most about in the world into this mess. Stole our chance at freedom from us.

He didn't even let me keep Lua. She ran off into the jungle, unnerved by the fighting, and Clancy forced me to march onto the helicopter before I could call her back.

He said he was sorry, but he didn't feel it. Not about anything.

I wasn't prepared for this level of agitation from him, though. My chest tightens. "What's going on?"

Clancy doesn't even look at me. "I got the call five minutes ago. The insurgents have invaded another village. My clients want us there ASAP." He grimaces at his laptop screen. "There are more of the fighters than usual—it's a bigger village. For us to overwhelm them without too many casualties…"

Inspiration hits me with Riva's steady voice carrying from the back of my mind. *It's only worth it if it's all of us.*

I approach the desk. "You were planning on going in with just a few of the Firsts, right?"

The red-haired man shoots me a narrow look. "I can't risk bringing all of them. Especially not after the stunt they just pulled. You know that."

I shrug. "I know they've realized how hopeless trying to escape is. And the six of us do have the strongest abilities by far. It'd go much smoother with all of us helping, along with however many of the younger shadowbloods you think could pitch in effectively."

I was trying to keep my tone cool and practical, as if I'm being totally logical about my suggestion, but a tremor of skepticism—maybe even suspicion—weaves through Clancy's whirl of emotions.

"Or they could screw me over," he snaps, and turns back to his computer.

I grope for a way to make the tactic easier for him to swallow. "They wouldn't all need to be in the field. You could keep Dominic back wherever you'll be monitoring the mission from—and maybe Andreas too? Just use his invisibility to scope out the scene before you send the others in. They'll be on hand if necessary, but having them right there, where you could put pressure on them if the others act out—that'd make for plenty of motivation to comply."

Clancy looks up at me again. "Did Riva ask you to push for this?"

Shit. How have I already started to lose the foothold I managed to gain with him.

"No," I say quickly. "We didn't talk about the possible mission at all. I only thought—"

I hesitate, feeling his wariness expand through the rest of his presence. My stomach lurches.

He isn't going to simply listen to me. The only chance I have of swaying him... is if I *really* sway him.

I haven't dared to use my powers on Clancy yet. I've been too afraid he might notice.

And now, after drawing my friends into his traps in the mainland facility, after compelling Celine to her violent death, even thinking about warping anyone's emotions fills my gut with nausea.

With every moment I waver, I'm losing ground with him. I was willing to *die* to see the others free—I have to do this.

I put on a calm expression and extend the slightest tendril of concentrated emotion toward the man in front of me. A thread of hope laced with faith.

You see a way through in the things I'm saying. You know I wouldn't lead you astray.

My stomach keeps churning, but I manage to keep my

voice even. "I understand why you're worried about keeping the Firsts together. But I think you're letting your fears cloud your better judgment. They wouldn't even be *together* or in contact with each other. Just somewhat nearby. And you could have at least two of them ready to be punished the second any of the others steps out of line, more easily than if you left some back here."

Clancy pauses. He *is* afraid, but it's a desperate sort of fear, like Andreas guessed from his memories.

He needs a victory. He wants to see a clear way to get it.

His suspicious vibe has faded but not vanished. I inhale slowly and apply a fraction more pressure to my imposing emotions.

"You could bring along a bunch of the kids too. Not just ones who can help, but the less useful ones who were part of the escape. The Firsts feel particularly protective of them. You'll have the perfect means to ensure they follow your orders to the letter."

Riva wants to get as many of the younger shadowbloods out as she can too, after all.

Clancy's shoulders relax just a smidge. He rubs his chin, the conflicting tensions in him starting to unwind.

"You might have a point there, Griffin. There's something to be said for a more immediate pressure point. And plenty of motivation."

"Exactly." I aim another smile at him and pray to whatever gods might exist that I've just opened a new doorway to freedom—not to our destruction.

THIRTY-ONE

Riva

The wind flicks grit in our faces. A tang of smoke and iron prickles my nose, leaving me with the impression that I've bitten my tongue.

I peer down the low slope through our cover of gaunt shrubs, studying the village of clay-brick buildings. In the thin dawn light, the shadows stretch long.

My pulse thumps at a frenetic rhythm.

.The insurgents gave the government of whatever country or state we've arrived in a deadline of twelve hours to meet their demands before they started a full-scale slaughter of the inhabitants. It took Clancy eleven hours to finalize his plans, transport us out here, and have Andreas conduct an initial survey of the situation while invisible.

We've got only one more to save the people huddled and hunched with fear in the broad courtyard at the edge of the village.

As many of them as we can still save. The terrorists have already murdered a few—whether because those civilians resisted or simply to make a point about how serious they are, I don't know.

The bodies of two men and a woman lie sprawled at the outskirts of the courtyard, dark stains marking the packed dirt beneath their corpses.

I swallow thickly, which rather than clearing the uncomfortable flavor from my mouth only intensifies it.

I don't want to be here. I don't want to be carrying out Clancy's mission for him or earning him money and acclaim.

But there've got to be at least a hundred innocent people down there in their tight huddle, many of them kids or elders, without much hope of defending themselves. I also don't want all of them to die if I can help it.

That's the worst part of our new circumstances, isn't it? If Clancy honestly wanted to help people out of the goodness of his heart, including us shadowbloods, I might have been okay continuing the life he set up for us.

If I could really be a superhero, sweeping in to save the day with powers that would suddenly seem more awe-inspiring than monstrous, would I turn down the opportunity so I could claim my own freedom instead?

I don't think I would. Not if it was a real choice with its own kind of freedom woven in.

And Clancy knows that. It's why he made his initial pitch to us the way he did, and why I didn't resist from the start.

He manipulated our emotions as deftly as Griffin can,

in his own way. Even now, he's arranging the scales so that any attempt we make to have lives of our own will result in someone else's death.

I am not a monster. Even though I'll never trust Clancy to put what's right over his own self-interests, even though I have no intention of returning to the island after today if I can help it, I'm still going to do all I can to ensure every captive below survives the day.

What happens after is on Clancy's conscience, not mine. He set the stage; we're just working with the scripts he gave us.

I've noted fourteen of the insurgents in their positions around the village, mostly where Andreas reported seeing them. Nine are stationed in a loose circle around the cluster of hostages, strolling a little this way and that, rifles held at the ready. Five others roam more widely around the village, keeping watch for new arrivals.

I don't need Griffin's sensitivity to read the wariness in their postures. They're perfectly aware that the officials they're bargaining with would rather kill them than give in to their demands.

They just aren't prepared for the resources those officials were able to bring to bear this time.

They aren't remotely ready to deal with us.

"I can see all eight of the men Andreas said were in the taller buildings around the courtyard," Zian says from beside me, where he's hunkered down behind the scrubs too. "A couple of them are in different rooms from what he reported, but that's all. If there's anyone else farther into the village, they're too far away for me to make out."

Jacob lets out a rough sound by my other shoulder.

"Drey searched the whole village. He'd have noticed if there were more. I'd only be worried if you couldn't find everyone he saw."

He lifts his head to eye the terrain down the slope leading toward the nearest buildings and the courtyard. "We should start with the pricks in the buildings. I can take them out at a distance as long as I know where they are—and without the others realizing anything's wrong."

I smile grimly. "The more of them we can eliminate before they go on the defensive, the better."

My scream is going to be the ultimate key to our victory, but as soon as that shriek careens from my lungs, we might as well have bellowed out a war cry. And I'm not sure if I can target the figures I can't even see while keeping my hunger for pain under tight enough control that I won't catch any of the civilians in its net.

A small herd of sheep stirs in a pen just beyond the courtyard. One of them pushes at the weathered boards of the fence with an emphatic bleat loud enough to reach our ears.

The nearest insurgent spins and squeezes his trigger.

The blare of the shot reverberates through the air. As I flinch, the sheep thuds over on its side.

Behind me, Griffin draws in a shaky breath. Whiffs of nervous pheromones tickle my nose from his direction.

He's never been right in a battle like this before. Never had to see the violence firsthand.

He speaks steadily enough, though. "I'll keep the attackers as calm as possible. If you think a different emotional effect would help more, just say the word."

Jacob looks over at Griffin and nods. There's still a bit

of tension in his stance when he interacts with his brother, but even when we were speaking apart from Griffin, he hasn't expressed the slightest doubt about his twin's loyalties now.

With the understanding they reforged that day in the jungle, he probably recognized Griffin's gambit with Celine more clearly than any of us.

We're back to how we were—or as close as we can get to the old days while there's damage not fully healed and Andreas and Dominic are back in Clancy's mobile military base, torture instruments poised to make them pay for any missteps on our end. We're all *here* as the family we were meant to be.

More than just the six of us.

I glance down the opposite side of the low hill to where the four younger shadowbloods Clancy sent along with us are crouched. He picked out the few he thought would be the most useful for the mission.

Lindsay can use her earthen talents to jolt the ground beneath our enemies' feet, setting them off balance.

The older teen who's joined us, a guy named Sully, can conjure distracting illusions. I have the feeling the five of us Firsts encountered his ability before, during our time out in the wider world, attempting to avoid re-capture.

George can hop not just over short distances but through walls, in case Zian notices something we need to grab quickly within one of the buildings.

And if worse comes to worst, Tegan can hit any attacker nearby with the toxic smoke she can expel from her lungs.

But having them with us means more people we

need to watch out for, more people to protect. I can't help suspecting that Clancy included them at least as much to ensure we'd take every care to pull off this mission well as because he thought they'd contribute with their powers.

He's keeping track of us through the monitoring bands around our ankles that we know from past experience are picking up our voices too. We have to be careful about what we say.

I catch the gazes of the three guys around me. "We're going to save everyone today."

Griffin dips his head. Determination hardens his features so that just for a moment, he looks even more like Jake's mirror image. "*Everyone.*"

His swift gesture encompasses the four of us and the younger shadowbloods behind us.

One corner of Jacob's mouth curls up in a harsh smile. "And take *all* of the villains down."

Zian bares his teeth. "Like they deserve."

We're all in agreement that after we destroy the terrorists, we're turning our abilities on the guardians who've terrorized *us*. Unfortunately, we won't be able to figure out exactly how to do that until we see what we've got to work with after this part of the mission is over.

I wet my lips, my pulse picking up to an even faster tempo. "Okay. So we split up now? Jake, you could go with Zian to pick off the men in the buildings—and bring George with you in case you need him to hop inside. I'll stay farther back with Griffin, Lindsay, and Sully where we can keep an eye on the bigger picture."

I hesitate at the thought of Tegan. Her talent won't do

any good unless she's close to her targets… but she's only twelve.

I don't care how useful her power could be in a pinch. Clancy is sick for sending any of the youngest shadowbloods out here, but especially her, when she only could be useful if she's right within reach of a murderous attacker.

"She'll come with us," Jacob says firmly. "Zee and I can make sure nothing happens to her."

Somehow it's a relief to have one decision taken out of my hands.

We scuttle down to the younger shadowbloods and convey the plan in murmurs. Sully's expression firms with the resolve of someone who's been in the line of fire before, but the younger kids look understandably jittery.

"Stick close to us, and don't do anything unless Griffin or I say so," I murmur. "If everything goes the way we're hoping, you might not need to get involved at all."

Lindsay clenches her hands. "I want to help if I can." But she doesn't look any less terrified.

I squeeze her shoulder. "I know. Come on—we don't have much time left."

We creep back to the crest of the hill, diverging into our two groups when we reach the top. My heart stutters as I watch Jacob and Zian pull away from us, even though I can sense exactly where Jacob is whether I can see him or not.

We can do this. We can protect these people, as much as this mission is really designed to protect them, lull Clancy into a brief complacency, and then strike at him too.

The scattered scrubs and gnarled trees give us enough shelter that we can steal halfway down the slope without being seen as long as we stay close to the ground. We move in spurts, Griffin gesturing when none of the men are looking in our direction and he can sense a lapse in their wariness, holding up his hand to stop us when they start to turn our way.

He's scanning the emotions of everyone in our vicinity —including the insurgents staked out in the two-story buildings that give them a higher vantage point over the village and its surrounding terrain. After a few minutes, he pauses and lifts his hand toward me with his forefinger raised.

Jacob has taken out one. Seven more to go.

It'll be slow going for Jake. He has to know exactly where his targets are, and he can't risk them noticing something's wrong before he gets a grip on them.

He'll be relying on seeing them through windows, but at least they should be staying near those while they keep watch.

As we crouch in our new positions, close enough to the sheep pen that the pungent odor of manure laces the air, Griffin raises his hand again and again.

Two down. Three. Four.

I study the men stationed around the villagers. None of their faces betray any heightened concern.

One of the insurgents patrolling farther out strides past us, just twenty feet from our crouched position. Next to me, Lindsay quivers.

I think I can direct my scream at both the men around

the hostages and the five who are patrolling the outskirts at the same time without my control slipping. They're far enough away from the main cluster of figures that it shouldn't be too hard to distinguish them.

But if Jacob and Zian can deal with some of them first as well, that'd be better.

Griffin indicates five gone, and then six. After he lowers his hands, he picks up a stick and draws a Z and a line in the dirt.

We don't dare speak here, but I understand. Zee managed to tackle one of the men on patrol.

Two more are left in the buildings near the courtyard, four on the outskirts, nine surrounding the villagers. We're closer and closer to our goal, and so far, no alarm has been raised.

A murmur carries from the group of hostages. Some of the figures near the edge of the huddle are stirring.

The voices that reach my ears hold the edge of a hushed argument. I tense, spotting a woman clutching at the arm of the man next to her.

Is one of the villagers thinking of rebelling? Can't he see the insurgents will simply shoot him?

But the locals don't know that we're already in the process of freeing them. He might assume they'll end up dead either way.

Two of the terrorists march over. One of them barks something in a language I don't know at the source of the disruption.

The villagers go still, but it's too late. And what the insurgents do is even worse than I expected.

The one who spoke reaches into the huddle and yanks a kid out by the elbow—a little boy who can't be more than five or six years old. He squeals and babbles in terror as the woman who must be his mother grasps after him.

The insurgent hefts up the kid, dangling, and points his rifle right at the boy's face.

My gut lurches, and my lips spring open before I've even thought about it. But Lindsay is even faster.

The dirt beneath the gunman's feet juts upward in a sudden bump. He stumbles, losing his balance, and the kid slips from his grasp.

Griffin's face has gone taut with concentration, no doubt trying to rein in the violence. But the other men scramble to snatch up the kid, and one grabs another child from the far side of the huddle.

Her cry wrenches at me. I might not understand their words, but their harsh voices tell me they're determined to punish the villagers for even considering resisting.

God only knows what'll happen if they start firing. Maybe they'd cow the rest of the villagers—or maybe they'd provoke a larger rebellion that will end with them slaughtering so many more.

The boy wails as he's jerked around toward the second man's rifle, and I can't hold back any longer. All the anguish of watching the villagers' pain bursts from my lips in a monstrous shriek.

The sound peals out of me and hurtles across the landscape to smack into my targets. The hunger inside me twitches and yawns, eager to be sated after weeks of denial, but I narrow the jabs of my power to lance only into the nine gunmen poised around the hostages.

I can't feel the more distant patrollers right now—and I'm afraid to loosen my grip even enough to seek them out. This has to be enough.

Please, let my fellow shadowbloods manage to handle the rest.

My power radiates through all nine men, freezing them in its clutches, but I can only tear apart one at a time. I pitch the shriek louder, harder.

My latent senses know exactly how to break and rend each victim for maximum pain. My scream rips through one body and another, shattering bones, splitting sinews and organs.

The agony ripples back into me, flooding me with an exhilarating strength.

For a long time, the pleasure that came with the pain I deal out has horrified me. But in this moment, knowing how many lives are at stake, I give myself over to it.

I need the strength. I need every bit of might I can get to ensure the larger massacre never happens.

These men would have murdered little kids. They were willing to kill every person in this village to get their demands met.

They don't deserve the life I'm tearing out of them.

My fingers dig into the dry earth, claws jutting out. Body after body crumples in their ring around the hostages.

I'm distantly aware of cries and shouts, but I can't even decipher where they're coming from while my focus is trained on my targets. I have to trust that my friends and colleagues are holding their own.

Then there's only one left. The man that first hauled

the little boy out of the crowd, the one who stumbled at Lindsay's shove.

I propel a sharper scream from my lungs, snapping his feet, then severing the tendons at the backs of his knees. Raking destruction up through his body swiftly but methodically.

Drinking down the last swell of agony before his life blinks out.

Then I sway forward, my own body caught in the rush of power. The sound fades from my throat.

Griffin touches my back, helping to ground me. His voice spills out in a rush of relief. "We got all of them. Jake and Zee and the others caught the sentries before they could hurt anyone—Sully helped divert them with his illusions. We—"

"Someone's coming!" Zian's frantic holler splits through the air from farther away. "I can hear it."

The words have barely left his lips when I hear it too—the roar of what sounds like a dozen engines. I leap to my feet, thinking that if we can just hurry the villagers to safety in time, it won't matter.

But I don't know where we could take them that *is* safe. And as I straighten up, a barrage of brown armored trucks careen into view over the top of a nearby ridge.

Did the insurgents here realize something was wrong in time to summon reinforcements, or were these men already on their way? Are they even with the original terrorists, or are they some new hostile group?

It doesn't matter. A hail of machine-gun fire blares across the landscape, and all I can do is yank Lindsay down with me as we flatten ourselves to the ground.

Our battle isn't over. It looks like it's barely even begun.

THIRTY-TWO

Riva

I hug the earth through another thunder of bullets, grit prickling into my mouth.

Tires are grating against the hard-packed dirt as the trucks grind to a halt. Voices holler unfamiliar words.

And a sliver of pain jabs me right through one of my marks.

Jacob's mark.

The chill of fear prickles through me. He's a few hundred feet away, farther down by the buildings and the courtyard—closer to the incoming attackers.

Griffin puts words to my fear where he's sprawled behind me. "Jake's hit. Zian too. They're still conscious. Jake's more pissed off than worried, but Zee's panicking a bit."

Shit. My own worry constricts my insides from my throat down to my gut.

I dare to lift my head to get a look at what's going on.

I only manage to make out a couple dozen figures with massive guns marching toward the courtyard before a few of them aim their weapons at the hillside again.

Bullets batter the soil and the twisted shrubs. Chunks of twig and leaf spray around us—and Lindsay lets out a pained gasp.

I twist toward her as she cringes closer to me. Blood streaks across the side of her arm where one of the bullets hit her.

It doesn't look serious, but guilt knots my stomach anyway.

"Stay quiet," I murmur to her urgently. "It'll be okay as long as we don't draw more attention."

Those definitely aren't any government soldiers come to thank us for our service. They were dressed similarly in earthen tones but nothing like an official uniform.

And I can already hear them yelling at the villagers with hostility rather than relief.

As Griffin shuffles closer to Lindsay with a bandage he's pulled from his pocket, I peer through the brush again. I have to get to Jacob and Zian—make sure they're okay, do what we can to pick up the pieces of our mission.

Frustration and fear tangle in my chest to form a prickling vibration. I'll scream all these assholes who've barged in to ruin our victory to pieces.

But when I judge it safe to lift my head so I can stare down into the courtyard, my spirits deflate.

The new arrivals have obviously figured out that something very bad happened to the insurgents who were here first. They're herding the hostages into the largest of the two-story buildings around the courtyard, shouting and shoving—many of them already inside.

Even with my practice under Clancy's supervision, I doubt I can keep track of who I'm tearing into with my scream when I can't even see who I'm aiming it at. I'd end up ripping through a bunch of the innocent villagers too.

Shit, shit, *shit*.

But if these men are with the first bunch, how long will they wait before *they* start killing more of the hostages in retribution for our attack? We don't have time to figure out a new plan.

Behind those walls, they could be slaughtering hostages to hold up as examples right now.

I feel like I'm going to vomit. I still need to reach Jacob and Zian, help them if they need it.

What is Clancy going to do if we have to pull out to get them to Dominic for healing?

Too many thoughts are whirling in my head. Just move—figure it out one step at a time.

I drag in a rough breath and glance at Griffin. "I'm going to the others. Keep making the insurgents as calm as you can manage."

"Riva—"

I don't wait to hear what he's going to say. The seconds are slipping past me—I might already have wavered too long.

The last of the gunmen is disappearing into the building. I heave myself forward, scuttling along the slope staying as low to the ground as I can, following the line of spindly shrubs for the cover they provide.

Jacob hasn't moved much from where I sensed him

before. Hopefully Zian and the younger two are still with him.

I have to run the last short distance from the patches of vegetation to the fence around the sheep pen, and then another short dash to nearest structure by the courtyard. Thankfully, I've already passed out of view of the building the terrorists ushered their captives into.

As I sprint to the mud-brick wall, the boom of a single gunshot splits the air from the other direction.

My wince radiates through my body. The scream swells in my lungs, but I don't have a proper target.

I dash around the corner of the structure—and make out a shed I can sense Jacob is behind up ahead. My footfalls echo the pounding of my heart.

I dart around the shed and freeze with a sharper lurch of my gut.

Jacob is leaning against the side of the shed, looking pissed off just like Griffin said. Blood has pooled beneath his thigh and is seeping through the hasty bandage already wrapped around the wound.

He might not even be able to walk like that.

And Zian looks even worse off. He must have caught a bullet in the side—the hem of his shirt and the left hip of his pants are dark with blood.

Tegan huddles close to him, helping him press a couple of balled bandages to the wound in an effort to stop the bleeding. She looks all right.

But George lies in the dust just around the corner of the shed, back of his skull blasted right open, the rest of his white-blond hair drenched red.

Zian somehow looks twice as upset when he takes in

my expression. "I'm going to be all right," he insists with a hint of a growl. "But he—I couldn't get to him in time..."

Lindsay lifts her head, her wide eyes flicking from him to me and back again. "I think the bleeding is slowing."

Jacob hefts himself farther upright. "That's what matters. Just tore up a little muscle on this hulk."

He taps Zian lightly with his elbow, but his face is tight with concentration. His jaw works when he glances at George's body.

His expression hardens even more at another crackling gunshot. He catches my eyes. "They're killing the hostages?"

I nod, my mouth dry. "Must be. I don't know..."

I don't know what we do now. I don't have the slightest clue how to salvage this mission.

For all we know, if we go back in failure and Clancy loses control over the guardianship... the remaining guardians will decide that Engel was right and murder us after all. Or send us off to be lab rats the way Clancy's always threatened.

But how the hell are we going to take down all those gunmen when only one of us who's much good at killing anyone has all her flesh intact?

Jacob is still watching me. "You tell us what you need, Wildcat. We'll do whatever we can."

None of us can touch the insurgents without getting inside the building. And I can't see Jacob or Zian launching themselves into a full-out brawl with their injuries.

Which leaves just me.

But how the hell could I manage to take down all of

our enemies in an enclosed space without them shooting me first? Without slaughtering all the innocents with them at the same time?

Even if I got in there and brought every supernatural talent I have to bear as quickly as possible…

The quivers of the exhilaration of my last scream still thrum through my veins, but that's not enough to take on an entire squad of terrorists unscathed.

Not on its own. I need more.

A restless bleat reaches my ears. My head jerks toward the sheep pen.

The bottom of my stomach drops out with the idea that's just occurred to me.

I can't deny the solution that's right in front of me, no matter how horrific I find it. If I have to become more of a monster to save us all, so be it.

I won't be able to save *anyone* if the mission completely falls apart.

"I need to see what I'm working with out there," I say.

Jacob pushes to his feet without another word, gripping the side of the shed for balance so he isn't putting too much weight on his wounded leg. Zian sways after him.

A protest tumbles from my lips. "You should—"

Zee shakes his head. "We're in this together. Like always."

Tegan looks terrified and fierce at the same time. "I'm coming too."

The truth is, no matter how powerful I get, I'm not sure I can pull this off alone. So I grasp Jake's arm to help him, and we shuffle as quickly as the guys can manage through a narrow gap between two of the buildings to where we can peek into the courtyard.

The sheep are pacing in their pen back the way I came from. The building with the hostages stands almost directly opposite it.

There's a pane-less window on the second floor, large enough that I'm sure my small frame could fit through it without a squeeze.

Two more shots ring out just in the brief moment I'm taking it in. My jaw clenches so abruptly I bite my lip.

I don't know how easy it'd be able to climb that material, not the same construction as the bricks I tackled before. It might give our enemies enough time to hear me coming and shoot me on sight.

There is another way I could get up there, though.

I jerk my gaze across the bodies of our first targets still strewn around the courtyard. One several feet away has a smaller rifle that looks easier to handle.

I touch Jacob's arm for his attention. "I need you to pull that gun over here. Once I have it, I'm going to circle around until I'm close to the building they're in. When I run for it, can you throw me through the biggest window on the second floor?"

Jake blinks at me, his stance tensing. "With that much effort, you know I don't have the best control. I could hurt—"

"You won't," I interrupt, my tone firm. "Just fling me up there, and I can handle the rest. Once I'm ready."

Zian frowns. "What are you going to do?"

I can't bear to answer him.

Jacob extends his power to the gun and drags it over to

us. I pick it up, backtrack between the buildings, and dart along a dusty street until I can slip through a passage that takes me within ten feet of the front of my goal.

There, braced between two of the neighboring buildings, I fix my gaze on the sheep and open my mouth.

The shriek seeps out, constrained so it's low but still piercing. I'm hoping the terrorists won't notice it.

The hunger inside me squirms eagerly. I aim all its reverberating power at the undeserving livestock across the courtyard.

My scream rips through one animal and another even more easily than it cut down the men before. I shatter their windpipes first to cut off any bleats or groans that might have alerted my next targets.

But only to silence them, not to kill them just yet. I need them to live through plenty more agony if their sacrifice is going to mean anything.

Wrench. Snap. Puncture. Crack. Flesh rent and bones smashed.

Pain floods my chest with each four-legged corpse toppling to the ground—and transforms into a nauseating flare of strength. The sense of power flows through my limbs and tingles all the way up to my scalp.

More and more and more. I'll need every bit if I'm going to have any hope at all.

I can only imagine the guys staring at the carnage from their vantage point. I hate to think what Tegan is making of the slaughter I'm carrying out.

Blood is starting to creep across the ground beneath the pen's fence. But there are still a few more sheep standing.

I propel the shriek from my lungs, drinking in every drop of anguish. My body vibrates with the unnerving thrill of it, as if I've been lit up with an electric current.

Please, let this be enough. Please, let them not have died for nothing.

The last sheep crumples. I tuck the rifle under my arm and race toward the building before one fragment of the power I've dragged into myself can dissipate.

My feet fly across the packed ground faster than I've ever felt, even with my usual supernatural speed. The wind warbles in my ears.

I stare up at the window I'm hurtling toward—and Jake is there for me. An invisible force whips me off my feet, straight toward the opening.

Between my speed and his shaky control, my shoulder might have glanced off the edge of the frame, but I twist sideways the second I see the danger. Then I'm careening into a crowded room over the heads of dozens of sitting hostages.

All my instincts spark to life with the hum of bottled power within my body. My hands whip out, and a shriek sears from my lungs.

It isn't even hard to figure out who my targets are now that I can see them—they're the only figures standing. I ricochet across the room, each spring of my feet adding to my momentum, and carve a path through them.

Bullets from the rifle I grabbed burst open several skulls. The claws of my free hand slash through one throat and another.

And my scream echoes off the walls, gutting the rest of the insurgents from the inside out.

Several of the hostages yelp or add their own shrieks to the mix, but thankfully they only duck lower. One of the terrorists charges at me, raising his gun, and I lance my scream straight through his innards so he crashes to the ground with a spurt of blood over his lips.

I'm flying, nothing but strength, speed, and fury—but this is only the upper floor. The instant I see the last of the terrorists around me collapse, I throw myself toward the stairwell.

The pain I drank in from the latest targets of my shriek replaces the energy I expended in my attack. I blaze down the stairs and slice through four more militants with my shriek and my gun before anyone below has a chance to think about reacting.

Then the rifle's trigger gives a hollow click. I toss it aside, rebound off a wall to tear one man's head right off his body, carve open another with the force of my scream—

And the front door bursts open.

Zian barrels into the building with a feral roar, his face contorted with its full wolf-man visage. The transformation must have rallied his own strength, because he slams one gunman into the wall and gouges open another's chest in the space of a blink.

Most of the hostages are crying out now, their terror pricking at me. I can't imagine Zian likes hearing how our rescue is being received either, but he rampages on, focusing on the insurgents who were gathered around the doorway.

The second he's tossed the last aside, I let my scream

fade just long enough to call out. "Get out of here! Hide in your homes until it's safe!"

I gesture with my arms at the same time, knowing it's likely none of them can understand my words. Zian stumbles back out into the courtyard.

The hostages hesitate until I crash into the last remaining terrorist with another vicious shriek. Then they scramble toward the doorway with a babble of panic.

The rush of pain-powered strength ebbs in my limbs. My breath stutters with a jitter of my nerves.

I won't be able to bring this heightened state all the way back to Clancy—but I have to use it in every way possible while I can.

Bending down, I smash my fist across the monitoring band clinging to my ankle.

I have just enough pain-driven might left to crack the metal and then to yank the band the rest of the way off me. I stomp on it to a sizzle of sparks.

We can tell Clancy it was destroyed in the fight. Technically that's even true.

When we meet him again, I don't want him to have a single clue what's going on inside me.

THIRTY-THREE

Riva

I leap through the doorway to rejoin the others. The hostages have scattered across the village, ducking into the other buildings. Doors thud decisively.

Not a single additional gunshot rings out. No armed men appear around the boundaries of the courtyard.

I wait for several beats of my heart, my ears pricked, but no further catastrophe descends on us.

We did it. It wasn't tidy, but we did it.

Zian has slumped down on the ground, his face returned to normal and shining with sweat but a broad grin baring his teeth. Jacob is hobbling over to him with Tegan helping balance him.

"We have to get out of here," I say, knowing my voice will carry through their own ankle bands—that it'll tell Clancy that I survived even if my own monitor didn't. "Regroup with the guardians—Dominic will be able to heal you too."

I pause with a fresh punch of nausea. There'll be no healing George.

I'm just opening my mouth to speak again when a faint rustle reaches my ears. Jacob has whipped his arm upward before I can even turn around.

The purple poisoned spikes jut from the side of his forearm—and spring free. They zing through the air like a set of darts and spear the insurgent who was still alive enough to drag himself to the doorway across the chest.

The man sprawls, his eyes glazing. The gun he was raising toward me slips from his limp hand.

Jacob stares at his arm. "I— They've never done that before."

I swallow thickly, thinking of the power that pealed through me just moments ago, more than I've ever felt in my life. "Our abilities are still evolving, apparently."

Jacob's mouth sets in a slanted line as if he isn't sure whether to be happy about that development. Then he motions me toward him.

"You're right. We've got to get going. I'm pretty sure whoever hired Clancy would rather we cleared out before they show up. Where's my brother?"

As we tramp across the courtyard, Jake, Zian, and I all pause briefly to confiscate a weapon. We don't speak about it, not when our voices would be transmitted straight to the guardians, but the solemn glances we exchange say enough.

We still have another fight ahead of us.

Griffin, Sully, and Lindsay emerge from the brush along the slope to meet us as we hurry over. Griffin makes a beeline for his twin and lifts Jacob's arm to support him.

"I can manage," Jake mutters, but I think I see him relax a little at the same time.

Sully glances at the sheep pen with its blood-stained earth and mangled corpses. He doesn't need to say anything.

My shoulders tense. "I did what I had to do."

His jaw works, but he nods.

Jacob lets out a rough dismissive sound. "Better us than them."

Lindsay is scanning the courtyard behind us, her face tight with worry. "Where's George?"

Zian winces. "He—when the new trucks first showed up, spraying bullets everywhere—we didn't get to shelter in time."

I hate the shadow of anguish that crosses her face. She's silent for a moment and then asks, "What about the hostages? Are they okay?"

My mind trips back to the scene in the building I just unleashed my powers on. A few of the bodies that remained after the hostages fled were villagers, but most of the corpses were the terrorists I destroyed.

"Almost all of them," I say, turning that fact over in my mind. The insurgents decided not to punish too many of the villagers even though everything had gone wrong.

Griffin directs us toward the van we arrived in, concealed about a mile away. "They were greedy. I could feel it, the whole time—the bunch of them were angry when they saw what had happened, but mostly they were still hopeful, hungry… wanting whatever it was they demanded as ransom."

"They didn't want to lose too many of their bargaining chips," I fill in with a shudder.

Zian lets out a rasp of a chuckle. "If they'd given up after our first round, *they* would have lived too. Guess they got a little too greedy."

"Maybe it works out better for Clancy this way. He'll get everything he's owed."

I keep my tone even, but I know the guys pick up on the extra meaning in my last words. We all know what he's earned from us.

Griffin nods. "Andreas and Dominic will be worrying about us, but they were ready for whatever might happen. When they see us and what state we're in, they'll jump in to help."

They're waiting for us to take the lead in our rebellion, he means, and then they'll pitch in however they can. That makes sense.

We're the ones who've had the chance to arm ourselves. We'll have the most room to maneuver when we make it back to the temporary base Clancy set up to monitor the mission.

As the cluster of trees that hide our vehicle come into view up ahead, my mind starts spinning through the possibilities. But even once we've clambered in and buckled up, I'm still not sure.

With their injuries, Zian and Jacob won't be able to maneuver quickly. Griffin isn't much of a fighter, no matter how he was trained.

I'm going to be the key, again. That's just the way it is.

Clancy and his guardian colleagues have Drey, Dom, and a few of the younger shadowbloods with them as their own kind of hostages. I don't think they'd hesitate to go as far as killing the younger ones if they realize we're defying them.

It's only the six of us Firsts they really think are valuable, after all. Clancy proved that when he all but dared Dominic to kill Celine.

And they won't be kind even to Dom and Drey if they catch wind of our rebellion too soon. Our friends won't be able to help us if they're drowning in agony.

I need to tackle him first. Without him giving the orders, it'll be so much easier to deal with the others.

Where would he make a fatal misstep that could get him killed? What is he afraid to lose, enough that he might act without thinking?

The answer soars up from the depths of my mind like a signal flare: It's us.

That's all there is to it, isn't there? He's spent his entire career working to get us under his control, and now we're essential to taking on the savior-hero role he's obviously been dreaming of.

There has to be a way I can use that fear.

I reach into my shirt to pull out my cat-and-yarn necklace, allowing myself to carefully click it open and snap it back together. The simple, familiar rhythm melds with the rumble of the van's engine.

The start of a plan forms piece by piece. I can't see how it'll end, because so much depends on exactly how Clancy reacts. But the longer I sit with it, the surer I feel.

"When we get back to the base," I say quietly, "wait for me. Then do what you need to."

Jacob squeezes my hand from the seat next to me, and

Zian lets out a grunt of acknowledgment from behind. Behind the wheel, Griffin doesn't give any visible sign at all, but a flicker of emotion passes through me, all warm acceptance.

A wordless message that says all it needs to.

Clancy's base squats on the side of the dirt road, a military-style truck attached to a long trailer with most of his monitoring equipment, both of them painted in camouflage colors. As we crest one last hill before it comes into view, his even voice crackles from our radio.

"Park twenty feet away and walk the rest of the distance. Enter through the back of the trailer."

We're not using the guns we grabbed, then. They're all too big to conceal under our clothes.

Griffin cruises to the indicated spot and parks. We clamber out and head toward the trailer.

I hang back, letting the others go ahead. Dragging my feet across the ground as if I can't quite lift my feet.

Clancy knows I'm not dead, that my monitoring band must have simply been broken. He'll have no idea what else might have happened to me.

He's probably already been on edge, hoping that my ability to speak coherently means there isn't an outright emergency.

Well, he's going to get an emergency now.

As our procession comes up on the attached truck, I purposefully stagger. My knees buckle under me.

I fall, catching myself with my palms in the dirt and swaying. A groan breaks from my lips.

"Riva!"

I don't think Jacob even needs to fake his panic. He

lurches back to me as fast as his wounded leg allows, his face paling.

Zian follows with a defensive snarl, his gaze skimming the landscape as if searching for new foes.

I slump over on my side, letting my head loll. And through the slits left by my nearly closed eyelids, I see Clancy burst from the truck.

I hadn't known if he'd simply send Dominic racing over or come himself. Maybe I should be gratified that he cares enough, even if it's for totally selfish reasons, to stick his neck out.

Although it might not even be his motivation alone. Griffin heard my instructions too—he's smart enough to have realized an extra shove of panic would work in our favor.

Even so, a sudden pang of loss ripples through me. This man has been a monster to us, but he's also the only guardian who's ever attempted to give us anything remotely close to a real life.

We're giving up on that dream the moment I go through with my plan. We'll be nothing but fugitives again—nothing but monsters ourselves.

To them. I know, with a resolve that steadies me through the pang, that we can be so much more for ourselves than even our new keeper ever imagined.

Another guardian hustles out behind Clancy. As they race over, I shudder and go limp again.

"Come on, get her legs—we'll carry her into the back for Dominic," Clancy says to his underling, his voice taut with concern. He bends over to grasp my shoulders.

My claws slide from my fingertips. It's now or never.

For the little bit of good he tried to do amid the bad, he deserves at least to have his death witnessed.

Opening my eyes, I whip my arm upward to rake my hand across Clancy's throat.

His blood splatters down over my face and hair. There's just an instant before his body crumples when he stares down at me, shock and denial and the briefest flash of emerging rage contorting his features.

You asked for this, I think. *You wanted us too badly to let us go.*

As Clancy's dying body hits the ground, the other guardian starts to yelp—but the sound is lost in the crack of Jacob's talent wrenching her neck around. Before she's even fallen, I'm sprinting for the trailer.

I throw open the doors to total chaos. Andreas and Dominic must have taken their cue and run with it.

Three of the guardians are circling each other and yelling in what sounds like bewilderment. Dominic has a stranglehold on another with one tentacle.

Another sprawls at Andreas's feet, still twitching from the jolt Drey must have given the man with the baton he's snatched.

I lunge forward, determined to end this now. To end everyone who'd have continued our torture.

I'm not sure the guardians even know what hit them. I sever one's throat and plunge my claws into another's chest, and then Zian is there behind me, bashing a skull into the trailer's floor.

Dominic's jaw clenches, and the man he's clutching purples as the tentacle around his neck squeezes and sucks the life out of him simultaneously. Andreas yanks a knife from one of the other guardian's belts and jabs it into the back of the man he toppled.

We stop, all of us panting. My nerves jangle through my body as if waiting for another shoe to drop. "That's—that's all of them?"

"That's all," Dom says, quiet and grim as he releases his victim.

I exhale with a sound like a sob. My knees wobble for real this time as all the pent-up stress and effort catches up with me.

We don't know what country we're in or where we're going next. But right now, we're more free than we've ever been before.

THIRTY-FOUR

Riva

We might be free, but we're not exactly done.

Dominic hustles over to Zian, having spotted the evidence of his wound on his clothes. As he ushers him outside to find a shrub or tree to draw healing power from, I turn toward the three younger shadowbloods crouched in the back of the trailer.

Devon is there, and Booker, and a fourteen-year-old girl named Harriet who was caught up in our escape but mostly kept stoically quiet. Clancy decided to separate the two couples who were part of our earlier escape, leaving Ajax and Nadia behind, maybe to give him more leverage over their significant others as well as us Firsts.

They peer at the carnage left in our wake in silence and then at me. Clancy's blood still saturates my hair and smears my skin.

I swipe at my face with my sleeve, but it's a little too late to make a cleaner entrance. Booker's jaw works.

We didn't have any way of looping them in on our plans. This is a much gorier revolt than the first one they joined.

"We'll go back to get the others," I promise. "Right away. Without Clancy giving orders, the whole organization falls apart, at least while the guardians are scrambling to figure out what to do next. We'll head back to the plane, and a few of us will make the pilot take us back to the island to get the rest of the shadowbloods while the rest figure out a safe place for us to regroup. Okay?"

Devon rubs his hand across his mouth with a little shudder. "Are you going to kill all the guardians on the island too?"

"Not if they don't get in our way," Jacob mutters. "It'll be up to them."

He slips from the back of the trailer at Dominic's beckoning and limps over to our healer. Griffin comes up beside me and squats down to put himself eye to eye with the younger shadowbloods.

"It makes sense that you're unsettled," he says. "You're probably not all that sure about me either. We all wish we could have let you in on what we were planning sooner, but there wasn't any way that wouldn't have tipped off the guardians too."

Andreas dips his head, his voice low and rough. "There was no way they were letting us go while they were still alive. I think if you look back on everything you've seen of the guardians, you know that."

Booker hesitates. "They were ready to hurt us, maybe even kill the three of us, to keep you in line."

"Yeah." I grimace. "You should never be in that position again—not you three or Nadia or Ajax—or any of the others. We look out for each other. We're blood, and they can't take that away from us, no matter what they do."

Harriet's head droops. "I don't want to go back to the island. Or any other facility. I never liked any of it."

"You won't have to," Griffin assures her. "Will you come with us? I think we'd better leave the trailer behind."

Andreas glances around the interior at the slumped bodies, the splattered blood, and the tools the guardians meant to use to torment their "leverage" if we disobeyed. "Yeah. It'll only slow us down."

The younger shadowbloods cautiously creep forward. As Griffin ushers them out of the trailer, I turn to Andreas. "What did you do to the guardians to get them so confused?"

His mouth twists at a pained angle. "I wiped one guy's memories completely so he had no idea who he was or what he was doing here. Then I wiped another from all the others' minds so they didn't understand where he'd come from. And after that, I threw a bunch of projected images into the mix to throw them off even more."

A thread of strain winds through his voice, and I don't think it's just because of the energy using his ability to that extent took out of him. He's no more comfortable with the most monstrous side of his abilities than I am with mine.

I squeeze his arm. "We all did what we had to do. Now we can really take charge of our lives."

"Yeah." He leans in to give me a quick but heated kiss

and brushes his forehead against mine. "I'm right here with you every step of the way, Tink."

We gather the guardians' phones and weapons for possible later use and clamber out of the trailer to find Zian already unhitching it from the truck.

"We're going to need both of them to carry all of us," he says, nodding to the van we arrived in.

Tegan watches the proceedings with her arms wrapped around her chest, hugging herself. "Even after we get everyone off the island, aren't the other guardians going to keep chasing us?"

"I can handle that," Andreas tells her. "At least partly. Once we have the other kids out of there, I'm going to erase Clancy from everyone's minds. If none of the guardians can remember him, they won't remember his project or where he organized it or any of that. There'll be records, but it'll take them a while to piece things together—time we can use to cover our tracks completely."

I peer into the front of Clancy's truck, where Jacob has taken the driver's seat. "Does this one have a working radio? If there are any local stations, we can figure out where exactly we are on the drive to the plane."

He frowns at the controls. "Looks like it. Let's get out of here, and we can check in with each other before we get to the runway to decide the final details."

"Sounds good to me." I like the idea of putting some distance between us and Clancy's worksite, if only because I have no idea how aware his clients are of the details of his operations—or when they might arrive to confirm his success.

Dominic comes up beside me, resting a gentle tentacle on my waist. "You're completely okay, Riva?"

I smile at him, letting myself lean into his offered embrace just for a moment. "Getting there. I'm looking forward to my next shower, though."

He gives a rough chuckle and presses a kiss to my cheek, heedless of what I recently wiped off my skin. "Here's hoping we can give you that soon."

We climb into the vehicles—Jacob, Dom, me, and the kids from our mission in the truck while Griffin, Zian, and Andreas head to the van with the guardians' hostages. Jacob guns the engine and spins the wheel to take us back onto the road.

"Good-bye and good riddance," he says without a backward glance.

The van roars ahead of us, and Jake speeds after it. I take a long breath, feeling my nerves just beginning to settle down, and shift in my seat to check on the others behind me.

Just as I turn, an explosion booms and sears through the air beyond the rearview window.

It's the trailer—it's just blasted apart in a surge of flames. The impact jolts the ground beneath the tires, and Jacob swears.

"I didn't think we were going to—" he starts.

Dominic is shaking his head, his body tensed. "That wasn't us. That—"

Another force wallops into the side of the truck, wrenching away his voice.

Our vehicle skids and tumbles into a roll.

The doors fly right off their hinges. We crash into the

dry earth on the side of the road, my head smacking the steel frame.

Jacob lolls, dangling from his seatbelt, mumbling. Dominic has been flung out onto the roadside just beyond my reach.

Not that I seem to know *how* to reach anymore. My head is aching and spinning at the same time.

I can't collect my voice; I can't remember how to move. Pain washes through my limbs in waves.

Footsteps thud across the cracked dirt. I have a blurred impression of two figures standing over me—a broad-shouldered man and a wiry woman.

"You did a good job, my shadowbloods," the man says in a roughly amused baritone. "You did half of *my* job for me."

My mouth opens and closes as I grasp for words. For a shriek. For anything.

The man turns to the woman. "Toni, we need them to know right from the start that I'm no one to fool with. That one first—the one with the tentacles."

He points, and the woman raises a gun I hadn't noticed clutched in her hand. "Of course, Mr. Balthazar."

"No!" I choke out, barely a whisper. I manage to jerk my arm forward—

And something slams into my head from behind, knocking all the thoughts out of my head.

Right before the darkness closes in, the last thing I hear is the blare of a gunshot.

ABOUT THE AUTHOR

Eva Chase lives in Canada with her family. She loves stories both swoony and supernatural, and strong women and the men who appreciate them. Along with the Shadowblood Souls series, she is the author of the Heart of a Monster series, the Gang of Ghouls series, the Bound to the Fae series, the Flirting with Monsters series, the Cursed Studies trilogy, the Royals of Villain Academy series, the Moriarty's Men series, the Looking Glass Curse trilogy, the Their Dark Valkyrie series, the Witch's Consorts series, the Dragon Shifter's Mates series, the Demons of Fame series, and the Legends Reborn trilogy.

Connect with Eva online:
www.evachase.com
eva@evachase.com

Made in United States
Troutdale, OR
07/27/2023

11596149R00243